Praise for *My Little Eye*

'A great premise which sets up lots of twisty, paranoid intrigue. Top notch.'   Mason Cross

'An original and compelling take on the serial killer story.'
Rod Reynolds, author of *Black Night Falling*

'Deftly plotted, authentic and creepily plausible.'
Amanda Jennings, author of *The Cliff House*

'Fresh, original, has a rip-roaring plot and is totally addictive.
David Young, author of *Stasi Wolf*

'This is a multi-layered, gripping read steeped in authenticity that will keep you up at night.' – Catherine Ryan Howard, author of Distress Signals

'A clever, twisting, nightmare-inducing read.'
Chris Whitaker, author of *All The Wicked Girls*

'A masterclass in pacing and such an original take on the serial killer thriller.'
Eva Dolan, author of *This Is How It Ends*

'Ingeniously plotted and perfectly chilling,'
Susi Holliday, author of *The Deaths of December*

'*My Little Eye* is a one-sitting read: gripping, clever and worryingly plausible.'   Mick Herron

'Enthralling, intriguing and twisty.'
Liz Nugent, author of *Lying In Wait and Unravelling Oliver*

Stephanie Marland has worked in the university sector for over ten years and has published research on how people interact and learn together in virtual environments online. She's an alumnus of the MA in Creative Writing (Crime Fiction) at City University London, and an avid reader of all things crime fiction, blogging about books at www.crimethrillergirl.com. Steph also writes the Lori Anderson action thriller series (as Steph Broadribb) for Orenda Books.

My Little Eye

Stephanie Marland

First published in Great Britain in 2017
by Orion Books,
an imprint of The Orion Publishing Group Ltd
Carmelite House, 50 Victoria Embankment,
London EC4Y 0DZ

An Hachette UK company

1 3 5 7 9 10 8 6 4 2

A CIP catalogue record for this book
is available from the British Library.

ISBN 978 1 4091 7197 3

Typeset by Born Group

Printed and bound in Great Britain by Clays Ltd, St Ives plc

MIX
Paper from
responsible sources
FSC® C104740
www.fsc.org

www.orionbooks.co.uk

For Grammy –
who encouraged me to be brave, and let me steal her name!

PROLOGUE

Kate can still feel his touch on her skin. He only held her hand. No, less than that, he put his hand over hers, just for a few seconds – nothing in the grand scheme of things. A comforting gesture because she was upset, that was all, she tells herself. A few days ago he'd walked into the break room at work just as she'd hung up on Mart after yet another argument. He'd seen she was crying, and he'd held her hand; a totally normal thing between colleagues – no, friends.

Since then, she's thought about that moment, their moment, a lot. It felt exciting, and she hasn't felt excitement for what seems like forever. She liked the feeling. A part of her wants to feel it again.

She refuses to feel guilty about it.

She's almost at the flat now. She looks up at the first floor out of habit, expecting to see darkness, but there is a soft glow behind the curtains, a light on inside. She frowns. Wasn't Mart working tonight? She's sure he'd said he had a late set at the club. Wasn't that why he'd waved away her excuses for doing overtime on the late shift? Hadn't he said he didn't care?

Setting the two jute bags of groceries down on the step, she fumbles in her jacket pocket for her keys. Her hands are numb from the cold and it takes her a couple of attempts to grasp them. She adds 'buy gloves' to her mental to-do list. The folks back home had told her it never got properly cold in central London. Now, in the middle of a dark, rainy November, Kate knows they were talking bollocks.

She unlocks the door, picks up the bags and pushes the door open with her shoulder. As it closes behind her the automatic light in the communal hallway comes on. She blinks at the brightness reflected back from the cerise-painted walls, sidesteps around the upstairs neighbour's bike and heads towards the stairs. Glancing at the stacks of mail on the tatty side-table as she passes, she spots a pile for her and Mart.

'Fucksake,' Kate mutters, snatching it up. 'Do I have to do everything?'

She leafs through the envelopes; two bills and a piece of junk mail plus what looks like a credit card statement for Mart with *Final Demand* stamped in angry red across the top of the envelope. She sighs. Shakes her head. He really is crap with money.

Tucking the post under her arm, she picks up her bags and trudges towards the stairs. She starts working out how much cash she's got stashed away across her savings accounts – the one he knows about, and the other two. No matter what her mum tells her about Mart being a rubbish freeloader and that she deserves better, Kate has always bailed him out. She knows he thinks she will again.

But that would mean she can't have that holiday in Dubai she's been saving for. The thought of having to stay in cold, damp London all winter pisses her off even more. The bags feel heavier, her legs more tired. She tries to remember if there is any wine in the fridge. She has a horrible feeling the answer is no.

Sod it. She won't bail him out again. She's going to Dubai with Eva.

Reaching the door to the flat, she drops the bags again and undoes the lock. Pushing the bags inside with her foot, she enters and closes the door behind her, calling, 'Hey Mart, I'm back.'

No reply.

Great, she thinks, hoisting up the bags again. Don't help me, will you. Since they've been living together he's treated her more like his mum or housekeeper than his girlfriend. When they first moved in they split all the chores down the middle; he cleaned and shopped, she cooked and did the ironing. Now he's always too busy with his music, the implication being that what she's doing is less important. That he thinks *she* is less important.

Kate pushes open the door into the living area. Halts a few steps inside.

The corner lamp is on, the low lighting giving the place a dusky haze. Two glasses of red wine are sitting on the glass top of the coffee table. There's music playing over Mart's high-end speakers, some ballad from the eighties that she vaguely recognises as one her dad likes. Not Mart's usual kind of tune, but maybe he's trying to be retro and romantic. It's been a while since he made that kind of effort; the sweet love notes and surprise gifts of their early days are long in the past.

'Mart?' she says.

Nothing.

She puts the bags down and takes a few more steps into the room. Listens hard, but can't hear him. 'Mart, where are you?'

Still nothing.

Kate moves forward to the coffee table and picks up a glass. Takes a sip of wine. It's the good stuff, delicious. She needs it after doing a double shift. Needs it to help her forget the hand holding, and remind herself not to feel guilty, more guilty. She takes another sip and glances round the room again. That's when she notices the red splodges on the carpet near the bedroom door. The door is ajar, a chink of light visible through the gap.

As she draws closer she recognises what the splodges are. Her heartbeat quickens. Guilt tightens in her chest. This is big, unexpected.

Kate stares at the rose petals scattered around the entrance to the bedroom and wonders what's got into Mart to go for such a grand gesture. Whatever's caused it, it's about time. She'd been thinking the relationship was on its way out, but if he's making this amount of effort, maybe they still have a chance.

'Mart?' she says, her tone soft, playful.

The bedroom door opens halfway.

Kate gasps. The cream duvet on their bed is strewn with rose petals. Candles encircle the iron bedstead in flickering light. 'Mart, it's beautiful.'

She steps onto the threshold, transfixed. Remembers the good times; sharing candlelit baths, talking for hours about anything and everything. Mart is the guy for her. This proves it. She wonders if he's about to propose.

Kate takes another pace forward. 'This is amazing. Where did you—'

The lights cut out. Plunging her into darkness, aside from the candlelight.

To her right, the door jolts back, bashing the wall and making her jump.

She feels movement behind her. Inhales a cocktail of unfamiliar scents. Lemon. Vanilla. Something else she can't place. 'Mart?'

He says nothing, but she feels his touch; a lingering caress from her temple, across her cheek, towards her mouth. She starts to turn towards him. 'I—'

His hand clamps across her lips and nose, yanking her backwards. She braces against them, lashes out with her hands, trying to break free.

Fails.

Loses her balance.

Falling.

Another hand slides round her arms, her waist. Pulls her back against a body, a chest. Holds her prisoner. She struggles harder. Tries to scream beneath the suffocating force. Her cries muted against flesh.

His grip tightens round her jaw, digs into her cheek, forcing her head to the left. She feels a sharp sting against her neck by her ear. Gasps.

The room seems to tilt, the candlelight dancing, the scarlet petals and cream duvet kaleidoscoping patterns in front of her. Her mind seems sluggish. Tiredness weighs her body down. Her eyelids feel heavy.

The pressure across her mouth disappears. She feels hands clasp her shoulders, spinning her round.

Dizzy. Nauseous. Afraid.

His face looks blurred, distorted by the flickering of the candlelight.

He reaches towards her. Strokes her cheek. 'Sleep now, my love.'

She tries to shake her head. Tries to speak, to say his name, to ask him why. Tries to tell him to stop hurting her. That she'll do whatever he wants.

The darkness takes her before her lips can form the words.

4

MONDAY

1
CLEMENTINE

They say I was dead for three thousand and six seconds. They say that when I woke I was different, but I don't know if that's true. What I do know is that my world became a different place once every one of those precious seconds had expired. People – Mother especially – seemed to move around me at double speed, talking, always talking, while I remained stuck on go-slow, unable to shift the fog of sleep that remained in my head, no matter what I tried.

They said I'd get better, that everything would be OK. I just needed to give myself more time. But even then, through the bewildering haze of the drugs and the pain, I knew that they were lying.

Reality was the problem. The facts could not be hidden under my bandages. A word, a single whispered truth, repeated inside my mind over and over again, and I knew that it was right.

Murderer.

First the doctors made excuses; said I'd suffered extreme trauma, that stress and shock took time to heal. They spoke of the panic I must have felt in that place, the terror as the flames surrounded me, the horror as I watched his life ebb away.

I don't remember those things. What I do remember is the shouting; the fury burning my mouth as I spat the words 'I hate you'. The rage building inside me until I couldn't control it, didn't want to control it, until I let it control me. Since that moment, I've felt nothing.

As seconds became minutes, minutes added into days and days to months, I got used to the nothingness. Like the skin grafts, it became a part of me. Sometimes I wonder if that's when I truly changed, but I cannot remember. It's possible I've always been this way.

One thing I can attribute to that night, though, is my fascination with 'what if'. What if I'd been at school that day? What if Father hadn't got so angry? What if I hadn't killed him?

Before, I lived in the moment. After, I dwell on the possibility of future moments, hiding behind theory and hypothesis, never taking action. Never feeling alive.

I want to change.

I think I know how.

You see, I've been watching them for a while.

2

DOM

The shrill, repetitive beep of his mobile jolts Dom awake. He fumbles for it on the floor beside his bed, his sleep-addled brain making him clumsy. The caller rings off before he can answer.

It's too bloody early, still dark outside. Groaning, Dom rolls over, his back muscles aching as he reaches out for Therese. He's only forty-three but he feels bloody ancient. Her side of the bed is cold and it makes him remember; she's not stayed here in nearly two months.

He's sore from the two-hour workout last night. A session that only ended because the gym was kicking out at half eleven and he couldn't persuade any of the fitness team to stay late. He didn't stretch. Didn't drink enough water. He knew he'd pay for it, and he is; his head is pounding.

The training session hadn't helped him sleep anyway. So he buried himself in the murders he's working, going back through the case files he shouldn't have brought home. Two young women – Jenna Malik found dead four weeks ago, and Zara Bretton who died six days ago. He's still got nothing to connect them except for the way they were killed, and the anguish on their loved ones' faces when he broke the news. Even after nineteen years on the force it never gets easier. The memory of their distress is a constant reminder that Jenna and Zara were real people, with real lives, and their deaths affect others; the devastating ripple effect of murder. It makes the fear even greater. A killer like this always kills again, if they aren't stopped, if Dom doesn't stop them. He doesn't want that on his conscience, there's enough weighing him down already.

He tried to sleep, but was still awake at three, thinking about her. Always her. Just like every other night since things went to shit, he couldn't stop the memory of their last argument replaying in his mind. He'd screwed up big time. He never meant to hurt her.

The phone in his hand starts to ring again. 'This is Bell.'

'Guv?' The nasal tone of Abbott. 'We've got another one.'

Shit, so much for having a day off.

It feels like his brain is bashing against his skull. Dom rubs his forehead, hoping it'll ease the pressure. It doesn't. 'What do we know?'

'She was found at home, by her boyfriend. He didn't recognise her straight off because she looked so different – changed hair, everything. When the first responder saw the scene he connected it to our case and made the call.'

'And it looks like our guy?'

'Jackson thinks so. He green-lighted bringing you in.'

Dom frowns. He's the lead on these murders, but he'd have thought DCI Paul Jackson would've jumped at the chance to have someone else work the case. Not just because he's not found the killer yet, but because with the IPCC taking over the investigation from Professional Standards – leading the hunt for what, or who, caused the operation he was part of last month to go bad – Dom's surprised he isn't already flying a desk.

Dom cradles the phone between his ear and shoulder as he pulls on his trousers. 'All right. Where?'

'Near Angel. I'll text you the address.'

'Right.' He stands, staggers to the wardrobe to grab a fresh shirt. His legs feel leaden, sluggish.

'Word is there's already rubberneckers outside.' Abbott's voice sounds strained. 'The media will be next.'

'I'll be there.'

'Just don't let the Rats catch you. They've set up on Fulham Palace Road again, the bastards.'

'Bastards,' Dom says. Traffic police were scum. Every real officer knew it. Getting to Angel by car could take an hour, more if he was unlucky. 'I'll take the tube. Should be there in thirty.'

He hangs up. The time on his phone shows it's just gone 6.30 but he barely registers that. It's the photo background on the screen he's staring at. Therese smiles out at him. She's lying in his bed with her long blonde hair draped across the pillow. The look in her eyes is playful, enticing. Her skin is tanned and glows with health. She looks like a different person from how she'd looked the last time he saw her. Four days ago her skin was pale. Her eyes had dark circles beneath them. Her hair was lank, the roots dark and more obvious than usual against the contrast of the white bandage covering her wound. Her injuries. His fault.

He pushes the thoughts of Therese away. He has a case to solve. He clicks off the screen, watching Therese's image fade to black, then grabs some shoes and pulls on his black denim jacket.

He hurries through the flat. In front of the door a small black cat is stretched out along the length of the mat, asleep.

Dom opens the door a crack. Looks at the cat. 'You're going to have to move, mate.'

The cat opens one eye but stays put.

'Come on, BC.'

The cat looks at him disapprovingly before closing its eyes again.

Shaking his head, Dom inches the door wider until the pressure forces the cat to move. Ignores its furious glare.

Outside, with his head still pounding, the crisp morning air makes him feel even worse. He knows from experience a migraine at a crime scene is never fun. Pulling a blister pack of codeine from his wallet, he swallows a couple of tablets.

His phone beeps once. A text: Abbott. Dom reads the address, and heads towards the tube. Guilt vibrates through him with every step.

Not another dead body.

3

CLEMENTINE

This morning things got interesting.

I'm one coffee and two cigarettes into my day when the news hits Twitter. It's 5.42. Streetlights reveal the cluttered pavement of St John Street on bin day, but not the sprawling extent of its filth. From my attic room four floors above I watch the meat lorries trundle past on their way to Smithfield Market, then turn back to my laptop and reread the tweet.

> **@DeathStalker** The Lover strikes again. Woman's body found near Angel. Blue lights on scene.

Taking a long drag on my cigarette, I watch the retweets continue to rise: four, nine, thirteen, twenty-one. True-crime fans never sleep. They're always waiting for a new case, another body; a fresh hit of adrenaline. Fantasists, most of them. Most, but I don't think all.

I stub the cigarette out in the overflowing ashtray and reach for the keyboard. I click the shortcut to CrimeStop, the specialist social networking site for true-crime fans. The homepage loads. Its logo, a blood-splattered microscope, is as familiar to me as the people who inhabit this virtual space.

The icon in the corner of my screen shows twenty-three notifications. I click to read the alerts:

> **Death Stalker** posted in True Crime London
> **Mysteries Solved, Blood City** and twenty others commented on a post in True Crime London

I click the first alert and it takes me to the private area for London-based crime fans. Death Stalker's post tops the feed:

Breaking News: 'The Lover' strikes a third time?
My inside source says dead woman's appearance was totally changed. Rose petals found around the body. Has London's 'Lover' struck again? My images attached.

There are three photos. The quality isn't great, but they're geo-tagged. The first is the outside of a building; terraced red-brick flats above a takeaway. Crime scene tape has been strung along the pavement outside.

The others are exterior shots too. One is the doorway; three stone steps leading to a black door, the number forty-three above the brass doorknob. The other shows the first floor window. I double-click the image, enlarging it, but curtains block any glimpse of the interior. There's no caption, but that doesn't matter, it's easy enough to guess what these photos mean. Death Stalker, the unofficial leader of the True Crime London group, is at the scene of the crime.

I reread the post and wonder who the inside source is. Glancing at the avatar beside Death Stalker's username – the outline of a face, the photo too dark to make out any features or even their gender – I wonder who *they* are; young or old, male or female? Online you can be anyone you want.

Flicking back to the first photo, I zoom in, focusing on the reflection in the window of the takeaway. Behind the light-flare from the flash, just visible, is the outline of a person. My heart rate quickens. The picture is too dark to make out much detail but, from their silhouette, I can be sure of two things: first, the photographer is wearing a hoodie, and secondly, Death Stalker is a man.

I see you.

Reaching over last night's Thai takeaway carton for my journal, I jot down the wording of Death Stalker's post and the points of interest from the photographs. I note the details of the figure reflected in the window and beside it I write: *gender reveal – intentional or accident?*

If it's an error then it's the first I've seen him make, and I've been watching for a while. It's nineteen months since I first

12

gathered data for my doctoral study. Back then CrimeStop was one of many websites on my list, and true-crime fans were just people I used in order to explore my hypothesis – that no matter what gossip might be spread across the internet, in reality crowd-sourced crime solving would never be achievable.

True Crime London made me rethink all that. Specifically, Death Stalker caused my rethink – he knows things the public shouldn't, with access to protected data from contacts close to the investigations. He has the case information gathered by the police, but without the bureaucracy and protocols that hamper them. It gives him, and anyone working with him, the chance to solve a crime faster than the police.

Now a new question inhabits my mind: could this group of true-crime fans solve a live murder case?

I think they have the potential to, and I think some of them believe that too. In the months I've been watching, several members of the group have talked about taking on the challenge of a live case. Every time another incidence of police incompetence or corruption hits the media the debate is had again. Each time the Lover has killed, the conversations have turned more serious.

The likes are increasing on Death Stalker's original post. Interest is rising. I copy the geotag into Google Maps and it zooms in on a side road near the back end of Islington High Street. It's a more daring choice of kill site – an area busy with foot traffic and cars most times of the day and night. The Lover is getting bolder.

There have been two murders in the last four weeks – one in Camden, the other in Crouch End. Two women are dead, both found in their bedrooms with the lights dimmed, candles burning and rose petals scattered around their naked bodies. Now, six days after the second murder, it seems there's been a third; the kills are increasing in frequency.

An alert pings at the top of my screen:

Death Stalker posted in True Crime London
Question: Can we find the murderer before another victim is taken? Funding to public services is at an all-time low. Police

budgets have been slashed. We can't rely on the Met to bring this 'Lover' serial killer to justice — they simply don't have the resources to cope. It's time for us to step up. Who's with me?

The comments are stacking up beneath the question:

Bloodhound I agree. This government doesn't seem to have any kind of plan for how to tackle policing. I blame Brexit. Something needs to be done. Perhaps this is how we show the folks in Whitehall just how bad things are. I'm with you.

Crime Queen Great idea @DeathStalker — I'm so up for this. @Witness_Zero might be interested too, I know he's been following the case.

Justice League I don't think he's a serial killer yet. Isn't it four kills before they're called that?

Robert 'chainsaw' Jameson @JusticeLeague Serial killer 101 — they get serial status when kills tally three or more with a cool-off period in between ergo the Lover is a serial killer.

Justice League @Robert 'chainsaw' Jameson I stand corrected. @DeathStalker I agree the MET don't seem to be directing enough resources towards this case. This man needs to be stopped; the devastation he's leaving in his wake is horrific. I want to help

Robert 'chainsaw' Jameson it's a dreadful business. @DeathStalker I am, of course, with you

Witness_Zero agreed. I'm in

Ghost Avenger It's shocking the Met can't divert more officers to this case. The Lover's signature is so specific. How the fuck haven't they got leads on him? I don't like the idea of going all *Lord of the Flies*, but what other choices are there? This killer can't be allowed to murder again. I'm with you — let's find the sick fucker.

Death Stalker By my count that's seven of us ready to take an investigation live. I'm going to cap the team at eight. So this is the final call for the last spot. Any takers?

Glancing out through the grimy window, I watch the sunlight peeping over the rooftops of the terrace opposite and know the rest of London will soon be waking. The story will hit the mainstream media in time for the breakfast news bulletins. If I want to be part of this, I need to decide now.

Death Stalker has invited you to a secret group: Case Files: The Lover
Click here to accept this invitation

This is crazy. I study this stuff, I don't take part in it. My studies are in psychology and human – computer interaction. My doctoral thesis explores the relationship between theoretical concepts of self-identity and how individuals construct, maintain or adapt their identities when interacting online.

Everyone lies. With some it's an airbrushed photo and a few pounds knocked off their weight, or an adopted happy-go-lucky persona to conceal the sadness inside. Others hide their weakness behind spite and hate, spewing poisonous bile to deflect from their own inadequacies. I'm fascinated by how and why they lie, and watching how it shapes their relationships. But the members of True Crime London are fascinating for a different reason; they concentrate on the lies and failings of the police, the corruption within the system that lets killers stay free. I have a vested interest in that type of lie.

As I click to accept the invitation I can't deny the fizz of anticipation. It takes me to a new page. Unlike the main pages, this is open only to Death Stalker, Crime Queen, Ghost Avenger, Bloodhound, Justice League, Robert 'chainsaw' Jameson, Witness Zero and me.

Death Stalker posted in secret group Case Files: The Lover
Initiation: Our goal is to reveal the Lover's true identity before the police. So, listen up, here are the rules of engagement. I'm the team leader. To be part of the team you must (i) live in London (ii) contribute actively to our investigation (iii) share all the intel you gather (iv) wait for my say before making information or suspects public – either online, to the police or the media.

I read the rules twice. They're simple enough, but there's something missing; how will they know for certain if they've identified the killer? Does this investigation end when they've agreed who they *think* the killer is? That can't be right; it's not resolution. I need to know their planned end-game.

I click in the comments box and start typing my question. Beside my online handle – *The Watcher* – my avatar appears. It's a close-up image of my left eye, the aquamarine of my iris vivid against the black of my lashes. I press return and my comment appears beneath Death Stalker's message.

> **The Watcher** @DeathStalker What do we do once we know the killer's identity, do we inform the police?

I wait for a response. There's nothing at first. Then the replies start to rack up, but none from Death Stalker.

> **Ghost Avenger** Good point @TheWatcher we need to share our findings with them asap so he's caught, yes?
>
> **Robert 'chainsaw' Jameson** I'd say so. The whole point is to get him off the street.

They want a wolf hunt, to run the murderer to ground and get their justice. By running with them I put myself in danger; a wolf in women's clothing, hiding among them as they call for blood.

A new message appears:

> **Death Stalker** @TheWatcher Aren't you confident? Excellent. Once we agree on the killer we can decide the specifics of how we reveal them. It'll be important to maximise media coverage if we're going to show Whitehall the error of their ways. This isn't just about one killer, it's about restoring order to society. Don't lose sight of that.

First I'm worried. Then I'm irritated by his condescending tone. The irritation wins. Death Stalker talks of 'we', but so far he's been very clear about this being his investigation. I'd bet money he's already decided what happens if and when we identify the killer but, for now, I'll play along. The literature says a key ingredient for group bonding is trust. If I collude with him it should help me lay the foundations for trust. Then I'll be able to influence the direction of this hunt.

> **The Watcher** @DeathStalker Of course. Thanks for clarifying.
> **Death Stalker** posted in Case Files: The Lover
> To succeed in our investigation we must be organised, focused and fast. To get us off to a good start I've compiled a list of tasks. Each person will be allocated a task and must complete it and report back within twenty-four hours to show they are serious and remain part of the team. To help me assign tasks, I need you to enable the location finder on your profile so I can see where you're based. Please do it now.

I don't disagree that we need to be organised and fast, but once I've enabled the location finder I'm exposed – all those in the group will know where I live.

One by one a location appears beside each person's name. I hug my arms around myself, pulling my tatty woollen jumper tight. I'm alone, but it feels like everyone is staring at me.

I glance towards the door. Four bolts, a deadlock and a security chain divide me from the outside world. That's how it's had to be for me to survive. Caged by the fear that just by looking into my eyes people will know who I am, *what* I am.

For the past twelve years I've been almost invisible from the world. Even the university doesn't have my real address; only my PhD supervisor – Professor Wade – does. I feel safe in my cyber bubble, watching others but not being watched. Hiding behind my own careful lies. Trying to understand those of others.

But something is shifting; this little group within True Crime London has enticed me to break cover because we share a common belief that the police are at best ineffective, and at worst inherently corrupt. Their goal to catch The Lover fits with one I've been coveting for a very long time – to expose the police for what they really are; to prove the system is broken. To show people that no one is safe.

I'm bored with hiding. Twelve years of exile is long enough; I do not want to make it thirteen. What I want is to move among people in real life, undetected. To feel alive, and prove I'm more than just words on a page; that I can have a life outside of my research, like my PhD supervisor Professor Wade tells me I should.

Maybe if I do this, if I help this group catch the Lover and beat the police, and I succeed in hiding my true nature from them, I'll feel something more than the nothingness I've lived with for every second of the past twelve years.

It's a risk, though. What if they discover the truth?

They shoot wolves; don't they?

4

DOM

The rain starts as soon as Dom reaches the crime scene. It's in a side road off the end of the High Street. The uniforms have moved fast: the outer perimeter has been taped off, blocking the road. Fifteen yards inside, a second cordon surrounds the part of the terrace housing a chicken takeaway and the entrance for the flats above.

He spots Abbott hovering in the area between the outer and inner cordons, his lanky frame swamped by an oversized navy parka. Seeing Dom, he raises his hand in an awkward wave.

Bowing his head into the rain, Dom strides across the road to meet his DS. Either side of the cordon people are watching. The press have commandeered the side of the barrier closest to the residential entrance. Dom recognises that ratty-looking bloke from the *Mail*, and a chain-smoking woman from Sky. In a group of older guys stands a youngish chap with a pudding-basin haircut and an SLR in a waterproof casing. It won't be long before more arrive, and they start yelling for details. He fucking hates that.

Reaching the tape, Dom ducks underneath and stops next to Abbott. 'See we've got company.'

'They showed up about ten minutes ago.'

'Better let Jackson know.'

'Already done.'

Dom glances back at the twenty or so people gathered at the other barrier. 'What about them?'

'Public, not media.'

Dom does a quick scan of their faces and reckons Abbott's right. Some he recognises; regulars brought out by the sniff of blood and the hope of getting a photo of the body onto Instagram.

A woman at the back is clutching a coffee. Dom wishes he'd got one. It's too late now. 'How the hell are they here already?'

Abbott shrugs. 'Word gets around fast these days, guv.'

Dom glances towards the building. A female uniform is standing beside the black front door. 'You been inside?'

Abbott grimaces. 'Yeah.'

Dom studies his sergeant's expression. It takes a lot to get Abbott riled, but this case is making him increasingly twitchy. 'So it's our man?'

'I think so. There's no sign of forced entry.'

'She let him in?'

'Looks that way, same as the others. The building's split into four flats, all rentals. Ours is on the first floor. Her name's Kate Adams.'

Dom nods, grateful Abbott keeps the information brief. He's glad his DS humours his idiosyncrasies; his need to not hear any personal information about the victim until after he's had the chance to observe the scene. Details come later; first he needs to get a feel for the crime scene, observe the victim without making a prior judgement.

Dom glances towards the reporters. More have arrived in the few minutes since he's been here. He knows what they're thinking – that this is his fault – another dead woman, one who'd still be alive if he'd already caught this bastard.

An old boy in a flat cap notices Dom looking. He waves. 'DI Bell, can you confirm this is another Lover victim?'

A blonde in a cream mac rushes to the barrier, thrusting a voice recorder towards him. 'A third victim in four weeks, have you got a suspect yet?'

Fuck. The press are going to roast him and, even though he loathes them, a part of him knows he deserves it.

Ignoring the questions, Dom turns to Abbott. 'Come on, let's get on with it.'

Abbott ushers him to the inner cordon. He flashes his warrant card to the uniform on duty, tells her their names for the scene log and heads inside.

Dom follows. The familiar cocktail of adrenaline pulses through his blood – apprehension mixed with anticipation. He's used to it, but this time there's something else. It sits like ballast in the pit of his stomach. Guilt.

With a final glance towards the gathering crowd, he goes up the stone steps and enters the building.

5

CLEMENTINE

I'm not bored any more. I stand on the outskirts of the crowd, a few feet away from the others. Inside the restricted area, a tall black guy wearing a navy parka strides over to greet a newcomer.

I step closer to the crowd to get a better view. The newcomer stands, shoulders hunched, with his back turned to the driving rain. The denim jacket he's wearing is already sodden, his dark hair plastered against his skull; dishevelled-looking, but not unattractive for an older man. He looks like the picture I've seen of the lead detective on the Lover case. He looks seriously pissed off.

As if sensing my scrutiny he glances this way, so I turn, angling my face away from his line of sight, and hope my hood shields my features from view. Out of the corner of my eye, I watch as he and his colleague start walking towards the building, heading for a black door that I recognise from the photo Death Stalker posted. As they reach the entrance the guy stops and looks back, scowling. I feel like he's staring right at me, but I know that's ridiculous; with me standing here behind the crowd he'll barely be able to see me.

I twist the lid off the takeaway cup of green tea I got from the coffee place on the High Street, and raise it to my lips. The heat coming off it feels scorching. I blow on it rather than drink, and can't resist glancing back at the detective. As I do, he turns away and steps inside the building. The black door closes. I gaze at it for a moment and wonder what he's doing now. Then I focus back on my task.

Pulling my phone from my pocket, I open the CrimeStop app and reread Death Stalker's last post.

First assignment: All actions must be completed within 24 hours and useful intel contributed. Anyone who doesn't

achieve this will be removed from the group. Post intel gathered online here. I'll message each of you your task privately.

I tap the messenger icon. My brief appears. It's the first and only
private message I've received.

Death Stalker to **TheWatcher** Attend the crime scene (you're
closest). Document activity, take photos, listen for information
shared by police and media. Find something useful. You have
until 06:23 tomorrow.

The deadline stresses me. Panic flutters in my chest. It's almost
7.30; in theory I have twenty-three more hours, but the crime
scene is live now and there's no way for me to get through the
barrier. I can take photos but I'll need more than that. I have to
find something useful, or I'll be ejected from the group. I can't
let that happen.

The noise of an engine on the road behind me draws my attention. A police van halts at the cordon sending a burst of watery
spray over the tape and the small gathering of people standing
beside it. A uniformed officer rushes over to them. She's pointing
along the barrier towards the rest of the crowd, telling those near
her to move. There's some head shaking and muttering, but most
of them obey and shift along the barrier. A couple sharing a pink
golfing umbrella stop a few feet to my right. Their heads are bowed
in conversation. He's speaking in a low voice, but she's no way
near as cautious. I can't help but overhear.

'. . . told him I had an early briefing . . . God knows how long
the street will be closed . . .' the woman says. Her pink lipstick
is the same shade as the umbrella. '. . . little bastard won't cover
for me . . . told you this was too risky . . .'

If they're having an affair she should be more worried about
the news crews setting up their cameras on the other side of the
barrier.

I snap a couple of shots of the police van easing through the
cordon into no man's land. As I do, two girls in front of me

start talking about the victim – Kate, they're calling her. From their comments about her boyfriend and the unhappy state of their relationship it sounds like they knew her, although they don't seem upset that she's dead. That I find strange. From my observations I've found death makes normal people feel sadness; they cry, or frown, or their voices sound strained. I don't detect any trace of that here.

I shuffle closer to try and hear more. The blonde turns – her dark eye make-up and red lip-gloss are total overkill for this time in the morning. She looks at me, but doesn't smile. Instead she nudges her friend and they move away.

Inside the crowd I feel invisible again. But I'm not. There's a man looking right at me. I inhale sharply. I recognise him, well, a version of him anyway. With his disappearing hairline and rounded paunch, there doesn't seem to be anything much 'chainsaw' about Robert 'chainsaw' Jameson in real life, but it's him, definitely him. He smiles and starts making his way through the crowd towards me.

I fight the urge to bolt. Tell myself that he can't know who I am – my profile picture only shows my eye. Even so, my heart's bouncing in my chest at double speed. My free hand curls into a fist inside my pocket. I glance round, checking my exit route. There's a clear path to the High Street. I could leave. If I go I'll be home in half an hour. But, if I do, I won't be able to complete my task. I'll have to forfeit my place on the investigation.

I watch Robert 'chainsaw' Jameson weave through the crowd. He's ten metres away and closing.

Stay or go?

Fight or flight?

I clench my fist tighter. This is my first test. I will not run from it. I'll find out if he can tell who I am, what I am.

So I let the tubby, balding version of the man whose face is so familiar from his twenty-years-younger profile picture come to me. Online he's the group know-it-all. If you're after random case facts, or the details of strange forensic anomalies, he's your man. But online behaviour does not necessarily follow the same pattern as real life interactions. I'm going to find out if that's true for him.

He gestures to the taped-off area and the building beyond. His wispy, overlong eyebrows rising as he speaks, testing the water. 'They say a woman's been murdered.'

His words might be serious, but the glint in his eye gives him away; he's excited, delighted. This is the most fun that's happened to him in years. I nod. 'That's the rumour I've heard.'

He leans closer and I catch a whiff of Old Spice. Tapping the side of his nose with his finger, he says, 'Stop pretending. I know.'

Am I that obvious? My breath catches in my throat.

Robert 'chainsaw' Jameson smiles, not noticing my fear. 'You're TCL, right?'

I stare at him. He's waiting for a response. There's little point denying it; somehow he's worked out who I am, and it's too late to run. 'How did—'

He grins. 'Your eyes, love. Never seen green-blue eyes like yours in real life.'

'Impressive,' I say. Him noticing such a small, subtle detail is more than I'd have given him credit for.

He looks pleased by the compliment. I file that knowledge for future reference. Flattery is easy, and those susceptible to it are among the quickest to manipulate.

'It wasn't hard. Death Stalker mentioned you were tasked with coming here.' He nods at my eyes. 'Are they contacts?'

I shake my head. Death Stalker told another member my task but wouldn't share the tasks with the group? From that I have to assume he and this short, pot-bellied man know each other well, that he is part of the inner circle.

He holds out his hand. 'Robert "chainsaw" Jameson,' he says. Leaning closer, he gives me a conspiratorial wink. 'But you can call me Bob.'

I hesitate a moment, then clasp his hand. I keep my expression friendly, hiding the repulsion I feel from his clammy skin touching mine, and give his hand a firm shake.

25

'I'm The Watcher,' I say. The name feels odd on my tongue, like it's not designed to be spoken out loud, but it has to do. I don't want this man, or any of True Crime London, knowing my real name. I force a smile, faking a happy emotion to hide my discomfort. 'It's nice to meet you.'

Bob's yakking on, continuing the blow-by-blow account of his tube journey to the crime scene. I don't do the tube. Can't. So its inner workings hold no interest for me. I tune him out. Bob doesn't seem to notice.

I start to appraise him. He's in his early sixties I reckon, but not in good condition. I clock his blotchy complexion and the purple thread veins zigzagging across his nose. High blood pressure, I suspect, most likely with a high alcohol consumption kicker. As a threat to me, physically he doesn't rate highly.

He grins, and from the intensity in his gaze I guess he's expecting me to agree to something. I say nothing. Wait.

'Look, I'll show you,' he says, and starts rummaging in his trouser pocket. He pulls out a mobile. Angling it towards me, he starts swiping through photographs.

Bob's been busy. His glee at having a found a fellow TCLer, someone he deems a worthy audience, is unbounded. He doesn't notice my irritation. He flicks through picture after picture. In his accompanying monologue, he highlights the obvious subjects in each: the crowd, the police, the media and the location. There must be seventy images. He's completed my task before I've begun.

'The crime scene photos are my task.'

He smiles. 'It's no trouble, love. I like attending scenes up close. Helps me get a feel for a case. Crime's my passion, you see. I like being at the heart of the action, try to get as close as possible to the body. There's nothing like the mystery of a good murder, is there? At my age it's good to have something to pit your wits against, stops the grey cells dying off.' He swipes to the next photo. 'And here's you.'

The image is taken from a distance. It's a little pixelated, and my hood hides my hair and most of my face. Only if you look closer can you make out a few stray wisps that have escaped.

Unless you know me well, and I can count the number of people who do on less than one hand, less than one finger, it's unlikely someone would recognise me. I don't like it, though. 'Promise you'll delete it.'

Bob looks rather crestfallen, and I realise my error.

I lean closer to him, as if I'm taking him into my confidence. 'With us doing our own investigation, don't you think it's best if there's no photographic evidence of us at the scene?'

Bob's eyes widen. 'You're right, love. Can't be too careful these days. Eyes everywhere.'

He deletes the picture.

'Thanks, I appreciate it.'

'Not a problem,' he says, giving my arm a squeeze. 'I've got more pics on here. You'd be surprised how addictive this crime lark is once you've a taste of it.' He goes back to the picture menu. The photo albums number into the hundreds. 'I've got a great shot of a dead body on one of them.'

Before I can reply, thunder rumbles overhead and the rain starts again in earnest. Bob tucks his double chin into his collar and turns away from the wind.

'Maybe later,' I say, gesturing towards no man's land. 'So, what usually happens at these things?'

His porky cheeks flush pink. 'This is the exciting bit. All the key people are here – detectives, forensics and the coroner. They're all doing their thing inside the inner cordon. It's a real shame we can't see inside. If you're quick enough to the open air ones you sometimes get a look before they screen it off. A residential one like this, the most we'll see is the trolley when they wheel it out – everything will be covered though.'

I ignore his glee over seeing dead bodies. His delight at murder seems rather distasteful, even to me. 'It'll be a while before the road's opened again then?'

'Well, they can't let the public through until they've got all the evidence. If they open it too fast we'll contaminate the scene. Could make them miss something vital. Can't have that, can they.' He points towards the police van inside the cordon where a couple of uniformed officers are loading plastic boxes into the back. 'Looks like it might not be too much longer.'

Dampness has penetrated through the seams of my jacket. Shivering, I think longingly of my warm, dry apartment, but I can't leave yet. 'I should get on,' I say. 'I need to take the photos for the group before they finish.'

'No need, love. I'll upload mine.'

'I need to do it, it's been assigned to me.'

He gives me a hard stare. 'Well, we can both upload them.'

Not helpful. 'Or you could let me—'

'I can't and I won't. I always upload pictures to my profile page. I'm not making an exception; I've got a reputation to uphold.'

Shit. 'If I don't contribute something I'll be ejected from the team.'

He shrugs. Shifts his weight from one leg to the other. Then raises a hand at someone in the press area. 'Just spotted an old mate,' he says, not meeting my eye. 'I best go and see what he knows about this murder.'

As Bob scuttles away like a portly cockroach, I wonder if sabotaging my task was his main purpose for coming here. Whether beneath the affable persona is a ruthless competitor who wants to keep the group as exclusive as possible.

I can't let him force me out. I glance around the crowd. Death Stalker must have been here earlier, when he took the first photos. I wonder if he hung around.

Opening the CrimeStop app on my phone, I search for Death Stalker's profile. The location finder isn't enabled. Cursing, I send him a private message:

The Watcher to @DeathStalker Are you still at the scene?

I wait. Ten seconds pass. Then twenty. A green light appears beside Death Stalker's name – he's come online. Moments later an answer appears.

Death Stalker to @TheWatcher No

I wonder where he is. Why he's not shared *his* location with us, despite his call for transparency.

> **The Watcher** to @DeathStalker I'm not the only TCL here. They've taken pictures. Is there any point me continuing? Do you want to reassign me?

From the High Street, I hear the siren of a police car or ambulance. It passes and gradually fades from earshot as I wait.

Three dots appear beside Death Stalker's name. He's typing.

> **Death Stalker** to @TheWatcher That's irrelevant. The crime scene is your assignment. If they've already got photos then find something better.

I glance across to where the journalists are gathered. Bob's there, deep in conversation with a man in a tweed cap.

Tension builds like an overloaded valve in my chest. I have to stay part of this. I need to test if I can hide in plain sight. To beat the police at their own job and demonstrate why they are no longer fit for purpose. To prove my PhD conclusion right – crowdsourced crime solving could be the future.

> **The Watcher** to @DeathStalker What if I can't?
> **Death Stalker** to @TheWatcher Then you're off the team.

6

DOM

The hallway is painted bright cerise. It'd be migraine-inducing enough at the best of times, even if his head wasn't already pounding from dehydration and lack of sleep. Dom looks up the stairs. They're steep; typical Victorian with those narrow treads that he can get barely half his foot on. He glances at Abbott, who's making slow work of zipping his suit. 'Better get up there.'

Abbott nods. Waits for Dom to go first.

Dom knows why. This many years into the job and you've got a flood of crime scene memories; so many dead bodies, too many. It's like your brain tries to second-guess what you're about to find, or floods you with old images in an attempt to desensitise you before you see the real thing again. It doesn't work, though. Can't. It's not like any dead body is ever a good thing.

He grasps the banister and takes the stairs two at a time. Abbott keeps close behind. The stairs creak.

Stepping into the flat, he takes a moment to get a sense of the place. It's a decent size for a one-bed in this part of town, newish furniture, with lots of glass and leather in the open plan living space – modern, with a nod towards pretentious. Stripped floorboards. The walls are painted burgundy. Kate Adams and her boyfriend must earn a decent wage to afford this place. The look is contemporary, like a copy of some celebrity pad. Dom imagines that matters to them.

On the glass coffee table there are two glasses of red wine. One looks half-drunk, the other untouched. An indication Kate Adams had company before she died. Dom nods at the glasses. 'Same as the last two.'

'Yeah. CSIs are on it,' Abbott says. 'Unlikely he's left prints, though.'

'True.' He hadn't at the homes of the previous victims. 'Her wine or the killer's?'

'I'll get that checked with the boyfriend.'

Dom nods.

'Photographs are done.'

'Good,' Dom says, but he doesn't mean it. He was last to arrive, and the team are professionals; there's no reason they should have waited for him, he knows that.

He unclenches his fists a finger at a time. Rolls his shoulders, once and again. He needs a clear, logical head on for what comes next.

'Nothing looks out of place, no sign of a struggle . . .'

His DS doesn't say it, but Dom hears the implication: for all their poking, the CSIs haven't found anything useful yet. 'Noted.'

'Bedroom?'

Abbott points him towards the doorway on their far right. 'Over there.'

The CSIs look up, and he sees one of them roll her eyes at the other. He tries to ignore it. Spots Emily Renton, Pathologist, standing in the doorway. The white paper suit does nothing for her mumsy figure.

She raises an eyebrow. 'So nice of you to join us, Dom.'

'It was meant to be my day off, all right?'

She laughs. Her glasses slip down her nose, and she pushes them back into place with a gloved finger. 'So I'm told. And did you have a nice rest?'

As usual with her, he can't help but smile. 'For about two minutes.'

'And now you're here.' She nods into the bedroom; her tone becomes more serious. 'Seems we've got another one. Similar MO, but—'

'Give me a minute, yeah? I need to take a look before we dive into the detail.'

'Not a problem.' Emily moves into the bedroom, speaking to people out of Dom's view. 'Can we clear the room, folks. Take ten.'

Two techs file out, Emily follows. 'All yours.'

He nods his thanks. Ignores the mutters of the techs, who've stopped in the lounge. He can guess what they're saying – that the IPCC are after him, that he's not long for this job. Keeping his gaze low he steps into the room. Inhales a faint aroma of vanilla. Out of the corner of his eye he sees candles, burnt down low, which line the floor at the foot of the bedstead. He catches a glimpse of rose petals bright scarlet against the cream of the duvet.

He doesn't look up, not yet. Knows that he's stalling. Also knows that if this *is* like the previous two crime scenes, she'll be on the bed. Part of him doesn't want to look. So he stands there, not moving. Every sound seems magnified: his breath, his heartbeat, the steady dripping of a tap in what he assumes is the en-suite. He's still got the headache; it's worse now, jabbing at his temples.

He turns to face the bed.

Déjà vu.

It's her, but, of course, it can't be. But she's an exact replica of the last two victims – of Jenna Malik found in her musty bedsit in Crouch End, and of Zara Bretton in her canal-view studio flat in Camden. He takes a step closer. Keeps looking. She's got the same loosely curled shoulder-length hair, in the same shade of medium brown, and from this distance her face seems identical: fresh, dewy skin, a pinkish bloom to her cheeks and lips, pretty. She's wearing the same make-up too – black eyeliner, peacock-blue eye shadow, purple lipstick – very eighties.

She's naked.

He stops at the boundary made by the candles. Her face is clearer in close-up. The resemblance is unnerving, but now he sees her healthy glow is from make-up, not life. Her lips are full and slightly pouted. Her eyes are fixed open, again like the others. He looks into her unseeing gaze.

Peaceful. That's the first word that comes to him. There's no blood, no obvious cause of death. He's not fooled, though. This is how the other victims looked, and there was nothing peaceful about what had been done to them. He keeps looking at her. Needs this uninterrupted time to get a sense of the place, to try

32

and feel what she felt, to understand more about the killer. The silence helps him find what others miss.

One thing here is different.

It's not here. She's the same, like a carbon copy of the other two, but the MO *is* slightly different. There's no rose.

What does that mean?

He checks again, slower this time. Scattered on the duvet, rose petals form a circle around her, but there's no actual rose here. Dom turns, scanning the room, looking to see if the rose has been placed somewhere else.

Like the lounge, this room looks normal, if there ever is such a thing. There's no hint of a struggle, nothing seems knocked out of place or broken. Dom's gaze lingers over the dressing table. He notices how shiny the surface is, like it's been freshly polished. It's the only furniture that has. On top of the mirror there's a layer of dust, same with the bedside cabinet.

Something else draws his attention. Make-up and potions are heaped in a messy pile on the floor beside the dressing table. It's an anomaly. Everything else about this flat is clean and ordered.

He nods at Emily for the CSIs to re-enter the room. Beckons one over to the dressing table. Dom's seen her before, at another crime scene; petite with freckles. He tries to remember her name, Penny, Paula, something like that. It doesn't come to him. 'Hey, err, hey . . .' He points to the bottles and pots heaped beside the table. 'Make sure you get these.'

The CSI nods, unsmiling.

'Cheers.' Dom wonders if the media are the only ones who've been losing faith in him.

He turns back to the girl on the bed.

What happened, Kate? Why did he do this? Why do it to you?

Behind him, Abbott clears his throat. 'She's twenty-six years old. Only child, parents live in Twickenham. Works for NHS 111. Lives here with her boyfriend, Mart Stax. He's the one that found her.'

He doesn't look round. 'Lived.'

'Sorry, sir?'

He knows he's being pedantic, but doesn't stop himself. Those pots heaped by the dressing table are still bothering him. And the fact there's no rose. The previous two victims had a single rose placed along their sternums, between their breasts. Why has the killer changed that this time? He needs to think. Doesn't want Abbott's input, not yet. 'She *lived* here with her boyfriend. Past tense.'

Abbott says nothing.

Dom stares at the girl. Tries to think, but his concentration's shot. Abbott's words repeat in his mind – twenty-six years old. Twenty-bloody-six. What sort of an age is that? Nothing. A total waste. 'What do we know?'

'As I said, her boyfriend found her, called it in.' Abbott hands him a framed photograph of a pretty blonde lying on a sun lounger, wearing a pink-and-white-striped bikini and raising a cocktail to the camera.

Dom glances from the photo to the naked brunette on the bed. She's almost unrecognisable. He hands it back to Abbott. 'Anything else?'

Emily clears her throat. 'Like before, her lips were glued together and her eyelids glued open. It was intricately done, the eyelids especially. Glue was applied to the tips of her eyelashes and fixed to the upper eyelid. It looks remarkably natural.' She moves past Abbott, pointing to the girl's wrists. 'There's localised bruising here and on her ankles. She was restrained before he moved her to the bed. From the angle and depth of the marks I'd say he used cable ties.'

Dom glances at the chair beside the dressing table; solid arms, sturdy-looking. Bound and unable to cry for help; there's nothing loving about this killer. Dom stares at the body of Kate Adams. The details of how the killer transforms their victims – the changed appearance and use of superglue – haven't been given to the media. 'So we're sure it's the same guy?'

Emily nods. 'As far as we can be at this stage.'

Dom clenches his fists. A third victim, he's let this fucker take a third victim. 'Jenna Malik was killed four weeks ago. Zara

34

Bretton died three weeks after her. The gap between her and Kate Adams is six days.'

'The time between kills is reducing,' Abbott says. 'A classic serial pattern.'

Dom exhales hard. 'Yup.' He looks at Emily. 'Sexual assault?'

She nods. 'There are signs of tearing.'

'Post-mortem, like before?'

'I'll need to confirm that later.'

Dom glances at Abbott. His DS has a grim expression; lips pursed together, eyes away from the body. He's holding his shit together, just. Dom understands. 'Cause of death?'

'Nothing obviously physical,' Emily says. 'I haven't found the needle mark yet, but I'm assuming death was chemically induced, as before. I'll need the tox screen before I can be conclusive.'

Dom looks back at the girl. He walks around the bed.

He's on the opposite side from Abbott and Emily when he spots it; the symmetry is out. Whoever killed her has been so careful, so precise, in the way she's posed. She lies on her back, perfectly straight, thighs just slightly apart, toes pointing down. Except her hands are angled differently. Her left arm lies against her side, palm upwards, but her right hand is curled into a fist, knuckles against the duvet.

Dom moves closer. Crouching so his face is level with her hand, he peers into the gap between her curled fingers.

'It's a piece of paper.' Emily's voice cuts into his concentration.

He keeps staring.

'It's interesting, he gave us the rose last time, this—'

'Her,' Dom says, cutting Emily off.

'Her, what?' There's no banter to Emily's tone now.

Abbott gestures to the girl. 'The killer gave *her* the rose. He lays it on the victims, the women, who've all been made up to look like the same person. It's for them, for her, the rose. Not for us.'

Emily shakes her head. 'Fine. Before he left a rose. This time, it's that paper.'

'Can you get it?' Dom says.

35

'Of course. I was waiting for you.' She moves alongside him and uses a pair of tweezers to ease the paper from the girl's fist. She hands it to Dom.

Five lines of prose, printed in a swirly font. He reads the note aloud:

'Farewell, my love, but it is not, and cannot ever be, goodbye. I carry your image with me, as part of me; your smile, your beauty, your grace. It sustains me, comforts me, providing a dash of hope as the hours pass. I cherish your memory, holding it dear until the moment we are reunited and I can bathe again in the radiance of your eternal light.'

Emily shakes her head. 'What does it mean?'

'It means we've got a big fucking problem.' Dom looks at Abbott. 'I need to speak to the boyfriend.'

'Parekh's sitting with him, they're waiting in the flat upstairs.'

DC Narinda Parekh was a smart choice for that job; steady and observant, she'd get a read of the boyfriend without him even realising. 'Good. Is Biggs around?'

'Should be.'

'Start him knocking on doors. We need a timeline here, sightings, anything potentially relevant that'll point us in this bastard's direction. And get him to speak to the neighbours in this building first. Find out if they heard or saw anything and make sure everything is cross-referenced back to the first two crime scenes. Look for similarities, patterns, anything that could be connected.'

'Yes, guv.' Abbott steps away and makes a call.

Dom knows Emily's staring, that she wants him to give her back the note. He ignores her, keeps looking at the body.

She doesn't take the hint. 'Dom?'

He half-turns. She's looking at him expectantly. Instead of answering he asks, 'Time of death?'

'At this stage, I'd say in the last twelve hours. I'll know more once I've taken a proper look.' She nods to the note still in his hand. 'We need to check for prints.'

He hands her the note.

'I'll get it bagged.' Emily takes it away, talks in hushed tones to the male CSI over by the window.

Dom turns back towards the bed. He pulls the blister pack from his wallet and swallows another couple of codeine tablets.

First he gave the victims a rose, now it's a note. Why the change?

'I told Parekh we'd head up now,' Abbott says.

Dom doesn't look at his DS.

Abbott clears his throat. 'Guv? The boyfriend. You wanted to . . .'

Three women, all made to look like the same person.

Dom swings round to face Abbott. 'You were right. His MO hasn't changed.'

Abbott looks confused. 'I didn't say it—'

'He gave *her* a rose in Camden and he gave *her* a rose in Crouch End. We, I, assumed that's part of his ritual, his calling card. It isn't. His ritual is to give her a gift. A rose, this note, they're love tokens.'

Abbott frowns. 'But why?'

Dom thinks of the last line of the note: *I cherish your memory, holding it dear until the moment we are reunited and I can bathe again in the radiance of your eternal light.*

'To remember him by, until he sees her again.'

Abbott's frown deepens. 'But he can't see her again, she's—'

'Dead? Yeah, they all are – Kate and Zara and Jenna. And the time between kills is getting shorter. My guess is it'll be three days, maybe four, until the next. We've got to find this fucker before then.'

7
DOM

In the upstairs flat, Dom hasn't said a word, but Mart Stax sitting in the chair opposite already looks broken. Perched on the end of the sofa, Dom thinks about his first question, how to word it. There's no way to soften this, nothing he can do to make things better whatever platitudes he spouts, so he doesn't even try. 'Tell me about finding her.'

Stax doesn't look up. When he speaks, his voice sounds shaky. 'I came home from work. She was . . .' He chokes up, tries to hide it with a cough.

Dom waits to see if he'll start talking again. On their way upstairs, Abbott had filled him in: the boyfriend, Mart Stax, is twenty-nine. He's a DJ at one of the clubs at the other end of the High Street. He and the victim lived together for eighteen months.

The bloke's still silent. Dom glances past him to Abbott, who's sitting on an uncomfortable-looking stool at the breakfast bar. Unlike Kate Adams and Mart Stax's contemporary pad, this second floor flat is rustic and tatty, rather like the occupier, grey-haired widow, Mrs Bradley.

His DS nods, implying this is how Stax has been since they found him. Dom decides to prompt him again. 'Look, mate, I know it's hard. Take your time. You want a drink? Tea or something?'

Stax shakes his head. 'No, thanks. I . . . I finished work, came home and she was . . . she was . . .'

This might take a while.

Dom gets that he's in shock, and needs time to process what's happened, but he still has to push. These first few hours are critical; it's the one chance to examine the scene with its integrity preserved, the memories of any witnesses will be at their clearest, uninfluenced by the media, and any suspects will have had less time to hide their crime. If Stax saw something useful, Dom's got to know. 'What time did you get in?'

'The usual, I think . . . must have been two thirty?'

Dom's still not had eye contact. He stares at Stax's bowed head, wonders if he realises his hair's thinning on top. 'I need you to describe everything that happened from you leaving work up to finding her.'

For the first time, Stax looks up. 'Describe it? I just came home. Why does it matter? She's dead. I wasn't here, and . . . she's dead.'

Dom leans forward, grasps him on the shoulder. 'I know, and I'm sorry for your loss. But to give us a head start at catching this bastard, I need to know everything you saw and heard.'

Stax doesn't look convinced. He looks petrified.

Dom smiles encouragingly.

'I left the club, I dunno, around two, quarter past? I'd had a few drinks after my set, to chill me out, same as usual. Walked back. Got—'

'Did you pass anyone, when you were walking?'

His eyes dart right and left, like he's thinking, trying to remember. 'No . . .' Stax shakes his head. 'I don't know. Streets were pretty quiet.'

'So tell me what you did when you arrived home.'

'I let myself in. Thought it was odd the lights were on, Kate's usually in bed by the time I'm back, unless she's been out herself.'

'Had she?'

'No. She'd had a girls' night the night before, said she was doing a double shift last night, she was saving up so we could go to Dubai, have a holiday together.' His voice cracks as he says the final word.

Dom nods. 'So, as far as you know, she was at work. What time would she have come home?'

'Dunno. Maybe around ten.'

39

'Did you see anyone near the flat, meet anyone on the stairs?'

'No.'

'And did you notice anything different inside the flat – stuff missing, or moved?'

Stax rubs his forehead. 'Like I told the other copper, no, the only thing I noticed was the lights, and then . . . then I went through to the bedroom, and I saw . . .'

Dom notices how pale Stax's face has gone. He gives him a breather, waiting a couple of seconds before asking the next question. 'In the past few days or weeks, did Kate mention a man she'd not talked about before? Or was there anyone she was worried about, someone acting strangely towards her?'

'No, nothing like that.'

'Can you think of anyone who'd want to harm her? Someone with a grudge?'

Stax inhales sharply. 'A grudge? What grudge would make someone do . . . that?'

Dom waits, doesn't respond. On the wall behind Stax a shabby-looking cuckoo clock noisily ticks off the seconds. Each one seems like an age.

Stax shakes his head. '*Everyone* loved her. Kate was just one of those people, you know?'

'Everyone?'

Silence. More head shaking. Stax's lips are moving, but there's no sound; it's as if he's on mute. Dom keeps eyes on him. He's one of those trendy types – although Dom supposes trendy isn't a cool word any more and, now he thinks about it, he isn't so sure *cool* is either. But, whatever the word, he has on those low-slung skinny jeans that only the young can get away with wearing, with a v-neck tee and some designer jacket. His hair's mussed up with a shedload of product – the sort of bed-hair that comes with a high price tag. 'And how were things between the two of you? Any problems, money worries, that sort of—'

'Nothing. We were good. Great.'

He's obviously into appearances, Dom thinks: carefully put-together image, smart flat, pretty girlfriend. Stax isn't even his real name. Abbott confirmed it'd been changed by deed poll three years ago. Stax goes with the DJ image better than his original last name – Buttram.

Dom wonders what he might do if his pretty girlfriend did something, someone, he didn't like. There'd been no sign of forced entry. Keeping his tone neutral, Dom asks, 'Was your girlfriend seeing someone else?'

'Jesus! What the—'

'Another man? A woman?'

'I . . .' Stax meets Dom's gaze, then looks away fast. His eyes are red-rimmed and bloodshot with grief or alcohol, probably both. '. . . a woman?'

Dom leans back, gives him some space and softens his tone. 'Look mate, I have to consider all the possibilities.'

'I . . . I'd have known.' Stax shakes his head, looks like he's tearing up and trying to fight it. 'She wasn't. She'd never . . .'

Dom believes him about Kate, but there's something lurking behind his expression, more than just grief. Something he's ashamed of. 'Are you?'

This time Stax meets his gaze and holds it. 'No.'

Dom doesn't look away; neither does Stax. For someone who's hardly made eye contact, this is unusual. The look he's giving is too strong, trying too hard. 'You sure about that?'

Stax keeps staring. 'Yes.'

There's definitely something not right, but Dom senses Stax won't give it up easily. He needs to check some facts and take a second run at him. Dom catches Abbott's eye as he gets to his feet. 'All right then, thanks.'

Abbott slides off the stool and moves towards the door.

Stax looks confused. 'Is that—'

'Like I said, I'm sorry for your loss.' The words sound less genuine than Dom would like. He is sorry about Kate, but he's not sure about Stax. He needs to keep him onside, though, for now, so he tries to inject a bit more warmth into his tone. 'You've been helpful, Mr Stax, thank you. The team will keep you updated.'

As they exit the flat, Dom turns to Abbott. 'Keep Parekh with him and get his alibi checked. I want to know what he was doing every minute of last night.'

Abbott frowns. 'You think he's good for it?'

Dom glances at his DS. He's doing that irritating thing where he bites his bottom lip with his front teeth; it makes him look like a damn rabbit. 'I'm not sure yet, but he's hiding something. I want to know what.'

The phone rings when he's halfway down the stairs. Pulling it out of his pocket, he sees the familiar number and presses answer. 'This is Bell.'

As ever, DCI Jackson skips the pleasantries and jumps right to the point. 'How's it looking?'

Dom halts on the first floor landing and gestures at Abbott to go and check Emily's progress. Abbott nods and moves away.

Dom pauses before speaking. Nothing he's got to say will please Jackson. 'The changes to the victim's appearance and posing of the body are similar to the Malik and Bretton murders.'

Jackson mutters something under his breath. 'Any leads?'

Dom notices a flap of cerise Anaglypta has curled away from the wall where it meets the banister. Beneath the paper, the wall is vomit green. 'Nothing noteworthy, not yet.'

'I suppose forensics giving us something useful is out of the question?'

He reaches out and presses the flap back against the wall. As soon as he removes his finger the paper peels away again. 'It's too soon to be sure.'

'We're going to need something for the press, something positive if we can. They're already—'

'I know. There's a load outside my crime scene. I'll give them the usual holding statement – it's all I've got right now.'

'I've tasked my assistant with arranging the press briefing.'

Dom swears. The DCI's assistant is super-efficient. The briefing will be organised before he has a chance to catch his breath. 'There's no point until we've got—'

42

'Anyway, that's not why I called.'

He waits for Jackson to continue. Theatrical pausing is something his boss does whether he's on camera or not, usually right before he delivers shitty news.

'The IPCC want you over the river for that interview. Ten thirty. No excuses.'

Dom glances at his watch. It's almost half nine. 'What, today?'

'You've been stalling too long. They're threatening all kinds of nonsense if you don't go.'

Dom hears the rattle of metal on metal. Looking round, he sees the doc's people wheeling a gurney out of the flat. He turns away. Lowering his voice, he says, 'But I gave Professional Standards a written statement weeks ago.'

'And now the IPCC have taken over the investigation, they want to hear you say it.'

Dom exhales hard. He's been dodging their calls all week. Now they've gone over his head and got Jackson to pull rank. Bastards. 'Didn't you tell them I'm running a murder investigation? There are three dead women and bugger all leads. But, slap in the middle, you're giving me a timeout to—'

'It'll take you an hour, two at the most.'

Conscious the medics are still on the stairs, Dom tries to keep his anger in check. 'Two hours at a critical point in the investigation. I need to tell the victim's parents—'

'Send Abbott to do that.' Jackson raises his voice an octave. 'My advice, Dom, is get this interview done. You keep avoiding Holsworth, you'll only end up with more grief.'

The unsaid implication isn't lost on Dom. If he hadn't been vague in his original statement five weeks ago he wouldn't be having this grief at all. Operation Atlantis had been well researched and thoroughly planned. After months of work they were ready to bring down criminal kingpin Markus Genk. The team were competent and reliable, or at least they should have been, with his mate DI Simon Lindsay leading the team on the outside and Therese on the inside. But their cover got blown and the raid went bad. Dom's hand goes to the slight indent in his forehead above his right eyebrow; the spot where he was knocked unconscious by the blow that buggered his memory. He rubs the skin, wincing from the pressure against the still tender area. 'I don't know what they think I'm holding back. I got injured. I've told them what I can remember of what happened, what I saw.'

'Look, things like this, they're distracting. They make good people screw up. Do the interview then focus on the case. We both need a win on this one.'

Dom sighs. 'Yeah, fine. I'll get it over with.'

'Good man, just tell them anything you remember, answer their questions and you can move on.'

Dom thinks about that night. About the darkness and the confusion. He *can* remember, but the faces, and the facts, are blurred like an old movie projected onto a threadbare sheet. He flinches at the memory of the gunshot. The thumping in his head starts again with greater vengeance.

Move on? If only it were that simple.

8

CLEMENTINE

In my sights are the two overly made-up girls from earlier. They seemed to know the victim. I want to know what they know. They're deep in conversation, scarlet-painted mouths working overtime. They haven't noticed me.

'Excuse me,' I say. My mouth feels dry and my words crack against my lips. 'I'm trying to find out more about the victim, can you help?'

They stare at me, all frowns and disinterest. Say nothing. My heart's punching against my ribs so hard it hurts. I pull the notebook and pencil I always carry with me from my pocket. Wave it towards them like a weapon. 'I'm doing research.'

'And you're what?' says the taller one with the ratty brunette extensions. 'One of them reporters?'

I nod. What does a lie matter, after all? I'm already assured of a hotspot in hell. 'That's right.'

Their expressions soften and they beckon me closer, under the protection of their umbrella. I step into their space and ask, 'So how do you know the victim?'

'Don't know her that well, to be honest,' the brunette says. 'I mean, I seen her about and that.'

'Right stuck-up little cow she was, you know?' The dumpier blonde one with the too-tight skinny jeans cuts in. 'Thought she was better than us. Bitchy little princess.'

I make a few notes in my book. Look back at the shorter girl. 'So you argued?'

'Nah, not really argued.' She glances at her friend. 'Just felt sorry for her man, you know? Mart Stax, he's a DJ, right? Really good, but she never went to the club or nothing.'

The taller one is shaking her head. 'It's not right to treat a man that way.'

The blonde nods. 'They've been living here about a year and a half. Reckon she'd let herself go a bit, you know, not making an effort for him. A year back she was always at the club.'

I don't comment. Make a few more notes. 'So they were having problems?'

The girls shrug.

I'm guessing they don't want to drop Mart Stax in the shit. I lean closer and give them a conspiratorial wink. 'Go on, you can tell me.'

They glance at each other and step back in unison leaving me standing in the rain again. The brunette shakes her head. 'Can't really say any more. Don't know nothing else.'

The shorter one nods. Stays silent.

I've blown it. I open my mouth to try and save the situation but they're already turning away. Shit.

I stand on the pavement and watch them move through the crowd. My jacket has given up any pretence of being waterproof, my cashmere jumper is damp and clinging against my spine like a cold flannel, the backs of my jeans are saturated and heavy. The siren call of a hot bath is alluring, but I can't go yet. The information on Kate Adams and her boyfriend is interesting but it's not concrete fact and there's no obvious lead from it. I need to find something better.

The door to the flats opens, and a hush descends on the crowd. Two medics emerge, a portable gurney with the body on it between them. A pulse of energy surges through the crowd and those around me push forward towards the barrier, eager for a look-see. The medics don't look at the crowd. They move fast, propelling the gurney from the building to the van in a matter of seconds.

I glance across to the other side of the cordon and see Bob, camera in hand, braced against the tape. He'll have a close-up shot of the body bag, no doubt. I snap a couple of pictures, but I know it isn't enough.

The medics emerge from the back of the van and slam the doors shut. Moments later the vehicle starts up and inches towards the outer cordon. There's murmuring among the crowd. Everyone's watching the van.

That changes when the door opens again and the detective and his sidekick emerge. Now all eyes are on the pair, including mine.

It's definitely him – Detective Inspector Dominic Bell. He looks just like the pictures on my Google search. His hair's drier now, making its trademark curl more apparent. Bowing his head against the wind, he takes long strides across the cordoned-off area. The lanky black detective has to hurry to keep pace.

On the opposite side of no man's land the growing media pack are jostling for position, shouting to the detectives, waving to get their attention, their smartphones and voice recorders outstretched towards the two men. DI Bell says something I can't hear.

The journalists yell more questions. I can hear *them* well enough.

'Detective Bell, is it the same killer as in Camden?'

'Dominic, over here, tell us what you found.'

'Early thoughts, DI Bell?'

'Did the Lover do this? Why's it been four weeks and there's still no arrest?'

He doesn't break his stride as he growls, 'Press briefing at six.'

Maybe he's been told not to engage with the press and is following the chain of command, but there's something angry, contemptuous, about the way he ignores their questions. I wonder what his story is.

The van reaches the outer perimeter and brakes, waiting for a uniform to remove the tape and let it through. The two detectives look like they're heading towards the gap as well.

I see my chance; there's nothing more for me here, but if I can find out more about the police effort, that would be information of value to Death Stalker and the team. I wait, using the rubber-neckers as camouflage until the detectives have gone past, then ease through the crowd away from the barrier. No one gives me a second glance.

In terms of threat, Detective Inspector Dominic Bell spells danger; if he finds out about True Crime London and what we're doing, he'd close down our citizen's investigation, I'm sure. Like a poisonous snake, he requires careful handling. I watch as he and the other policeman exit the cordon and head down the side road towards the High Street. I can't see their faces, but it's clear they're having a heated debate.

I wait three seconds then follow.

At the junction with the High Street, they stop. I'm far enough behind not to look suspicious, but too close to stop without drawing attention to myself. I keep going. Drop my head so the hood of my jacket droops lower over my eyes.

As I draw nearer, I hear the sidekick talking.

'So what's the urgent—'

'Errand for Jackson. Non-negotiable.' DI Bell's tone is hard. It's obvious the subject isn't open for discussion. 'Shouldn't take too long, all right?'

'I'll let you know if something comes in.'

'Yeah, do that. Thanks, Abbott.' DI Bell strides away. He turns left up the High Street and disappears.

My fingertips tingle. It's a small triumph, but now I've got both their names: Detective Inspector Dominic Bell and his sidekick, Abbott.

I keep walking. Go past Abbott, and take a left. Now it's just Bell and me. He walks fast and I have to take two paces for every one of his to stop him extending the distance between us.

We reach Angel tube station. It's a busy spot, people bustling in and out, others loitering on the street outside – magazine sellers in dripping raincoats with stacks of soggy papers piled beside them; a line of people huddled at the bus stop, backs pressed against the glass of the shelter, trying to keep dry. The traffic along the road is as relentless as the weather.

DI Bell heads inside. He crosses the foyer towards the turnstiles. I hover on the pavement, unsure of my next move. I don't go on the tube. Not ever. I don't want to let him go, though. He's my best shot at finding something better to bring to the group.

I follow him. I'm passing through the cattle crush of the turnstiles as DI Bell reaches the escalator. Inch by inch he disappears. I push past a fat man in an expensive-looking suit as I hurry to catch up. I can't lose sight of the detective now. From his tone it sounded as if he didn't want his sidekick to know where he's going. That can't be normal in the middle of investigating a fresh crime scene? I hope it's not normal. I need it to be something unusual and interest-worthy.

I have to get enough information to stay in the team.

I'm halfway down the escalator when the first symptoms manifest. My breath catches in my throat and I start coughing. The woman in front, a skirt-suited forty-something, turns round to glare at me. Fighting the urge to keep coughing, I ignore her until she turns back round.

By the time I'm at the bottom it feels like there's a leather strap being tightened notch by notch around my chest. I fight through it, keep my eyes focused on DI Bell, as I navigate the swarm of people in the tunnel. He's eight, maybe ten metres in front of me as we round a bend.

Papery moth wings flutter in my chest and I swallow hard, trying to force them away. Doesn't work. My throat's too dry and I cough, louder this time. Keep coughing. My legs feel odd, weightless. I wobble, unable to maintain pace behind the detective. More coughing. No one around me makes eye contact.

The crowding is worse on the platform. There's a tube train already here and people are barging towards it. Those inside are already rammed tight. I stand on tiptoes, scanning the platform for the detective. Where is he? Have I lost him?

The door alarms beep. An announcement sounds over the tannoy: *Please stand back from the closing doors.*

That's when I spot him along the platform to my right. He jumps into a carriage; it's too late for me to follow. The doors slam shut behind him.

This train is about to leave. Stand back from the platform's edge. The next train will arrive in one minute.

'Stand back,' shouts an irate guard. 'This train is leaving, the next one is right behind.'

The people closest to the carriages shunt backwards. There's no room. It's hot, so hot – stifling. Something sharp, an elbow or the corner of a briefcase, smacks into my back. I stumble deeper into the crowd. Panic surges through me. It feels like I'm suffocating. I have to get out.

Twisting round, I shove my way back towards the tunnel. I hurtle back up the escalators, blast through the turnstiles and I'm free. Stumbling onto the pavement, I take a few steps to get clear of the heat and the people, and stop. Leaning against the iron railings with the rain pouring down on me, I fish in my pocket and pull out a soggy packet of cigarettes. Lighting up with shaking hands, I inhale, deep and slow.

I tell myself it's OK. I know that it's not, though. Dominic Bell has got away.

The clock is counting down to Death Stalker's deadline.

I've still got nothing.

9

DOM

The atrium of the IPCC offices is vast, and far grander than any police building. With the curved reception desk, the granite-clad walls and the huge flower displays, it's more like some fancy hotel. The young guy behind the desk watches Dom approach through black-framed glasses.

Dom nods at him. 'I've got a meeting at ten thirty with Mr Holsworth.'

Dom watches as he brings up a diary on the computer. From the look of Holsworth's schedule, he's the only appointment the investigator has that morning. Hopefully they can make it quick.

The reception guy looks back at Dom, smiles with an air of smugness. 'That's fine. I'll let him know you've arrived. Take a seat and someone will be along to collect you shortly.'

Dom hates this place already. The echoing space and high ceiling makes him feel uncomfortable, out of place. He sits down heavily on a cream armchair.

He crosses his legs, then uncrosses them. Jigs his left heel up and down as he thinks about what he'll say when Holsworth asks him about the raid. The brief for the undercover operation was clear enough; get Markus Genk to take the bait that would let them destroy his sex trafficking business and arrest him. DI Therese Weller had been in the lead. She'd initiated contact with Genk, handled the communications and got them close to him. As far as their target knew, Therese was a criminal looking to do business. Dom had been her her back-up. DI Simon Lindsay, his mate from their rookie years, and DS Darren Harris, boyfriend to his sister, Chrissie, had been leading on communications. The memory of the raid is jumbled in his mind, the thump on the head saw to that, but he knows someone had to have tipped off Genk, and someone must have helped him get away.

He jigs his leg faster. For someone to tip off the target they'd have to have been part of the team, people he counted as friends as well as colleagues. One of the team had been much more than a friend: Therese. Now he's no idea if he should trust any of them.

Dom glances towards reception. Above the desk, screwed into the black and pink granite, four clocks show the time in London, Hong Kong, New York and Sydney. Dom has no clue why people in this office need world time information. He stares at the London clock, watching the minute hand move from 10.30 to 10.40 and beyond, and feels more pissed off with every second. Holsworth had nothing in his diary to delay him, so why the wait? Dom assumes it's a power play. That pisses him off even more.

His phone rings. Dom recognises the number on the screen. Presses answer. 'Abbott?'

'Guv, there's something you need to see.'

'What is it?'

The signal is cutting in and out, and his sergeant's voice sounds metallic, like a Dalek.

Dom looks at the London clock; it's 10.48. The bastard's kept him waiting twenty minutes already. He's in the middle of a murder inquiry, there's no time for this shit. 'Where are you?'

'Back . . . base . . . got a new . . . interesting, could be . . .'

Sod this.

Dom stands. 'I'll be there soon as I can.'

He's almost at the exit when the reception guy calls, 'DI Bell?'

Dom glances over his shoulder. 'Tell Holsworth I couldn't hang around any longer.'

He steps into the revolving door and escapes the building. Operation Atlantis is over; picking through the carcass of that cock-up won't change things. Right now, there's a killer out there and three dead women waiting for justice; the best way to atone for the past is to find the truth for them. Sod the procedural bullshit. Whatever questions Holsworth has, they'll have to bloody wait.

10
CLEMENTINE

Twenty minutes' walk and four flights of stairs later, I'm home. Inside, I fasten the deadlock and slide each of the four bolts into place. I close my eyes a moment, then open them and look again at the bolts to confirm they're closed.

Next, I press my finger against the shaft of each bolt, tracing along the barrel to where it passes over the edge of the door between the two brackets. Locked. Rationally, I know they're all locked.

I want to turn away, to go and get dry, but I can't. Again, I press my finger against the top bolt, checking that it's pushed completely home. I count out loud as I double-check each one in turn. 'One . . . two . . . three . . . four.'

Exhale.

I repeat the process in reverse, bottom to top. 'Four . . . three . . . two . . . one.'

Checked. Double-checked. Triple-checked. Done.

Forcing myself to turn away, I yank off my boots and the mismatched green and orange socks beneath, and dump them beside the door. Unzipping my jacket, I let it fall onto the sodden heap, and pad barefoot across the wooden floor of the living space. I look back at the bolts only once. I count that as a small triumph.

The flat is warm, the old radiators competent enough at spewing out heat, but still I start to shiver. I rid myself of the damp jumper and keep going, stripping off everything until I'm naked. The floorboards feel cold against my feet. There's a draft from the sash window in the corner. The cold air tickles across my patchwork skin, the grafted places on my arms and legs feeling the temperature change less acutely.

I step past the sofa, between the piles of books surrounding my desk, and pick up the thick fleece blanket folded over the back of my chair. Wrapping it round me, I sit down. My laptop is on but hibernating. I tap the space bar to wake it and open the CrimeStop website.

Crime Queen and **Robert 'chainsaw' Jameson** posted in Case Files: The Lover

I click to view their posts. First up is Bob's. It's long, with waffle dirtying up the facts, but he's managed to get some information from his journalist friend. As well as the time of tonight's press conference, he's gathered details on the victim similar to those I got from the neighbours. Unconfirmed as yet by the police, the journalist says the dead woman is Kate Adams, twenty-six. She lived in the flat with her boyfriend, Mart Stax. Bob says the police questioned Stax while we were outside the building.

I wonder what secrets Kate Adams's boyfriend had to tell, and if he told them, or if he kept quiet like I did when the police questioned me twelve years ago.

Murderer.

I push the word away and refocus on the screen. Bob doesn't know if Mart Stax has been arrested. He's having a beer with the journalist tonight to find out more, but that's not why I curse. Attached to the post is a new photo album with eighty-two crime scene photos.

I decide to upload my photos anyway.

The Watcher Here's my first upload from the crime scene. I also spoke to a neighbour. They confirmed victim as Kate Adams and that she'd lived with her boyfriend Mart Stax, a DJ, for about one and a half years. They implied the relationship had problems but wouldn't elaborate. Attached: New photo album – crime scene task [forty-three photos]

'Fuck you, Bob,' I say as I press return. It might not be enough to keep me in the team, but it'll do until I find something better.

I scroll to the next post. It's from Crime Queen and links to a website – www.darkstreetsdarkcrimes.com. I click it and a new window opens. It's a true-crime blog, Crime Queen's I assume, dedicated to the celebrity of serial killers. This surprises me. We're trying to catch the Lover, but from the fangirl-style posts on her blog, it looks like Crime Queen is considering him as a future husband. The title of today's blog post is 'Who's Hunting the Lover?' I scan the text. The piece is more puff than content, like some trashy gossip magazine.

Amid the fluff are three photographs. The first picture is of Emily Renton, Pathologist. She's a mousy-haired, chubby-looking middle-aged woman. Plain, but with sharp eyes that look straight at the camera.

I scroll to the second picture. It's the lanky black detective I saw chatting with DI Bell earlier – Detective Sergeant Abbott. The third photo is the lead detective himself.

Leading the search for the Lover is Detective Inspector Dominic Bell – a bit of a hottie by anyone's standards. He's DS Abbott's boss and has been in charge of the case since the first murder victim was found four weeks ago but it remains to be seen if he's a match for the Lover. Spotted earlier at the crime scene, Bell (pictured) refused to comment for the media.

I double-click on his image to enlarge it. He's glaring at the camera. I scan the background, see the tape that marked the outer cordon of the crime scene and the corner of the police van. Bob and me weren't the only True Crime Londoners at the scene; Crime Queen must have been there, too.

Goosebumps rise along my arms and I shiver. Did she not introduce herself because she didn't recognise me, or because she wanted to operate below the radar? What is she hiding?

I'm assuming she's a woman, not because of the name – that could be male or female – but because of her online interaction pattern, responses and blogging style. Her comments feature in my thesis; she's one of the key group members pushing the others towards solving live cases, and she's got increasingly more dominant in the group over the nineteen months I've been watching. Now I want to know who she is.

I move the mouse to my research database, but before I click it, a red number one appears beside the CrimeStop icon. As I watch, the number rises: two, three, five. I click on the icon.

Ghost Avenger added six photos to the album The Lover: Victims
Robert 'chainsaw' Jameson and five others commented on a post in Case Files: The Lover

Clicking the first alert, I go to Ghost Avenger's post. Ghost Avenger, usually the joker of True Crime London with his daily postings of puns and gifs, has uploaded some pictures with maximum shock value.

I scroll through them. First there's a hand, with pastel pink-painted nails that look at odds with the grey tinge of the skin. Next is a close-up of an ear, framed by mid-brown curls. There are two piercings in the lobe, but no rings or studs. Then, a closed eye, lined by thick lashes, wearing no make-up; the skin of the eyelid looks almost translucent.

As I keep scrolling the images repeat – a hand, an ear, an eyelid. That's when I realise. The pictures aren't the same. The set-up is, but the subject is different – there are two women, not one. I study the second set more closely. The skin of the hand is pale, but more olive-toned than the first. The piercings in the second ear are closer to the bottom of the earlobe than the first, and one looks newer, raw. The lashes of the eye in the final picture are a shade darker.

These photos look like trophy shots, the kind of mementos a killer would keep. I shiver again, wonder what the hell I've got myself into; who is Ghost Avenger? Frowning, I scroll back, looking for an explanation, but there is none.

Another notification appears:

Ghost Avenger added two photos to the album The Lover: Victims

I follow the link to the new images. As they appear side by side I see Ghost Avenger has captioned these pictures. On the left is

Jenna Malik – the Lover's first victim. To the right is Zara Bretton, his second. The photos are full body shots. Both women lie on a metal surface, a pale green sheet covering their nakedness from knees to collarbone. These photos were taken in a clinical setting; my guess is a mortuary. Ghost Avenger isn't joking now.

I lean forward, peering closer. Even if they hadn't been taken in a mortuary I'd have known these women were dead. There's an absolute stillness about them, a different quality to when someone's unconscious or sleeping, a slackness to their features as if they've been de-animated. It's mesmerising.

Dead. Fascinating. Dead fascinating. There are no boundaries now, no taboos; the web is a portal to every kind of horror. Whether dead bodies are your thing, or you enjoy watching torture, or get off on snuff videos – whatever you want is available at a click. I'm not interested out of morbid curiosity, though; for me it's more personal.

I zoom in on Jenna Malik's face. Trace my finger over her cheekbone to her lips. She looks so peaceful. I wonder if I looked that way in the minutes I was dead. I wonder if I felt peace. I haven't since.

Sometimes I wish the paramedics hadn't arrived in time.

Jealousy needles at me like a thousand tiny pinpricks. Peaceful has to be better than empty, doesn't it? Empty just feels like vast, endless nothingness. Often I've thought perhaps the reason I feel nothing is because I shouldn't be alive; that I cheated death, but I'm not meant to exist, that the numbness is a punishment for me to atone for what I did, for the fact that I'm still here, breathing.

It's not enough, though, just existing. Not any more.

I want to feel like something.

I pull back from the close-up and study the two pictures side by side. Both mortuary-cold women look peaceful. But it's not just the peacefulness that's similar; it's their whole appearance. I frown. Jenna Malik and Zara Bretton shouldn't look this similar. Opening another window, I type their names into the search engine, hunting for news reports on the Lover's previous kills.

Thousands of mentions are listed, the media feeding frenzy on their cases has spawned articles galore – broadsheets, tabloids, online magazines, blogs – everyone wants to get in on the action. From the read-counters that tally into the millions it seems the public's appetite is barely sated.

I open a tabloid article. I see Jenna Malik beaming from the photo; it's a graduation picture – her in a cap and gown, fresh-faced with minimal make-up, French-manicured fingernails clenched around a plastic scroll. Her hair is light brown.

I search for Zara Bretton. Her picture looks like it was taken at a birthday party. She's holding a cupcake decorated with a silver number 21 and a sparkler, grinning at the camera. Her hair is blonde.

I toggle back to True Crime London. Both women in the mortuary pictures have hair the same shade of mid-brown. I zoom in on Zara Bretton's image, magnifying the area around her hairline. There's no root growth visible. I do the same with Jenna's photo. Again, no growth, meaning both women had freshly dyed hair when they were killed.

Flicking to the comments section, I see the messages beneath Ghost Avenger's post are stacking up. The pictures are proving controversial.

Crime Queen WTF?? Details . . .
Ghost Avenger I'm just delivering my contribution to the group.
Please treat these pictures as strictly confidential and do not share them wider, I would hate for the victims' families to see them.
Robert 'chainsaw' Jameson These are real? How so?
Justice League Just referring to my notes, these are the first two 'Lover' victims, yes?
Ghost Avenger @JusticeLeague Correct
Ghost Avenger @Robert 'chainsaw' Jameson I have access through my job
Bloodhound YOU SHOULD HAVE PUT A WARNING ON THESE! I don't want to look at pictures of dead people! It's perverse. I can't believe you've forced me to see these images.
Ghost Avenger @Bloodhound This was my assigned task. Apologies if you're upset but it's data for our investigation. These are similar to the pictures taken by the police. It brings

our level of awareness of the victims closer to theirs. You're not supposed to get off on it and that was never my intention!
Bloodhound @GhostAvenger 'Get off on it'? Jesus! That's vile.
Ghost Avenger @Bloodhound Exactly my point. These women have been murdered. If we're serious about investigating this case, and finding their killer, we need to be prepared to tolerate looking at fucking horrible things.

Rationally, I know that murder is wrong. Taking a life, that's as forbidden as it gets. But I don't experience outrage at the wrongness like Bloodhound. Theoretically, I understand why he is revolted by these images. I cannot feel it, though, and that means I need to be careful – I can't have the group realising I'm different – so I wait a little longer to ask my question.

Crime Queen @GhostAvenger What's your job?
Robert 'chainsaw' Jameson What is your job?
Ghost Avenger I'm a mortuary technician. That's how I got close enough to take these pictures. Obviously I'm not supposed to, so please keep photos confidential
Robert 'chainsaw' Jameson Useful for our investigation. Thanks for sharing
Death Stalker @GhostAvenger Good work

I assume that Death Stalker knew about Ghost Avenger's job. It makes sense to give him the task of getting images of the victims; a role in the mortuary gives him unique access to their bodies. But it's four weeks since the Lover's first victim was found, so when did he take these photos? Does he photograph all the dead in the mortuary? I wonder about these questions, but I ask something different.

The Watcher @GhostAvenger Has Kate Adams been brought to your mortuary? If so, what colour is her hair?
Ghost Avenger I'm not on shift right now. When I get in later I'll check for you and report back.
Bloodhound All this gawping over dead bodies is ghoulish.

Crime Queen It's necessity not fun.

Bloodhound Keep telling yourself that!!

Robert 'chainsaw' Jameson There's no need to get offensive. Some of us consider this a public duty.

Bloodhound Bollocks. You enjoy it.

Death Stalker This discussion has taken an unhelpful deviation. As moderator of this group I'm imposing sanctions. This place is for serious investigators only please desist from this line of conversation @Bloodhound or I will remove you from the group.

Bloodhound doesn't respond. I can see why Death Stalker intervened. I guess some addicts prefer their true crime pre-sanitised and sanctioned as entertainment by Netflix rather than raw and unfiltered. Maybe it's easier to pretend they're not feasting on the remains of someone's life that way.

I'm still thinking about it when the number one appears beside the messenger icon. It's Death Stalker. He wants to speak privately.

Death Stalker to @TheWatcher Hair colour?

The Watcher to @DeathStalker Jenna Malik's hair was naturally light brown. Zara Bretton was blonde. In these pictures they have the same mid-brown shade, freshly dyed. I'm assuming this is the Lover's work? The news reports say the victims' appearance had been changed. I think he's making them look like someone else.

Death Stalker to @TheWatcher Nice observation.

It feels like I'm being patronised. From Death Stalker's reaction I'm thinking he knew about the hair colour already. I'm pretty sure he's holding information back from the group. I wonder if he's trying to make me complicit by messaging me privately rather than replying on the forum.

The Watcher to @DeathStalker You knew already?

Death Stalker to @TheWatcher Patience

Condescending bastard. I stare at his avatar, the outline of a face in shadow, and want to punch it. Slowly, I breathe into the anger. Why is he holding back information? Doesn't he want the investigation to succeed? The thought I've been deliberately ignoring since this all began surfaces insistently: is Death Stalker involved in the killings somehow?

> **The Watcher** to @DeathStalker I'm not good at being patient.
> **Death Stalker** to @TheWatcher Find some good crime scene intelligence and submit it by 06:23. Once you're confirmed in the group I'll share everything I know. We need everyone on the team 100% committed. This is an important investigation, we have the chance to shake up the status quo and make the government and the police see just how far they've strayed from their responsibilities to the people of this country. I need to know I can rely on you. Complete your task, then we'll talk again.

I'm right, he knows more. Maybe, as he says, he's leading the investigation to increase debate on social justice, or maybe he's involved somehow. The only way of finding out is to make the cut for the team and learn all he knows. I need more information.

A fresh barrage of rain pelts the window beside me, and I shiver. The fleece blanket isn't enough to keep the cold at bay. It's as if the damp has chilled through to the marrow. I'm too cold to think, and I need to plan my next move; get some information of value before first thing tomorrow.

Hugging the blanket tighter, I get up and walk to the bathroom. The aged taps squeak as I turn them on full. I squeeze a dollop of lemon-scented bath foam into the tub and, as the steam swirls into the room like mist, I step into the water. A quick bath to get warm, then I'll be able to focus, to think.

Lying back, I sink low until every bit of me from the neck down is submerged beneath the bubbles. I exhale. Try to relax as the warmth spreads across my frozen skin, and close my eyes. I let myself slip lower, my mouth beneath the water. Breathe in through my nose, a long breath, and slide below the surface.

11
DOM

It's just gone 11.30, and the office is almost empty. The few detectives at their desks blank him as he passes. Trying to ignore the snub, he finds Abbott in the small meeting room they've commandeered as the incident room for the case. He's facing the murder board, staring at his phone as he eats.

'What have we got?' Dom says.

Abbott switches off the phone's screen. He's not quick enough, though. Dom clocks the red and white logo of one of the bitchier online news sites – *News Byte* – and reads the headline: *Met lets the Lover strike again*. From the way they reported it you'd think he'd *wanted* another murder to happen.

Finishing his mouthful, Abbott says, 'Just catching up on Twitter. You got back quick.'

'Yeah.' Dom looks away from the phone. It's easier to pretend he didn't see the article. 'How'd it go with the parents?'

Abbott looks grim. 'Shit. That's why I called. They want to speak to you.'

Dom's surprised. Most people want to avoid him these days. 'Why?'

'Wouldn't say. Just said they wanted to speak to the lead detective. They're here. Downstairs. There's a FLO with them.'

Dom nods. There's no point putting it off. 'Better get down there then.'

The interview room is a rubbish place to talk to Kate's parents. Wherever you are it's a shit job, but if they'd been in their own home they'd have had familiar surroundings, been more comfortable. The scuffed lino floor and pale green walls of this room aren't designed for comfort. The fluorescent lighting is harsh, unforgiving. When Dom enters Kate Adams' parents – Bernard and Lucielle – are sitting side by side on two plastic chairs, their backs to the door. The FLO is on the opposite side of a table. No one is speaking.

'I'm sorry you had to wait,' Dom says by way of introduction as he moves round the table. 'I'm Detective Inspector Dominic Bell.'

They don't get up. Kate's father, Bernard, reaches for his wife's hand. They're both still wearing their coats – his green Barbour is undone over a country check shirt, her pink Puffa is zipped tight. They're immaculately turned out, even in grief.

Their expressions are those of two people caught on a tightrope of emotion; they've not come to terms with the horror of what's happened, but they're hoping he has some answers. Or that it's a mistake.

It's not a mistake, though, and he has no answers. Dom can see they're trying to hold it together but the strain is evident on their faces. He ploughs on. 'DS Abbott said you wanted to speak with me?'

Bernard nods.

Neither of them speak.

Dom sits down and waits. Lets them take their time.

'It's that boyfriend of hers. Mart Stax,' Bernard says. His voice has a tremble that's at odds with his stern expression. 'We've never liked him.'

Lucielle sniffs loudly. The sound seems strange coming from such a petite, bird-like woman. Her words come in a rush. 'He bled her dry, always had her paying off his debts, liked living way above his station.'

'Had she told you they were having problems? Was he violent towards her?'

Lucielle shakes her head. 'Nothing like that, she's just such a kind soul, wants to help people, that's why she took the job at NHS 111. And she's always seeing the good in people. Even Mart. Always helping him out of trouble.'

Bernard grunts agreement.

'Had she mentioned anyone else, or anything else, that was worrying her?'

They shake their heads. Bernard's cheeks flush and Dom can tell he's steeling himself to ask a question.

'What did they do to her?'

Dom hates that he's asked. Wonders if he really wants to know the answer.

'They're saying on Twitter she was killed by the Lover. Is it true?'

Fucking Twitter. Dom shakes his head. 'It's too early to say, sir. We're following multiple lines of enquiry. It'll be—'

'So it's possible . . . oh God . . .' Bernard's words trail off. He clutches his wife's hand tighter. When he speaks again his voice is strangled, forced. 'Did they . . . I need to know . . . did they violate her like the others?'

Dom doesn't speak. He's not supposed to give details out at this stage; they'll still need to do a proper interview with Bernard and Lucielle once they've had a chance to process what's happened. But the anguish in the man's eyes is killing him. Dom looks down. Gives a slight nod.

As soon as he does Lucielle buries her face into Bernard's chest. Bernard struggles to stay strong, but fails. He grimaces as he tries to hold back his emotion. The effort twists his features and tears stream down his cheeks.

Dom stays sitting on the chair, watching Bernard howl and Lucielle trying to soothe him, and feels utterly fucking useless.

An hour later, back in the incident room, Dom tries to focus. He looks at the murder board. Photos of the victims are tacked along the top. Abbott has added Kate Adams's picture. Dom stares at it. The smiling blonde in the picture is totally different from the dead brunette he saw a few hours ago. He follows the dotted line from the photo to the picture below; her partner, Stax. He looks back at Kate, at the block capitals written above her photo: DECEASED.

Tracking back along the pictures he looks from Kate Adams to the second victim – Zara Bretton. The photo at the top is from her twenty-first birthday party. The original picture had been of her and two friends – they'd cropped it around Zara and enlarged it for the board. He stares at the photo, at Zara Bretton's broad smile. Like Kate Adams, Zara was blonde, although not a natural one. She was younger, too, only twenty-three. She'd worked at an artisan sandwich shop while looking for acting work. She thought she'd get her big break. Instead she got killed.

Six days ago she'd been found dead in her canal-side apartment in Camden by her best friend; naked on the bed, surrounded by rose petals and the stubs of burnt-out candles. A single black rose between her breasts. Five dotted lines go from her photo to others below. All are men. Each has a thick black cross over them. Five lines of enquiry, five possible suspects – all followed through and cleared.

He moves on to the picture of the first victim – Jenna Malik. She'd graduated that summer and moved out of a shared student house to a friend's flat in Crouch End to house-sit while the friend was away on a gap year. According to her parents she'd originally planned to travel herself, but when she was offered a place on a prestigious graduate training scheme she decided instead to start work. She was smart, motivated, and then four weeks ago she was killed. With her light brown hair cut into a heavy fringe and her make-up-free face, she'd looked much younger than her twenty-one years. It'd taken two days before she was discovered – one of her work colleagues raised the alarm. Jenna has three dotted lines to three male suspects; each different from those below Zara Bretton and Kate Adams, each is crossed out.

Three dead women; nothing to connect them. There's got to be something. Has to be.

He glances at the picture below; Jenna Malik again, but how she was found at the crime scene. She looks older; the eighties-style make-up ageing her, the darker brown curls making her look pale and washed out. Zara Bretton's crime scene photo is almost identical. Her skin tone is ever so slightly darker, but everything else looks the same. From memory, he thinks Kate Adams's crime scene picture will match just as closely.

He's still staring at the photos when his mobile vibrates in his pocket. Pulling it out, he sees Parekh's name flashing on the screen and answers.

'Guv, I'm with Mart Stax, we've been talking about the night before Kate was killed. He says she seemed twitchy, was acting a bit funny when she got in from her night out with the girls.'

'Does he know why?'

'No, but he reckons her friend might. Eva Finch. They worked together and were both out that night. Told each other everything, he says.'

'All right, thanks. Get the friend's details and text me?'

'Will do.'

Dom hangs up and hurries into the open plan. It's still deserted aside from Abbott over at his workstation, talking into his mobile. Dom catches his eye and jerks his head towards the door. Keeps walking.

Abbott catches Dom up. 'Central Control are sending CCTV footage over.'

'Good.'

'So where now?'

Opening the door to the stairwell, Dom marches through. 'To see what Kate's best mate can tell us.'

12

He's pleased their schedules align. Her routine is to swim at lunchtime, every day, but that isn't always possible for him. Today he has the time, and for that he is grateful. Because although he knows he will see her tonight, a whole day is too long to wait. He pines when they are apart.

When she left her office at 12.30 he was waiting outside for her. They took the short walk to Breeze's Gym, then changed quickly; her into the blue and orange racing-back swimming costume, him into black swimming shorts. Her hair is pinned up on the top of her head in a messy bun. He favours a swimming cap, black, to cover his, and a pair of goggles. He doesn't want to be recognised.

He's already in the water, in the deep end of the leisure area, when she emerges from the changing room. He treads water as he watches her. Admires the elegant way she slides into the pool. Her impeccable stroke as she swims lengths in the fast lane. She is so close, but he cannot touch her. Yet.

He savours the delayed gratification. It feels just as it did that first time, in the dusty old barn deep in the sun-scorched South African bush. He'd been the youngest, the pale, skinny kid from England, allowed to tag along with his older cousins and their friends as long as he did as they said. That afternoon they'd told him he had to do her. She had been his initiation – part of his journey to becoming a man. It had felt good.

He swims breaststroke as he watches her complete her twenty lengths. When she exits the pool, vaulting up onto the side rather than using the steps, he knows he will have thirteen minutes until she leaves the gym and walks back to her office. He waits until she's out of sight before he hurries from the pool.

He is faster at changing. He's sitting in the relaxation area facing away from the changing rooms, coffee in hand, baseball cap on his head, when she walks towards the exit. As she passes he inhales. She smells of orchids and peach blossom. He's dizzy at their proximity. Wants to reach out and touch her.

But he doesn't. And he doesn't follow her either. Not again. Not in daylight.

The waiting is part of the thrill.

He cannot wait much longer.

13

CLEMENTINE

My lungs feel like they're about to explode. Still I hold back, fighting the urge to breathe. Getting this close to death makes me almost feel alive.

The image in my mind's eye isn't the usual one. I'm in the reception area at school waiting for Father. I've been sitting on the wooden bench for a while, a long while. My bottom has got pins and needles. The sun has moved round the building as I've sat here, its light peering through the high windows at me, casting shadows across the stone-flagged floor.

Miss Penton, the receptionist, glances across at me again. Clears her throat. She doesn't think Father's coming, but I know he will. My father is a hero; he has important police work so he's often late, but he'd never, ever let me down.

That's when I hear the growl of an engine. Tyres on gravel. The slamming of a car door. Jumping up, I run outside. 'Father!'

He lifts me up, pulling me into a bear hug. I wrap my arms around his neck, giggling. He smells of soap and tobacco, and I breathe in the smell so I don't forget. I never know how long it will be before I see him again.

It wasn't always this way. When I was really little we lived as a family; Father, Mother and me. I went to the local school and we did things like other families – weekend shopping, cinema, football in the park. But after Father's promotion he started going away for months at a time, and Mother seemed permanently cross with me. Now Father and Mother are divorced and I live at school.

I try not to be lonely.

'Happy birthday, Twinkle,' he says. 'Eleven years old already, I can't believe it.'

'It's true. Miss Sue baked me a cake. Do you want some?'

'Maybe later, don't want to ruin our appetites.' He gestures to the back seat of his car, at a wicker hamper and a tartan rug. 'I thought this would be fun.'

Grinning, I nod. This is going to be the best birthday.

We walk through the grounds playing I Spy. I spy B for buttercups, S for squirrel. Father spies E for the gold earrings I'm wearing, and says he's sorry he wasn't there when I had my ears pierced.

When we reach the biggest oak tree, Father spreads out the rug and we plonk ourselves down onto it. I chatter away as he lays out the feast. I wait for him to give the nod, then we dive in, loading our plates and stuffing ourselves on quiche, triangle sandwiches, crisps and sausage rolls.

As we eat he asks me about school. I tell him my grades are mainly As, my piano playing isn't going so well, and that I've got the part of Nancy in the next school play – *Peter Pan*. He listens, smiling and nodding as I talk, but he seems distracted. He keeps glancing at his phone.

'Are you OK?' I ask.

He smiles. 'Just work stuff, nothing you need to fret about.'

I grin, and eat a fondant fancy to show I'm not bothered. Father's frowning, though. He's changed, aged, in the four months since I last saw him. His black hair is clipped shorter and has more grey. The lines around his eyes are more heavily etched. His brown eyes are just as bright, but there's a worry in them I've never seen before.

'Tell me about this job,' I say. 'More bad people doing bad things?'

He puts down the sandwich in his hand. 'Lots of bad people, lots of bad things.'

I lean forward, wondering if he'll give me details. He never usually gives me details. 'Are you working undercover? Will you get another medal?'

He sighs. 'I don't think anyone will give me a medal for what I'm doing.'

'Why is—'

His phone rings. He looks apologetically at me then gets up, answering the call in a voice rougher than his own. 'What?'

I can't hear what's being said, but as he listens to the caller he looks angry. Then he's speaking, shaking his head, saying he *can't do that, won't do it*. A minute or so later he agrees to whatever they're discussing and hangs up. As he walks back towards me I eat another fondant fancy and pretend I wasn't eavesdropping.

He starts packing away the picnic. 'I'm sorry, I've got to go.'

'Already? But you only just got here.'

He avoids my eyes. Puts the sandwiches back into their carton, wraps the sausage rolls in cling film, folds up the blanket. 'It's the job.'

My lower lip quivers. 'Yes I know.'

Father looks sad. 'Sometimes it makes me do stuff I don't want to. It's a hard world out there, Twinkle. You have to make tough choices or you won't survive.'

Fighting back tears, I breathe in. Water floods my lungs and I'm choking.

Arms thrashing. Hands grasping. I fight myself free. Bath suds and water cascade over the sides of the bath as I struggle to sit up. Gasping. Coughing. The taste of soapy lemon foam makes me retch as his words repeat in my mind: *Make tough choices or you won't survive.*

Back at my desk, I nurse a coffee in one hand and a cigarette in the other. I stare at the Twitter feed under #TheLover while I think about my next move.

@dexy457: #TheLover has killed again? Seriously people, are the police even trying to catch this guy?

@bigben95: Don't go out alone ladies. I'll protect you #TheLover #crime

@donaldgee: London just got less safe - #TheLover is in town

@witness_zero: Something needs to happen #TheLover

@mspaulabeale: #TheLover tip: stick to the south, all victims have been north

Idiots and fantasists, that's what a serial killer flushes out in
the Twittersphere. I encountered plenty when I was doing my
research. Hundreds took part in my survey, always super-eager
to talk about their passion, pathetically grateful I was taking
an interest. True Crime Londoners seemed different, but after
meeting Bob I wonder if they really are. I remember my idea to
reacquaint myself with their survey responses.

Before I've opened my database, a new alert appears.

Death Stalker to Case Files: The Lover We're seven hours
into the first tasks. So far Ghost Avenger, Robert 'chainsaw'
Jameson, Bloodhound, Witness_Zero and Crime Queen have
successfully completed [guys — I've messaged you with new
tasks] and are confirmed members of the group. Justice
League and The Watcher, we need more from you — you've got
seventeen hours to deliver.

He's goading me, piling on the pressure with his ticking clock
countdown. I hate how I've fallen into this trap, this desire, of
wanting to stay part of the group.

The Watcher @DeathStalker No problem

Back when Father was a police hero, my hero, I asked him how he
coped with working undercover, pretending to be a different person,
for so many months at a time. He told me, when you're walking
into a situation where you have little control, having confidence in
your skills is the key. If you don't have that, he'd said, bluff.

I'm trying. But this bluff will only work if I can find more
information in the next seventeen hours. I open my research
database and pull up the True Crime London file. If I have their
specialist knowledge, maybe I can spot a gap or opportunity to
find new information. That way I'll bring something fresh to our

investigation and earn my place in the group. There's another benefit, too; knowing all I can about this group helps me understand them, their motivations and how best to handle my interaction with them. Helping me keep my disguise in place.

The survey responses were supposed to be anonymous. In truth, they're simple enough to identify by running a basic algorithm. I make a quick scan of the data, looking for markers to help me identify the people in Case Files: The Lover.

At first it's easy. In the end of survey comments box, three of them left their contact details in case I wanted to chat further. This gives me Bob's email address, and the real name and email of Justice League and Bloodhound.

I like to see data visually. Getting up, I grab a dry marker and start to write on the whiteboard beside my desk. At the top of the board I write CASE FILES: THE LOVER. Above it, over to the left side, I write ROBERT 'CHAINSAW' JAMESON. I list all the details I have on him – mid-sixties, retired, bobjames69@hotmail.com. I write his weaknesses – flattery, ego, need to be right.

Next up is BLOODHOUND. Real life name: Colin Blunt. A Google search finds nothing about him, but in the comments box of my survey he included his date of birth. I do the maths and make him thirty-one, a few years older than me. CrimeStop gives his location as Shepherd's Bush. Opening the document where I've stored my observation notes on True Crime London, I see at the time of the survey he was a temp on a computer help desk, and that he has a fascination with Sherlock Holmes. From a post he made a couple of months back, it's likely he's in financial debt. I note this on the whiteboard.

Moving on to JUSTICE LEAGUE, I write her real name: Jennifer Lenfield. I like the symmetry of the JL initials. In the survey she listed her occupation as student. In the comments she said she's an undergrad in criminology at Birkbeck. That makes her harder to age, as that university has mainly part-time students – she could be studying alongside a job or family responsibilities, or she could be a recent school leaver. She left the age question on the survey blank, so I've no way to know for sure, but her leaving the question unanswered makes me think she's more likely to be older.

Online, she's given few details about her personal life. Again, this lack of sharing makes me think she's more mature. She's located in Hounslow. Her writing style is considered, analytical, and she usually posts during the day, and not often at the weekends, suggesting a busy family life. At a guess I'd say she's middle-aged and looking for a bit of excitement. I note down my thoughts; that's the easy bit done.

Four more remain – Crime Queen, Ghost Avenger, Witness Zero and Death Stalker. I start with Crime Queen, write her name in block capitals to the right of the whiteboard along with her blog that she linked to. Her location is Henley-on-Thames – Buckinghamshire, not London. It's curious that Death Stalker allows her to be part of the group when his first rule said members must live in London. It makes me wonder about her London connection; does she work here? It makes me wonder about her relationship with Death Stalker, too.

I scroll through the survey data and find her responses. She's marked her age in the eighteen to twenty-four range, and states her interest in true crime as professional. That intrigues me. Maybe she's an undercover police officer spying on True Crime London, hiding behind an online persona like me. It's possible, but why also blog about crime? Surely the bigger the lie, the harder it is to maintain. I think about what other professions might fit and it strikes me that she could be a journalism student; she's the right age, assuming her answers are true. Maybe she sees blogging as her way into a career. Or maybe she's just a fanatic daydreaming about having a prison marriage with a serial killer. Maybe she fantasises about being a killer too.

Whatever her plan, the answers she's given aren't very illuminating. She's stuck to mid-scale responses, safe and conservative, unlike her often challenging comments on True Crime London. From her online behaviour I've seen she's competitive and attention-seeking – both traits that could cause trouble in the investigation.

Ghost Avenger is next. I note his location – Ealing. Now I know his job, his survey response is easy to identify. In the comments he's put he works as a mortuary technician at the Cellular Pathology Service near Euston. What's interesting is he's stated his fascination with true crime as personal. He's added he wants to understand more about those who kill, to make sense of how some people do the things they do that result in a person ending up on a slab in the mortuary. It's deeper stuff than I'd have credited him for, from his jokey interactions on True Crime London, up until today anyway. There's more to him than I'd previously thought.

Witness Zero completed my survey but left all the personal data fields blank aside from first name; Steven. He said he enjoys being part of online groups and debating current affairs, hence his interest in crime. Compared to the others, his motivation seems weak. I refer back to my observations of True Crime London, search the file for his name. In real life he lives in Brent. Online, it seems he's a transient member of the group, dipping into conversations for a few days then disappearing and resurfacing weeks later. It remains to be seen how much he contributes to our investigation.

Last is Death Stalker. I write his name in the middle of the whiteboard and stare at the blank space below. I've no survey response that's identified as his, and he's not enabled the location finder on CrimeStop. I jot down the scant details I have – male, dominant, secretive. Death Stalker has the most knowledge of the case, and the power to let me continue within the group, but there's something not right about him that I can't put my finger on. He knows too much, finds out about the Lover kill sites before any of the media. Knows details no one else seems to, but is holding back on them, playing the team off against each other rather than sharing what he knows. How does he know these things? Why doesn't he share?

What secrets is he hiding?

14

DOM

Abbott drives. As he eases his Golf out of the parking spot and into the slow-moving traffic, Dom taps the address for NHS 111 into the satnav. It finds the route; eighteen minutes to their destination.

Dom fiddles with the seat, pulling the backrest more upright. He's no idea why Abbott's missus always sets the thing at half-mast, but it's bloody annoying. Finally it clicks into place.

Abbott nods, and asks, 'So why the friend?'

'Stax told Parekh that Kate seemed twitchy after their night out. The next evening she was killed. Girls talk. If Kate was worried about something or had a bit on the side, she'd have told her mate.'

Abbott keeps driving. The top speed he's managed so far is barely pushing twenty. 'You still thinking Stax is suspicious?'

'Maybe. I want a clear run at him next time, with as much info in my pocket as I can.' Dom glances at his DS. Assumes that beneath his polite exterior he's thinking the same shit about him as all the rest. 'You don't?'

Abbott takes a left. Accelerates. 'I didn't say that, sir.'

The phone buzzes in Dom's pocket. He checks it: a text from Jackson.

Holsworth says you didn't show. Call me asap.

Shit. The last thing he needs is another earbashing. The clock's ticking; he has to have something of substance before the press briefing tonight. Has to. Deleting the text, he shoves his phone back into his pocket.

Dom glances at Abbott then nods at the road. 'Hurry it up, yeah.'

Fifteen minutes later they arrive. At first glance it's just another soulless call centre; banks of desks crammed in tight, magnolia walls and a few cheesy motivational posters. Only the NHS logo on the far wall, flanked by the call waiting and average call time screens, gives away this is part of a healthcare institution.

'She worked down that end,' the skinny team leader with the fuzzy curls says, pointing towards the desks at the farthest point of the office. 'With the Ones.'

'The Ones?' Abbott asks.

'Non-emergency calls – NHS 111. Our emergency call handlers, the Nines, sit closest to the entrance.'

Abbott raises an eyebrow. 'Why's that?'

The woman shrugs. 'It's a hierarchy thing.'

Dom stays silent. All the desks are occupied, people with headsets are talking, typing as they speak. On the big screen, twelve calls are flagged as queuing.

The team leader continues chattering as she escorts them through the office. '. . . after you called and told us about Kate, well, we were all so shocked. I mean, you read about these things, don't you, but to think it could happen to someone you know, that you actually work with . . . it's horrific. Is there anything you can—'

'How long did you know Kate Adams?'

The woman looks taken aback by Dom's interruption, but recovers fast. 'Well, she'd not been working for us very long, only a month, but she was lovely, you know, really sweet, everybody liked her.'

Dom nods. 'Did she do fixed shifts?'

'No, we work on a rota. She was great about that too, didn't moan if she had to work a late or night shift. Always happy to do overtime.' The team leader gives a sad smile. 'That made us like her all the more.'

'And did you notice anything strange about her mood recently? Had she called in sick or arrived late?'

'No, nothing. She seemed the same as always. No sick days, no lateness.'

'OK, thanks.' Dom glances across the office; the banks of desks and partitioned workspaces make him think of a battery farm for humans. He looks back at the team leader. 'You said Eva's working today?'

'Yes, yes. She's been in since eight o'clock.' They reach the end of the office and take a right round the last line of desks. The team leader points to the door a few feet ahead. 'Been waiting in meeting room one since your call.'

Abbott slows his pace, smiles. 'Thanks for your help.'

Letting his DS handle the pleasantries, Dom steps past him and opens the door. The meeting room has more of the same bland decor – pale walls, cream carpet, cheap table and blue chairs. A petite twenty-something woman with brown hair cropped into a pixie cut sits statue-still on the far side of the table.

'Eva Finch?' Dom says.

She looks up. There's a dark shadow of sadness beneath her eyes, and her cheeks are blotchy from tears. 'Yes.'

Dom steps towards her. 'I'm Detective Inspector Bell.' He gestures to Abbott who's closing the door. 'This is DS Abbott.'

Eva nods. 'What do you want to know?'

He's surprised at her directness, but senses the best approach is to match it. He sits down. 'Kate Adams's boyfriend, Mart Stax, told us she seemed upset after your girls' night out two evenings ago. Can you tell us why?'

Abbott winces. Dom figures he'd have come to the question more gently.

Eva doesn't seem to notice. 'We had a fun night. She was fine.'

'Are you sure? Her boyfriend said she seemed unusually twitchy.'

Eva grimaces. 'I bet he bloody did!'

Abbott interjects. 'Meaning?'

'Nothing.' Eva sighs. 'Look, it was a good night, generally. A few dodgy sorts, but nothing we couldn't handle.'

'Any problems between Kate and her boyfriend?'

Eva looks away. 'They were fine. She was happy.'

Dom stares at her. She looks nervous, more than upset at the death of her friend. There's something she's holding back. 'You sure?'

She nods.

'OK, tell me about the dodgy sorts in the bar then.'

'They were nothing, really.'

Dom waits. He glances at the clock on the wall opposite. It's gone half past one. He can virtually hear the seconds ticking closer to the press briefing. He's almost given up hope of getting anything when Eva speaks.

'Mostly they were nothing, but there was this guy, in the pub.'

Dom leans forward. 'What did he do?'

She shrugs. Doesn't elaborate.

Inside his pocket, Dom's mobile starts vibrating. He takes no notice. 'Where exactly was this?'

'The Wetherspoons on Euston Road. We went there for Blue Lights Night.'

Abbott glances at Dom.

'Emergency Services night,' Dom says. 'Cheap drinks for police, fire and health workers.'

Abbott shakes his head. Dom supposes that in between feeds and nappies, their new baby doesn't give Abbott and his wife much time for partying.

He looks back at Eva. 'It would really help if you could tell us about the man. For Kate.'

Fresh tears cascade down Eva's cheeks. She gives a little sob. 'There was this guy up on the mezzanine, leaning over the railing. I remember because he was alone, and every time I looked up he was watching us, staring, like a right perv.'

Abbott pulls out his scratchpad. 'Can you describe him?'

'Shit, no.' Eva pulls a face. 'I'd run out of contacts, and I couldn't go out wearing these.' She gestures to her navy-rimmed glasses; the left arm has clear tape holding it together. 'But without them I can't see more than a couple of metres ahead. I didn't get close to the guy. I remember he had dark hair, though, does that help?'

Dom nods, trying to be encouraging even though the description is hopeless. He's being too abrupt with Eva and he knows it. She's just lost her friend. 'Is there anything else you can tell us about him?' Dom keeps his tone gentle, trying to soften the words. 'Without a detailed description . . .'

Eva looks gutted. Dom knows the feeling. He glances at the clock; it's dead on two. There are four hours until the press briefing and he's got nothing solid. He starts to stand.

'Wait, hold on. When Kate went to the loo she said some guy came on to her really strong.'

'The man you saw on the mezzanine?' Abbott says.

'I don't know. But she was totally freaked out. That's what made us move on to Fusion early.'

Dom feels his phone going again. Ignoring it, he shifts forward in his chair, keeps his eyes on Eva. 'The club near Paddington?'

'That's it.'

'So how long were you at the Wetherspoons?'

'From about eight until nine thirtyish.'

'And Fusion?'

'We got a cab from the bar, and stayed until about two. After the bar we didn't see him again. There were plenty of guys trying to get close to Kate on the dance floor, but she wouldn't have it. She was loyal, you know.' Eva's voice cracks with emotion. 'A good person.'

They're halfway back to base. Dom stares through the windscreen, watching the rain pelt down. It's mid-afternoon but seems much later. His headache is back, thumping at his temples in time with the rhythmic squeak of the Golf's worn-out wiper blades.

Pulling out his wallet, he pops another couple of codeine tablets. Tries not to fixate on the dull ache leeching across the right side of his skull, and wonders again if the doctors got it wrong in saying it wasn't a fracture. He looks at Abbott. 'What did you take from that?'

'Two girls on a night out, a few drinks. A dark-haired guy, who may or may not have been watching them. Another guy, or possibly the same one, who came on to Kate strong enough to make her leave the pub. Maybe two suspects.'

'Or none.' The killer is well prepared, smart. Being so obvious as propositioning Kate in a public place with witnesses and cameras isn't a mistake Dom would expect him to make.

Abbott taps on the steering wheel. 'Don't you—'

'I'm not convinced, but we need to follow up both. Can you talk to the bar, get any CCTV they've got for when Kate was there, and the club too. Cross-reference them, see if we've got men appearing in both places.'

'Will do.' The brakes lights flare on the car in front, Abbott slows in tandem. 'So what's your theory?'

'Nothing much yet, but we didn't have any reports of the first two victims – Malik and Bretton – getting hassled by a dark-haired bloke, did we?'

'There was no mention of it in the interviews.'

'Yeah. So I'm not seeing a pattern there.'

Abbott inches the Golf forward in the traffic. 'The friend said the victim was happy, that there were no problems between her and Stax. Are you buying that?'

Dom's quiet for a moment. 'Eva Finch said that, but I'm not sure she believed it. Something's not right there. We need to find out. Find someone who doesn't just tell us how fucking happy she was.'

I don't think anyone's ever that happy, Dom thinks. His phone vibrates again; the continuous rhythm of a call. As he pulls it from his pocket it stops. On the screen it says five missed calls. Two voicemails. One text.

'Problem?' Abbott asks.

'Nothing to do with the case.'

Abbott doesn't pry. Dom likes that; he's not a nosy bastard. He's not freezing him out like the others, either; hasn't branded him a rat just because Professional Standards, and now the IPCC, keep calling him in.

He checks the text first. It's from Chrissie, his sister, reminding him he's due at hers for dinner at eight, and telling him to bring wine. Next he dials the voicemail service.

The first message is from Holsworth's assistant. She tells him they urgently need to reschedule the appointment he missed that morning. The second voicemail is from Jackson. His tone is pissed off, and his orders more direct. He makes it clear that if Dom

81

isn't in his office within the hour there's going to be a massive shitstorm heading his way.

Dom deletes the messages.

Abbott's fidgeting in his seat; trying to look like he's not overheard the voicemails and making a poor job of it. Dom wonders if he should be worried, but decides no. His DS is a straight arrow. He won't talk out of turn.

He looks at Abbott. 'Be a mate and drop me round the back.'

Abbott nods.

Dom doubts that containing the shitstorm will be as easy.

15

DOM

There's a click as the incident room door opens. DS Biggs and DS Abbott saunter in, with DC Parekh following a few strides behind.

'All right, boss,' Biggs raises his mug in mock salute.

Tosser, thinks Dom, struggling to keep his expression neutral. Biggs is too full of it for his taste, but so far his work's been solid. A long server with almost twenty-five years on the job, he has the experience but lacks the work ethic. Dom watches him pull out a chair and flop down onto it. With his curly brown hair tufty behind a receding hairline, he reminds Dom of an ageing clown. 'You done with the door to doors?'

'All those in the building and within two hundred metres of the scene,' Biggs says.

Parekh moves past the guys and perches on the table to their right. She looks at the board, then at Dom. 'Stax might stay with a friend for the next few days. I've got the address. I told him not to go far without telling us first.'

She's the opposite of Biggs, thinks Dom, young, only a few years into the job, and keen. Unlike Biggs in his faded suit trousers and tieless shirt, Parekh's skirt suit is professional, her long black hair smoothed into a ponytail. He looks at Abbott. 'Any luck getting the CCTV?'

'It's just come in.'

'We need to get on it.'

Abbott nods. Looks uncomfortable.

Parekh steps closer to the board, looks at the smiling photo of Kate, then at the shot of her dead. 'Changing their appearance, that's got to take a while. He makes his victims look younger, and—'

'Every woman's dream,' Biggs mutters.

'Right,' Parekh says. 'We all want to look good dead.'

Dom stares at Biggs. 'We're working here. Don't be a twat, yeah?'

Biggs doesn't reply.

Parekh shakes her head, but she's smiling. 'He must have gear, you know? Make-up, hair dye and stuff. That's got to be a pain to lug about.'

'So our man isn't an opportunist. He stalks his victims first, waits for a time when they're alone, then acts.' Dom looks at Abbott. 'Any luck with the pub?'

'I spoke to the assistant manager. He was helpful, he's sending across their camera footage.'

Dom glances at his watch. It's gone five. The press briefing is less than an hour off.

'Anything on the note, Abbott?'

'Sorry, I haven't got to it yet, I'll do it after the HOLMES searches.'

'I can work on it if you want?' Parekh says. She looks eagerly from Abbott to Dom.

'Actually if you could get cracking on the CCTV that'd be great, Parekh.' They need to find out what the note means, but if there's footage of the killer on CCTV that's got to be the priority. He looks at Biggs. 'Anything worth following up from the door-to-doors?'

Biggs shrugs. 'Bugger all, really. No one in the flats heard anything unusual.'

The sergeant won't meet his eye. Still smarting from the knock-back, no doubt. 'So nothing?'

'Well, the downstairs neighbour remembers our vic returning home from work around quarter past ten because she heard the door slam.' Biggs coughs, not bothering to cover his mouth. 'Other than that no one seemed to have much to say, or didn't want to tell me. Everyone's so bloody distrustful these days, even of us police.'

Dom grabs a marker and draws a timeline along the bottom of the board. At 2215 he notes Kate returned home, then adds Stax's return at 0230. 'So we're building a picture of who entered and left the flat.'

'Interesting symmetry with the jobs,' Parekh says. She steps to the board, taps a bullet point listed below the photo of Zara Bretton, then another below Jenna Malik. 'All three victims were new in their jobs. Zara had worked at the sandwich place seven weeks, Jenna had just started as a graduate trainee and Kate started as a call handler last month. I know the employers are different, but it seems rather a coincidence.'

'Yup, good point.' Dom underlines the corresponding bullet points. 'We checked that out after the first two murders, but with Kate we have another angle. Get on to Kate's employers and find out how they recruited her, see if they use the same agency as the others, or if there's another connection between them. Maybe we'll get lucky.'

'Will do, sir.'

Dom looks round the room. 'Anything else?'

Silence.

Abbott flicks through his notes. 'I had a call from the doc's office. The PM's scheduled for first thing tomorrow.'

Dom hates the things. He's tempted to send Biggs, but feels he owes it to Kate Adams to be there. 'All right, pencil me in. You too.'

'OK.'

'Anything back from the lab?'

Parekh shakes her head. 'No, guv. I'll chase them, but it's likely to be days rather than hours.'

Different case, same old shit. 'Keep on at them. We're flying blind without it.'

'I'll request a fast track.'

'Ask hard, yeah.'

Biggs sniggers.

Dom glares at him. 'If you've finished knocking doors, get digging into the relationship between Stax and Kate. Something there's not right, we need to know what. Talk to family, friends, colleagues. Check Stax's story, every minute of his movements. Also Kate's parents said she was often lending him money – check that out too.'

'Fine.'

Biggs looks like nothing could excite him less. Dom figures he'd act the same whatever task he assigned. He wishes he'd get over himself.

Abbott gestures towards the clock. 'We need to . . .'

Twenty past five. Shit. Dom can't delay any longer. He has to prep for the press briefing. Jackson likes to call the soirées 'media partnership' meetings; he's had a special room tarted up and dedicated to them. Still, at least today isn't the full works, just a verbal update, a request for specific information to be included in news coverage and a brief Q&A, no cameras.

Dom looks around the team, catching each person's gaze in turn. 'OK, good work. You know your tasks. Full team meeting tomorrow, four o'clock. Until then, Parekh, you're up as office manager. We'll feed all info in through you.'

Parekh smiles. Looks pleased.

Dom isn't, though. In thirty minutes he'll be standing in front of the press with virtually fuck all to say.

16
CLEMENTINE

At five o'clock he posts the reminder in Case Files: The Lover.

> **Death Stalker** Remember, there's a press briefing tonight at
> 6pm @Robert 'chainsaw' Jameson – you're our eyes on this.
> **Robert 'chainsaw' Jameson** I've managed to get a press pass
> via my friend. I'll take notes and report back.

I have to find a way to stay in the group. The memory of my
eleventh birthday with Father still lingers in my mind. *Make
tough choices or you won't survive.* Well, his choices were bad, and
I need to do more than just survive. I want to beat the police. I
have to show there's another way to get justice.

I stare out of the window, watching people scuttling along the
street below. It's dusk. In a few minutes the sun will be gone. It's
harder to observe in the gloom, and that makes it easier to go to
places you shouldn't.

It gives me an idea; to get inside the crime scene. The briefing
at six is my opportunity. The detectives will be with the press. If
I'm lucky the uniforms will be gone too. It's the perfect time to
make a return visit.

I grab my boots and zip them up over my leggings. Pull on my
coat, and put my phone and purse into the pockets. I plait my
hair into a loose braid and pin it up on the top of my head, then
pull on a black beanie. I try to ignore the fluttering in my chest.

I'm ready. I'm determined to do this. I'm terrified.

It's 5.50. The rain has stopped but the streets are slick with damp.
I'm careful not to slip as I carry my bags along the pavement
towards the Chick-o-Lick takeaway. I bought a few items at the

store around the corner – teabags, a few packets of crisps, a magazine – just enough to give the impression I'm an office drone who's picked up a few essentials on the way home from work. It's prime commuting time, and I'm passed by plenty of other people whose jaded expressions look just like mine, although theirs, I assume, are real.

As I walk past the open door of the chicken place I spot a pack of youths loitering inside by the counter. I catch snatches of their banter, goading each other to take their chicken with maximum chilli. A couple of older men sit by the window eating chicken dripping with grease.

I look away, keep my pace steady and my head bowed as if seeking respite from the wind. I'm not, though. I'm scanning for threats, checking the environment, looking to see if a uniform is still stationed at the crime scene.

The building entrance is up ahead. There's no one keeping guard. A lone strand of police tape flaps from one side of the black door; the only clue something unpleasant occurred here. I don't stop. The sturdiness of the door tells me the front isn't viable. I could try and pick the lock, but the old boys eating chicken are facing the pavement, they'd see me. I need to find another way.

I continue along the street. The chicken takeaway must have a place round the back where it stores rubbish, and although gardens are rare here, these old houses might have some outdoor space hidden behind their street-facing facade. It's my best hope.

A few hundred metres on the left, I spot a narrow side street, just wide enough for a single vehicle. I turn down it, following as it snakes between the houses, curving back towards the chicken place. There are no streetlamps, but in this city it's never truly dark. Bright windows in the buildings either side of me light the gloom and I start to relax. The contrast with the bustle of the neighbouring streets is pronounced. Here I am alone.

Perfect.

The smell of cheap meat is heavy in the air. I follow it, knowing that as the odour grows stronger I'll be drawing closer to the back of the house. The wall is too high to see over, shielding the terrace from view. I keep going, looking for a way in.

I find one a couple of metres before the boundary with the chicken takeaway – a wooden gate. Stopping beside it, I rummage in my pocket and pull out my cigarettes. I don't need a smoke, but it's a good cover. As I light up, I double-check I'm alone.

The street is clear. Inhaling hard, I let the smoke fill my mouth, and chuck my cigarette into the gutter. Exhaling, I move closer to the gate and reach for the latch.

Stepping through the gap, I find myself in a small paved area cluttered with garden furniture. On the other side is what I'm looking for – a back door. I squeeze past an old barbecue to reach it.

The lock looks basic enough. I swipe my phone awake and replay the YouTube clip I'd found as I walked here – how to pick a lock in three simple stages. I press play.

The clip's almost done when I hear it. A male voice with a strong East European accent, singing tunelessly on the other side of the fence, '. . . and you're the one. The one I've been waiting . . .'

I curse under my breath. Pause the video. Wait. Hear the scuff of metal on metal, followed by the clatter of glass being tipped into a bin. More singing.

'. . . turn around, let me see your angel . . .' The voice fades as the man moves back towards the building. A door slams shut.

With my heart hammering against my ribs, I pull the two long pins from my hair and try to copy the actions shown in the video. After a couple of minutes of wrangling I feel the mechanism yield and the lock undoes. I step inside the building.

My heart thumps harder. Anticipation makes me hyper vigilant and adrenaline floods my body. I breathe into the feeling. It reminds me of another act, one I must never speak of. One I chastise myself to never do again no matter how strong the urge.

I force myself to focus. I'm in a narrow hallway. My boots sound loud on the tiled floor. A plug-in nightlight illuminates the passage enough for me to navigate. Stepping lighter, I advance towards the stairs.

The light in the main hallway comes on automatically and I pause a moment as my eyes adjust to the brightness. The walls are painted a garish pink. Taking care not to touch the handrail, I take the stairs to the second floor.

At the top of the stairs I pause. Listen hard. Hear nothing.

It seems the residents have left this place. People are funny like that, not wanting to stay where another person died, as if somehow that person's bad luck will transfer to them – as if death is something you can catch. As if it's something to be afraid of.

Still, I keep my carrier bags clutched tight in my left hand, ready to use as props in my cover story if I meet anyone. I'll say I've brought Mart Stax some supplies, that I'm a friend. It's plausible enough to let me get clear of the building before they start wondering how I got inside.

Crime scene tape is fixed diagonally across the door to Flat B. I fiddle about with the hairpins until I manage to pick the lock, and duck beneath the tape to go inside. Glancing across the room, I see the curtains are still drawn from when the police were here, a narrow border of light from the street visible between the material and window frame. I wonder how Detective Dominic Bell approached analysing this crime scene.

Using the torch on my phone, I sweep the light around the room. I want to get a sense of the place, a glimpse into the life of the victim, Kate Adams. The way other people live, the clutter they choose to surround themselves with, is far more revealing of their personality than the things they say. All through university I found my fellow students' rooms and possessions the best way to assess them. Snooping among their things gave me insights that allowed me to feign interest in what they liked, helping me seem like them, letting me pretend I fitted in. I got pretty good at faking. But tonight isn't about fun or faking; I need to stay on task.

If this is another Lover murder then the victim will have been found in the bedroom. I move, light-footed, across the room. The torch on my phone highlights the dark powder residues on the glass table and across the worktops of the kitchenette. It makes the place look grubby. It also shows that no one has cleaned up since the forensic team left.

Switching the phone to camera mode I enable the geotagging function, then, being sure to get the room in focus, take my first picture – Kate Adams's bed. It's been stripped of linens, just an iron bedstead and memory foam mattress remains. I can't take my eyes off it. I wonder how the bed looked before the forensics team took away the parts that had contact with the victim. I wonder how the victim looked.

I snap another picture. These images, with the geotag identifying where they've been taken, *have* to get me included in the group.

A bang makes me jump.

I spin round in the direction of the noise. It came from the front door, I'm sure of it. The door is closed, but there's a strip of light visible beneath it. Something has activated the automatic light in the hallway.

My mouth's dry, my heartbeat's thunder-loud in my ears. I fight the urge to scream. Fear roots me to the spot. I listen hard. Am I imagining it? Is my mind playing tricks?

No.

Something bangs against the door a second time. The handle turns back and forth; someone's trying to get in. Is it the police? Could the killer be returning?

The only way out is through that door. I'm trapped.

I watch the door inch open.

17
DOM

Heading to the press briefing, Dom can't shake the feeling he's a dead man walking. Up ahead, by the doorway, is Jackson. Tall and broad, the DCI is an imposing figure at the best of times. As Dom approaches he makes a show of looking at his watch.

Dom knows he's cutting it fine: that's the point. He didn't want to arrive early so Jackson could badger him about the missed meeting and why he'd been avoiding his calls.

He stops beside Jackson. Addresses him more formally than usual. 'Sir.'

The DCI nods in acknowledgement. From the silence, Dom knows his commanding officer is seriously pissed off. Abbott scoots round them into the briefing room.

Jackson readjusts his tie and runs a hand across his bald head, smoothing imaginary hair into place. His tone is deadpan as he says, 'See me afterwards. No tricks.'

Dom nods. The indent in his skull starts to throb.

The DCI's assistant scuttles from the press room into the corridor. She beams at her boss and Dom, oblivious to the tension between them. 'They're all here. Ready whenever you are.'

Jackson gestures at Dom to go into the room. 'You're running this show, Bell. After you.'

Dom feels like such a twat. He's sweating, a lot. Beside him, Jackson looks a picture of neat professionalism. Dom wishes he was sitting at the back with Abbott, observing the crowd rather than being the main act, or main course if this lot get their way.

The room is full. The murder of an attractive young woman in a good part of town always gets the roaches crawling out for a feast.

As Jackson launches into his usual 'thank you for coming' spiel, Dom scans his notes, trying to memorise the key points. The more he does, the more he thinks about the things he's omitting – like the note and the women's changed appearance.

'And so,' Jackson's voice gets louder, breaking into Dom's thoughts. 'I'll hand over to Detective Inspector Dominic Bell, who will take you through the briefing.'

His throat feels tight. He grabs a glass of water from the table and takes a gulp, wishing it were gin. He resents sitting here doing a show-and-tell to this lot while the killer's still out there. He hates that he has to overanalyse every sentence to make sure they can't twist his words.

'In the early hours of this morning, the body of Kate Adams was found by her boyfriend at their home. We believe she was killed between 10.15 p.m. and 2.30 a.m. There were no signs of forced entry to the property. We're still in the early stages of our investigation, but given the circumstances in which she was found, there's a strong likelihood Kate Adams's death and the murders of Zara Bretton and Jenna Malik are connected.' Dom pauses. The journos are listening; most of them are tapping notes into iPads. He takes a quick sip of his water, and continues, 'At this time, we're following initial lines of enquiry and would like anyone who has any information that could relate to this case to come forward. You'll find images and further details of the victims in your briefing packs.'

Jackson's assistant leaps into action, hurrying along the rows as fast as her five-inch heels allow, giving each person a copy of the handout.

Dom waits for her to finish. Calling the two sheets of A4 a briefing pack is a bit crap, really, but that's what Jackson likes to call the press notes. It's all part of the spin, the *partnership*.

'So, we'd appreciate your support in getting this crime, and our appeal for witnesses, into the public eye. The incident room number and the anonymous Crimestoppers number are printed in your pack.'

Beside him, Jackson's nodding. Dom forces a smile. 'Thank you all for coming. We've time for a couple of questions if you've . . .'

Several hands go up. Dom nods to the bearded guy in the back row.

'You said early signs indicate this murder and the Crouch End and Camden murders are linked. When will you be able to give us confirmation?'

'We're waiting on forensics to confirm. As soon as we have it, we'll make sure you're updated through the usual channels.'

The bearded guy puts his hand up again. 'So if you don't have forensics yet, why do you think it's the same killer?'

'I'm sorry, I'm not able to give you that information at this time.'

The bearded guy shakes his head and scribbles something on his pad.

Another journo with a pudding-basin cut asks, 'Is it because of the rose petals?'

Dom frowns. He recognises the bloke as a freelancer who covered the previous Lover murders, but the media shouldn't know there were rose petals at the Kate Adams crime scene. 'No comment.'

The journo continues. 'Or because there were two glasses of red wine found at the scene?'

What the actual fuck? How has the media got the information about the red wine? Is there a leak in his team? 'Like I said before, no comment.'

His heart's banging, but he tries to stay professional. He moves his gaze to a skinny chap with a receding hairline with his hand up. 'Go ahead.'

'Is this the work of a serial killer?'

Given the note he'd read that morning, Dom's gut response is yes. Instead he answers, 'It's too early to say.'

Sandwiched in between a big bloke from one of the locals and the old boy from *The Times* is a woman. She's scribbling in a notebook, head down, blonde hair falling across her face. Dom stares at her. From this angle she looks the spitting image of Therese. He bites his lip. Remembers how they'd laughed about the thing between them being their secret. How she'd tease him by sitting at the back whenever he gave the Operation Atlantis briefings. How she'd give him that look, all playful and enticing. How he couldn't wait for them to get away from their colleagues and be alone.

The blonde glances up and smiles. She doesn't look a bit like Therese.

Dom looks down at his notes. Tries to push away the pain, the regret, of how things ended. He should have played it cool; not told Therese he loved her. Not put pressure on her when she'd smiled and said, *'Don't spoil things, we're having fun, aren't we?'*

Casual is better than nothing. He knows that now.

'Detective Inspector?' A man's voice cuts into his thoughts.

Dom jerks his head up. Shit. Did the man ask something and Dom didn't hear? The questioner is the journo with the pudding-basin haircut again. He's staring at him expectantly; eyebrows raised, smug grin wide as a Cheshire fucking cat.

Dom glances at Jackson. The DCI nods, like he's giving Dom permission to speak, which is no help because he hasn't got a fucking clue what the question was.

The silence is getting more uncomfortable by the second. The blonde in the front row catches his eye then glances away like she's embarrassed for him. He clenches his fists. He doesn't want her pity.

Speak. Say something.

Dom looks at the guy. With his narrow tie and slim-cut suit he looks like he really fancies himself. In Dom's experience, all that type want to do is to catch you out and make themselves look clever. He decides to gamble that that's what's going on now. 'What's your theory?'

Jackson gives him a worried glance, but Dom ignores it, keeping his eyes on the freelancer. The bloke looks pretty chuffed.

Twat.

'Well, I think the killer *is* a local. The fella's picked three local girls, and got into their homes without a fight. You'd need prior knowledge for that.'

Dom tries to keep his expression neutral and act as though they're talking professional to professional, like Jackson's always reminding him to with the press. It's hard, though. The bloke's looking more punch-worthy by the second. 'It's possible, and it is a line of enquiry we're pursuing, but at this stage there's no evidence to confirm either way.'

The freelancer cocks his head to one side. 'Stands to reason, though, doesn't it? It's been a month since the first one. Long time for a tourist or whatever to stick around – means they're more likely local than not.'

Great. Everyone's a sodding detective now.

'No.' Dom's deliberately curt.

Jackson inhales sharply.

Dom gets the hint and gives a tight smile. Tries harder to play nice. 'It could be they're a regular visitor to this part of the city, or here on an extended stay, or any number of other scenarios but, as I said, there's no conclusive evidence either way.'

The guy glances at his iPad, frowns, then opens his mouth like he's about to ask another question.

Jackson shifts in his seat and opens his hands out wide, like he's the Prime Minister giving some national address. 'Well, I'm afraid that's all the questions we have time for this evening. Thank you all for attending and for helping keep our partnership strong in the fight against crime.'

Most of the journos start to file out through the door. The blonde in the front row is having her ear bent by the old boy from *The Times*. She's nodding as he speaks, but her gaze is on Dom. She takes a business card from her bag and puts it onto the seat she's just vacated, then glances back at Dom and smiles. The old boy beside her is still wittering on. As they pass Dom, she mouths the words, 'Call me.'

Dom knows that he won't.

His mobile buzzes in his pocket. The mouthy journo starts heading his way. Ignoring him and the business card left by the blonde, he hurries towards the door. Pulling the phone from his pocket, he checks the screen, expecting it to be one of the team. It isn't. He halts, staring at the caller ID. Lindsay, it reads. DI Simon Lindsay. A good mate, or at least he used to be.

'Bell?'

Jackson is weaving through the crowd, coming his way. The journo is a few steps behind, closing fast. Shit. Dom declines the call and heads for the door.

The DCI catches him, leans in close. 'A word, Bell, now.'

Jackson's expression tells Dom there's no point trying to bullshit his way out of this. The journo's halted a few feet away, watching. Rock and hard place springs to mind, so Dom shoves his mobile in his pocket and follows Jackson back to his office.

As they walk, Dom knows he should be preparing his story, but he isn't. All he can think about is Simon Lindsay, and why he'd be calling now.

The DCI's office is a depressing place at the best of times. Its colour palette, inspired by twelve shades of shit, does nothing to liven up the laminate desk and metal filing cabinets.

Jackson drops his briefing file onto the desk and glowers at Dom. 'Shut the door and sit.'

'I'd rather stand, thanks.' Dom halts behind one of the visitor chairs, resting his hands on the faux-leather upholstery. An old newspaper, one of the tabloids, is lying in the in-tray. *Met on the take?* screams the headline. His grip on the chair back tightens.

Deep breath. Play it cool.

Jackson is sitting ramrod straight in his high-backed chair. It's the only non-standard item in the room. The official line is it gives the best lumbar support for his sciatica, but Dom has always reckoned the DCI chose it to make himself look more imposing, like a modern-day Henry VIII on his throne. Today it's working.

Jackson stares at him stony-faced. 'I said, sit down.'

Dom decides he'd best do as he's told. As soon as his arse hits the chair, Jackson lunges across the desk, slamming his fists hard on the laminate. The tumbler of water beside the computer wobbles. 'What the hell are you playing at?'

Dom doesn't show any outward sign of surprise, but he feels his heart rate increase all the same. 'I—'

'Shut up! I'm the head of this unit, and you're in the middle of an investigation.' Jackson's face is turning beetroot. 'I need to be kept in the loop on *everything* going on, not having to chase you down at the sodding press briefing.'

Dom points to the folder. 'Paul, you've . . .'

Jackson grabs the file and tosses it into his in-tray. 'For God's sake, man. I'm on your side here, but you're making it bloody hard work.'

Dom stays silent. However his boss feels personally about the IPCC stuff, he's still got a job to do.

'So why didn't you attend the meeting like we agreed?'

'Something came up with the case.'

'Tell me, or you and I are going to have a problem.'

Dom nods. He can't afford to alienate the one member of the brass who's on his side. If Holsworth lives up to his hatchet-man reputation, things aren't going to be pretty. Dom's going to need all the support he can get.

'Holsworth was running late. I had a call from Abbott, the parents of the deceased, Kate Adams, wanted to speak with me personally. It was important so I prioritised the case.'

Jackson sighs. 'Look, I've done your job, Dom. I'm not some career desk jockey, I know what it's like out there, working a case. So I get it, really, but Holsworth won't go away by you shutting your eyes and pretending he's not there. You've got to meet him halfway, answer his questions, let him fill out his forms and write his report. No matter how inconvenient you think it is.'

Dom thinks about the last night of Operation Atlantis, when everything got fucked up and his job and family life collided in the worst possible way. He knows all about inconvenience, about doubt and guilt, but he can't tell Jackson his fears; that someone in the team fed inside information to the criminal gang they were targeting, and that the three people he'd trusted most – Therese, Simon Lindsay and Darren Harris – are the most likely suspects. He can't say that's why he's avoiding the interview; that he's been waiting, hoping, for his memory to return. He needs his memories back to get answers, but it hasn't happened yet. Now he's run out of time.

'They've rescheduled your meet for one o'clock tomorrow. Be there.'

Shit.

The post-mortem is scheduled for the morning. To be at Holsworth's office for one, he'll have to leave straight after, no time for following up anything, no time to brief the team. 'But we've got the—'

Jackson puts his hands up. 'Don't start. I don't want to hear it. Just get to that meeting. Once you've played Holsworth's game, you can put the thing behind you and move on.'

'Paul, I—'

'I mean it.' Jackson holds his gaze. 'Whatever comes up, you do that interview. Abbott can hold the fort for an hour or two.'

Dom nods. He'll have to make the timings work.

'Good. And once you've finished with Holsworth, you find this Lover bastard and get us an arrest.'

Dom flinches at the mention of the media's name for the killer. He hates that shit.

Jackson doesn't notice. 'The last quarter stats aren't doing us any favours with that lot.' He gestures in the direction of the press room. 'Or with the big cheeses either.'

Dom keeps his expression serious. 'Yes, Paul.'

Jackson cracks a smile. 'All right, Dom. That's enough. Sucking up doesn't suit you.'

Dom senses the conversation is over. He's almost reached the door when he stops and looks back at his boss. Dom remembers what he'd said about not always being a desk jockey. 'The media shouldn't have known about the rose petals and red wine.'

Jackson looks up. 'Wouldn't they have just put two and two together from the other crime scenes? You said they could be connected, it's an easy leap.'

'For the petals, yes. But we've never released any intel on the red wine.'

Dom sees the gleam in his boss's eye, like an old terrier that's spotted a rabbit and is recalling the thrill of past chases. 'You think you've got a sieve?'

'I think there's one somewhere.'

'Any idea who?'

'Not yet, but I'll bloody find them.'

Jackson's expression is serious. 'Find them, and find them fast. We can't afford for things to leak. Is there anything else I should know?'

Dom shakes his head.

'Well, keep on it. And I meant what I said about an arrest. There are a lot of eyes on us right now – inside and outside. Your last job might have been set up by a bit of political posturing, but here we operate under the old rules, measurement by results, and you know how that goes. You're only as good as the last case you worked.'

Yeah, Dom thinks as he exits Jackson's office. I know all about how that works.

18

CLEMENTINE

The hooded figure stumbles into the flat, kicking the door shut behind them.

From my hiding place behind the half-closed bedroom door, I peer through the gap between the door and frame, watching. My mouth is dry. My pulse pounds at my temples. Adrenaline courses through me, urging me to run. I can't, though. It's impossible to get out unseen.

The lights come on and the man staggers across to the kitchenette. He trips and, swearing, grabs for the worktop to steady himself. His shoulders rise and fall, as if he's taking deep breaths. Then he turns, yanking his hood down to reveal bloodshot eyes and blotchy skin on an otherwise attractive face. Whoever he is, he's totally wasted.

Leaning back against the worktop, he pulls his phone and wallet from his jeans and dumps them onto the granite top. More gently, he feels inside his other pocket and extracts something thin and red. He holds it up close to his face with a shaking hand. Stares at it.

It looks like a small, narrow paintbrush.

He keeps staring. There are tears in his eyes.

I want to know what it is. Where it came from. But I'm too far away and my view through the gap is too limited to get a proper look.

He keeps staring at it until his phone rings. We both jump.

He answers. 'This is Mart.'

It's Mart Stax; the victim's boyfriend. I think about taking his photo, but decide against it. I can't risk him spotting me.

I listen to his side of the conversation. His words are slurred. 'Got it here now . . . I know.' He stares at the brush again. 'I don't know why I picked it up . . . may be I'll call Detective Parekh . . . tomorrow . . . I might . . . don't know . . . enough.'

He flings the phone and the brush back onto the worktop and starts weaving across the room towards me. I freeze. Press myself tighter against the wall.

Mart stops a few steps into the bedroom. He's so close, just feet away. I'm terrified he'll be able to hear me breathing. But he's not interested in me. He's staring towards the bed. His eyes look vacant, spaced out, like he's on something.

A strangled sob comes from his lips. He staggers to the en-suite and shuts the door.

This is my chance. I need to run.

I move out from my hiding place and across the living space. Mart's words on the phone and the way he looked at the brush mean something, I'm sure of it. I think he found it here before the police came; it could be a clue to the killer.

I want it.

The brush is sitting on the worktop. It's about five centimetres long, with silver letters embossed against the red. I try to read the letters, but they're too faded. It's a brush, a broken brush, split from midway to the end, but not a paintbrush. It's not soft enough for that. Instead it has five short, rigid bristles.

Death Stalker's post this morning said the victim's appearance was altered, and I know from Ghost Avenger's mortuary photos that the first two victims had their hair dyed. Chances are the killer made them up differently too. Perhaps this is one of his brushes; maybe it broke while he worked, maybe it got damaged as she struggled.

A shiver of excitement tingles across my skin. I glance back towards the bedroom. The door to the en-suite is still shut. Quickly, I decant the groceries from one of my carrier bags into the other and scoop the broken brush into the empty bag. Stax didn't seem convinced he'd take it to the police, but if it's connected to the Lover it's evidence; it needs to be analysed. I will make that happen.

I wrap the plastic tight around the brush and push it deep into my pocket. With my photos from inside the crime scene and this brush, I must have done enough to be validated as a proper member of the team. Imagining the likes and positive comments

I'll get when I post them, I smile.

The toilet in the en-suite flushes.

I run.

I'm halfway down the stairs when she sees me.

She's standing in the hallway, looking at the piles of post on a scuffed-looking table. She's in her late fifties, and carrying a few extra pounds round her middle. She's also carrying two paper grocery bags. She glances up at me. Frowns. 'And you are?'

Remembering my cover story, I try to sound normal even though I feel like I might be sick. 'A friend of Mart's,' I say, holding up my carrier bag. 'Brought him some things, but I don't think he's in.'

She nods to the paper bag under her left arm. 'Snap. He needs to keep his strength up. Damn police interviewed the poor love for hours.'

Her tone suggests she doesn't like the police. I shake my head. 'I heard that.'

'I understand they need to investigate what happened to Kate, of course, but he'd just lost her. Seems cruel to put him through an interrogation.'

I edge towards the front door. I need to leave before she wonders how I got access to the building without Mart to let me in. 'I should—'

'It's a terrible thing, though. And I must have been right here, in my home, when it happened. I dread to think what that poor girl went through.'

I need to leave, but this woman knew the victim. It's an opportunity I can't miss. 'You're friends with Kate and Mart?'

She laughs. 'Don't sound so surprised, I'm not that old! They moved in here just after I lost my husband. Kate was such a sweetheart, checking in on me to make sure I was OK. Mart does any odd jobs I've got. I mean, he needs a bit of nagging sometimes, but he's a good lad.'

'So you don't think he's involved?'

Her expression darkens. 'Of course not.'

'But the police seem to have him as a suspect. I don't understand.'

'Good job I didn't tell them what I saw, then,' she mutters.

'What you saw?'

'I want to mention it to Mart, though if he's gone away, I'm not sure when I'll get the chance. Yesterday, on my way in after the bingo, I saw a man going into Kate and Mart's flat. It was just as I was unlocking my door, and he was on the landing below so I didn't get a proper look. He looked a bit like Mart: slim, wearing those tight jeans he likes, but he had his back to me and his hoodie up so it's hard to tell.'

If it wasn't Mart, it could be she'd seen the Lover. 'What time was it?'

She thinks for a moment. 'Well, I left the bingo at eight, it wasn't my night, so I must have got back here about quarter to nine.' She shakes her head. 'At the time I thought it was Mart. I said good evening, but he didn't respond. It was only this morning, after hearing the terrible news about dear Kate, I realised Mart would have normally been at work at that time.'

I clutch the carrier bag in my hand tighter. 'But you haven't told the police?'

'I can't really tell them anything. It was a man in a hoodie, that's all I saw.' She lowers her voice. 'After the way they treated my son Duncan when he got into a bit of bother, I don't really trust them anyway.'

I nod. I know that feeling. I learnt that lesson the hard way too.

The police are rotten, right to the core.

19

DOM

I'll make you dinner, Chrissie had said, we'll have a few drinks. You can relax. You need a break from the case. He'd said OK. Hadn't wanted to let his sister down. But now he's here, in the two-bed new build flat near Twickenham that she shares with Darren Harris, Dom feels anything but relaxed.

'So what's going on with you?' Chrissie says, as she slides the pasta bake into the oven. 'You've been so remote these past few weeks.'

'Sorry, little sis.' Dom takes a swig of his beer. It's going down too easy and he knows he needs to pace himself. He puts it down on the wooden countertop. 'It's the case. I can't seem to make any headway. It's driving me nuts.'

'You always let your cases become all-consuming. Just like Dad.'

Dom nods. Their dad had been Fraud Squad. He'd worked cases until two weeks before he died. Bowel cancer, diagnosed too late. 'I always wanted to be just like him.'

Chrissie tucks the blue-striped oven gloves away. 'And you are. But sometimes you need to look up from the case you're working and remember there are other things, good things, in your life.'

Dom knows she's right. When Dad died he'd already started in the Met. He was too caught up in work and his own grief to see the warning signs; how his mum had taken to her bed, how there was never any fresh food in the house. Three weeks later, Mum was dead; officially it was suicide, a razor in the bath. In reality, Dom knew she'd died from a broken heart.

Chrissie was the one who found her. The shock turned her into a full-on wild child. When a video surfaced of her having sex with a group of men three times her age in the toilets of a seedy club, Dom was shocked out of his own grief. The pubs and clubs where he used to drink became places he'd trawl to find Chrissie if she didn't come home. The low-rent drug dealers he'd bust in his job became the first people he'd call if the school phoned to say she'd missed registration. He cooked, cleaned and put his own love life on hold while he devoted himself to saving his little sister. It wasn't easy, but he got Chrissie back. Unfortunately she was already pregnant by then.

'Dom?' Chrissie flaps a dishcloth at him. 'Don't go zoning out on me.'

He rubs his eyes. 'I'm just tired. Sorry.'

'You're working too hard.' Chrissie uses the cloth to wipe down a chopping board. 'It's not healthy. You need some balance.'

Dom doesn't meet her eye. 'I can't let him do it again.'

Chrissie brushes away a stray curl that's flopped over her eyes. Tilts her head to one side. 'You sure it's just the case? Nothing else going on?'

'I'm sure.'

'So how's the secret romance going?'

Dom doesn't say anything. He grabs for his beer. Drains it. Feels worse.

'Shit, I'm sorry.' Chrissie puts her hand on his arm. 'When?'

'A few weeks ago.'

'Did she—'

'Mum, I need to do my story,' Robbie, Chrissie's son and Dom's godson, shouts from his bedroom. 'The bean one.'

'Coming,' Chrissie shouts to Robbie. She gives Dom her serious look. Squeezes his arm. 'Don't think you're getting off this easy. When Robbie's asleep we're going to talk about this more. And don't shake your head. You'll just bottle everything up otherwise.'

Dom knows he won't tell her about Therese, but he smiles anyway. She's come a long way from the teenage tearaway that used to drive him crazy. 'I'm so proud of you.'

Chrissie gives him a half-smile and shakes her head. 'Don't get all gushy on me, bro. Just turn up a little more often.'

'I'll try.'

'That's all I ask.'

*

Dom grips his beer tighter. Through the thin wall he can hear Chrissie reading to Robbie – *Jack and the Beanstalk* – her voice rising and falling as she adopts different accents for each character. Dom can hear Robbie laughing. Here in the lounge the atmosphere is very different.

Darren's just got home. He sits at a right angle to Dom at the other end of the grey corner sofa. He's clutching a beer, too, but he's not drinking it. So far they've avoided eye contact. It's been five weeks since they've seen each other. The last time was a few days after the Operation Atlantis raid, when Darren had turned up at Dom's flat to see how he was doing.

Spaced out on painkillers and bruised from the beating he'd taken, Dom had barely followed the conversation, but he remembered Darren saying Internal Affairs suspected there was a mole, that one of their team had been on the take and that Darren had looked as shifty as fuck. He'd asked Dom who he remembered seeing in the house. Dom said his memory was wrecked and asked Darren what he'd seen, but Darren said he'd never gone inside, never saw the target. Dom had let it go, not pushed Darren further. But even through the fogginess clouding his mind, he couldn't shake the feeling Darren was hiding something.

Darren clears his throat. 'Got interviewed by the IPCC today.'

Dom nods. Takes a swig of beer. Doesn't want to talk about it.

Darren does though. 'It was really fucking unpleasant.' He's picking at the label on his beer, shredding it from the bottle. 'Three of them roasted me. Holsworth and his henchman, henchwoman.'

Dom listens to Chrissie's voice next door, trying to work out how far through the story she is; Jack's climbing up the beanstalk. Dom wishes he could climb a bloody beanstalk out of here.

Darren leans towards Dom. His pupils are pinpricks, like he's high or stressed or both. 'What happened in there? How did it go to shit? It was supposed to be our moment of triumph.'

Yeah, thinks Dom. It should have been the high point to end the eighteen-month op – arresting the players at the top of the Mohawk gang and disabling a sex trafficking ring operating across the capital. For Dom it was the last hurrah of his secondment south of the river, a chance to gather extra bonus points with the brass before heading back to the MIT in the north. 'I dunno, mate.'

Darren is staring at him. A muscle above his eye is twitching. 'Was the intel bad? You were on the inside, haven't you heard anything?'

All these questions; this was the reason he didn't want to come round. Dom feels his hands starting to shake. His stomach lurches, and he feels the nausea rising. He doesn't want to discuss what happened with Harris, but he can still hear Chrissie reading the story next door, not giving any signs of finishing. Putting his beer on the table, he gets up. 'Just going for a piss, mate.'

In the bathroom he puts the toilet seat down and sits. He'd had no clue they were being set up, and he doesn't know who by, but he has his suspicions, and that's what's making him feel sick. The lavender plug-in air freshener makes the nausea worse. Yanking it from the wall, he rests his head in his hands, blotting out the Nemo bath mat and shower curtain, and tries not to vomit.

'Fuck,' he mutters, as the memory of the operation comes flooding back.

It went down at ten; a prearranged meet at a large end-terrace house not far from the power station. Therese set it up, her undercover identity established through months of fieldwork, trust building and witnessing some nasty shit. Dom was with her, acting as her muscle. He'd played the role a good many times over the past eighteen months. It felt almost normal. Almost.

They parked a street away and walked the rest, partly to get a feel for the place, partly to give the rest of the team and their armed response colleagues the chance to get a fix on their position. The location had changed at the last minute, the house a switch-in for the original place, an old warehouse they'd had under surveillance for the previous forty-eight hours. Here they were going in blind.

It was raining. Dom and Therese strode towards the house, brisk enough to look like they knew where they were going, not so fast to make them look nervous. Markus Genk, the head of the Mohawk gang, had a reputation for getting easily spooked. Anyone acting twitchy around him tended to wind up dead in the river. With this guy, appearance was everything.

As they walked, Dom noticed how uneven the pavement was along this stretch. Cracks zigzagged through the slabs making them tilt beneath his feet. He glanced at Therese. Dressed in a black leather jacket, skinny jeans and low-heeled boots, her clothes weren't so different from how she dressed as DI Weller from the Organised Crime Squad, but she had on more make-up than usual, her lips painted red rather than natural, and her shoulder-length blonde hair was loose rather than tied back.

He remembered their argument the previous night; how she'd wanted to keep things between them casual and he didn't. She'd refused to talk about it that morning, said the subject was off limits, for now. Instead she'd tried to distract him from thinking about the future. She was good at distracting him. Her hair had tickled across his belly as she'd taken him deep into her mouth and—

'You ready?' She stared at him, her green eyes narrowed as though she'd guessed what he'd been thinking.

'Yep.'

'So let me do the talking. Usual drill, you're the help as far as Genk's concerned. Whatever's said, let me handle it, OK?'

'I was at the briefing, Therese, I know—'

'Good.' She pointed to an alley on their right. 'This runs along the back of the houses. The text said to enter that way.'

They turned into the alley at a brisk walk. Taking care to dodge the dog shit and split bin bags spewing rubbish across the path, they strode the last twenty yards to the back gate. Dom tried to look relaxed and in character; tried not to think about last night, when he'd told Therese he loved her and she'd told him she wished he'd not said that. He needed to get his head in the game. From here on in, they had to play their roles just right.

As she lifted the latch, Therese turned to him. A streetlamp a few yards away illuminated her face. She looked serious. Gazing up at him through her thick mascaraed lashes, she said, 'Keep your mouth shut.'

Meaning: are you ready?

'Yeah.' Undercover was all about trust; you lost that, you were screwed. Therese was the lead in the field on this operation, she'd got them this far, Dom knew he should trust her decision. When he opened his mouth to say more Therese had already turned away. She opened the gate and advanced on the house. He followed.

They ascended the steps to the back door in single file. Reaching the top, Dom glanced behind. He saw nothing, but knew that lurking out there in the darkness would be Lindsay and Harris, listening in on the comms channel. The armed response bunch should have eyes and MP5s trained on the building, ready to back them up on Lindsay's say-so, if it came to that.

He glanced at Therese. Hoped she realised the danger. Genk was one hell of a slippery bastard. Operation Atlantis had got closer to him and his business than any previous attempt. When the team was put together, they'd had to start from scratch. Genk never left survivors.

As if sensing his concern, Therese caught his eye and gave him a brief smile. Then she opened the door and stepped inside. Dom followed.

Therese turned. 'Shut the door.'

Code for 'we're in'.

From the tiny magnetic earpiece nestled deep inside his ear, Dom heard Lindsay say, 'Acknowledged. Have fun.'

Being sure not to angle his head towards the button mic sewn onto his shirt pocket, Dom said, 'Yeah, yeah.'

The room was in darkness. The windows had been lined with cardboard, blocking the view and the light. The open door behind them allowed a dim glow from the streetlamp to illuminate the doorway. Beyond that the room was black and silent.

Therese flicked the light switch. Nothing happened.

Dom felt the hairs along the back of his neck rise to attention. Why cut the power if you're planning a meet after dark?

'Come on,' Therese said, switching on a small aluminium torch. 'This way.'

Dom took a torch from his pocket and turned it on. They

advanced through what, in the small discs of light, looked to be a tatty kitchen, and towards a door at the far end. In the silence, each sound seemed magnified: his breath, his heartbeat, their footsteps. As Therese moved to open the door, he put his hand out and stopped her from turning the handle. 'Let me.'

Code for 'something's wrong'.

'It's fine.' She batted his hand away, shoved the door open and stepped forward. 'Remember your place.'

Meaning: proceed.

He followed. In the gloom he saw a hole-riddled sofa and four mattresses with sheets, unmade. Getting closer, he glimpsed a roll of duct tape and three syringes discarded on the nearest mattress. No sign of Genk or his people.

Dom didn't like it. He knew Genk would be careful, take precautions, but careful was extra bodies and more guns, not dark rooms and silence. Dark and silence was a set-up.

Therese is wrong. I need to give the amber code word, tell the gang to get prepped.

'It's—'

Crack, the pain in the front of his skull was instant, immediately followed by the urge to vomit. His vision blurred. He staggered, off balance, arms spread wide as he tried to regain control. Suddenly Therese seemed a long way from him.

The second attack came from his right. He saw the bat swinging towards him too late. Took the blow to his ribs before he'd a chance to defend himself. Fell left, his torch clattering to the ground. It felt like every ounce of breath had been pushed from him.

Lying prone on the musty-smelling rug, Dom couldn't see his attacker. All he could see was Therese up ahead standing silhouetted in the doorway. Behind her was the bright glow of a working bulb. Illuminated in the light was Genk.

Dom coughed, spitting blood. He slid his hand across the dirt-crusted rug, trying to claw his way to Therese. 'Eclipse,' he croaked.

Code red. Danger. Send in armed response.

In his earpiece he could hear Lindsay talking crap with another of the team, some shit about a girl. They hadn't heard him.

Dom's vision morphed in and out of focus. 'Eclipse,' he repeated. 'Bring the rain.'

Lindsay kept prattling on about the girl's tits.

They can't hear me.

A bang on the bathroom door makes him jump. He hears Chrissie's voice on the other side, 'Dinner's up. Come and get it, bro.'

He can't spend any longer with Harris. He just bloody can't. He'll want to keep talking about the investigation, the interview he had and the one that Dom will have tomorrow. He'll want Dom to tell him it'll be fine, that it's routine; that because of what happened to Therese they need to pay due diligence. He'll keep asking Dom questions.

Dom shakes his head. He won't tell Harris anything, so there's nothing he can say that won't sound trite or total bollocks. All he has are some incomplete memories and a head full of suspicions. Tomorrow Holsworth wants answers – he wants someone to point the finger at. Tomorrow *he'll* be asking Dom the questions, and Dom knows he'll be forced to give up what he knows, even though it's incomplete.

'Dom, come on, you been in there ages.' Chrissie sounds worried. 'What's going on?'

He flushes the loo. Unlocks the door and opens it.

She smiles when she sees him, then frowns. 'You look like shit, bro.'

'I feel it,' he says, and it's the truth. Someone set them up, made the raid fail, and one of them will hang for it. If that's Darren it'll kill Chrissie – he's the first man she's allowed herself to love since a drug-pushing bastard left her pregnant at fifteen. Darren is the only dad that Robbie, Dom's godson, has ever known.

Dom steps into the hallway. He can see the table in the lounge has been pulled out and set for dinner. Three places. Chrissie, Darren Harris and him.

He shakes his head. It's killing him to go, but he can't stay here and play happy families. 'I'm sorry.'

He sees the disappointment in her expression and hates himself even more.

'I've got to go.' He holds up his mobile like it's a doctor's note for getting out of PE. 'Work, you know.'

'I know,' she says. Her tone is dull, resigned. 'It always is.'

He's still feeling like a shit as he exits Chrissie's building. He hates it when she's disappointed in him; they used to be so close, and he knows she's confused by him keeping his distance. Trying not to dwell on it, his thoughts turn back to the missed call he had earlier from Simon Lindsay.

Why's Lindsay calling now? He's been dodging me for weeks.

He hasn't spoken to Lindsay since the debrief of Operation Atlantis. They'd been tight enough before; often going out for a pie and a pint, and putting the world to rights for the evening. But, after everything went tits up, nothing.

Dom pulls his phone from his pocket and looks at his missed calls list. Lindsay's number is at the top.

Better to know than not.

He presses the number. Hears the call connect and the ringing start. His palms feel hot, the phone slippery. He grips the handset tighter as he waits. It pisses him off that he's this nervous.

Three repetitions later the call is answered. 'Lindsay.'

'It's Dom. You called?'

'I did. We need to talk.'

Dom says nothing. Waits out the silence. He wants to ask why Lindsay has called him now, why it's taken over a month, what has suddenly changed, but he doesn't. He's realised that he already knows.

'So you know Therese woke up three days ago?'

'Yeah.'

'And the IPCC's proceeding with the inquiry?'

There's a nasty taste in his mouth. 'Yep, they've been in touch. I've an interview tomorrow morning.'

'Then you're the last. They've spoken to the rest of us. Wasn't pleasant – they're looking for a scapegoat, gunning hard.'

'So this is, what, a heads-up?'

'No, there's something else,' Lindsay says. '*She* wants to see you.'

20

CLEMENTINE

Professor Wade is waiting for me outside my flat. Pacing three steps along the pavement, then turning and repeating; back and forth, the hem of his long mac flapping in the wind. I curse under my breath. I don't want to face an inquisition now, I need to get inside and upload my photos, prove I'm good enough to make the team.

He stops pacing when he spots me. 'Clementine. Where've you been? I've been waiting ages.'

'I told you never to come here.' I walk past him and up the steps to my front door. Touch the key fob to the lock and hear the clunk as it disengages. Shoot him an irritated look. 'I'm busy.'

'We need to talk.'

I push the door open but don't go inside. 'Like I said, I'm busy.'

He runs his hand through his hair. As ever, it looks just that shade too black. I'm convinced he uses dye. 'I've sent you thirteen emails,' he says. 'You've not opened any of them.'

He must have put a read-receipt tracker on his email. Typical Wade. 'I know.'

'And you haven't accessed the university systems for over a fortnight.'

I raise an eyebrow. 'You're checking up on me?'

'Of course.'

'Don't.'

'It's my job.'

'Not any more.' I step into the hallway, ready to close the door. 'Look, I've handed in my thesis. I met the deadline. There's no problem.'

Wade exhales. His breath clouds into the frigid night air. 'You met the deadline, sure, but you're wrong about there not being a problem.' He leans closer, softens his tone. 'I'm worried about you. This obsession of yours with that true-crime group, it's not healthy.'

'You said I should get out more, get a hobby.'

He looks stern. Shakes his head. 'Fixating on an online community group for months on end isn't getting out more. Changing the conclusion of your thesis to some cock and bull idiocy that says crowdsourced crime solving is possible in real time isn't a hobby. It's lunacy, truly. I'm in half a mind to call in Student Services.'

I fix him with a hard stare. 'Do not do that.'

He nods. 'But we do need to talk.'

I sigh. 'Fine.'

'Tomorrow. Twelve o'clock. The tea shop.'

The tea shop is always Wade's preferred place for a face-to-face meet. It's not on university grounds, letting him play the 'maverick professor' card he so loves.

'Come alone.'

'I always do.'

'Don't be late, Clementine.'

I resist the urge to make a sarcastic retort. He knows I'm always late. Instead I shut the door in his face.

It's almost nine but I'm too buzzed to think about food. What I'm hungry for is acceptance – I have to know if I've made the cut.

I've uploaded the photos. Eighteen pictures from inside the crime scene, each geotagged to prove I'm not bluffing; the co-ordinates matching those on Death Stalker's photos uploaded this morning.

The comments have been building beneath my photos.

Crime Queen Chilling to think that bed is where Kate Adams died.

Ghost Avenger You must have nerves of steel! I was nervous enough taking the victim pictures at work, but at least I was allowed in the room. You've taken things to a new level.

Witness_Zero Nice work.

Justice League I wish I could have been there with you – it must have been fascinating to witness the crime scene first-hand. Did you notice where the forensic team had dusted for prints?

The Watcher Thanks guys. It looked like they'd dusted for prints on the coffee table, the dressing table and a few other surfaces. It was dark though, so hard to tell.

Robert 'chainsaw' Jameson It's lucky you live so close to the crime scene — easier for you to get back there!

Bloodhound Lucky you weren't seen. Breaking and entering is a crime! Although we're investigating a more serious crime, we should try to stay within the limits of the law!

I haven't said anything about the red brush and my conversation with the neighbour yet. I'm still weighing up if I should, gauging their reactions to the photos and my infiltration of the crime scene. Bloodhound's reaction makes me think it's better not to share.

The Watcher @Bloodhound True. I thought it was worth it though.

Robert 'chainsaw' Jameson Definitely worth it.

Bob's right; it was. I reckon that's the closest I'll get to a well done from him, but I don't care about his faint praise. I care about Death Stalker's thoughts, and he hasn't passed comment.

On the right of the screen all the members of Case Files: The Lover are listed. The dot beside Death Stalker's avatar remains white. He's not online at the moment.

I move the cursor to hover above Death Stalker's name. A text box appears: *User last online ninety-two minutes ago.*

It's been forty minutes since I uploaded the photos. Doesn't he get alerts on his phone? Isn't he paying attention?

I stare at his avatar. Twist the butterfly ring around my index finger. The skin beneath the silver is raw from the motion.

Where is he?

Why isn't he online?

Why isn't he replying to me?

I twist the butterfly ring faster. The metal bites into my flesh. I close my eyes and count to ten, concentrating on my breath. Refocus. Gain control.

I need a distraction. Bob's comment about me being close to the crime scene has given me an idea. Getting up, I cross the room to the bookcase on one side of the fireplace and run my fingers across the books as I search for what I need. I find it halfway along the second shelf – a map of London.

Unfolding it, I grab some Blu Tack and attach the map to the wall next to my whiteboard. With a black marker I plot the locations of the three Lover murders, the police building DI Bell and DS Abbott work from and my address. Then I mark other places of significance – the homes and places of work I know of the members of Case Files: The Lover.

Overall the plotted points appear random, with one exception. Almost equidistant between the three murder sites is a location well known to one of the group members – the London Cellular Pathology Service, workplace of Jonathan Pike, aka Ghost Avenger.

Interesting. There's no evidence to say Ghost Avenger has been to the crime scenes, and no indication he has greater knowledge of the murders than the rest of us, aside from what he's observed in his job. But the more I think about it, something about him does seem out of kilter.

Leaning back in my chair, I think about what I know of Ghost Avenger: his online interactions, and how he never disclosed his work to the broader group until the task assigned to him made it necessary. I wonder why he held it back. Telling his online peers about what he did, what he had access to, would have elevated his status; instead he'd sought favour through sharing cartoons.

In response to my questionnaire he'd said he joined True Crime London to help him understand more about those who kill, to help him make sense of how some people do the things that result in another person ending up on a slab in his mortuary. The answer reveals his deeper side, and his enthusiasm to join the investigation is unquestionable. But this behaviour seems incongruent. He's chosen to join a group that are working closer together, sharing *more* than in the main group, the very opposite of what he's been doing for the past eighteen months. Question is, why the change in behaviour, and why now?

Studies on the personality profiles of people who spend higher proportions of time interacting in the virtual world rather than the real world, like many true-crime fans, show them as high in the need for affiliation and fulfilment. A significant proportion self-report as introverted. They're more comfortable sharing things online, and are prone to oversharing. Not so with Ghost Avenger. He's withheld knowledge rather than sharing it. He's an outlier, an anomaly.

Grabbing a dry marker I jot down my thoughts under Ghost Avenger's name on the whiteboard: secretive, located centrally to crime scenes, change in online behaviour inconsistent with previous interaction – why? An idea occurs to me. I open a new private message and type Ghost Avenger into the recipient field.

> **The Watcher** to @GhostAvenger Thanks for your kind words about my nerves. It was pretty scary, but exciting too. I really wanted to contribute something to the investigation. It's so ridiculous the Lover is still out there, don't you think?

A couple of seconds pass, then three dots appear. Ghost Avenger is replying.

> **Ghost Avenger** to @TheWatcher Totally. Kate Adams shouldn't have died. The police should have caught the killer before this. It's been four weeks, but they're operating on minimal staffing and long hours. Overstretched, just like we are at the mortuary. It needs to change.

Interesting.

> **The Watcher** to @GhostAvenger So how did you get interested in true-crime stuff?

The three dots appear. Then disappear. Then appear again. He must be typing, then changing his mind and deleting what he's written. A message appears.

> **Ghost Avenger** to @TheWatcher Kind of a long story. Let's talk at the meet.

I frown.

> **The Watcher** to @GhostAvenger The meet?
> **Ghost Avenger** to @TheWatcher Don't worry, you'll get an invite. Death Stalker will tell you. Look forward to meeting IRL.

I'm no further forward. I want to know what this meeting is, and who else is invited; I want an invite. For such a significant change in Ghost Avenger's behaviour there must be a powerful motivator: I need to find out what it is.

There's still no response from Death Stalker.

I raise my arms above my head and feel my back muscles, cramped up from sitting at my desk for far too long, begin to stretch out. I'm fed up with waiting.

My laptop pings. There's a new comment beneath my photo album post. I smile when I see who it's from.

> **Death Stalker** Good work. Great to have pictures from inside the crime scene.

I force myself to wait ten minutes before responding.

> **The Watcher** @DeathStalker Thank you. This investigation is important to me. I wanted to contribute something useful.

I wait for more – another comment, a private message – something to tell me I've made the final group. Nothing comes. The dot beside Death Stalker's name is still green. He's online. Why isn't he talking to me? I want him to talk to me.

There's a way I can get him to talk. It will also let me test how much of a team player he really is. I select his name and type.

The Watcher to @DeathStalker I have more information.

He replies in nineteen seconds.

Death Stalker to @TheWatcher From the crime scene?
The Watcher to @DeathStalker Yes
Death Stalker to @TheWatcher Tell me . . .

I smile.
    Got you.
    I wait four minutes before answering.

The Watcher to @DeathStalker I spoke to a neighbour – it sounds like she might have seen Kate Adams's killer entering the flat last night.

The reply is immediate.

Death Stalker to @TheWatcher Did she see his face?

21

CLEMENTINE

I don't reply immediately. There's something about the message, the speed he sent it or the way it's worded, that makes me uneasy. I'm considering how to respond when another message appears, and then another.

> **Death Stalker** to @TheWatcher Can she describe him?
> **Death Stalker** to @TheWatcher Has she told the police?
> **Death Stalker** to @TheWatcher Is she going to tell the police?
> **Death Stalker** to @TheWatcher This is important! Answer me!

It's scaring me. I lean away from the screen. Why is he reacting like this?

> **Death Stalker** to @TheWatcher Please answer.

I wait thirty seconds before I respond.

> **The Watcher** to @DeathStalker She said he was wearing a hoodie. She didn't get a look at their face, she thought it was the boyfriend at first – Mart Stax. But he was at work.
> **Death Stalker** to @TheWatcher Has she told the police?

I wonder why he keeps asking that. Does he think this information gives us an edge over the police, or is he trying to hide something more sinister? He was at the crime scene early this morning. Now I'm wondering how early.

> **The Watcher** to @DeathStalker No, she doesn't trust them.

Forty-six seconds pass before he replies.

> **Death Stalker** to The Watcher: Good work. Anything else to report?

The red brush is sitting on the corner of my desk. I'm worried by Death Stalker's reaction to the neighbour's sighting of the killer. I'm not sure I should trust him, but who else can I tell? I can't go to the police; they'd want to know how I got it.

> **The Watcher** to @DeathStalker At the crime scene I found something. It's a broken brush. Stax had it in his pocket, he was all upset over it. I grabbed it on my way out.
> **Death Stalker** to @TheWatcher Wait, you saw Stax??
> **The Watcher** to @DeathStalker He came back while I was there. I had to hide then run when he went to the bathroom.
> **Death Stalker** to @TheWatcher Respect
> **The Watcher** to @DeathStalker Shall I post a pic for the team? I could tell them about Stax and the neighbour, too.

The answer comes in under ten seconds.

> **Death Stalker** to @TheWatcher No, let's keep this to just us for now.

The hairs on the back of my neck stand on end. I pull the fleece blanket around me, suddenly cold. He's letting me into his confidence, but it doesn't feel good. There's something dangerous about this man. I should stop, log out, delete my profile; but I don't. I can't leave the investigation now.

> **The Watcher** to @DeathStalker What do you suggest?
> **Death Stalker** to @TheWatcher I know a guy who can run analysis for us. Bring the brush to the meet tomorrow. We can talk more then.
> **The Watcher** to @DeathStalker What meet?
> **Death Stalker** to @TheWatcher Check the group page tomorrow and you'll see.

The Watcher to @DeathStalker OK
Death Stalker to @TheWatcher Have a good evening. You've
earned it.

I start to type a response. Before I press return the dot beside
Death Stalker's name turns white, and I know he's gone. I take
a deep breath and try to calm my racing heart rate. I can't stop
shivering, I feel sick to my stomach.

I tell myself it doesn't matter, I've made the final cut, I'm in;
but it doesn't help. The sense of dread I have about Death Stalker
is growing. His controlling nature, the secrets he keeps, and the
way he reacted tonight are scaring me, but it's more than just
that – perhaps we are alike, him and me.

What if he's the killer?

22

He misses her even though he's been less than fifteen feet from her most of the night. He misses touching her, that's the difference. He hasn't been able to touch her tonight. He had to watch instead.

He watched his rival, some scruffy blond idiot, collect her from her flat at twenty past eight. He followed behind them, just within line of sight, on the eleven-minute walk to the Italian restaurant. He heard her laughing. Watched his rival grab her arm when she caught her heel in a crack between the pavement slabs. Felt the jealousy needle through him.

He took a corner table for one towards the back of the restaurant. Ignored the candlelight, the piano music and the hushed conversations of the other couples around him. He ignored the man she was sitting opposite at the table halfway into the restaurant. He had eyes only for her. But he had a book with him, the latest John Grisham, for disguise. He played with his phone a bit too; social media, messages. It made him just another lonely businessman reading for company over dinner; someone to feel sorry for, someone to discount and forget.

But he doesn't forget. He couldn't forget her. She'd had prawns as her starter, pulled off their heads and tails with a smile on her face, licked their juice from her fingers afterwards, savouring their taste, just as he would savour hers.

While he ate his goat's cheese salad, she had steak for her main, cooked pink. He watched the blood spill as she sank her knife into the flesh. A fine spray misted across her wrist and he felt himself harden. Shuddered. Knew he wouldn't be able to hold back for long.

She didn't have dessert. Instead the scruffy man paid the bill and they walked the eleven minutes back to her apartment. At

11.32 they both went inside. He didn't like that. He curled his fists round the napkin he'd taken from the restaurant, her napkin. Put it to his face and inhaled the scent of her. Breathed her in until the anger started to dissolve. Kept watching.

From the shadow of the neighbouring building he watched the light go on three storeys above in the apartment he knows to be hers. Moments later she appeared, just briefly, at the French doors onto the Juliet balcony. Like a tease, she paused, looking out into the night as if she knew he was there, watching. Then she pulled the curtains closed, and was gone.

He groans. He has had enough of watching.

TUESDAY

23

CLEMENTINE

I dreamt of death again. As I hovered in the dark place between sleep and consciousness, the day I last saw Father began to replay in my mind.

I'm fifteen years old and it's my first time playing truant from school. I got a postcard from Mother yesterday, our first contact in months, telling me she's just got married for the fourth time. This husband is Denny Lyle, an American, a realtor she calls him; he has a yacht. She gives no phone number, no reply address. I read it twice before tearing it into tiny shreds.

So I decide to visit Father. I call his work, but they say he's taking some time away, so I call his flat in London but get no answer. I guess he must have gone to the cottage; an old thatched place in rural Oxfordshire, less than an hour from school. I can hitch my way there without too many problems, so I do.

But there's no one home when I arrive. Figuring I'll wait, I fetch the spare key from beneath the fungus-riddled log to the right of the back door, and let myself in.

That's when I find the letter. Father has been suspended from duty pending investigation into misconduct. He's been off the job for almost a month. It makes no sense. My Father is a hero. He's been awarded the Queen's Police Medal for bravery. He's devoted his life to the force, the job. He's police through and through – one of the good guys – it's all he knows.

The letter implies otherwise.

My breath comes in gasps. Tears stream down my face.

Both my parents are AWOL. I feel even more alone.

Next to the sink is a half-drunk bottle of whisky. Picking it up, I collapse onto the battered leather chair beside the Aga and take a swig from the bottle. I grimace at the sour taste and burn in my throat.

After a few more mouthfuls I start to quite like it.

The memory jumps to later that evening.

The stench of petrol is acrid in my nostrils.

I grip the matches tighter.

The memory shifts forward again.

Father is back and he's shouting but I don't want to hear what he has to say. The fury within me is as hot as the fire leaping higher between us. The lights shut off as the electrics blow.

The flames chase along the timber beams, the embers glow orange like captive fireflies. Father lunges for me. I jump back out of reach towards the door. He loses his balance, staggers. A beam above him cracks and pops, buckling from the heat. There's a deep groan as the beam crashes down.

That's when I wake. Inferno hot. Heart racing.

I throw back the duvet. Shivering as goosebumps rise along the grafted skin that covers the scarring on my arms. The room is dark. I fancy there are human shapes in the shadows. As I watch they morph from crouching to standing, from the chair to the bed, surrounding me.

Murderer. They chant. *You should be dead. Murderer.*

I close my eyes. Shut them out. Breathe slowly, as I've been taught to when I feel a panic attack coming on. In through the nose for eight beats, then out through the mouth for eight. Repeat. Repeat. Repeat.

By the eleventh repetition I'm feeling more in control. The shaking has subsided. I tell myself that I'm OK, try to convince myself by saying the word out loud over and again. Pretend that I believe it.

My heartbeat flits, skittish and unsettled. Switching on the lamp, I snatch a cigarette from the pack on my nightstand, light up and take a couple of quick drags. I check my phone; it's almost six. There's no way I'll get back to sleep.

Taking another drag on my cigarette, I get out of bed and pad barefoot to the kitchen. I make coffee, then root about in the cupboard and find a dusty bottle of whisky with a few measures left. I pour a double into the coffee and take a gulp.

Clutching the mug in both hands, I cross the living space to my desk. I need a distraction, something to chase the memory away with.

There's a new post in Case Files: The Lover.

Justice League shared an article with Case Files: The Lover
Justice League Found this online about the DI. Useful bit of background . . .

I click the link. It takes me out to an online news website – *News Byte*. The article is headed *Investigation called into Bungled Raid.* I scan the text. It talks about a sting operation that went wrong and hints at police negligence. It says one of the team was shot and is in a coma. I check the date of the article; it was written almost a month ago. At the end it states the incident is being investigated by Professional Standards. I wonder how far they've got.

The photo accompanying the article is a close-up of DI Dominic Bell. He's looking past the camera, his jaw set firm, his mouth a thin line, his expression one that would be easy to read as anger. It's not, though, I can tell. The upper half of his face gives him away in the dip of his eyebrows, the haunted look behind his gaze. Guilt.

Another bent copper.

This flat belonged to my father. I inherited it on my eighteenth birthday. Before I moved in I had everything put into storage and redecorated. I couldn't bear to be reminded of him, and how he let me down. I erased him, all except for one thing.

I glance at the mantel. On it is a wooden box that belonged to my father. A thick layer of dust mutes its royal-blue colour, but it's what's on the inside that Dominic Bell has reminded me of.

I move across to the fireplace. Press my toes against the edge of the hearth and feel the cool smoothness of the ceramic tiles. Breathe in deep, and lift the box from the mantel. It's a long time since I last held it, and it feels lighter than I remember.

I twist the gold clasp and lift the lid. Father smiles up at me. He's young in the photo, no more than my age now. He's with his colleagues, they're getting some award, all are in uniform. He looked so happy, carefree, back in the days before he was selected for undercover work and taken deep UC. His face doesn't have the hard lines, the tense edge, I remember. His eyes don't have the haunted look.

I put the photo to one side. Underneath is a jumble of medals and awards, their ribbons faded from age, and a smashed-up memory stick, black, with the word COBALT printed along the side. Scooping them aside, I pull the folded letter from beneath them, open it out and read the text. The key words leap out at me: *findings of our investigation . . . dishonourable conduct . . . fraud . . . criminal charges.* He was dead before they charged him, but they found him guilty just the same. My father, the decorated hero, the man I'd looked up to for my whole life, was just another bent copper.

I never got the chance to ask him why.

Shoving the letter back into the box, I push it back onto the mantel and return to my laptop. DI Bell's picture is still on the screen. I stare at him. His sadness draws me in; the overwhelming strength of it is the very opposite of the nothingness I feel.

What did you do?

Why did you do it?

Are you guilty?

I sit, transfixed, gazing into his pixelated stare and, for a fleeting moment, I imagine I feel a twinge in the place where my heart ought to be.

24
DOM

Something lumpy is sticking into his cheek. His neck aches, the muscle across his left shoulder is stretched tight, pins and needles prickle at his fingers.

'You slept here?' Abbott's voice booms from above.

What the . . .?

Dom opens his eyes. He's at his desk, his head resting on the edge of the keyboard. There's a half-eaten cheese toastie on a paper plate in front of him. He sits up, rubbing the sleep from his eyes. 'What time is it?'

'Just gone seven-thirty.' Abbott says between mouthfuls of breakfast. He's holding a bag of muffins. 'You look like crap. Why didn't you get a room at the section house? It's only—'

'Did a long session in the gym before coming back here. I must have fallen asleep while I was working.'

Abbott looks concerned.

'What?'

'Look, I know it's none of my business, guv, but are you all right?'

'Like you said, it's none of your business.'

'Guess I asked for that.' Abbott gives a rueful smile and offers Dom a muffin.

Dom shakes his head. He's not usually one to spill his guts, but he trusts Abbott. Maybe it would be helpful to talk about some of the crap flying around in his head. 'Sorry for being off. It's this case, you know, all the dead ends and the media bitching. And having the IPCC thing hanging around at the same time, well, it's pretty shit.'

'Sounds it.' Abbott nods. He starts eating a second muffin. 'Mind you, some days I'd happily swap with you. After a while the novelty of dirty nappies wears a little thin.'

Dom smiles. 'I bet.'

'Sometimes I wish I was single,' Abbott says.

I wish I wasn't.

Dom doesn't want to talk about relationships. He shoves the cold remains of the toastie into his mouth, then picks up the photocopy of the note they'd found in Kate Adams's hand from beside his keyboard. 'I started working on this last night.'

'Get anywhere?'

Dom nods. He taps the mouse to wake his computer and enters his password. The screen unlocks, revealing a Google results page, the first link taking him to Amazon. 'It's from a book called *Black Rose Chronicles*. It's out of print, has been for a few years, but you can get used copies on Amazon.'

'*Black Rose Chronicles?*' Abbott says, peering at the screen. 'Guess that's why he left the rose.'

Dom turns, scanning the office. Parekh and Biggs aren't in yet, but this book needs further investigation. The note isn't the killer's words, but text from a book. That has to mean something; this book could detail the scene – the woman – that the killer is trying to recreate.

He sends Parekh a brief email asking her to check out the book as a priority, then glances back at Abbott. 'Any luck with HOLMES?'

'What, on other cases matching the MO? No, not yet.'

'Reassign it to Biggs.' They need to get going to make the PM on time. Dom stands up. He stretches, trying to ease the tension. Feels a muscle in his lower back start to spasm. 'Be ready to go in ten.'

In the Gents', Dom splashes water on his face and peers into the mirror. Abbott's right, he does look like crap; his eyes are bloodshot, his stubble heavier than it should be, his hair's bushing out like a wild man.

Pulling off his t-shirt, he swaps it for the spare from his locker. Rinsing his hands under the tap, he runs his fingers through his hair, smoothing it into some semblance of order. He tries to smile but thoughts of the three victims mingle with the image of Therese lying in her hospital bed, and the effort seems too great.

She wants to see you.

Fuck.

If she wants to see him, why didn't she call him herself? He knows Lindsay has been visiting her in hospital, the nursing staff told him, but why did Therese ask Lindsay to call him?

He needs answers, but he can't see her, not yet, not until he's worked out what happened during the raid; he has to know who's responsible and who he can trust. Until then he needs to avoid them all – even if the urge to visit Therese feels like it's tearing him apart.

He glares at the mirror, at the grumpy-looking sod reflected back at him, and wonders when the hell he got so old. Maybe Therese was right to be keeping her options open.

25

DOM

He's always hated this part. Having toughed it out for the best part of three hours, Dom's relieved it's almost over. He looks at Abbott. He's staring at Emily as she finishes up, eyes on her face rather than on what she's doing. Dom understands that. However you try to rationalise things, the mechanics of a post-mortem are brutal.

Kate Adams lies on the gurney. Naked, again – there's no dignity for the dead, not in a murder case. Logically Dom knows why post-mortems are important, that they can provide vital clues to help break a case, but he's never been able to reconcile the clinical violence they inflict on the deceased's body. It got harder when he read the PM report on his mum.

Emily is sewing up the chest cavity, working head to toe and back again as usual, her pattern the same with every body. As she ties off the sutures, she glances at Dom. 'Shall we run through the key points, to be clear?'

Dom knows Abbott's been scribbling notes but he prefers to wait until the end, then talk out the anomalies. The debate helps his thinking. 'I'd appreciate that.'

Emily peels off her gloves. Once white, now the latex is stained dark with blood and other bodily fluids. She puts them in the clinical waste bin. Taking the notes her assistant, Ted, has been making as she works, Emily walks round the gurney to where Dom and Abbott are perched. 'OK then, so how was the view from the cheap seats?'

Abbott smiles, as always. Dom doesn't. He knows Emily's trying to make the situation more bearable with humour. He's heard about her infamous turns at Comedy Crossroads on amateur night, and that she writes material for her wife, Jacquie, who's semi-professional now, but comedy around dead bodies, dead people, doesn't work for him; it never has. Death is not a joke.

He looks past Emily to the body on the gurney; cold and exposed in this room furnished with stainless steel and easy-wipe surfaces. It's a clinical space, purpose-built and hygienic, but the last place a young woman like Kate Adams should be.

Abbott's scanning through his notes, asterisking some of the points and underlining others. 'You said the tox screen was similar to the other vics?'

Emily clears her throat. 'It's my show, if you don't mind, DS Abbott. How about I do my solo first before you jump in for the singalong?'

Abbott blushes. 'Sorry, of course.'

'Excellent. So, the headlines then: as we saw at the crime scene, the victim has localised contusions and minor skin abrasions on her ankles and wrists. The angle and depth of the marks are consistent with restraint in a seated position from a narrow shackle, approximately one centimetre diameter. Traces found in the wounds indicate a nylon paracrystalline carbon mix.' Emily glances at Abbott, flicks her gaze to his notebook and gives a little smile. 'Cable ties, most likely, same as with Jenna Malik and Zara Bretton.'

Abbott makes a note.

'The contusions are recent. Their presence indicates the abrasions were incurred pre-mortem. She also has superficial contusions on her upper arms, shoulders and neck. The severity is consistent with physical compression, and the placement and shape leads me to conclude they were made by human fingers. Not her own, and not enough to kill her. Those marks were concealed by make-up.'

Dom frowns. 'But not the bruises on her wrists and ankles?'

'No, but that could be because of the abrasions.'

Perhaps, Dom thinks; although something tells him that's not the case. 'Seems strange, though, don't you reckon? Whoever did this went to a lot of trouble to cover up her skin blemishes, but left the marks from tying her up. Why?'

'Practicality?' Abbott says. 'If he'd got her tied he might not have been able to conceal the restraint marks, the make-up would've got rubbed off.'

'That's possible,' Emily says. 'But he could have concealed them when he transferred her to the bed.'

'He might not have wanted to,' Dom says.

Emily shakes her head. 'I can't comment on motivation, only the facts.'

Dom looks again at Kate's body, at the purple bruising circling her wrists and ankles, and the lacerations caused by the ties. She must have struggled hard. He clenches his fists. What kind of person would conceal a spot on her neck, but leave the cuts exposed? 'All right, go on.'

'You were keen to get to the tox screen, DS Abbott. Let's do that next. Generally, her blood work is as I'd expect in a well-nourished twenty-six-year-old female, but there are two interesting facts. Firstly, the toxicology shows a blood alcohol level of 0.08, consistent with a couple of glasses of wine at dinner, and confirmed by the contents of her stomach.'

Abbott clears his throat. 'Well, a twenty-six-year-old having a few drinks, that's not really unusual, is—'

'Again, Sergeant, you're coming in too early. That in itself isn't surprising. The standout thing is the high level of Alfetanil present.'

Abbott frowns. 'What's—'

'Alfetanil is a synthetic opioid analgesic,' Emily says. 'An anaesthetic, if you'd like it in plain English. It's fast-acting, and in the quantity found in this young woman's blood, fatal.'

Abbott doesn't look up from his scratchpad, still writing as he says, 'So the cause of death is an overdose of anaesthetic, same as the first two victims?'

Dom shakes his head. 'Not the same. Zara Bretton had Levorphanol in her system – so did Jenna Malik.'

Emily smiles. 'Excellent memory, Dom. And you're right, DS Abbott, in that both drugs are anaesthetics, but they are quite different.'

Dom fixes Emily with his gaze. 'Different how?'

'As we discussed last time, Levorphanol is an effective anaesthetic, but slow-acting. Alfentanil is different. It causes respiratory depression. The effect is accelerated when taken with alcohol, and in this volume the drug would have stopped the victim's breathing within minutes.'

Emily's still talking, but Dom's tuned her out, thinking instead about this change, this clue. The killer is refining his method. He interrupts, 'The killer's skill at altering the victims' appearance made me think he'd done this before our three victims. But if he's still refining his method, experimenting, I'm thinking the murder part could be new.'

Emily shakes her head. 'I can't comment on that, but the change in anaesthetic is interesting. Your killer could research the different types online, but getting access to them wouldn't be as easy.'

Abbott stops scribbling. He looks at Emily. 'So you're saying they're in the medical profession?'

'Could be.'

'Any way to trace which hospital the drugs came from?'

'No; each batch would be identical, and they start to be absorbed by the body pretty fast. We're lucky there were enough markers left for us to identify them. That's only due to the massive dose he gives them. Anyway, it's not just hospitals that carry these drugs. All this tells us is that the killer can access controlled drugs.'

Shit.

'There is something else that's interesting.' Emily steps over to the gurney, gesturing for Dom and Abbott to follow. Stopping on Kate's left, she points out a minuscule mark just behind her ear and another under the armpit. 'These are needle sites. They're not the easiest positions to inject someone, especially if they're struggling. Yet your killer found a vein and made both injections first time. That's quite a skill.'

Abbott's flicking back through his notes, looking for something. 'Jenna Malik and Zara Bretton were injected in the neck and in the vein above the index finger on their right hand. That's an easier place. Why the change?'

Good question, Dom thinks.

He looks down at Kate's arm. Her skin is so pale. Tiny purple veins thread around the needle-stick site under her armpit like thermal springs around a geyser. There's no life here, though, no warmth. He tries not to look at the aftermath of the post-mortem but fails. The ugly stitching, crude and out of place, makes her look like a badly handcrafted rag doll. He swallows back anger.

The facts crowd in on him: the changed anaesthetic, the different injection site, the marks on her wrists and ankles left unhidden and the little details consistent in all three murders. They have to mean something. 'The killer's trying to conceal it better.'

'From us?' Abbott asks.

Dom shakes his head. 'No, he's not bothered about us. He wants to hide it from himself.'

'But why?'

'He's recreating a scene where the victim was bound by their wrists and ankles but not injured anywhere else.'

'From where, another murder?' Abbott asks.

Emily's nodding. 'It would explain why some marks are covered and others aren't.'

Dom meets Emily's gaze. 'You're sure he assaulted her?'

Emily frowns. 'You doubt me, Detective?'

'No, I just need to be clear that—'

'She was sexually assaulted, yes. All the indicators of penetration are present. Post-mortem, as with the previous victims.'

Bile rises in his throat. He swallows hard, not wanting to let the others see his reaction. Coughs. Even after all his years on the job. Even when you're expecting to hear it, nothing makes that shit more bearable. Nothing. 'DNA?'

'Came back with no matches, like before.'

Dom slams his hand down onto the bench beside him. 'How's that even possible?'

'You don't need me to tell you that,' Emily says.

Dom stares at her, too pissed off to speak.

Abbott fills the silence. 'So there's nothing to go on?'

'Not quite,' Emily says. 'We found traces of a latex-silicon compound across her breasts, stomach, inner thighs and inside her vagina.'

'Meaning, what?' Dom asks.

'Within the compound were propellants consistent with what you'd expect in an aerosol spray. My best guess? The killer used it to cover his skin to prevent leaving trace evidence, DNA, at the scene. Unfortunately for him it didn't work.'

Abbott makes a note. 'Do we know who makes the compound?'

'I've asked the lab to look for a match.'

'No DNA match. No fingerprints.' Dom can't keep the frustration from his tone. 'Basically, zero forensics.'

'I'm afraid so.' Emily flicks through the notes on her clipboard. 'We're still waiting on the lab for a couple more things. We've sent samples of the glue used to seal her lips and keep her eyes open. It was also used to fix her right hand into a fist to hold the note, so we have a decent sample size. I've asked them to identify the manufacturer if they can.'

'Why do you think he uses the glue?' asks Abbott.

Dom frowns. 'I'd have thought it's bloody obvious. He wants her to keep quiet, and he wants her to see want he's doing to her.'

'Not necessarily,' Emily says. 'It's worth ruminating on further, the eyes especially.'

'How so?'

'If he'd have applied the glue while she was conscious I'd expect there to be more mess – excess glue on the eyelids, lashes missing or pulled out as she struggled against him. There's nothing to indicate that, so, and I'm theorising here, I suspect the glue was applied either while she was unconscious or after she was dead.'

Abbott frowns. 'Why would he do it after she was dead?'

Dom swears under his breath. Shakes his head. 'To force her to look at him while he fucked her.'

'Precisely.' Emily looks from Dom to Abbott, pausing a moment before continuing. 'Just so you know, I also took scrapings of the make-up before we cleaned her up. I've asked the lab to look for a brand match.'

Abbott opens his mouth to speak.

Emily puts up her hand. 'Yes, yes, Sergeant. I've asked them to be treated as a priority.' She looks at Dom. 'That's about all, gentlemen.'

What with the first two crime scenes being so clean, Dom hadn't expected much from this one. He needs something more than a change in anaesthetic in order to catch this killer.

He looks at Kate, lying naked on the gurney. His stomach churns. The lights seem too bright. He fights the urge to cover her with a sheet, his jacket, anything. She's been violated enough.

Dom looks back at Emily. 'Call me as soon as you have anything, yeah?'

'Of course.'

He reminds himself it's not Emily's fault there's no evidence. Forces a tight smile. 'Cheers, appreciate it. I'll be on my mobile.'

As they stride along the corridor to the exit, Dom checks his watch. It's just after twelve. He needs to get a shift on if he's going to make the meeting with Holsworth at one o'clock. Turning to Abbott, he says, 'Can you check in with Parekh and update her?'

'Will do, guv. Are you not coming back to base?'

'Not yet, I've got to do that IPCC interview. I'll not be long.'

They wait at the double doors for a tech in scrubs to wheel through a trolley piled with medical equipment. The tech's hunched over the handles, his dark hair flopped forward over his face. White cords feed up from beneath his tunic to his ears. Dom can hear thrash metal pulsing from them.

The tech looks up as he passes. As he meets Dom's eye, his mouth curls into a lopsided smile. 'Thanks.'

'No problem, mate.'

The tech nods, holding his gaze a fraction too long.

26

CLEMENTINE

The 'tea shop' is neither a shop nor a place that serves tea. It's the third bench round the lake when you enter Regent's Park from Marylebone Road and follow the path anticlockwise. I know the special name and obscure location are important to Wade, but with the morning's freezing fog lingering into lunchtime I wish that, for once, we were meeting at an actual tea shop.

I approach clockwise. It's three minutes to twelve and I can see Wade standing in front of the bench, feeding ducks and a squirrel with bread from a plastic bag. Aside from a female jogger further along the path, only visible due to her fluorescent-pink jacket, we're alone.

'Hey,' I call. My voice sounds overloud in the quietness of the park.

Wade turns, looking startled. His cheeks are ruddy from the cold. Tiny droplets have formed on the tips of his quiff. He scans the path behind me. 'You're on time, Clem.'

I don't answer. He's called me Clem on purpose, even though he knows I never respond to the abbreviated version of my name. He's started the power play early today. I won't rise to it. Won't give him the satisfaction, not when I so clearly got the better of him last night.

'Clementine.' His tone is firmer now, more authoritative.

I wait a beat before I look at him.

He runs a hand carefully over his hair. He's smiling, attractive in the way of an ageing rock star. When he speaks his tone is conversational, amused. 'You know we have to talk about what happened.'

'We don't.' I keep my tone professional. He usually values that, likes to stay focused on the work, most times anyway. Not the time he wants to discuss, though. 'You said you wanted to talk about my thesis, so talk.'

His smile sags. 'OK, walk with me.'

We stride along the water's edge, our footsteps crushing the frosted grass, leaving partially thawed footprints in our wake. I match Wade's pace and wait for him to speak first.

'I'm disappointed in you, but you know that. The conclusion in the version of your thesis that you submitted deviated from the one I'd signed off.'

It's true. I don't deny it.

He exhales, his breath pluming in the cold air. 'Why?'

'It's the right conclusion.'

'Based on what, your online games with these true-crime fanatics? What research are you using as a model?'

I don't answer; it's a trap.

Wade looks at me. Raises an eyebrow. 'Go on. I'm waiting for you to impress me with your innovative use of a human-computer interaction theory. One that is so very outstanding that you thought it OK to break the rules and go over my head.'

I lengthen my stride so I edge ahead of him. Stay silent. There's no defensible position for what I've done. There isn't a theory that endorses it. He knows that.

'I didn't think so.' He pauses at the water's edge and opens the plastic bag. He takes out a few pieces of bread and throws them to the ducks swimming alongside us.

I stare at the ducks, the water, the mucky plastic bottle floating half-submerged further out; anything but at Wade.

'You've left me wide open.' He sounds disappointed. 'I told the Faculty your thesis would be special.'

I dart a look at him. Narrow my eyes. 'So it's about you, not me?'

He shakes his head. 'You went behind my back. Submitted a conclusion I don't agree with, but will reflect on me because you're my student.'

The memory of him naked beneath me flits across my mind's eye. I hold his gaze a beat longer than appropriate, then say, 'I am, aren't I?'

From the way he flinches, I know he gets my meaning.

'So are we done?' I say.

He frowns. 'We agreed a true-crime group couldn't solve a live crime. All the theory points to that. Most of the data, too.'

'Exactly, *most* of the data. I kept thinking, what if—'

'Jesus! What is it with you and your what ifs?'

I stop, facing him. I don't hide the anger from my voice. 'Look, the thesis is submitted, it's too late to change it, so if you're going to question me, hear me out first, before you start laying into my answer.'

He smirks. Chucking the last piece of bread to the ducks, he scrunches up the plastic bag and slips it into his pocket. 'Fine, I'll play your game of Let's Pretend. Tell me why this group is so impressive.'

I haven't told Wade everything, but I've told him enough for him to see I'm serious. As we walked around the water he listened to the information I have on each member of the group, to the assignments Death Stalker gave us and the details we have on the police investigation.

Wade's asked me questions about each of the team – their online personas and the details of their real world lives. He's been far more OK with it than I imagined possible. That changes when I tell him I don't know Death Stalker's real life identity. He doesn't speak, but his mouth purses and frown lines appear between his brows.

'Problem?' I ask.

Wade slows his pace. It's a stalling tactic. The park entrance is in sight and he won't want to take another lap of the lake; he never does. 'It's more dangerous if you don't know who they are. It's the unknowns that increase the risk.'

I shrug. 'Not much, though. I know something about all of them aside from Death Stalker, and he's interacting with me more each day. Anyway, I've—'

'Interacting how – private messages? About what?'

I roll my eyes. 'The case, obviously. I found out some things and he asked me to keep them secret from the rest of the team for now. We're going to talk about it when we meet.'

Wade halts. There's a pained expression on his face. 'He's singled you out? I don't like the sound of that. He could be dangerous, Clementine. Have you stopped to think for a moment that he might actually be the killer playing some sick game? Why else would he be so desperate to start this investigation?'

'Any of them or none of them could be the killer.'

'So you admit you're in danger.'

I don't tell him that I slept with a knife on my bedside table last night, just in case. Instead I shrug, look unbothered. 'We're all in danger every moment of every day. You could fall downstairs and break your neck tomorrow, or I could be run over by a bus on my way home. It's all—'

'You're not thinking about this rationally.'

'I've got it covered. I'll go along to the meeting, meet Death Stalker and find out all about him. It'll be fine.'

'Perhaps.' His jaw is clenched tight, and there's a vein pulsing at his temple.

He meets my gaze. 'This Death Stalker character hasn't revealed his location, yet he's made the rest of you do so. He hasn't told you his real name either. He's got an agenda here, no question. You need to find out what.'

Keeping my tone light, I say, 'He says he's all about social justice, that he wants to get the government to fund the police better. But does it really matter if that's true? Maybe he's just looking for glory. If the group solves the case, maybe he'll get it. And as I've predicted it as part of my thesis, if I'm part of the group that succeeds, it'll give more weight to the post-doctoral funding bids we talked about—'

'It's a risk, a big risk.'

'It's a risk *I'm* taking. I need to prove—'

'A PhD isn't about proving what ifs. It's not about indulging personal whims, either; it's about demonstrating you can follow the rules of research. When you have your PhD, that's the time to indulge your fancies.'

I raise an eyebrow. 'Like you?'

He ignores my comment. 'You must earn the right to break the mould, Clementine. Right now you need to prove you're able to fit inside it.'

'But what if this group does solve—'

'It can't happen. They, you're, at a disadvantage. You've no solid data: it's all smoke, mirrors and chat. Your thesis really could have been something. It's like you're deliberately trying to sabotage yourself.'

The park entrance is less than fifty metres ahead. Through the gap in the hedge I see people scuttling along the pavement. There's a flash of red as a bus passes along Euston Road. If I'm going to succeed in my viva and be awarded my PhD I need Wade on my side. 'I'm just hypothesising that if they got the data, and were faster at investigating without all the red tape the police have to contend with, it could be possible.'

He keeps walking. 'But they won't get the data.'

We're forty metres from the entrance. The noise of the traffic is now a permanent drone.

Twenty.

I'm almost out of time. If I want to sway him to my way of thinking I need to do it now. I reach out and put my hand on his arm. 'Maybe. Or perhaps they already have it.' I pause, letting the implication of my words sink in, before adding, 'Look, you know I'm good at this stuff, that's why you picked me to supervise. I'm aware that what I'm suggesting is a gamble, but it's potentially groundbreaking, too. What if this action research *does* prove my thesis correct? What if I'm, *we're*, the first academics to have predicted it happening?'

Wade stops. He turns to me. He's close, very close. His expression is guarded, but not well enough. I can see the glint of competitiveness in his eyes. 'Tell me, do you really think this group of true-crime freaks can beat the police at their own job?'

I hold his gaze for a long moment. 'Yes.'

27

DOM

Dom's been in the interview with Holsworth for twenty minutes. The bastard has a smug look about him; his two colleagues – Jan Ekman and Donald O'Byrne – do too. They've switched on the interview recorder and finished the formalities, checking name and rank for the record. Dom's confirmed he was medically suspended for seven days after the raid because of the minor head injury incurred in the line of duty, that he was signed fit to return to full duties and has been back in the Murder Investigation Team for the past month.

All three nodded, made out they knew what it was like to serve as a police officer, like they knew the realities of being on the MIT, the day-to-day stresses of the job, but Dom knows they're full of shit. Independent Police Complaints Commission investigators don't have to come from a police background, and none of these three do. Holsworth came from criminal law – a legal liar – while the other two are from the civil side. IPCC aren't like Professional Standards, real police officers you had a begrudging respect for. The IPCC just wanted to nail you to the pole to hit their monthly quota.

Holsworth wants to know about the last night of Operation Atlantis. He's asked the question and is silent now, his piggy eyes staring at Dom as he waits for an answer.

Dom likes the silence. What he doesn't like is how Holsworth's question has brought the memories to the forefront of his mind. He keeps it brief. 'Like I put in my statement, Therese and I went into the property alone. An assailant took me out with a blow to the head. The comms failed.'

Jan Ekman, all glossy black bobbed hair and high-buttoned shirt leans forward. 'What else do you remember about the comms failing? Can you show us your decision log?'

Fuck. Dom shakes his head. 'I was injured in the line of duty. I went to hospital, didn't complete my decision log straight away.'

'So you didn't follow procedure?' Donald O'Byrne's voice has a tone of disbelief. 'But you're a senior officer, DI Bell. Surely you're aware of proper—'

'Of course I'm aware. But I was knocked unconscious.' Dom points to his forehead. 'I've got a bloody dent in my head to prove it.'

'Now, now, DI Bell. There's no need for that kind of language.' Holsworth can barely contain a smirk. 'We're just trying to get the facts clear.'

Dom doesn't answer. He'd waived his right to be accompanied by a union rep, thinking it showed he had nothing to hide. He's only meant to be being interviewed as a witness after all, but with the line of questioning they're taking he's beginning to regret that decision.

Ekman smiles. 'Let's refresh your memory about the comms.' She taps a couple of keys on the laptop in front of her. Turns the screen to face him so he can see the audio file. Clicks play.

The comms feed sounds crackly. Then he hears Therese's voice, confident and clear, 'Keep your mouth shut.'

Dom hears their stilted conversation replayed, ending with his own gruff 'Let me.'

Ekman stops the tape. 'Why did you use "*Let me*", the code for "*something's wrong*"?'

'I had a bad feeling.'

'A bad feeling?' Holsworth repeats, raising his eyebrow. He nods at Ekman to continue the recording. 'Your colleague DI Weller didn't have any such qualms.'

The audio restarts, and Therese's voice is decisive as she tells Dom, 'It's fine. Remember your place.'

Ekman stops the audio. Raises her eyebrow.

'There was no sign of Genk or his people, that felt wrong,' Dom says. 'We knew Genk would be cautious but had expected people, guns.'

O'Byrne sniffs. 'So why didn't you give the amber code word and get the back-up prepared?'

'I wanted to. Should have. But Therese, DI Weller, was in command and she wanted to proceed.'

'So it was DI Weller's fault she got shot?' Ekman says.

'No it fucking wasn't. She . . .' Dom takes a deep breath, mustn't let these fuckers see how riled they're getting him. Exhales. 'Look, it was a tough call to make. We'd been setting this up for eighteen months – no one wanted to leave empty-handed.'

Ekman doesn't comment, just restarts the tape. They hear the crack as the baseball bat hits Dom's skull. The clatter as he drops his torch. The thud as he hits the ground. After that there's only white noise.

'I said "*Eclipse*",' Dom says, staring at Holsworth as he speaks. 'I said it twice, then "*Bring the Rain*". I told them we were in trouble. I told them to send in CO19.'

'Did you know the comms were down?'

Dom shakes his head. 'I didn't until the confirmation failed to come. I still had DI Lindsay's voice in my ear gobbing off about some girl.'

'Did you deliberately turn off the comms?'

Dom glares at Holsworth. 'No I didn't.'

O'Byrne makes a note. Ekman turns the laptop screen back to face her.

Holsworth doesn't acknowledge what he's said. Instead he asks another question. 'What else do you remember before DI Weller was shot?'

Dom doesn't answer right away. Things had happened fast. He was immobilised on the ground. 'I remember trying to clear my sight. To my right, almost outside my field of vision, were three pairs of trainered feet facing away from me, and Therese's boots, toes pointed in my direction. I heard a voice – male, Russian-accented – it had to be Genk – say, "*You should have come alone*" and Therese reply that she'd told him she wasn't coming alone and he'd overreacted.'

'What did you take that to mean?' Ekman asks.

'I took it to mean she was pissed off with him for hitting me.'

Holsworth gestures for him to continue.

149

'The pain in my skull was intense. Their voices became raised. I tried to follow the conversation but I kept losing consciousness.' Dom looks down. Doesn't want Holsworth to see he's hiding something. The moment Therese lost control of the interaction with Genk replays in his memory.

Therese's voice: 'The police know about you, they—'

'This is not news. Of course they know. You waste my time. Go back to your whore business.' Black brogues stepped into Dom's field of view; Genk was leaving.

'I'm the officer in charge of the operation to bring you in,' Therese's voice is too quiet for the mic to register, even if it was working.

The black brogues halted in front of Dom's face. At close range, he could see Markus Genk was trembling.

Therese again: 'I'm here to offer you a deal.'

Dom's head pounded. What the hell was Therese doing? This wasn't the agreed script. She was supposed to keep her cover as the owner of a bunch of massage parlours looking for product. Their objective was to get evidence proving a direct connection from the trafficked girls arriving weekly in the capital, all the way up the chain to Genk; proof that would put the bastards away for a very long time. They were so close.

Genk pivoted round and strode back to Therese. The trainered guards parted, letting him closer to her. Dom heard Therese gasp, then Genk's voice again: 'You little cunt.'

'Did you see DI Weller act in an inappropriate manner?' O'Byrne says.

The dent in his forehead aches. Dom massages it with his left hand, trying to fool himself that it'll help. It won't, and he knows it. The pain is as much in his mind as physical. Had Therese acted inappropriately? Fuck. She'd gone off-script, but he'd been injured; maybe she felt their cover hadn't stayed intact. Therese wouldn't be the first officer to try to convince a big player they were willing to play both sides, and it could well have been a ploy to get him back onside because she thought she'd lost him.

Dom shakes his head. Holds back the fact Therese told Genk she was a police officer. He has to believe she did it to try and salvage the operation, because if she didn't, if she really was offering to play both sides, it means he'd have to admit that he really doesn't know her at all, and he doesn't want to believe that's true.

Holsworth frowns. 'For the tape, DI Bell is shaking his head.'

Ekman shifts in her seat. 'What else happened before CO19 went in?'

Dom looks at her. Takes care to maintain eye contact and keep his tone calm. 'Another body had entered the room. I didn't see their face.'

O'Byrne makes a note on his pad. His spidery writing is angled steeply backwards.

Holsworth leans forward, narrows his eyes. 'What *did* you see?'

An image of Chrissie, all smiling and happy, her arms wrapped around Darren Harris, floats across his mind's eye. He forces it away. He can't lie on record. Won't. No matter how much he wants to. He has to answer a direct question with a truthful answer. Always knew he'd have to. 'High-laced cherry-red Doc Martens. That's what I saw.'

'And you recognised them.' More a statement than a question, but the pause afterwards tells Dom that Holsworth's waiting for him to go on.

Dom's head starts to pound. 'DC Darren Harris wore boots like that, but he wasn't deployed undercover. He stayed behind the scenes, supporting us with intel on the comms. Whoever entered the room before CO19 knew Genk.'

He rubs his forehead again. The question he's been trying to answer ever since that night loiters at the front of his mind; how could Darren know Genk?

Holsworth leans forward across the table. 'What made you think they knew each other?'

'Whoever it was shouted a warning before opening the door. Genk recognised him, told him to come in. They sounded friendly.'

Holsworth smiles as he smooths down his goatee; it makes him look like a cut-price psychiatrist. 'Interesting. Did it sound like Harris?'

Bastard.

Dom remembers the pain in his ears, the fogginess in his brain and the sickness. 'I couldn't tell. My hearing was screwed.'

'Could it have been Harris?'

'Possibly.' Dom glares at Holsworth. Hates him for pushing him into a corner. 'I don't know for sure.'

'What exactly did he say?'

'I don't know.'

'I think you do. So tell me. It's your career on the line here.'

Dom glares at Holsworth. 'I told you, I can't bloody remember.'

O'Byrne jots something onto his pad, then shuts it so Dom can't read what's written.

Dom forces himself to keep his arms relaxed, hands resting in his lap. It's hard. What he really wants is to shove the pad up O'Byrne's arse.

Holsworth's voice cuts into his thoughts. 'So this man enters, with boots like DC Harris. Then what?'

Dom remembers the light, the explosion. The room filling with smoke. 'A flash-bang disorientation grenade went off.'

'Go on.'

'I couldn't see or hear much, but I sensed movement around me. There was shouting, I think. Then gunfire.' The memory replays in his mind. Therese was shouting, Genk too. Feet moved past his face, he couldn't tell whose. Everything was hazy. The noise alternately muffled and deafening. Then it happened. Dom flinches at the memory of the whip-crack sound. Gunfire. One of the trainered guys fell forward onto the sofa. A quarter-second later, Therese dropped limp to the floor. Her eyes were wide, her mouth open, blood gushing from the wound in her head. 'DI Weller was shot.'

Holsworth picks up the file on the table and flicks through the pages until he reaches a report printed on yellow paper. 'It states here that the shot was a through-and-through. The bullet killed one of Genk's men, but continued on and grazed the side of DI Weller's head. The medical report says you applied pressure to the wound using Black Nasty and your hands until help arrived.'

Dom remembers the blood flooding through the gaffer tape, and the bloodstains that never seemed to fade no matter how hard he'd scrubbed his hands. 'Yeah.'

'Any reason you were able to move then, when you'd been incapacitated until that moment?'

He'd asked himself that question a thousand times. 'No.'

'I see. So you were quite the hero.'

'Therese, DI Weller, was in a coma for four weeks. Genk got away.' Dom shakes his head. 'There's nothing heroic in what I did.'

Holsworth stares at him, unblinking. 'That's for me to establish.'

The interview is done, for now at least. From the questions, and the way the smug-faced bastard looked at him, Dom knows things are going to turn bad. As he heads to the tube, Dom replays the meeting in his mind. He'd answered the questions as well as he could, and as honestly as he was willing to, but he knows his answers sounded weak. There are too many holes in his story. It's obvious Holsworth wanted him to confirm the person with the Doc Martens was Darren Harris, and maybe he should have, but he feels bad enough for saying as much as he did.

Shit.

Chrissie is so happy with Darren, and after all the heartache she's endured she deserves some happiness. When she met Darren it was as if both she and Dom were finally moving on with their lives. They sold the house they'd grown up in and bought flats in different parts of town. Dom got promoted and began to date for the first time in years. Chrissie got a part-time job, and started making plans. For just over two years she's been in a happy, stable relationship. Now Dom knows he's jeopardised it all by putting Darren squarely in Holsworth's crosshairs.

He hurries along the pavement. A constant stream of traffic passes along the road beside him: cars, cabs, a bus and a skinny lad on a pizza delivery scooter. He steps off the kerb to dodge round a group of slow-moving tourists, then weaves across to the other side to avoid the solid mass of a sightseeing walking tour.

Dom wishes, just for once, that the street wasn't so busy. That he had more space to think, to breathe.

He's almost at Embankment tube. He tries to push the interview from his mind, but he can't. All he can think about is Holsworth; that smile he gave whenever he asked a question. The way he'd grilled him about Therese – had she acted inappropriately? Holsworth had known Dom was keeping something back, and Dom knows Holsworth will keep pushing, digging, questioning until he finds what it is.

She wants to see you, Lindsay had told him on the phone.

He doesn't need this shit. He needs to focus on the case, on getting some kind of justice for Kate and Zara and Jenna. He has to prevent the killer from killing again. But the memories, and the questions, from that last night of Operation Atlantis are pinging around in his head. Taunting him. He hates to admit it, but he needs answers just as much as Holsworth. The not knowing is driving him insane.

Why did Therese tell Genk she was police?

Was it Darren who came into the room before shots were fired?

Why was telling Therese he loved her such a bad move?

Why did she ask Lindsay to call?

He jogs up the steps and enters the station. Pressing his Oyster card to the reader, he goes through the turnstile and follows the flow of people towards the escalator. He stands on the right, still thinking. He has to be able to focus. Maybe if he sees Therese, speaks to her and gets some answers, then he'll be able to concentrate on the case.

She wants to talk. Maybe we need to.

28
DOM

He finds her in the steel and glass new-build part of University College Hospital, rather than one of the original red-bricks. A flash of his warrant card to the efficient-looking receptionist helped him discover that Therese has moved from ICU into a private room. His relief mingles with the nerves he feels about seeing her again. He loves her, and she pushed him away. It still hurts.

When he gets to her room on the third floor, the door is shut and the glass panel has the shade drawn down. He almost bottles out, but just manages to hold his nerve. He needs to see her.

He knocks twice, and opens the door.

She's sitting in bed, watching TV. Her frown turns into a smile when she realises it's him. 'Hello, stranger. Trust you to pitch up without calling first.'

'Lindsay said you wanted to talk.'

'Not brought me chocolates? No asking how I am? Jesus, Dom. Some people might not think you cared.'

He stares at her. Can't believe she's acting this casually with him. She looks smaller than usual, paler too. Her cheekbones are more pronounced and there are dark shadows beneath her eyes. The energy buzz he always associates with her is gone.

'Don't you pity me,' she says, pointing a finger at him, 'and don't say you don't, because I can see it all over that mug of yours.'

He loiters at the foot of her bed, unsure whether to kiss her or keep his distance. 'How's it going then?'

'As well as I can hope, I guess. The doc says I have to be patient, that I need to rest . . . blah, blah, blah.'

'And are you?'

'For now.' She lowers her voice. 'Lindsay said you had an interview with the IPCC . . .'

'They did me today.'

'Holsworth?'

'Yeah, and his two sidekicks.'

She straightens up a little. Winces. 'He came here yesterday. Asked me a few questions, background stuff to do with Atlantis. Said he'll be back.'

'Did you—'

'I didn't tell him we were screwing.'

That wasn't the question he'd been going to ask. He's silent, not sure what to say next. He wonders if the only reason she wanted to see him was to talk about the IPCC investigation. He's winded by how much the thought hurts.

'It's none of his business and it was just a bit of fun, wasn't it? Nothing serious.'

It was for me.

Dom clenches his jaw, holding back the questions: was that all it was to you? Why don't you want more? Aren't we good together? His jaw begins to ache. 'Did Holsworth ask about what happened?'

'Not really.'

Is she being evasive, or just answering the specific question he's asking? Dom's not certain. He asks her again, more direct this time. 'So what did happen?'

She smiles. 'You checked out.'

He feels the guilt, hot and spiky, like chilli powder in his blood. 'I'm . . . I . . .'

She laughs. It makes her cough. He can tell the movement hurts. 'Don't get all humble, Dom. Doesn't suit you. Some bastard twatted you with a bat, I'm surprised it isn't you lying here.'

Him too. 'I've got a hard head, that's what the doc said.'

'Yes.' There's amusement in her tone. 'I could have told you that.'

He suppresses a smile. Can't let himself get sidetracked; he needs answers about what happened, why she did what she did. His tone is harder than he'd intended as he says, 'I heard you and Genk. Heard you telling him—'

'What I thought I needed to say to keep us alive.'

'Is that why you did it?'

She gives him that look, the one that gets him in his heart and his pants. 'Don't you trust me, Dom? After everything . . .'

'I want to.'

There's emotion in her voice as she says, 'You were down. Genk was suspicious. I had to do something to get him to incriminate himself.' She pauses, wheezing, the effort of speaking becoming too much. 'Telling him I was police was the first thing that came to my mind. I thought if he was willing to work with a corrupt—'

'It was risky.'

She glances down at her body shrouded in the white sheet, and at the monitors she's hooked up to. 'I'd say so.'

Seconds pass; neither of them speak. The machines continue to beep. In the corner, the characters of a dreary-looking daytime soap prattle away on the flat screen TV, the volume on low. Dom watches the liquid in Therese's IV drip through from the bag to the line.

'They tell me I'm dehydrated.' There's a quiver to her voice that he's never heard before. 'I'm sure it's nothing a wine or two couldn't fix.'

He doesn't respond. He's still thinking about what she's said about her and Genk. What she did makes sense; she made a fast decision in the moment. It could have worked, and rescued the operation before it totally went bad. Dom wants to believe her, thinks that he does, but there's an uneasy churning in his gut, as if he's drunk four pints on an empty stomach. Is this what closure feels like? He doubts it.

She's the one to break the silence. 'It would have been worth it if we'd got him.'

Dom nods. 'Yeah, it would.'

'Did you tell Holsworth what you heard?'

'What I heard you say to Genk?'

'Yes.'

He looks away, wondering again if this is the real reason she wanted to see him, to find out if he'd grassed her up. Wonders if she's been using him all along. 'I didn't tell him.'

'Thanks,' she says, the word whisper-quiet.

He tries to meet her gaze. Can't. He still loves her, but he doesn't trust her. He focuses just below her eyes instead. 'Did you see who came into the room before the shots were fired?'

'I don't remember. My head's still jumbled from the . . .' She gestures to the adhesive patch fixed over the wound on the side of her head. 'Well, you know.'

'Yeah.' The machines seem louder; the beeping of the heart monitor, the clicking from the morphine pump. Outside in the corridor, two men are talking loudly.

'So I hear you're working a serial killer case,' Therese says. 'How's it going?'

'What have you heard?

'I've heard you're respected by your team and that Jackson rates you.'

'But?'

'Word is, you're nowhere on the investigation.'

'Is that right?'

'It's a high-profile case, and coming right after Atlantis . . .' She shakes her head. When she continues her voice is softer. 'With the way the media are crying for action, some are saying it's going to get you bumped.'

'Some being Lindsay?' His tone is bitter.

Her expression betrays nothing. 'Is it true?'

He stays silent. Wants to know why Lindsay's taking such an interest in Therese's well-being. He needs to know the answer, but doesn't want to know.

'Dom?'

'I've got to go.' Turning away, he heads for the door.

Fuck Lindsay, and fuck the media. He can't get bumped off the case. He has to find this killer, needs to find who's responsible. Kate, Zara and Jenna deserve that.

'Dom?'

He glances towards the bed, towards Therese.

She smiles. Looks apologetic. 'Thanks for coming.'

He wishes he hadn't.

29

CLEMENTINE

Death Stalker posted in Case Files: The Lover
Death Stalker This is the team – Crime Queen, Robert
'chainsaw' Jameson, Justice League, Ghost Avenger,
Bloodhound, The Watcher, Witness_Zero and me as your team
leader. Tonight we meet to plan our strategy. 19:00 at the
Wetherspoons on Euston Road. Here's the link.

I'm going to meet them, meet Death Stalker, face-to-face.
It's perfect.
It's terrifying.

30
DOM

Therese's words are still buzzing around his head. Thoughts of her and Lindsay are distracting him from the case. As he exits the tube, a vendor in a tartan coat thrusts a folded newspaper at him. The start of the headline catches his eye: *THE LOVER KI—*

What line are the press spinning now?

Forcing a half-smile, he takes the paper. 'Ta.'

Still walking, he reads the full headline: *THE LOVER KILLED MY GIRLFRIEND: Distraught DJ speaks of his heartbreak.*

Dom stops dead, speed-reads the piece, his grip on the pages tightening with every word he reads. Stax has used his girlfriend's death to get publicity. *Attention-seeking bastard.*

There's a large picture of Stax gazing soulfully into the camera. The article mentions his set times at the club and his aspiration for a recording contract. Aside from the headline and first paragraph, the story barely references Kate Adams.

Anger gnaws at his stomach, hollowing him out. Has Stax got no shame? Dom remembers how he acted when they met, that too-intense stare and the evasiveness. They need to bring in the weasel and really roast him. Find out what he's hiding.

The team meeting starts at four o'clock. They're gathered in the incident room, all facing the murder board, except Dom. He's perched on the table at the front, marker pen in hand. He glances at the pictures of Kate Adams, Zara Bretton and Jenna Malik smiling, not knowing how things would end. It's not fair, and him being distracted isn't good enough. They deserve better. He shouldn't have let himself get sidetracked by Holsworth, by Therese. This meeting needs to remedy that.

Abbott's perched against a table, scratchpad in hand. Parekh looks keen to start, unlike Biggs who's lounging back in his chair, playing with his phone. Dom clears his throat. 'OK, let's get going. Updates, first. Who wants to kick off?'

Parekh raises her hand. She looks excited. 'Guv, I've found something on the Chick-O-Lick CCTV. A man not matching the description of any resident or guest of a resident gained access to Kate's building at 8.42 p.m. and left at 1.58 a.m.'

Dom inhales fast. This is huge. 'What can you tell us about him?'

'Not much, unfortunately.' Parekh passes Dom a grainy black and white image. 'He looks about six foot tall, medium build and is wearing dark clothing. He never looks directly at the camera, and his hoodie is pulled low over his face, obscuring his features. He's carrying something in the hand farthest from the camera. It looks like an old-fashioned doctor's bag.'

'Do you know where he came from?'

Parekh shakes her head. 'I tried tracking him on the street cams but lost him two hundred metres from the crime scene, same on the way in. It's like he just pops up from nowhere.'

'Or he knows the exact range of the cameras,' says Abbott.

'Yeah.' Dom looks back to Parekh. 'Any luck with the CCTV from Wetherspoons?'

Parekh nods. 'I've been through it. Kate and Eva only appear when they're served at the bar. The place they stood the rest of the time, and the area on the mezzanine where Eva said the guy watching them was, are in the camera's blind spots. There's something useful, though. The guy who came on to Kate when she went to the loos? We've got the altercation on camera.'

'Does it look like the person of interest on the Chick-O-Lick camera?'

'No, the guy from the bar looks shorter and stockier.' She passes Dom a second image. 'Also, we don't know if the guy who came on to Kate is the same man who watched the girls from the blind spot, but I've found out who he is so we can ask him.'

Dom's impressed. Parekh's achieved a lot. 'Good work. Who is he?'

'POI 2 is Jon Leighton, twenty-three. He's an estate agent, works for that new high-end company, Padulous. He's been clean a few years, but in his teens he built up an impressive juvie sheet – disorderly misdemeanours mainly.'

Dom sticks the two pictures to the murder board, marks the Chick-O-Lick man Person of Interest 1 and the Wetherspoons guy Person of Interest 2. He adds their details beneath. Looking at Abbott he says, 'Get the first image circulated.'

Abbott nods.

Dom turns to Parekh. 'We should check Jon Leighton out. After this, yeah?'

She smiles. 'Yes, guv.'

Dom nods at Biggs. 'What have you got?'

'Not a lot.' His tone is gruff, bordering on rude.

Dom keeps his expression and tone dead serious. 'You were looking into Stax and Kate's relationship and money problems, you must have found something?'

Biggs shrugs. 'Not really, everyone I spoke to said they were happy. Golden. He's getting money in, it's just the bigger amounts are sporadic, like his better-paying DJ gigs. Only her parents thought something was up. I checked out the financials and they're right – his credit card debt was high, but he always paid in the end.'

'With Kate's money, from what they said.'

'Not always, and from what they said Kate was willingly giving him the money when she did.'

'Unless she refused,' Abbott says.

Biggs shakes his head. 'I found nothing suggesting that. They were happy, even if her parents weren't.'

Dom doesn't believe it. No relationship is ever that perfect, especially when the boyfriend is a tosser like Stax. 'So you're saying not one hint of trouble, then?'

Biggs picks up his mobile from the table and scrolls through what Dom assumes are his notes. 'Well, not much, but I talked to a few people who work at that club where he DJs. They said he's a good lad, and that the vic was devoted to him. He put her on a pedestal and all that bollocks, but something about the way they said it didn't stack up for me.' He chuckles at his pun.

Twat.

'Did you press them?'

'Course. But I didn't get anywhere.' Biggs puts his phone back onto the table. 'Maybe he's a stand-up guy.'

'I doubt that. Anyone seen tonight's news?' Dom throws the paper onto the table closest to Biggs. 'Stax, Kate Adams's *devoted* boyfriend, has talked to the press. Details-wise it's puff, but it shows us more about Stax's nature. He's playing the sympathy card, looking for his fifteen minutes. He talks more about his career than his murdered girlfriend.'

Biggs shifts in his seat. Looks uncomfortable.

Good, Dom thinks. Biggs was working the angle on Stax all day; that he's surprised by the article looks bad. Maybe this will jolt him out of his sulk. If not, Dom knows they'll have to have a serious chat about his future with the team.

'You think he's worth taking another run at?' Parekh asks.

'Yeah, I do. That story's a fucking disgrace. We need to squeeze the bastard.' Dom looks at Biggs. 'You talked to him today?'

Biggs shakes his head. 'Nah.'

'Why the fuck not?'

Biggs shrugs.

Dom clenches his fists. Wishes Biggs wasn't such a dick. He really wants another crack at Stax himself, but he can't be everywhere. They finally have a fresh lead – it needs following up fast. Biggs might be a bastard, but he's well capable of handling Stax alone. 'Well get it done tonight. I want his balls in a vice until you find what he's hiding, yeah?'

'Yes, boss.' Biggs's words sound far from genuine.

Dom glares a moment longer at Biggs, then looks around the room. 'What else?'

'The book, *Black Rose Chronicles*,' Parekh says. She consults her notes. 'According to Wikipedia it was written by Daphne Turtine in 1943. For a while it was used as a set book for O level English, but it got thrown out when GCSEs came in. It's pretty much been out of print since then, but according to Google it's still on reading lists at a few public schools for expats, mainly in

Singapore, South Africa and India. I've ordered some second-hand copies from Amazon. They should arrive tomorrow.'

Dom notes the information on the board and turns back to Parekh. 'Have you checked if Kate Adams, Zara Bretton or Jenna Malik had a copy?'

'Not yet, it's on my list to do next.' Parekh looks over at Biggs. 'Can you ask Stax when you question him?'

Biggs types something on his phone, one-fingered. 'Yep.'

'Guv?' Parekh says. 'I just wanted to add the book was made into a film in the late eighties. Not a good one, according to IMDb. The plot was the same as the book, which is pretty basic by modern standards – a young woman takes a job as governess to the young children of a reclusive widower who lives in a crumbling mansion. At first she barely sees him, but over time they develop a bond, etc., then she discovers the secret he's been hiding – the reason why he's withdrawn from society. She's conflicted, leaves, then realises she's in love with him and returns. Emotional reunion, etc., happy ever after.'

'There's no murder in it?' Dom asks.

'Not that I can tell from the plot synopsis.'

'I checked out pictures of the actress playing the lead. She didn't look like our victims, not in the film or in her personal life. Could be there's a supporting role that'll give us a link.'

'Maybe,' Dom says. 'Can we download it? Did the film have the same title as the book?'

Parekh consults her notes again. 'No, they shortened it to *The Black Rose*, and you can't download it, too lame for them to bother with, I guess. I've got DVDs on order, though. They should be here tomorrow.'

'Good work, Parekh.' He looks over at Abbott. 'Do you want to update everyone on the PM?'

'Can do.' Abbott reels off the information from the autopsy. Consults his notes for the name of the new anaesthetic used in Kate's murder and how the killer injected it into a hard-to-reach vein.

'It could be he stuck the needle in anywhere, maybe because Kate was struggling, but there are easier places to inject if that's

164

the situation. I think it tells us something about our killer,' Dom says, taking over from Abbott. 'I think he's deliberately trying to hide the mark from the injection, for some reason that's important to him—'

'You think he's re-enacting a previous kill?' Parekh says, leaning forward in her seat.

'I think he's re-enacting something. It could be another murder, or maybe something from this *Black Rose* book.' He gestures at the board, towards the crime scene pictures. 'Whatever it is, they're meant to *be* someone, *mean* something to him. He's careful, clean. The way their appearance is changed takes skill and time. But he's still experimenting, trying different drugs.'

Biggs shrugs. 'Maybe he'd run out of the other one. It could mean nothing.'

Dom stares at him. 'Or it could mean something.' He looks at Abbott. 'Can you run a check for recent drug thefts, specifically anaesthetics? Check hospitals, pharmacists, doctor's surgeries, anywhere that keeps these drugs.'

'Yes, boss. We're getting an extra indexer from Kelterman's team tomorrow. I'll get them on it first thing.'

'Great. Anything more from the lab?'

'Forensics got nothing usable from the scene, same as the others.'

'How about those samples Emily sent over this morning – the make-up, that compound and the glue?'

'Nothing yet,' Abbott says. 'It's still early, though.'

Working a case without forensics was like a cage fighter entering the ring with his dominant fist tied behind his back. Dom looks at Parekh. 'Any luck on that recruitment connection?'

'I spoke to human resources at the NHS Trust. They did their own hiring for Kate Adams's role. As we already know, Zara Bretton was put forward via an agency called Office Magic and Jenna Malik went direct through the graduate recruitment portal. I called both companies to be sure, though. They'd never heard of Kate.'

Dom had expected as much, but he still feels disappointed. He jots the new information onto the board. 'Anything else?'

Parekh clears her throat. 'Just to let you know I'm going through Kate Adams's diaries – work and personal – looking for any similarities with the first two victims.'

'Give her a gold fucking star,' Biggs mutters.

Dom glares at him, then looks at Parekh. 'Found anything?'

'Just the usual, really – nights out, doctor's appointments, hairdresser – that kind of thing. She had a dental appointment three weeks ago, and we already know Zara Bretton and Jenna Malik saw the dentist in the month before they died, but they're different surgeries, so not connected.'

Dom nods. 'OK, so until the lab work is back, our best leads are Stax and POI 2. Let's get them interviewed tonight, and regroup first thing.' He eyeballs Biggs. 'Call me when you've finished with Stax. I want to know what you find.'

Biggs nods, a face on him like a right miserable bastard. Dom guesses he's pissed off because it's almost six and he wants to go home. Tough.

As they leave the room Abbott falls in step beside Dom. 'Is there anything you need me on now?'

Close up, Dom can see how dog-tired his DS looks. 'Nah. You get off and see that little kid of yours. Pick up with the lab again tomorrow.'

'Thanks, guv.' Abbott smiles. 'Tomorrow's another day, and all that.'

'Let's hope so.' Dom lifts his jacket off the back of his chair and pulls it on.

Parekh heads his way, her orange parka and black fingerless gloves already on over her grey skirt suit. 'Ready, boss?'

'Yeah. Let's see what Jon Leighton has to say for himself.'

31
DOM

Padulous Estate Agents close at six, so Parekh drives straight to Jon Leighton's home address, a shabby ex-council high-rise with a good postcode. They park on the street, put a police notice on the dash and head to the building.

Leighton lives on the fifth floor. Dom and Parekh buzz the intercom for flat fifty-three and wait. After almost a minute, Parekh glances at Dom.

'Try it again.'

She presses the buzzer.

This time the intercom crackles and a man's voice says, 'Hello?'

Dom leans closer to the intercom. 'Are you Jon Leighton?'

'Who wants to know?'

'Detective Inspector Bell and Detective Constable Parekh. We'd like to speak to you. Can we come in?'

There's a pause, then Dom hears the door unlock. They enter the building and head to the lift. A few ceiling lights are blown, making the lobby seem gloomy. Over to the right a couple of bikes are locked to the emergency exit. Next to them a sleeping bag has been pushed up against the wall, some empty lager cans heaped up beside it.

'Nice place,' Parekh says.

Dom grimaces.

They step into the lift. The stench of piss is overwhelming. There's a wet patch in the corner; it ripples as the lift ascends. By the time the door judders open Dom can't wait to get out. They follow the corridor, counting off the numbers on the doors. The walls are grubby; a hodgepodge of sticky hands, furniture scrapes and the odd bit of graffiti.

Parekh glances at him. 'Hardly the Savoy, is it?'

Dom shakes his head but says nothing. He's thinking about the interview. This guy's a person of interest, but not a suspect, not yet. They need enough to take him out of play, or put him in. Parekh's a good detective but she's still new to this game; an interview like this is good experience. He meets her eye. 'You comfortable leading this?'

'Yes, guv.'

'Good.' Dom can tell she's nervous at leading the interview, but she's pleased he wants her on point too. 'Gently at first. Get the feel of him. Then decide the best way to work it.'

Dom knocks on the door. He notices the paintwork's fresh white, unlike the others they've passed. The wall on either side is cleaner, too, the scuff marks and handprints washed off.

On the other side of the door there's the sound of a bolt being drawn back, then the clunk of the deadlock releasing. The door opens. A stocky man, a couple of inches shorter than Dom, stands in the doorway. His suit is well cut, looks expensive. It almost hides his beer belly. 'All right, fella?'

'Jon Leighton?' Dom asks.

'That's right. Guess you want to come in?'

'If we can,' Parekh says. 'We've got a few questions you might be able to help us with.'

Leighton stands aside. 'Come inside.'

Parekh goes first. Dom hangs back, watching the way Leighton ogles the female detective's bum as she passes, and the way he follows too close behind her as he directs them to the living room. Dom doesn't like it. Suspects he knows what type of man Jon Leighton is, and why Kate Adams wouldn't want him near her.

The room is sparsely furnished. Leighton gestures towards a pair of cheap sofas with faded blue covers. 'Sit down if you want.'

His voice echoes, loud, not helped by the laminate floor and the lack of curtains.

'Thanks,' Parekh says, perching on the edge of the nearest sofa. Dom sits beside her, forcing Leighton to take the other one.

Leighton flops down onto it, and asks, 'So what's this about?'

'Were you at the Wetherspoons on Euston Road on Saturday night?' Parekh asks. 'It was the 999 night.'

Leighton gives her a suggestive smile. 'I went along for a bit, had some laughs. Why?'

Parekh doesn't answer the question. Instead she passes him a photo of Kate Adams. 'Do you recognise her?'

Leighton looks at the photo, saying nothing. He doesn't need to speak, though; Dom knows he remembers Kate, he saw it in the slight smile that flicked up the corners of his lips as he first looked at the photo. Often a person's physical reactions are as telling as the things they say.

Leighton looks at Parekh. 'Could do, can't be sure. Why, what's she done?'

'She didn't do anything. We need to know if you recognise her.'

Leighton shrugs. He tilts his head to the side and drops his gaze to Parekh's chest. 'Dunno, sweetheart, sorry.'

Sweetheart. The term of endearment sounds more like a come-on the way Leighton says it. Dom resists the urge to jump in, knowing he has to let Parekh keep the lead. If she can deal with Biggs she's more than capable of handling this prick.

Parekh hands Leighton a different photo; Kate Adams's face in close-up, her eyes staring lifelessly upwards, just as they'd found her. 'How about now?'

Leighton takes the picture. The colour drains from his cheeks. When he speaks the bravado's gone. 'What the . . . why are you showing me this?'

'This young woman was murdered last night. I'm asking you nicely right now, but if you continue to be obstructive we can take this back to the station.' Parekh pauses, letting her words sink in. 'So, tell me, did you see her in the pub?'

Leighton slumps forward. Hangs his head. 'OK, yes. I saw her.'

'Where?'

'Just in the bar, you know. Her and a mate were having a few drinks.'

'Try to chat her up?' Parekh asks.

Leighton looks at Dom. 'Might have.'

'Look mate,' Dom says. 'We're not auditioning you for a dating show here. Did you speak or not?'

Leighton looks embarrassed. Doesn't meet his eye. 'Tried to. But she wasn't having any of it.'

Parekh nods. 'Tell us what happened.'

'I'd clocked her downstairs earlier with her mate, but they were in some heavy conversation so I went back to the people I was with.'

'These people have names?'

Leighton reels off three names, adding, 'Dan's a nurse, that's how come we were there, for the free first drink.'

Parekh notes the names. 'Did you see her again?'

'So, yeah, later I spotted her on her own. She was going to the bogs. Well, I thought nothing ventured and all that, so I tried to have a little chat.'

'And how did it work out?'

'Not good, to be honest – she got all freaked out, saying I was hassling her. Seemed really high-maintenance.' He glanced at Dom. 'You know what I mean? So I left her to it, figured I didn't need that kind of crap.'

Dom keeps his expression neutral. He keeps watching Leighton: taking note of the anxious fiddling with the cufflink on his left sleeve, the rather forced laddishness, the frequent glances at Parekh's chest. Dom knows Leighton being a creep doesn't make him a killer; it does make him a twat, though.

'Did you see her after that?' Parekh asks.

Leighton shakes his head. 'Her? No. But there was this guy, he kept giving me the evil eye, ever since I spoke to her.'

'Was he with her?'

'No, but after she'd gone down to the bar it looked like he was watching her. Given the way she'd freaked on me I wondered if they were together or something, you know, playing some game and me butting in wasn't part of it.'

'So you thought they knew each other?' Parekh asks.

'Maybe.'

Dom leans forward. This could be important. 'What made you think that?'

'Dunno really. Something about the intense way he looked at her. And the way he looked at me after I'd spoken to her was, like, really angry.'

Parekh jots down what he's said. 'Anything else?'

Leighton's silent, thinking, his lips pursed tight together. 'Nah, don't think so.'

'Can you describe him?'

'Quite tall, medium build, I guess. Darkish hair, although it looked a bit weird, like he was wearing a rug or something, hard to tell in the pub.'

'Distinguishing features?'

'Not really. I guess you'd say he was all right looking.'

'How old?' Dom asks. This is good. The height and build is consistent with the man on the CCTV outside the flat. It also fits with what Eva Finch said.

Leighton shrugs. 'Older than me, I reckon.'

Parekh takes the photos back from Leighton. 'Thank you, you've been very helpful. We're going to need you to come in and make a statement.'

Leighton gives a weak smile. 'I can do that.'

'First thing tomorrow?'

He looks pained. 'I can't, not first thing. I've got some viewings lined up, can't miss them.'

'And this is a murder inquiry, Mr Leighton,' Parekh says.

Leighton sinks back against the sofa. The hems of his trousers ride up, and Dom glimpses the washed-out socks below have begun to fray around the top edge. The suit and the brown brogues he's wearing must have cost him most of five hundred quid, but the socks and the flat were own-brand value.

Leighton looks at Dom. 'I'm commission-only. If I don't show those properties, then—'

Dom nods. 'I get it, mate. What's the earliest you can come in?'

'Ten-thirty.'

He glances at Parekh, gives a little nod.

'Ten-thirty is fine,' she says, handing Leighton her card. 'Ask for me at the desk.'

They do a quick debrief back in the car. Dom knows better than to leap to assumptions, but he still feels a kick of adrenaline – it's possible Jon Leighton could identify their primary suspect.

Parekh's driving faster than she did on the way out. Dom doesn't mention it; he knows she's feeling the rush as much as him, that surge of excitement, of hope, when you hit on something that might help you solve a case.

He thinks about their next move. 'That CCTV from the Wetherspoons. I know you said the area on the mezzanine our voyeur stood in was a blind spot, but do they have a camera on the entrance?'

'They do, yes. I've got the footage back at the office.'

'Great. We need to separate out the face shots of all the men entering the pub during the hours Kate Adams was there. Then get Eva Finch and Jon Leighton to go through them. I know Eva said she couldn't see properly without her contacts, but if Leighton got a good look, between the two of them we might get an ID.'

'I'll get on to it first thing, guv.'

'Cheers.' The link's tenuous at the moment, but if Leighton and Eva Finch can pick out the man from the pub's CCTV then the techs could do a comparative analysis between that man and the one caught on camera by the takeaway. It could get them a damn sight closer to identifying who the hell he is.

Parekh turns on to Euston Road. The traffic's heavy as always. She crawls along behind the cab in front. Looks across at him. 'I'm joining a few of the team at the Drake and Castle. Do you want to come, sir?'

'Not sure I'd be welcome.'

'Maybe not, I guess.'

'Just drop me at the tube and go and have fun, yeah.'

Parekh nods. 'Yes, sir.'

She looks stoked, and he recognises the look. The rush you get from a new lead, especially in a case as frustrating as this one, can be more intoxicating than booze. He hopes she'll be careful. He knows from experience where a few drinks with the team can lead. He's *been* where it leads. An image of Therese in the Princess Victoria with a gin and tonic in her hand floats across his mind's eye; the end of their first week on the Operation Atlantis team. A drink and a chat, that's how it started. A few hours later they were fucking each other senseless in his flat.

He never meant to fall in love with her.

32

CLEMENTINE

The Wetherspoons is what's left of an old Victorian pub that's had its guts pulled out and been refurbished into something generic. Death Stalker's choice is an interesting one; according to his police source, this was where Kate Adams spent her last night out before she died. There's no media here, though. Tonight, the benches lining the pavement are vacant aside from a few hard-core smokers.

Pushing open the sturdy door, I step into the pub. It's busy. Most seats are taken and there's a ring of people around the bar. I scan the room, looking for Bob, but don't spot him. There's a group of people by the fireplace. I watch them, wondering if Bob's late and that's the rest of the group. No. Their laughter is shrill, and there are shot glasses piled on the table in front of them. I discount them and keep looking.

Another minute passes. I'm feeling awkward now. I can't stand by the door forever. I make my way across to the bar and order gin and soda. I don't usually drink alcohol in public; I can't risk the lack of control, the dulling of the senses it brings. The heightened risk that people will see me for what I am.

Tonight's different, though. Tonight I need some extra courage.

'Five pounds ninety,' the floppy-haired blond barman says. His accent's Australian, but his pasty skin has a proper London pallor.

I hand him the cash. 'I'm looking for a meeting of—'

'What's the booking under?'

I look blank. I don't know Death Stalker's real name, and the other option is going to sound odd. 'I'm not sure.'

The barman raises an eyebrow. He speaks slower, as if he thinks I'm stupid and unable to understand the question. 'What's the name of the person who booked?'

Over the noise of the bar, I say the only name I have. 'Death Stalker.'

He shows no surprise. 'Back room,' he says, nodding to the far end of the bar. 'Through the curtain.'

Weird. 'Thanks.'

Taking my drink, I move along the bar and through the gaps between the sofas cluttering the space by the fire until I'm standing in front of a black velvet curtain hanging ceiling to floor.

My mouth feels dry. This is my last chance to opt out. Once I open the curtain and step inside, they'll know what I look like. I won't be able to hide. I think of Wade's concern, and of the mystery surrounding Death Stalker's identity.

Walk away.

I take a gulp of my drink and hope it helps me hold my nerve. If I leave now I'll be cast out of the group. I can't let that happen; this amateur group has to beat the police. I have to prove it's possible, even if I fear the Lover could be one of them. I messaged Wade before I came here, told him the location of this meeting; thought it would give me some comfort, him knowing. It doesn't feel that way, though. Not now I'm here.

I take another mouthful of gin, then pull aside the edge of the curtain and slide between the wall and the swathes of black velvet to enter the private room.

It's smaller than I'd anticipated and has a whiff of stale beer. The walls are clad halfway with dark wood panelling, and the space above is painted burgundy. This, combined with the ineffective light from the wall lamps, makes the place seem murky, claustrophobic. I clutch my glass tighter and resist the urge to bolt.

It's too late to change my mind. In the centre of the room is a table, and sitting around it are six people. Five of them are looking at me.

Bob's the closest. He's wearing a green waistcoat that's straining at the buttons, and a keen smile. I give him a wave and he starts to ease his bulk off the chair.

'Great you made it, love,' he says, coming towards me. 'Thought you might have got lost.'

He looks like he might hug me. I step back, out of reach, and check my watch. It's ten past seven, so I'm hardly late. I shrug. 'Traffic, you know.'

Bob nods. 'Let me introduce you to the gang.'

I follow him to the table. My heart's thumping against my ribs. Every fibre of my being is telling me this is a mistake. I should have stayed alone in my apartment, anonymous – safe. I clench my fists tighter to stop my hands shaking. Fear that my grip might shatter the glass.

'This is The Watcher,' Bob says to the others. There's a note of pride in his voice, like he's passing on great wisdom rather than stating the bloody obvious.

A guy with dark shaggy hair, cute in an emo kind of way, meets my gaze. 'Welcome. I'm Ghost Avenger.'

So he's the mortuary guy. I force a smile. 'Hey.'

Beside him is a girl I recognise – Crime Queen. I realise she's in a couple of my photos from the crime scene yesterday, but always on the edge of the frame. She's young, late teens I'd guess, the bottom end of the age range she'd answered on her question-naire. Her purple hair is cut into a short bob that frames her elfin features. Her skin looks almost ivory against the blackness of her tight mesh top and ripped-at-the-knees jeans. Thick make-up covers her acne. She looks nothing like she does in her online photo – in it her skin is perfect, her eyes bigger and wider, her cheekbones more pronounced. It reminds me that however much we give in to our vanity and change our appearance online, we're still stuck with reality in real life. I make eye contact with her. 'Hi.'

She doesn't say anything. I notice how she leans a fraction closer to Ghost Avenger, laying her claim to him. Interesting. I file the alliance in my memory.

'Come, sit,' Bob says, gesturing to an empty chair beside his.

I do as he asks. The table is covered with newspaper clippings, photos and several laptops. I push Bob's clutter towards him, making space to put down my drink.

The middle-aged woman sitting opposite holds out her hand. 'I'm Jen, erm, Justice League.'

I shake her hand as that seems to be what she's expecting. 'The Watcher,' I say. The name still feels odd to speak aloud. But from Justice League's correction and Bob and Ghost Avenger's introductions, it seems that using online names is how the group operates in real life.

The dark-haired guy beside Justice League nods. 'I'm Bloodhound,' he says. He sounds rather embarrassed by the moniker.

'Hey,' I say. I force a smile, and the guy meets my gaze for a moment before glancing away. He looks tense, uncomfortable – how I'm feeling, although I hope I'm disguising it better than him. And he looks older than his online information says he is; more early forties than early thirties. That's the problem with knocking a few years off your age online – it only works if you never meet.

There's still one person I've not spoken to, a slim thirty-something with mop hair and a boyish face. Death Stalker, I presume. He's sitting at the head of the table, watching me. I meet his gaze and hold it. Wait for him to speak.

'Welcome.' His voice is deeper than I'd expected. 'That's all of us for now – Witness Zero is going to come later. Let's make a start.'

He doesn't give his name. Probably because he called the meeting and, as our leader, assumes he needs no introduction. From the hush that comes over the group it seems the others are willing to follow his lead, but I'm not so sure. The situation seems unnaturally surreal, like I've stepped through the velvet curtain and tumbled down a beer-smelling rabbit hole.

Death Stalker's monologue has lasted twenty-nine minutes yet he's said very little that's new. There's been bluster about finding the truth and us being in this together, but I think it's all for show. He calls us *his* team, and refers to the Lover investigation as *his* case. He's not a team player, that's pretty clear; he wants us to do the donkey work, while he gets to bask in the limelight if we succeed.

And to me, success looks unlikely. The investigation routes he wants us to follow seem disparate and unconnected to a wider strategy. Of course that could be how he wants it to appear – keeping us out of the big picture so he alone will be able to piece the information together – but that limits our ability to find the Lover and places all the responsibility to identify them on Death Stalker.

Although perhaps that's the point; if he is the killer, it gives him the chance to sabotage us if we get too close. I keep my expression neutral as I try to make sense of it. It's hard work, and the gin is fogging my thinking.

Death Stalker looks at each of us in turn and asks, 'Anyone got questions?'

Bob jumps in right away. 'That was very helpful. I wondered if we should set up a virtual murder board on our page. That'd let us record our findings and cross-reference them, and to spot patterns.'

Death Stalker nods. 'Yep, I like that. Can you set it up for me?'

Bob's porky cheeks flush, with pride I guess. He hasn't realised Death Stalker's fobbing him off. Death Stalker's not shared any information *he's* gathered since posting the initial photos. Without his input we'll only ever have a partial view.

I want to ask him what he's discovered, but I need to be careful not to alienate him. The books I've read on influencing put great emphasis on the use of language – saying 'and' in place of 'but' so as to appear to be building on a person's idea rather than implying it won't work. The key is to be non-confrontational.

I swallow. My heart rate accelerates as I open my mouth to speak. I need to try and appear confident. 'That sounds a great idea. *And* if we look at your intel alongside ours perhaps we'll spot a pattern faster?'

Bob is nodding. Across the table, Justice League and Bloodhound look expectantly at Death Stalker. Ghost Avenger's expression is hard to read, but Crime Queen's isn't – her frown implies I've crossed a line.

Death Stalker doesn't seem phased. 'I'll share anything I get, just as I have been doing. So far my energy's going into tapping up contacts in the police, finding out how their investigation is progressing so I can feed new leads to you guys.' He makes eye contact with each of us again. 'We need each other to beat them to finding the Lover. *I* need you all to be part of this team.'

The others are nodding, taken in by his performance of sincerity, but I'm not. He's avoided the question. Used a politician's trick to appear genuine; appealing to their desire to be needed, making them feel part of something important. I can see through it, though; I've had to learn those tricks to mimic normal human interaction. He doesn't fool me.

I consider what to do. Walk out? Go along with the charade? If this is all about him taking the glory I need to make myself indispensable, get closer to him, although I know that will make Wade worry. I press my palm against my jacket pocket, and feel the outline of the plastic bag and the broken brush within. I've got something Death Stalker wants. I have to use it to get into his confidence.

Not yet, though. With no further questions, the formal part of the meeting is over. Bob and Crime Queen huddle closer to Death Stalker, talking in hushed voices. Justice League, Bloodhound and Ghost Avenger move their chairs closer to mine. I feel hemmed in, claustrophobic.

Justice League catches my eye. 'So have you worked on any cases before?'

I shake my head. Don't speak. She keeps staring at me. I grab my gin and drain the glass. Because although I know how to respond in a way that will make her believe I'm just like her, really I am not. Everything about me is an act. And here in this group, I'm feeling more like an outsider than ever.

The fear is growing, too. This room is too small. The air is thick and lumpy, chewy on my tongue. I swallow hard. The moths are back, fluttering in my chest, their sharp wings cutting at my throat as my panic rises.

Leave. Go now.

'I have,' Ghost Avenger says, answering Justice League's question. 'I helped another group with a couple of cold cases.'

Bloodhound nods. 'I've done a few small ones.'

Justice League switches her attention from me to Ghost Avenger. 'Did you solve them?'

He shakes his head and his hair falls over his eyes. He brushes it away with a flick of his hand. I notice he's wearing black nail polish. 'Nah. Didn't get far, to be honest.' He gestures towards Death Stalker. 'This group is very different.'

From the tone of Ghost Avenger's voice it's clear he thinks this group is better. Am I ridiculous to think Death Stalker could have a darker motive for the investigation? Wade's suspicions have made me paranoid; my fear isn't founded on methodical analysis, it's borne from Wade's own fears that what I'm doing isn't good for my academic career or, more specifically, isn't good for his.

I've been a fool. I've let him manipulate me; planting the kernel of fear and then moving away as it grows in my mind just as he knew it would. He knows about my troubles with anxiety and my tendency towards paranoia, and he's used them to play me. I clench my fists and the moth wings cease their flapping. I start to breathe a little easier.

'Oh, yes,' says Justice League. She's ignoring Bloodhound and looking at Ghost Avenger like he's some kind of rock god. 'Different how?'

Ghost Avenger shrugs. 'More organised. With the other group I got the impression they just did it for a laugh, you know? This is more serious. We all want to solve this. Take the killer off the streets. It's not a game.'

Bloodhound nods along, but says nothing. I do the same.

Justice League looks thoughtful. 'How could they treat it as a game? Murder is murder. Doesn't get more serious than that, surely?' She lowers her voice. Glances down as if she's embarrassed. 'It's not meant to be fun, even if investigating is quite thrilling at times. That's not the point. The point is that we're making this world, this city, a safer place.'

From the way she's talking we should each have a superhero outfit, a cape or something. I wonder if she's got some kind of God complex, then discount it. She doesn't seem to have an inflated opinion of herself. 'True.'

Justice League gestures towards our glasses. 'Drink?'

We give her our orders and she disappears out through the curtain to the main bar. I look at Ghost Avenger. 'So did you tell the other group about your job?'

'No. I didn't tell them anything much, to be honest. Just read a few things and checked stuff out online.'

'You told us, though.'

Ghost Avenger gives a lopsided smile. 'I did. I'd already told Death Stalker a while back, thought it might be useful, when the first body ended up on one of my slabs.'

'Is that why you took pictures of them?'

Ghost Avenger nods. He glances at Bloodhound. 'DS said I should make a record, you know, in case we needed it. The police have their crime scene photos and post-mortem pictures. If we were going to investigate too then we'd need something similar.'

Good thinking, and good planning on Death Stalker's part. The chatter about hunting a serial killer started around that time and it seems Death Stalker was planning his investigation already, or his cover-up. I meet Ghost Avenger's eyes. 'What was it like, seeing the victims' bodies?'

Bloodhound stands. 'Back in a mo. Just nipping to the loo.'

I smile at him, then look back to Ghost Avenger.

His expression becomes wistful, his gaze focused somewhere over my shoulder. 'Amazing. It's spooky how each victim was changed to look like the same woman. Every detail was exact.'

'Sounds fascinating,' I say, leaning closer to him. 'How?'

He shifts forward. Slides his hands across the table, palms down. He smells of vanilla soap and musk. 'The Lover is a perfectionist. Every element of his kill is pre-planned – it has to be to achieve such perfection. He selects his victims carefully and follows his routine to the letter. There's an artfulness about it. An inevitability that the sequence will play out exactly the same every time.' His eyes close, as if he's picturing it in his mind. He opens his eyes and stares back at me. 'Even in death his victims are beautiful.'

There's an emotion in Ghost Avenger's voice that I can't identify. Whatever it is, it's clear that he's just as fascinated by death as I am. Leaning closer, I lower my voice and ask, 'So, how close have you got to them?'

He beckons for me to move to the seat next to him. I oblige, and he whispers in my ear. 'I've touched them.'

I draw back, increasing the distance between us.

Ghost Avenger sighs. 'You asked before what got me interested in true crime—'

'And you said it was a long story.'

'It's not that long, to be honest.' He looks at me. He's frowning, like he's trying to figure something out. 'OK, so when I was thirteen my best mate, Dan, was murdered. He was grabbed after football practice and found dead, strangled, the next day.'

'That must have been hard.'

'It was. They said it was a sexual attack.'

'I'm sorry. I don't know what to say.' Which is the truth. I don't know what to say, but I do feel a twinge of sorrow. It's an unfamiliar sensation. Am I feeling sorry for another person, for Ghost Avenger? 'Did they find who did it?'

Ghost Avenger picks up his glass before realising it's empty. He puts it back down again. 'That's the worst of it. They matched the DNA left on Dan's body with Mr Caldiene, our football coach. When they went to arrest him he was already dead.'

'How?'

'Hose from the exhaust pipe of his car. They found him locked in the garage.' He shakes his head. 'I thought he was a good man, you know? No matter how I tried, I couldn't make sense of it. Why would he do that to Dan? I mean, he'd known us since we were little. He'd trained the team for years. He had a fucking wife!'

'People keep all kinds of secrets.' As I speak, another twinge of sadness vibrates through my chest. It makes me feel queasy.

'I just wanted to know why he did that to Dan, but he topped himself so I can never ask him.' Ghost Avenger's voice cracks. He looks down, his hair flopping over his eyes. 'I want to know why.'

'So you joined this investigation because you want to find the Lover to help his victims' families get closure?'

Ghost Avenger nods. 'Something like that, you know?'

I do know. I also know that a higher percentage than you'd think of those affected by violent crime go on to commit violent crime themselves, but before I can question him further we're interrupted.

'I need to borrow The Watcher for a moment.'

Death Stalker's voice makes me jump. I twist round and see him standing to my left.

He gives a half-smile. 'Do you mind?'

'Not at all,' I say, but I do. Things were getting interesting with Ghost Avenger. He's experienced loss, seen death. Maybe even caused death. It was almost as if I was feeling something for him. Something like empathy, perhaps.

'Will you give me a hand at the bar?' Death Stalker asks me.

Back in the main bar, I wonder where Justice League got to; she's not here and it's been ages since she left to get more drinks. The place is packed. We've been waiting five minutes and the queue doesn't seem any shorter.

'Do you have the brush?' Death Stalker asks. I get now why he wanted us to buy more drinks; so we could make the exchange away from the others. He's keeping it from the rest of the group. It's our secret.

I nod. Try to hide my nerves, appear confident. 'Who's your contact?'

'Someone reliable.'

It feels weird talking in real life. 'I found it. I want to know where it's going.'

Death Stalker looks thoughtful. I hold his gaze. In my peripheral vision, over his shoulder, I see Crime Queen staring at me, her eyes narrowed. She's standing with Bob, holding the curtain open, but her attention is fixed on Death Stalker and me. Her stare is intense beneath her purple fringe. I figure I don't have long before she interrupts.

Lowering my voice, I say, 'I get that you want to lead this. All I'm asking is for you to let me in on this part of it. I'm a professional researcher. Let me help you.'

For a moment I think he's going to walk away. Then he says, 'All right, seeing as you found it, I suppose it's fair. A friend of mine works in a pharmaceutical lab, which one isn't important, but he's got access to the equipment needed to run the tests we want.'

That's more information than he's shared so far this evening. I slip my hand into my jacket and pull out the plastic bag with the brush. 'I want to know what it is, and how it fits with the information your contacts are feeding you.'

He holds my gaze for a long moment. Nods. 'Deal.'

I hand the bag to Death Stalker. He pushes it into his pocket.

I find Justice League in the back room. She's bought me another gin, as has Death Stalker. The buzz of alcohol is fuelling my confidence, making talking with these people less of a chore, but it's fogging my mind. I'm worried my act will slip.

'Sorry I was slow getting the drinks earlier,' Justice League says. 'The husband rang. Had a problem with the kids.' She takes a gulp of her wine. 'We've got three boys. You'd think he could manage them for one bloody night, wouldn't you?'

I've no idea. 'I guess.'

'It's not like I get to go out much.' She looks at me. 'And for much, read hardly ever. He's their dad. He should be able to cope for a few hours. I have them all the time.'

I take another sip of my drink. It's easier just to let her talk.

'Do you have kids?'

'No.'

'Husband?'

'No.'

'Keep it that way. It's much simpler, believe me.'

'I've never given much thought to having children, or a husband. Don't think it's for me. I like my own space,' I try to say it like it's not the understatement of the year.

'Wise words.' She laughs. 'So what do you do?'

'I'm an academic.'

'Really? Brilliant. I'm doing Criminology at Birkbeck as a mature student.' She laughs. 'Makes me sound ancient, right?'

I ask her a question before she can ask me more about myself. 'Do you enjoy it?'

She nods. 'I do. I know I've just moaned on about my husband and the boys, but they're great, really. It's just I felt like something was missing. Like I was only valid in relation to someone else – someone's wife, someone's mother – not in my own right. I wanted something for me, a sense of my own purpose.'

It amazes me that she's sharing so much about her life with me. I'm a stranger. I could be anyone, do anything with the things she's telling me. 'And studying gives you purpose?'

'It does, and criminology, it's a chance to give something back, for the public good, you know, like this investigation . . . who's that?'

I look in the direction she's pointing. There's a new guy standing beside Crime Queen. He's at least a foot taller than her, older, too – late thirties or early forties I reckon – and smart in a charcoal-grey suit and black shirt. His blond hair is cropped short, and his face has a rough charm that makes him quite attractive.

Witness Zero was running late. I wonder if that's him. I watch Crime Queen call to Death Stalker. He raises his hand and goes over to speak to the new arrival. They exchange a few words before the three of them disappear back through the curtain to the main bar.

'Blimey, he was a bit pretty,' Justice League says. Her cheeks are flushed pink, and she's fiddling with her hair.

For me, though, the feelings he evokes are rather different. Is he Witness Zero? I hate that I know nothing about him, and that he's seen me. Most of all I hate that he's close with Death Stalker and Crime Queen, and that the three of them have gone off alone.

I need to be in their inner circle.

Most wolves hunt in packs.

33
DOM

He's only been home ten minutes when he gets Lindsay's text: *She said you'd been by. Thanks. Fancy a beer? Old times and that.*

Dom texts back: *Yeah. Sounds good. Give me an hour.*

It's a lie, though. Meeting Lindsay doesn't sound good, but it could be a way to get some answers. He needs to know what's going on. Has to know.

Forty minutes later and he's almost at the Princess Victoria, the place they used to go drinking after shift on Operation Atlantis. He's been trying to think about the murder case, about the leads they've got, but the Atlantis stuff is buzzing around his head like a fly he can't swat.

It's busy by the river. As he jogs up the steps of the Millennium Bridge he's passed by office workers, still in their business clothes, and a fair few people out for the night, dressed up despite the shitty weather. All of them are bustling across the bridge, hurrying to get to wherever they're headed.

One person is different. He's sitting on the tarmac, staring straight ahead. His grey hair is matted against his skull, and his baggy suit trousers, scuffed trainers and dirt-covered raincoat look soaked through. There's an open bottle in a plastic bag lying at his feet. A woollen hat is upturned on the ground beside him. It's empty.

As Dom passes, he hears the old guy muttering, 'No, Albert, no. Not before you've done the dishes.'

Poor bugger.

He puts some change into the hat. 'Get yourself a tea, mate.'

The old guy mutters something Dom can't make out, and smiles. His teeth are yellowed and rotting. An image of the first victim, Jenna Malik, floats into Dom's mind: she's been in the ground four weeks. Deep in the soil and darkness, worms will be eating through her coffin.

Dom looks away.

The pub is fifteen minutes' walk from the river, hidden down a side road round the back of the Southbank Centre. It's an old building with big sash windows covered in a thick layer of grime. The brickwork is fretting, crumbling from damp and frost. The front door, pitted beneath flaking green paint, looks like it's suffering the same fate. Dom pushes it open and steps inside.

A blast of warm air hits him. The place is as he remembers, all dark wood and frosted glass, traditional. He spots Lindsay in the corner, tapping away at his phone. Smart, with his usual black suit and dark shirt accentuating the white blond of his hair, he could be a banker rather than a detective. He's already got the pints in.

Dom weaves his way through the tables and sits down. 'Hey.'

Lindsay looks up. Smiles. 'All right, chap.'

'Not bad,' Dom says, going along with the small-talk bollocks. 'You?'

'Can't complain.' Lindsay slides the full pint across the table to Dom. 'Heard your investigation's turned chilly.'

Dom keeps his tone light. 'Don't go there, OK?'

Lindsay laughs. 'No problem.'

Dom takes a mouthful of beer. 'So what's this about?'

'Why does it have to be about anything?'

'Nothing in weeks, then you call twice. Bit odd.'

Lindsay takes a long slug of his beer before answering. 'Look, you're the one who buggered off back over the river.'

'The operation ended. Therese was in hospital.'

'I know but, I've got to be honest here, I had no clue what was going on with you. You never told the lads you were going. You didn't visit Therese when she came round.'

Fuck this, and fuck you.

Dom takes another gulp of his pint. The sooner he finishes it, the sooner he can be away.

'You know, Holsworth visiting her in hospital really shook her up.'

Dom frowns. 'She seemed OK when I saw her earlier.'

'Putting on a good face, wasn't she. The whole thing's freaking her out. I told her not to speak to Holsworth. Said to give herself more time, but she didn't bloody listen.' Lindsay runs a hand through his perfectly styled hair. 'She should have made him wait.'

Why shouldn't Therese speak to Holsworth? Lindsay's over-reacting, playing the role of protector too much. Dom can't imagine Therese liking that. She's always blazed her own path. That's one of the things he admired about her. 'Since when were you her keeper?'

Lindsay raises his eyebrows. 'I'm just being a mate.'

Him and Therese had never told anyone about their thing, but from Lindsay's tone Dom reckons he suspects something. Dom changes the subject. 'How's your wife?'

Lindsay shrugs. 'Busy with the kids, as ever.'

'Doesn't mind you visiting Therese all the time then?'

'Why should she? Me and Therese have been colleagues a long time. You know how it is with this job, you can't help but get close, can you.'

Dom doesn't respond. Can't. He wonders if Therese has told Lindsay about them, about how it ended. He grips his pint tighter and takes a mouthful of beer – anything to avoid looking at Lindsay.

'Mate, are you all right? You've gone a bit pale.'

'Long day,' Dom says, and takes another swig of beer.

'Tell me about it. Holsworth had me in again this afternoon.'

'Yeah?'

'He kept asking about Darren Harris.' Lindsay shakes his head. 'Poor bastard. If Holsworth's got something on Darren then he's going to get screwed.'

Dom says nothing.

'He wanted to know if I'd had eyes on Harris for the whole operation. Really had a hard-on for him. Made me wonder why.'

Dom says nothing.

'Your interview was this lunchtime, wasn't it?'

'Yeah.'

'Did he ask you about Harris?'

Dom shakes his head. He doesn't want to talk about Harris. He knows Holsworth is on Darren's tail because of what he'd told him in his interview, because of the boots. 'I was disabled early, wasn't I? You were the guys on the outside.'

Lindsay looks serious. 'Didn't think you'd be getting out of there, know what I mean?'

'I thought that myself for a while.'

'You know, I told Therese I should go in with her, but she wouldn't have it, would she. Always has to know best.'

Bastard. Had Lindsay wanted his place in the operation? It takes all Dom's self-control to keep his tone even as he says, 'I'd partnered with her on the other ops, no need for that to change.'

'No, suppose not.'

'Did you see Harris do anything dodgy?'

Lindsay frowns. 'Did I hell! He did his job, and he was good at it. That's what I told Holsworth. When we lost the comms link he stayed calm, didn't freak out.'

Dom remembers the moment he realised their communications had failed. *Eclipse. Bring the rain.* But there'd been no response, no back-up arriving. 'Did they find out why the comms stopped working?'

'Dunno. All I know was one minute you were clear, the next it was radio silence. Couldn't hear a damn thing from either of you.'

'Did you try and fix it?'

Lindsay looks confused. 'What do you bloody think? I was going spare. Genk wasn't playing ball; he'd told Therese to go back to her whore business. From the intel we'd got I knew if he wasn't doing business with you, things could turn bad any minute.'

Dom sits very still. His pulse thumps at his temples. 'So what did you do?'

'We needed ears on. I got Harris to stay put while I moved location, thinking if the signal had hit a dead spot I'd have more chance getting you back that way.'

'And did you?'

'Not till it was too late – that's when I sent in the cavalry.'

189

Genk wasn't playing ball. He told Therese to go back to her whore business.

How the fuck did Lindsay know that? Genk hadn't spoken until after Dom was down, until after he'd given the abort command – the command Lindsay claimed he'd never heard. 'How'd you know?'

'Know what?'

'That Genk told Therese to go back to her whore business, that the deal was off?'

Lindsay's expression gives nothing away, but he holds Dom's gaze a fraction too long. Shrugs. 'Dunno. She must have told me.'

Liar.

'You sure about that?' Dom says.

Lindsay leans closer. His lips curl into a sneer. 'Oh, I'm crystal. But it's best to keep quiet in this type of situation. Wild accusations and career-limiting assumptions get made otherwise, don't they?' He fixes Dom with a glare. 'It's lucky none of us got killed, isn't it? Mate.'

Dom stares back. If Lindsay knew what Genk said, then he knew they were already in trouble, and he didn't call it in. He's hiding something, covering for himself or for Therese or for Harris, or for all of them.

Lindsay leans closer. 'You want to stay breathing? Keep your fucking mouth shut.'

34

CLEMENTINE

Home. My phone vibrates in my pocket as I'm unlocking the door. I wait until I'm inside, until I've fastened every one of the bolts, before I check it. When I do, I sigh. It's a message from Wade.

I wanted to be sure you're OK.

Kicking off my boots, I remove my jacket and hang it on the peg beside the door, then type: I am.

Good. I could come over?

I look at Wade's text and remember how he bent me over his desk and spanked me as he fucked me. I enjoyed the feeling of him inside me, and am tempted to let it happen again; to invite him over and let the rush of endorphins, the ecstasy of climax, chase away the nothingness for just a little while. But I don't.
Instead I text:

Met the team. They're all right if a bit weird. Something about Ghost Avenger seems off. Death Stalker too – it's obvs he wants control. We share what we find, he won't.

Wade's reply is immediate: How so?
I head to the kitchen. Grabbing a glass from beside the sink, I give it a quick rinse and fill it with water. I take a sip, then message back:

I asked. He gave some bullshit about tapping police contacts on their investigation, but didn't give details. He wants to unmask the Lover and keep the glory. That's my take.

Based on? Wade replies.

I take another sip. Text back: Observation.

Wade fires back: Not very scientific.

Shaking my head, I type: It's late. I'm going to bed.

Wade: Death Stalker's main ace is his contacts. It wouldn't hurt for you to have a police contact of your own.

I don't reply. Instead I think about DI Dominic Bell.

Sleep doesn't come easy. It's hours after Wade's texts, and I'm lying in the centre of my bed staring through the curtain-less window at the moon. It's round and full tonight. I find its glow comforting.

On the night Father died there was a full moon watching over me in the cottage. I remember glimpsing it through the window earlier in the evening, before the smoke grew too thick. Aside from that, the sequence of what happened evades me. I close my eyes, and try again to remember.

After reading the letter, I need answers. It's late, getting dark. The whisky makes me feel both numb and tearful. I struggle to process what I've learnt. I can't believe the accusations against Father. He's a hero, not a criminal. It has to be a mistake.

I need answers but Father's not here to ask, so I stumble upstairs on unsteady legs, heading to the study. The door is locked. It's never been locked before. He lives alone, so there's no need.

I know where the key will be, though. One time, when I was young and we were playing I Spy, I spied Father's special key drawer. It's the second drawer of the apothecary cabinet in the kitchen. He'd left the drawer slightly open, and I'd seen the keys. It was the only time he'd not laughed when I beat him.

I go downstairs. There are fewer keys in the drawer than I remember. I take all that look as if they could be a match for the study door, then try them in the lock until I find the right one.

Inside, the room looks different. Father is always tidy, but his large oak desk is strewn with papers and Post-its. Behind it, pinned to the wall, are scraps of paper with his spidery scrawl, newspaper clippings and photographs; lines of string connect them.

On the leather chair there's a navy sports bag; it looks out of place. I unzip it. I cannot believe what I see.

I spy with my little eye, rolls of banknotes held together with elastic bands.

I spy clear plastic bags filled with white powder.

A stack of obscene photographs.

I flick through the pictures. My hands shake. Tears stream down my face. Nausea gets stronger with every image I see. Each one is of a different girl, a girl as young as me, naked or in bra and knickers. Written in the top left corners are names and reference numbers. Beside the number is a price.

I drop the pictures and they scatter across the floorboards like dirty confetti.

They're right; my father isn't a hero, he's a monster.

I cover my face with my hands and howl.

That's where the memory ends. Every time. Leaving me feeling the fury. Preventing me from knowing what happened next, the actions that took place, before the fire that killed Father took hold.

My heart's racing. I count to ten. Count backwards from ten. Stare at the moon and damn it to hell for not telling me what it witnessed all those years ago. For leaving me with the horror of what Father did, all over again.

He was a dirty copper.

Father was disgraced, the investigation said he was guilty, I know that.

Dominic Bell is a dirty copper, too.

I start to tremble. Don't like where this thought process is taking me.

This wolf doesn't want to kill again.

WEDNESDAY

35
DOM

Abbott and Parekh have been in the office since seven o'clock. Dom's glad. Forty-eight hours after a murder can be the point where leads dry up and the energy directed at the case wanes. It's when the dread sets in; the worry you won't make an arrest. No one in the team wants that to happen; except Biggs, and it's hard to know what he wants. Dom looks up from his desk to see him saunter in. It's almost 9.30.

Biggs dumps the plastic bag he's carrying onto his desk, chucks his coat over his chair, then picks up his mug and heads towards the kitchen. He says hello to Abbott and Parekh, ignores Dom. He still hasn't updated him on what happened with Stax the previous night.

Dom gets up and follows him to the kitchen. He glances up as Dom approaches.

Dom halts just inside the doorway. 'A word, Sergeant. Now.'

Biggs steps over to the machine. 'I'm just getting a—'

'Leave it.' Dom's tone is dead serious. 'We'll talk in the meeting room.'

Biggs says nothing, but he leaves the mug on the counter and follows him. Dom can feel eyes on him as they walk through the open plan.

The room seems smaller than usual. The murder board dominates one wall, the pictures of the victims staring down from it. Biggs props his arse against the nearest table. Looks unbothered.

Dom gestures to the door. 'Shut it, yeah.'

Biggs nudges it closed with his foot. 'So what is it?'

'You were meant to call me with an update on Stax last night.'

Biggs shrugs. 'Wasn't any point, there was nothing of use. Guessed you'd have phoned me if you were that fussed.'

196

Trust Biggs to throw that at him. Dom hates that he's right; he should have called Biggs, but with Darren and Lindsay and the damn Operation Atlantis stuff, he'd forgotten. Dom glares at Biggs, doesn't back down. 'If I ask you to do something, I expect it done.'

'Yes, *boss*.' Biggs's tone is full-on sarcastic. 'That all?'

'No.'

Biggs looks bored. 'What then?'

Dom's temper flares. How can an experienced detective be so blasé in the middle of a case like this? 'Tell me what the hell happened with Stax.'

Biggs gives a weasel smile. 'He caved.'

'Meaning?'

'He's been shagging a bar girl at that club where he works.' Biggs smirks. 'That's what he was doing when his girlfriend got killed.'

Dom's gaze flicks to Kate Adams's picture on the murder board; she's smiling, unknowing. He tries to swallow down the disgust he feels towards Stax, the two-timing little bastard. No wonder he acted so shiftily; he wouldn't look nearly so good in the press if the truth came out.

Biggs looks like he doesn't give a shit.

'You find that funny, Sergeant?'

'Not especially. Just didn't think it was worth calling about.'

'I do. And I expect you to follow the chain of command.'

Biggs exhales, the breath whistling through the gap between his top teeth. 'But, see, the thing is, *sir*, word is you're not going to be here long enough for it to matter what you think.'

Dom's fingers twitch. He stares hard at Biggs, fighting to keep calm. 'Is that right?'

Biggs shrugs. 'It's what I hear.'

Dom resists the urge to shove the bastard against the wall. 'I wouldn't listen to rumour, *Sergeant*.'

Biggs looks him straight in the eye. 'Maybe you should.'

Dom lunges at Biggs. Stops himself just before making contact, his face inches from the sergeant's. 'Look, personally I don't give a flying fuck whether you want to work for me or not, because right now this isn't about you or me. It's about these dead women.' Dom jabs his finger towards the crime scene photos. 'Look at them, remember their faces, their names – Kate, Zara, Jenna – young women with hopes and dreams. Go on, take a good look, and then you tell me you think it's OK, no, you think it's funny, not to follow orders, not to work this case like it absolutely should be worked.'

Biggs opens his mouth to speak.

Dom doesn't give him the chance. 'So did you check with this bar worker that she was with Stax when he said she was?'

Biggs's stare is hard, angry. Five seconds pass before he shakes his head. 'Not yet.'

'I thought not.' Dom doesn't keep the contempt from his voice. He steps back, putting a bit of distance between them. 'You used to be a class act, Biggs. But all this crap you're pulling now . . . it's pathetic.'

Biggs stares at him. Doesn't speak.

'I know you wanted my job, but you didn't get it, yeah? I guess you liked it while I was on secondment, but I'm back now, so you need to suck it up, or find another team, because this crap,' Dom gestures between the two of them, 'whatever it is, can't carry on.'

Biggs is stony-faced.

Dom holds his eye contact for a long moment. Sighs. 'Go and do some bloody work.'

Biggs moves to the door. Opens it.

'DS Biggs?'

The sergeant turns, looks at Dom. 'Yes?'

'If nothing changes, you *will* be out of this team by the end of this case.'

'Like fuck I will.'

'Don't you—'

Biggs exits, letting the door slam behind him.

Tosser.

The last thing Dom needs right now is the bureaucratic nightmare of their disciplinary proceedings. He rotates his shoulders, trying to ease the tension. Knows Biggs won't suck it up. The best he can do is get him transferred.

Dom turns to the murder board and glares at the photo of Person of Interest 1, the man from the CCTV outside Kate's building. 'Who the hell are you?'

His phone starts buzzing. Pulling it out, he reads the caller name that's flashing on the screen: Chrissie. He presses reject. Feels guilty. Tells himself he'll call her back later, once he's made some headway on the case.

He looks back at the board, tracking the lines of enquiry from each victim. There are few meaningful interconnections. The only thing similar were their deaths and how they looked when they died.

There's a knock on the door.

'Yeah.'

Parekh pokes her head into the room. 'Jon Leighton's arrived early to do the ID. He's waiting downstairs.'

As they head to the ground floor to collect Leighton, Parekh tells Dom the tech guys have done a great job of cleaning the images for the identification.

'They've got this new bit of software that can isolate unique faces from video. It's cool, just out of beta testing. Did the job in a fraction of the time.' She raises the buff-coloured folder she's carrying. 'We've got four hundred and sixteen male customers and six staff for him to work through. I contacted the pub to email the staff photos across. Thought it was worth covering all the bases.'

'Great, good work.' He watches her for a moment. She seems on the ball, but there are dark shadows beneath her eyes. 'You all right?'

She blushes. 'Why wouldn't I be?'

Dom wonders which one she's shagged. Not Biggs, surely. 'Good night, was it?'

Her blush deepens. 'Yes, sir.'

He doesn't want to embarrass her. Nods. 'Lets get a positive ID, shall we?'

They reach the bottom. Parekh pushes open the door out of the stairwell and gives him a relieved smile. 'Amen to that.'

Jon Leighton looks knackered. They've been in the interview room for two hours; Dom and Parekh watching Leighton looking at the images. From over four hundred pictures, he's narrowed it down to four.

That was twenty minutes ago. The windowless room is depressing at the best of times, but today there's a bulb flickering maniacally in one of the ceiling lights.

Opposite him, Leighton's hunched over the table, staring at the pictures. Dom doesn't want to break his concentration, so he waits.

Leighton looks up at Dom. The laddish bravado of last night has long gone. He shakes his head. 'I don't know, sorry. He could have been any of these.'

Dom tries to look encouraging. 'I know it's tough, mate, you're doing well.'

Leighton exhales hard. He picks up one of the photos. 'It could be this one.'

From his tone it sounds like he's asking Dom rather than telling him. He needs Leighton to be sure. 'Yeah?'

'Maybe not. His hair might be too long.' The estate agent frowns. 'It's hard to be certain. I'd had a few, you know? Can't really picture him.'

Dom clasps his hands together beneath the table. Doesn't say anything.

'How about we try walking through what happened when you spoke to Kate Adams?' Parekh says. 'You can visualise yourself in the pub, what you did, the things you said.'

Leighton rubs his eyes. Seems unconvinced. He's looking at Dom when he says, 'Do you think it's worth it?'

Dom knows from the flush that's spread from the base of her neck up her throat that Parekh's pissed off with the way Leighton constantly defers to him. He doesn't blame her, but is glad she's keeping her feelings to herself – they need to keep this guy sweet until he's made an ID. He nods at Leighton. 'It's worth a go. Might help.'

'OK.' Leighton hunches over the table, elbows on the laminate, cradling his chin in his hands, and stares at the photos.

Dom looks at Parekh. 'If you're all right to carry on here, I'll go check how Abbott's doing.'

She gives a small smile. 'Yes, guv.'

Standing, he glances at Leighton. 'Take your time. Be certain.'

Leighton keeps staring at the pictures. Poor bloke looks like he's on the verge of going catatonic.

By contrast, Abbott tells him Eva Finch is super-chatty. She arrived forty-five minutes ago, but she's already worked through the images. Standing in the corridor outside interview room two, Abbott looks exhausted.

'So she hasn't picked anyone out?' Dom says.

Abbott shakes his head. 'She says she can't be sure. All she remembers is a vague blur.'

Dom supposes it was a long shot; she'd said when they first spoke that she'd not had her contacts in that night, but still, it's frustrating. 'I guess that's it for her then.'

'Actually, she asked to have a word with you before she goes.'

Eva Finch looks embarrassed. She's wearing more make-up than the last time he saw her, and her brown pixie cut is gelled into spikes, but even beneath the thick foundation he can see her blushing.

Dom sits down opposite her. Glad the lights aren't on the blink in this room, and that with the thin window running along the top of the side wall there was at least a small amount of natural light. 'You asked to speak to me, Ms Finch?'

She picks at the turquoise nail polish on her index finger. 'There's something I didn't tell you.'

'Go on.'

'It's not because I didn't want to help. It's just that Kate's a friend. I didn't want to . . . I wanted to protect her reputation.'

Dom nods. Waits.

'There was a guy, well, I don't really know if there was a guy or not. I mean, they're definitely friends, but I don't know if

201

they're a thing or . . .' She looks at Dom. 'I just thought you should know.'

'You're saying Kate was seeing someone else?'

Eva shakes her head. 'I don't know if they were seeing each other, I just know they'd got close recently, in the past couple of weeks.'

'Who is he?'

'This looks bad, doesn't it? Her parents are going to be so upset. I . . .' She sighs. 'His name's Patrick Bartlett. He works with us, he's one of the Nines.'

Dom pulls out his phone and taps the name into the notes function. 'What does he look like?'

'Tall, skinny. Brown hair, big beard. Wears those black-framed glasses.'

Doesn't sound like either of the POIs from the CCTV, but he needs to follow this up. Kate Adams had a secret, and secrets are often the things that get people killed. 'I'm going to need to take an official statement, and I need to interview Patrick Bartlett.'

36

CLEMENTINE

Death Stalker posted in Case Files: The Lover
New task list. Deadline: two hours (Bloodhound four hours).
Ghost Avenger: Kate Adams mortuary pictures
Witness_Zero: Follow-up witness from takeaway
Crime Queen: Kate Adams's background
Robert 'chainsaw' Jameson: Reporter intel update
Bloodhound: Cross-reference victim data
The Watcher: Zara Bretton's background
Justice League: Jenna Malik's background

My head's fuzzy from lack of sleep. My concentration is below par. I can't stop thinking about the late arrival to the meet, the blond; I need confirmation he was Witness Zero. I look at the private message I sent over two hours ago.

The Watcher to @CrimeQueen Sorry I rushed off last night. Was the blond guy @Witness_Zero?

There's still no reply. She was online two minutes ago, and she's read the message. It seems she's ignoring me.

I tap my fingers against the keyboard. Think about how to find out more about Zara Bretton, but it's no use, I can't concentrate. Opening a new chat window, I type a message.

The Watcher to @JusticeLeague Who was that blond guy last night?

Justice League is online. She reads the message immediately and three dots appear as she types her reply.

Justice League to @TheWatcher It was @Witness_Zero. Hot wasn't he?!

The Watcher to @JusticeLeague Is he friends with @CrimeQueen and @DeathStalker? When I left they were huddled together in the main bar. I messaged CQ earlier asking about him – she's read the message but not replied

Justice League to @TheWatcher Dunno re CQ/DS. Happy about WZ joining tho. Good to have something pretty to look at.

The Watcher to @JusticeLeague I guess. What's the deal with Crime Queen – is she serious about this investigation do you think?

Justice League to @TheWatcher GA says CQ's studying forensic psychology – something about social impact of celebrity culture vs serial killers. So serious enough.

The Watcher to @JusticeLeague Useful. Thanks. Makes more sense that she's part of the group now!

Justice League to @TheWatcher no problem

From what I observed last night, Death Stalker seems to have his favourites: Witness Zero and Crime Queen. I need to get closer to Death Stalker, become part of his inner circle or circumvent them entirely. To do that, I need to prove my worth. Complete my task. Build his trust in me, even if I don't trust him back.

Switching screens, I read the list of possible Zara Brettons that my Facebook search has generated – thirty-seven in total. I peer at the thumbnail profile pictures; some are faces, some random objects. Scroll down.

Thirty-two is a match. This Zara Bretton has a photo as their profile picture and a lax approach to online security. The profile is public, so I can see all their information, friends and photos; all their status updates. The twenty-first-birthday photograph used in the newspaper articles is there, along with more from that night and similar pictures from other nights out.

I learn that Zara's BFFs are Rach and Dan, that she likes clubbing and snowboarding and that she's a fan of a TV bake-off show. Her relationship status tells me she's not currently in a relationship. All these things make it appear as if she's alive. The posts on her virtual wall are what destroys that illusion.

> **Rach Wesbel** to Zara Bretton: Missing you babes. Every day. Love you xxxx
> **Lesley Pink** to Zara Bretton: Tragic. So sad ☹
> **Daniel Tyrone** to Zara Bretton: Nothing's the same without you. Love D xx
> **Anya Baskue** to Zara Bretton: Taken too soon. RIP xxx

I wonder why these people feel the need to post these public outpourings of grief. Does it help them get closure? Or is it driven by a need to be *seen* to be grieving? They look like they're trying to out-grieve each other, prove they are the most affected, the most sorrowful. As if only those emotions shared online count for anything. It's something I cannot understand. After all, it's not as if the dead can browse the internet. I wonder why Zara's family hasn't removed the page.

She was popular, that's for sure. I scroll through over a hundred messages before I get to the posts Zara herself made prior to her death. I speed-read them, searching for new information. I discover that she went speed dating three weeks before she was killed, but didn't get the number of anyone she met – too old, too young, not fun enough – and that seven weeks before she died she'd started working at The Sandwich Shack near Camden Market. From her status updates it looks like she enjoyed the job.

In the feed there's a video Zara posted the week before her death. The status beneath it is short, to the point: *Gr8t Nite!!!!*

I hover my mouse over the clip and it starts to play. I recognise the girls and guy from their profile pictures – Rach, Zara and Dan. They're near Piccadilly Circus, by the fountain with the four rearing horses; giggling at the camera, arms round each other. Six seconds, and the clip is done.

I enlarge the video to full-screen and play it again. I listen to their laughter, see the happiness in Zara's expression and the love between these three friends. I try to imagine what it must be like to feel that way about someone, to be as happy as Zara looks.

I do feel something, though; a quivering sensation in my chest, a tightness around my eyes. I click the video again. As it plays I feel my eyes tearing up and I wonder what the hell is happening to me. I have never met these people, and yet I think I am feeling something like sadness. It doesn't make sense.

I close down the video. Push away the feeling. Continue reading until I've got through two more months of status updates, photos posted and videos shared, but find nothing else of interest. So I switch back to Zara's profile and follow the link to her Pinterest page. I scroll through the images, reading the tags – hot guy, pretty updo, great shoes, straight teeth. There are a lot of images of smiles, all women's faces, some with lipstick, some without. It seems rather random.

My eyes are dry, itchy. I rub them, but it doesn't help. I need to get away from the screen. Cracking the window open to let in some air, I toggle back to True Crime London and the group page. It's time to report back.

The Watcher My online search for Zara Bretton has shown she was single and worked at The Sandwich Shack in Camden Market. Her closest friends are Rach Wesbel (Crouch End) and Daniel Tyrone (Camden). She was a regular on the clubbing scene.

I add links to Zara's Facebook and Pinterest accounts. Then I press return.

Ghost Avenger and 2 other people liked your post in Case Files: The Lover

Draining the last of my coffee, I'm thinking about getting a refill when Ghost Avenger posts the results of his task. As the pictures fill the screen it feels like déjà vu. I scroll through them, mesmerised again.

One – pastel-pink painted nails.

Two – an ear with two piercings in the lobe.

Three – mid-brown curled hair. Shoulder length.

The last is a full body shot: Kate Adams, lying on the metal gurney, a sheet covering her modesty. She looks just how Jenna Malik and Zara Bretton did in the pictures Ghost Avenger posted of them.

A ping alerts me to a new post.

> **Crime Queen** Here are the links to Kate Adams's Facebook, Twitter and Tumblr pages. They don't tell us much.

I linger over Crime Queen's dismissive reference to Kate's social media pages. It feels like a dig at the links I posted to Zara's profiles. I click each of the links in turn. Facebook and Twitter don't reveal anything obvious, but on her Tumblr feed I notice a lot of pictures of smiles; just like Zara's Pinterest page. I'm about to point this out when another post appears at the top of the feed.

> **Witness_Zero** Good to meet some of you last night. I've completed my task. Talked to Steven Ravenscroft – he works in the Chick-o-Lick takeaway. He thinks he saw a dark-haired man enter Kate Adams's building around ten o'clock the night she died. He hasn't talked to the police (he's got a bit of form, I think). Couldn't give me a description of the man, so no further intel.
>
> **Justice League** Do you think Steven would be willing to do an online eFit? I've got a link to an app that's similar to the police one (part of my uni course). We could use it . . .
>
> **Witness_Zero** I can ask him @JusticeLeague. DMing you now.

I exhale hard. Sit back in my chair and twist my butterfly ring around my finger. Steven Ravenscroft's sighting doesn't fit with the timing of the hooded man Kate Adams's neighbour saw entering the flat. Now Witness Zero is talking direct to Justice League, she is getting drawn closer to the inner circle and I am not.

This I do not like.

37

DOM

In interview room four, Patrick Bartlett is crying.

Dom's only asked him one question, but it set him off. He hasn't answered, though. Dom knows he's going to have to ask again. 'Mr Bartlett, Patrick, how did you know Kate Adams?'

Bartlett wipes his face with his hands, sniffs loudly. Dom passes him a tissue.

When he speaks, Barlett's voice is wobbly with nerves. 'We met at work. We started the same day, but were on opposite sides – I'm a Nine and she was a One.' He looks like he's about to cry again. 'We used to say we were like Romeo and Juliet.'

'So you had a romantic relationship?'

'No, not really.'

'Which is it?'

Bartlett sniffs into his tissue. Balls it into his fist. 'I wanted to, but she had a boyfriend. They were having a few problems – money stuff, the usual crap – and we talked on our breaks. She often got upset. It didn't feel like the right time, but I hoped we might . . .'

Dom doesn't think Bartlett killed Kate. They'll need to check out his alibi for the murder, and for Jenna's and Zara's, but this bloke doesn't look like he's got a violent bone in his body. 'You hoped if her and the boyfriend ended you'd be able to pick up the pieces?'

'Something like that,' says Bartlett, starting to sob. 'Not going to happen now, though, is it?'

An hour later Dom's standing in front of the murder board, wondering what the fuck to do next. He's added Patrick Bartlett and connected him to Kate Adams. Another lead, but not one he thinks will go anywhere.

He looks at the other Persons of Interest. From the CCTV there's still no identification of POI 1 – the man in the hoodie on the Chick-O-Lick camera. Next along the board is POI 2 – Jon Leighton. Dom puts a cross through his picture; Parekh chased down his alibis and they all check out. Leighton himself is a dead end, but he did eventually pick out two men from the Wetherspoons CCTV.

Their two pictures are stuck on the board alongside Leighton. Dom peers closer at them. One is staff member Enzo Metiz. Parekh's putting the other through the database, searching for a match. They're new leads, but Dom isn't hopeful. Neither of these men look right to him. Their body shapes don't match the man outside Kate's flat, and that's all they've got to go on at the moment.

The unreliability of eye witness descriptions are well known – they often identify people they've seen, but not always the person who did the crime. Wrong person, right place is a common problem. Given how much Leighton had been drinking and the sheer volume of people in the pub that night, Dom won't be surprised if that's what's happened here.

'Guv?'

Dom looks round to see Parekh hovering in the doorway. 'Yeah?'

'Jackson's looking for you, thought I'd give you the heads-up.'

Just what I need.

'Thanks,' Dom says. 'Anything new?'

Parekh shakes her head. 'Abbott's trying to get hold of Enzo Metiz. I haven't seen Biggs since this morning, and I'm waiting for a pingback on that other ID.'

Parekh leans against the door frame. She's rolled her shirt-sleeves up and Dom notices the intricate henna tattoo winding from her index finger, across her hand and up her arm.

She sees him looking. 'Big family wedding at the weekend, the celebrations started a couple of weeks ago.'

He nods. 'How's our new indexer doing?'

'Ploughing through, checking for drug thefts, but nothing that fits with the anaesthetics has flagged yet. I'll let you know if we get something.'

'Cheers. Appreciate it.'

Parekh disappears back to the open plan. Dom takes a final look at the pictures. The more he looks at them, the less he's convinced the men Leighton singled out are relevant.

Someone has to know something.

'Sir?'

Jackson is sitting behind his desk. He beckons Dom in.

'Parekh said you were looking for me?'

'Who the hell is talking to the press?' Jackson gestures to the websites open on his desktop. 'There's stuff in here about Patrick Bartlett. They're saying he's our prime suspect.'

Dom peers at the screen. Sees the photographs of Patrick entering the station, head down, looking guilty. 'What the—'

Jackson looks furious. 'Who did this?'

'No one in my team.'

'You sure about that?'

'Totally.'

'Because if he's not the Lover, it's going to look like one massive fuck-up. All the major news channels are running it. I've already had Bartlett's lawyer on the phone chewing my ear off. How serious a suspect is he?'

'We need to check his alibi, but I doubt it's him.'

Jackson curses under his breath. 'When the press find that out, you're not going to come off well – they're already gunning for you.'

Dom glances at words on the screen again. Words leap out: *befuddled, incompetent, shameful.* He looks back at Jackson. 'Yeah, I get that.'

'We need the press back onside, mitigate the fallout from the lack of arrest and the fact we're likely to clear Bartlett. It's nearly forty-eight hours since the initial press briefing about Kate Adams, so time we had another, a bigger one.'

Dom shifts his weight from one foot to the other. 'I think we need to release more information. Tell them some specifics of how the killer changes his victims' appearance. It might mean something to someone. We could appeal for them to come forward.'

Jackson shakes his head. 'No, it'll only confirm we've got a serial on our hands.'

Dom glances at the newspapers. 'They think that already, I really—'

'We'll bring in some relatives to make an appeal. Kate Adams's boyfriend, Mart Stax, and the parents of the second victim, Zara Bretton, I think.'

'We're still checking out Stax, he's—'

'It's decided, Dom. Eleven o'clock tomorrow.'

This is bullshit. Without the victims' changed appearance there's nothing new to give the media. They've already had the CCTV image of the man outside Kate's apartment, and that's brought back nothing.

Jackson's expression turns grim. 'There's something else. Biggs says you threatened him.'

Fuck.

'He was being sloppy, not working with his colleagues. I took him aside and made my expectations clear.'

'That's not the way he tells it. He's talking physical harassment here.'

'That's shit. I just told him to do his job.'

'So you didn't touch him?'

'No, I bloody didn't.'

Jackson looks unconvinced. 'You need to keep it together, Dom. I can't have you roughing up every officer who pisses you off.'

'I didn't. It's not a—'

The DCI gives Dom a knowing look. 'It would be to Human Resources.'

Dom stays silent. He stares at a poster on Jackson's wall; a red rose with blood dripping from the stem, the domestic abuse helpline in large numbers below. He shakes his head. How can Biggs call what happened between them harassment?

Jackson keeps his voice low. 'Look, this won't go away easily, but I've talked him out of an official grievance. You need to be careful, though, Dom. Don't push it.'

Dom frowns. Biggs is tough enough to keep on task as it is. If he's got to pussyfoot around him, it's going to be impossible. 'I have to do my job.'

Jackson nods. Looks serious. 'Yes, you do.'

Dom steps out of the lift. He needs fresh air, needs to clear his head. Biggs bitching to Jackson, it's pathetic. The bastard is just trying to make as much trouble as he can; acting out because he's got issues with Dom telling him what to do. Dom hates the bloody politics of it.

He halts. Across the reception area, outside the glass doors, he can see the press pack camped out, waiting for him. One of them spots him and starts shouting his name. Another joins in, then the rest. Shit. He steps back towards the lifts.

'Dom?'

He turns, surprised. 'Chrissie? What are you doing here?'

'I've been calling you all day. Left messages. This can't wait.'

Dom can see the anxiety on her face and hear it in her voice. It bothers him. Makes him feel responsible. He puts his hand on her arm and leads her across to the far corner of the reception area, out of sight from the main entrance. 'What is it?'

'They've called Darren in for another interview.' She exhales hard. 'I'm worried, Dom. Why do they want to speak to him again? This'll be the third time. He's told them everything he knows.'

'I don't know, Sis. Look, I spoke to Lindsay last night, he said they'd had him in again too. It's probably just fact checking, standard procedure.'

'You think?'

'Most likely.' He feels like a shit for lying to her, but what can he do? After talking to Lindsay, after Lindsay threatening him, he's certain he's hiding something about Operation Atlantis. Maybe Harris and Therese are in on it, too. But he can't tell Chrissie his fears, not until he's got everything straight in his own head. He can't risk sending her off the rails again.

212

'Look, it'd really help if you had a chat with him.'

'Why me?' Dom's tone is harsher than usual, distorted by the guilt.

'Because he's family, and he's freaking out.' Chrissie is talking faster, her voice growing louder. Tears fill her eyes. 'He needs to talk to you.'

'Why didn't *he* come, then?'

'He thinks you're avoiding him. The way you ran off last night, it was weird.'

Dom's silent.

Chrissie's eyes are on his. Her breathing's ragged, emotional. 'Are you avoiding him?'

Dom wants to tell her, but he can't. Not yet. 'Chrissie, let's not do this right now, yeah? I'm in the middle of a case. I've barely slept. You know how it—'

'The case is all-consuming, I get it, but we're your *family*, Dom.'

He can hear the hurt in her voice. Can't look her in the eyes as he says, 'Look, I'll try and get over later if I can, but I can't promise anything. It depends on the case.'

Chrissie sighs. She knows he's fobbing her off; that he'll text her later and say he's too busy. He hates that, and he hates the look of disappointment on her face, but he knows he'll do it anyway. It makes him hate himself a little bit more.

38

CLEMENTINE

Death Stalker wants to meet. He's got the results back from the lab but won't tell me what they are on the messenger app, says it's better to meet face-to-face; he's singling me out again. That excites me, and scares me.

I haven't told Wade.

The Coffee Palace is one of those chains that pride themselves on their overpriced coffee and faux Italian decor. I buy an Americano and spot Death Stalker sitting in a corner booth at the back of the shop. There's a silver laptop open on the table in front of him, but he's not alone. I'm disappointed. Bloodhound is there and so is Crime Queen. She looks different. Her purple bob has gone; now her hair is mid-brown and styled in shoulder-length curls. I can't help but stare for longer than I should. It's an exact match for the way the Lover leaves his victims.

They're deep in conversation, pretty heated. They don't notice me as I approach.

Death Stalker is shaking his head. 'Freya, these women are dying. You making yourself look like the victims is in really bad taste.'

'But I'm making myself into bait, don't you get it?' Crime Queen's voice sounds whiny. 'I know about serial killers, it's my thing, I can lure—'

'I just think it's a dangerous game to play, that's all,' Bloodhound says. 'Your choice, obviously, but it's—'

'Agreed,' Death Stalker interrupts. He looks at Crime Queen. 'You're putting yourself in danger.'

Crime Queen blushes. 'It's my—'

'Look, take the damn wig off, or you're out of the investigation,' Death Stalker says. 'I'm serious.'

None of them speaks. I clear my throat.

They turn, and notice me standing there. Death Stalker gestures for me to sit next to him. As I do, Crime Queen rolls her eyes. Bitch. I smile at Death Stalker and Bloodhound, and ignore Crime Queen.

Death Stalker glances pointedly at his watch and looks at Crime Queen. 'So, we're clear?'

'Fine,' she says, unfastening a couple of pins and pulling off the wig. 'Happy now?'

Death Stalker looks at Bloodhound.

Bloodhound nods. 'Thank you. It just seemed so disrespectful to the victims. I—'

'Fucksake,' Crime Queen says, scowling. 'I've taken it off, all right.'

Bloodhound gets up and slings a canvas messenger bag over his shoulder. 'Thanks,' he says to Crime Queen and Death Stalker, then nods at me. 'Nice to see you again.'

As he walks away, I take a sip of my coffee and wait for Death Stalker to speak. He's silent at first, while Crime Queen gets her coat on and head towards the exit. I check out the booths near us. Most are unoccupied; those that aren't have single drinkers, the majority tapping away on laptops or smartphones. No one is paying us any attention.

As the door closes behind Crime Queen, Death Stalker says, 'The lab found something interesting.'

'Yes?'

'It's not a make-up brush. It's for dentistry.'

I frown. 'Come again?'

Death Stalker looks impatient. 'It's a specialist dental brush. Used in cosmetic procedures like teeth whitening.' He runs his finger across the laptop's trackpad. There's an email open on the screen but it's impossible to read from this angle. 'The brush is part of a set of cosmetic dental brushes sold by a manufacturer called Dentiflex. It's a high-end product, not your average NHS-type thing. Expensive.'

'Did they test the bristles, had it been used for dental work?'

Death Stalker shakes his head. 'No, that's where it gets odd. There was a trace of one substance on the bristles, a powder.'

I lean back a little, trying to see what's on the laptop screen. 'What kind?'

Death Stalker closes the laptop. 'They gave me the chemical formula, but basically it's the residue of a cream powder foundation.'

'Did they match it with a brand?'

'Not yet, but they're trying.'

I think back to Zara Bretton's Pinterest and Kate Adams's Tumblr. 'Both Zara and Kate had pictures of smiles, teeth, on their social media. I thought it was odd, but maybe there's a connection.'

Death Stalker nods. 'It's a lead worth following.'

'There must be thousands of dentists in London. Assuming there's a link between the killer and the brush, it could still be impossible to identify them.'

Death Stalker smiles. 'I know. That's your next task.'

I expected as much. 'It'll take forever. What about the police investigation, have they got a line of enquiry on this? What's your contact said?'

Death Stalker looks away. He picks up the laptop and slips it into the rucksack lying at his feet. 'Not much.'

'Meaning you're refusing to share your intel with me?'

'No, it's not that. I don't think my police contact is being straight with me. They know more than they're letting on.'

'So push them harder.'

'I've tried, but it's not working. Look, you got into the crime scene, could you get into the police offices, find out what they've got?'

I laugh. 'You want me to break into a police building? Have you any idea how ridiculous that—'

'Do you want us to beat them?'

I hold his gaze. This is my opportunity to get into his inner circle. 'Of course.'

'Then we need you to get in there.'

'By *we* I'm guessing you mean the team, but that doesn't wash with me. You're keeping stuff back, making sure only you have the full picture.' I lean across the table. 'I'm OK with that for the wider group, but if you want me to take more risks, you need to tell *me* everything.'

He doesn't speak. Doesn't look away either, just stares straight back at me. Usually I feel awkward in this type of situation. I can see the person looking at me is experiencing some kind of emotion – I can see the changes in their expression. It isn't a problem with Death Stalker. His expression remains neutral; his eyes give nothing away. I break eye contact and take another sip of my coffee. I'm surprised how his lack of emotion unsettles me.

'Fine.'

I wait for him to tell me more.

'The police have been looking at Kate Adams's boyfriend as a possible suspect, but it's not looking likely. They're going through CCTV footage from a bar she was in the night before she died. So far they've got nothing to connect the three victims.'

'And the victims were all found with their appearance altered. Dyed hair, different make-up?'

'All of them looked like the same girl. My contact said Kate Adams's boyfriend didn't even recognise her. He thought there was a stranger in his bed.'

'Found naked?'

He nods. 'With candles burning and rose petals around the bed, just like the first two.'

I drain the last of my coffee. 'Sounds like you've got plenty from your contact.'

'They've gone cold since last night. Not replying to emails, not answering when I call. It's critical we're up to date with what they've got. Without their information we're dead in the water.'

He's right. I know that. But attempting to break into a police building requires a special kind of crazy, and specialist skills; I have neither of those things. 'Maybe they're just busy.'

'I don't think so. I think with the media attention the case is getting they're losing their bottle.'

'Then use whatever you have on them to get them to co-operate.'

'I'm trying.' His expression gives nothing away, but his voice sounds strained. 'But I need a back-up plan in case it doesn't work. I need to find the Lover.'

I keep my eyes on his. 'Why?'

He holds my gaze, and for a moment I think he's going to tell me. Then he shifts back in his seat, extending the distance between us, and says, 'So we can get him locked up.'

This time something in his eyes tells me he's lying.

39

DOM

Back in the open plan, Dom sees Parekh heading for him.

She holds up a scrap of paper. 'We've got the man Leighton identified from the pub, the facial recognition software threw up a match; Tommy Hodge. I cross-referenced with the database – he lives near Earls Court on Siltoe Street in one of those council high-rises, and he's got form.'

Dom tries to push the thoughts of Chrissie and their conversation away. He needs to focus back on the case, get out of the office. 'Good work,' he says to Parekh, then, turning to Abbott he says, 'Fancy making a house call?'

Tommy Hodge's flat is on the eleventh floor. They tailgate through the front doors behind a young mum with a double buggy and head straight for the lift. Thankfully this one doesn't smell of piss.

As soon as they reach the eleventh floor Dom hears the dance music. The building's not in bad nick. What's letting it down is the racket coming from Hodge's flat.

Dom knocks on the door several times. When there's no response he resorts to banging hard with his fist and shouting Hodge's name. It takes a few more minutes, but eventually the door inches open, the security chain in place.

'What?' a man's voice shouts over the din.

Dom can't get a proper look at him through the narrow gap. 'Tommy Hodge?'

'Who wants to know?' There's aggression in the man's tone, maybe a slight undercurrent of fear.

Dom notices the bare wood around the door lock – the original lock has been replaced with one of a different shape. There are grooves gouged out of the door frame. Dom knows the signs of a door that's been jimmied open. 'I'm Detective Inspector Bell and this is Detective Sergeant Abbott,' Dom shouts back. 'We need to ask you some questions.'

'Show me your ID. I know my rights.'

They produce their warrant cards and hold them up for him to read. Dom knows this isn't a new experience for Hodge; his rap sheet for petty theft and aggravated assault is on the long side, especially considering he's barely into his twenties.

When they've given him long enough to read, Dom yells, 'Now can we come in?'

The door closes. A few seconds later the music stops. Dom hears the chain being unclipped, and the door reopens. The man from the pub CCTV image is staring back at them. He's wearing grey jogging pants and an oversized hoodie; his feet are bare. He waves them inside. 'Knock yourself out.'

They walk through the boxy hallway, past a cat litter tray that looks like it's not been emptied in weeks, and into the living space. It's sweltering hot, the heating cranked up full blast. Over by the window, a skinny girl in tiny denim shorts and a vest is lounging on a scuffed leather sofa, painting her toenails. She doesn't look up. Beside her is a ratty-looking dog. It fixes Dom with its beady eyes and starts to yap.

Dom halts. 'We need to talk about Saturday night. Where were you?'

Hodge narrows his eyes. 'What's it to you?'

'We're investigating a murder.' Dom keeps his tone conversational, but straightens up, squaring his shoulders, just in case the bloke's thinking of trying something. 'So just answer the question, mate.'

'I was down 'Spoons, OK.' Hodge turns and shouts to the girl. 'Shut that little runt up, will you, it's doing my head in.'

Ignoring the kissing noises the girl starts making to the dog, Dom keeps focused on Hodge. 'You were there all night?'

'I reckon. Went there after work, stayed till they closed.'

Abbott jots down what he's saying. Hodge's gaze flits to him. He frowns.

'Were you alone?' Dom asks.

Hodge laughs. 'Nah, course not. I was with some mates, and my bird.'

Dom turns to the girl. Avoids looking at the dog. 'Is that right?'

The girl shrugs. 'Why'd you want to know? He didn't murder no one.'

Dom keeps eye contact with her. Waits. She looks young, eighteen, maybe less. Her expression is a mix of defiance and indignation. He wonders if that's her default attitude or whether she's switched it on for their benefit, if there's something she's trying to hide.

She rolls her eyes. 'Fine, I was with him.'

'What about after the pub shut?' Abbott asks Hodge.

'Got a kebab, came home.'

Dom keeps looking at the girl. 'And you?'

'What he said.' She licks her lips, slow and provocative. 'I was with him. All. Night. Long.'

Dom doesn't acknowledge the girl's comment. He looks at Hodge and says, 'We'd like you to take a look at a picture, mate.'

Abbott takes Kate Adams's photo from his pocket and hands it to Hodge. 'Do you recognise her?'

He shakes his head. 'Nah.'

'What's that?' The girl slams the bottle of nail polish onto the wooden floor and glares at Abbott. 'You saying my man, like, *knows* this bitch?'

Abbott ignores her and asks Hodge, 'Are you sure?'

'Course.' Hodge looks shifty. 'I never seen her, honest.'

The girl jumps up from the sofa and struts over to Hodge, the dog at her heels, yapping again. She snatches the picture. 'Who's the bitch? Tell me you didn't put your dick in this skank?'

Dom steps sideways, away from the dog. 'She's a murder victim.'

The girl spins to face him. 'He's not been shagging her?'

'She was at the Wetherspoons the night before she died,' Abbott says.

Dom's aware the girl is giving Hodge the evil eye. He ignores her and says to Hodge, 'Did you see her?'

'Like I said, not that I remember.' He turns to the girl. 'Woman, I don't know her, and I ain't shagging her.'

The girl is scowling. She looks at Kate's photo again, then back at Hodge. After a long moment she smiles. 'Course not, ugly bitch like that.'

Dom feels his heart rate rising. This girl has been told Kate Adams is dead and she's bloody smiling. It makes his skin crawl. He takes Kate's photo from the girl. Looks from her to Hodge, trying to keep the anger from his voice as he says, 'Give the names of these friends who can verify where you were to DS Abbott.'

Abbott takes the girl's name and the names of their friends; three blokes and two women. As she notes down their contact details, Dom scans the flat. It's messy as hell – old plates crusty with leftovers, crumpled beer cans beside a heap of musty washing that's not been hung up. Roll-ups in the ashtray that don't look like plain tobacco.

Dom's got a hunch. Hodge's defensiveness isn't linked to Kate, he's fairly sure on that, but there's something he doesn't want Dom to know. 'Tell me where you were standing in the pub that night?'

Hodge glances at his girlfriend, then shakes his head. 'Dunno.'

He sounds nonchalant, but Dom saw the way he tugged at the bottom hem of his hoodie; a nervous tick.

'Sure you do.' Dom looks pointedly at the ashtray and back to Hodge. 'Just take a moment to think.'

The girl saunters away, flopping down onto the sofa again. Dom can tell she's trying to look as if she doesn't give a shit, but he's not buying it.

He says more firmly, 'Mr Hodge, tell me where you were standing.'

Hodge tugs the hem of his hoodie again. 'I don't want any trouble, it's just a bit of fun with my—'

'Look, mate. Right now I'm not interested in whatever you were selling, what I want to know is where you were standing.'

'Midway along the balcony.'

'Why?'

'Why'd you think?'

'I'd like you to tell me.'

Hodge exhales hard. 'The camera has a blind spot, everyone knows it.'

Everyone knows it. Shit.

Dom glances at Abbott. He nods. They're both thinking the same; the killer could have known about the blind spot, too. He could have been at the pub, standing on the balcony, and if he'd avoided the front entrance, maybe sneaked in through a fire door, then it's possible he wouldn't be caught on CCTV anywhere.

Abbott pulls into the postage stamp of a car park a few hundred yards from the office and switches off the engine. They haven't spoken on the drive back. Not since Tommy Hodge slammed the door behind them. Little shit. He and his sulky girlfriend hadn't given a crap that a woman had been murdered, and trying to get a straight answer out of either of them had been a nightmare. Pointless, too. Tommy Hodge was just another dead end.

Abbott twists to face Dom as he releases his seat belt. He looks as disappointed as Dom feels. 'I'll contact the names Hodge gave us and make sure his story checks out. I'll look on the CCTV, too, confirm the girlfriend was there like she said.'

'Thanks,' Dom says. 'And let the Drug Squad know about his little business. They might want to check it out.'

'I'm on it.'

They head towards the building. As they approach the entrance, Dom recognises the bloke with a pudding-basin haircut loitering by the steps. Their eyes meet. There's a flicker of recognition on the bloke's face, and he bounds forward.

Dom speeds up, lengthening his stride so that Abbott has to hurry to keep up.

'What is it?' he asks.

Dom keeps his eyes on the door. His expression's grim. 'Bloody reporter, incoming.'

The guy cuts them off, and thrusts a voice recorder into Dom's face. 'DI Bell? I know you're very busy, but if you could just—'

Dom sidesteps him. The reporter's yakking away, but Dom keeps walking. 'Speak to the press office. They'll answer your questions.'

'About Operation Atlantis?'

Dom slows. How does this freelancer know the codename Atlantis? That information was never in the public domain.

The bloke's trotting alongside him, keeping pace. 'That other DI's out of the coma now, isn't she? Therese Weller? The hospital told me she's doing well. That must be a relief? You were close, weren't you?'

He glares at the reporter. Clenches his fists to stop himself from throttling him. The bastard's grinning, like he knows stuff he shouldn't, stuff about Dom, and about Therese. Who the hell is leaking this stuff?

Dom shakes his head. 'No comment.'

'Really? I'd have thought you'd want to—'

'I said, no comment.' Dom leaps up the steps and shoves the door into the foyer hard. The glass rattles in its frame as it swings open. As he looks back he sees the freelancer standing on the other side, watching him. He raises his hand and gives Dom a little wave.

The atmosphere in the incident room is sombre. It's gone seven and the team's energy is flagging. Dom understands that, he feels the same, but they can't slow now; they're still so far from an arrest.

He's sitting on the table at the front, his usual perch. 'I know you're all knackered. We'll make it quick tonight.'

There are nods from the team. Even Biggs looks grateful.

'OK, good,' Dom says. 'I'll kick off, then. Abbott and I checked out Tommy Hodge – one of the IDs Jon Leighton made – but it's a dead end. He's been alibied out by his girlfriend and a handful of others.' He looks at Parekh. Notices there's a bag of Maltesers open on the table beside her. 'You checked out Leighton's story, didn't you?'

She refers to her notepad as she gives her report. 'Leighton checks out. His alibis are good for all three murders. He was staying at his parents' house when Jenna Malik was killed, and out with work colleagues until 3 a.m., and 2.30 a.m., on the nights Zara Bretton and Kate Adams died.'

Abbott catches Dom's eye.

Dom nods. 'Yeah, go ahead.'

'No luck in getting hold of the member of staff at the Wetherspoons Leighton identified – Enzo Metiz. He's not answering his phone, although the pub say that's normal, it's his day off. The assistant manager confirmed Metiz was working the night Kate Adams was there, so I've asked them to contact me when he reports for work tomorrow. Till then I'll keep trying to get hold of him.'

'All right.' Dom picks up a marker and puts a black cross through the picture of Tommy Hodge. Turns back to the team. 'What else have we got?'

'It might be nothing, but I'm having trouble confirming Patrick Bartlett's alibis for each of the murders,' Parekh says. 'And he's eaten at the sandwich place Zara Bretton worked at a few times. I don't think we can discount him yet.'

Dom nods. 'Keep on it.'

'I'm still waiting on phone records for Kate Adams,' Abbott says. 'They're promising me them tomorrow.'

'OK.'

Biggs clears this throat.

Dom looks at him. He's sitting alone at the back of the group, arms crossed over his gut, a bored expression on his face. Dom nods.

'I looked into Stax's revised alibi, and talked to the girl he was shagging,' Biggs says. 'It's legit. I spoke with some of his colleagues, and they confirmed it. They apologised for not telling us before.'

'Thanks, Biggs. Good work.' Dom can barely spit the words out, but with everything else going on he can't afford a shitstorm over Biggs.

Biggs nods, accepting the praise like he's not a lazy bastard. Dom looks away, seeking out Abbott again. 'Anything from the drug theft searches?'

'Nothing reported for the anaesthetics we're interested in.'

'All right,' Dom says. 'How about the lab?'

Parekh opens a file. She flicks through the papers and pulls out a yellow form. 'Nothing on that latex compound, but we got some details on the glue and make-up.'

'When did they come in?' Dom's voice is gruff, showing his frustration. Lab work coming back; Parekh should have told him immediately. She's a good detective – hard-working. Her making a rookie mistake is bloody irritating.

'About an hour ago, while you were interviewing Tommy Hodge. Perhaps I should have called . . . I'm sorry.' She looks flustered as she fumbles with the file. Her cheeks colour as she scans the pages. 'There's nothing critical, I don't think, but I've got the details here, I can run through them.'

'All right,' he says, his tone a little softer. An hour's OK, it's reasonable to have waited for him to get back if there's nothing critical. 'What've we got?'

'The glue has been identified as Crystal Stick.'

'Go on.'

'That's it, really. Crystal Stick is the second-biggest selling superglue in the UK. The lab has identified it as the current formula, so it's been bought within the last three years as the formula was slightly different before that.'

'Anything else?'

'They've confirmed the same glue was used on all three victims.'

'And the make-up?'

Parekh picks up the other sheet of paper. 'That's more interesting. Unlike before, this time the lab's been able to identify the brand. It's Glam Max.'

'What do we know about it?'

'Not much. Glam Max wasn't widely sold in the UK. It was made by a South African manufacturer who went bust in the late nineties. I did a quick Google search but couldn't even find any for sale on eBay.'

'So are you saying the cosmetics were bought in South Africa?'

Parekh meets his gaze. 'It's possible, but I need to dig more to be sure.'

Dom nods. 'Quick as you can.'

'Oh, and copies of the *Black Rose Chronicles* and DVDs of the film arrived,' Parekh says, tapping the pile on the table beside her.

'I'll have a copy of the DVD,' says Dom. 'Everyone take something to read or watch tonight. Be vigilant for anything that might link to the case. And Parekh, chase Patrick Bartlett's alibis, that's the priority.'

'Yes, guv,' Parekh says as she passes Dom a DVD, then hands out the rest of the pile to the team. Biggs starts grumbling when she hands him a book.

Ignoring Biggs, Dom looks round the team and, trying to inject a bit of enthusiasm into his voice, says, 'If there's nothing else, then I've got one more thing. The DCI has called a press conference for 1100 tomorrow. It'll be the full works – cameras, relatives, and so on – you know the drill. We need more before that. Anything you find that could be useful information to release, talk to Parekh. We'll regroup first thing to see what we've got, and make a plan from there.'

Pulling out his phone, Dom checks the screen. He's got a new message – it's from Therese: *Got discharged so I'm back home. Thought you might want to know. Didn't want you turning up at UCH to find me gone.*

He stares at the words, almost oblivious to the team leaving the room. He can't put it off any longer. He needs to know if she's been playing him all these months.

227

40
CLEMENTINE

I wasn't going to come. I only told Death Stalker I would to keep him onside. After the day I've had, though; the frustration of calling over fifty dental practices and cosmetic surgeries pretending to be a Dentiflex sales rep, and finding that not one of them use Dentiflex products, I needed to do something. Even this, sitting in the bus shelter across the road from the police building, feels more productive than the past few hours.

Maybe that's why I'm content to sit here a while and stare at the building. It's one of those pale brick and glass constructions, sandwiched between a line of shops and an ugly sixties office block. The rush hour bustle is over. The street is dark and getting more deserted as the time edges closer to eight o'clock.

It's late. I wasn't expecting to see him.

He's wearing different clothes, but it's definitely him striding out of the building. His gaze is on the ground as he hurries down the stone steps. He doesn't see me, but I'm watching. I see you, Detective Dominic Bell, and I wonder where it is you're going.

He takes a left at the bottom of the steps, and, as he turns to hail a cab, I catch a glimpse of his expression. It's one I can recognise. He looks haunted, remote. I've seen that expression on my own face. It's there every time I wake from the nightmares and rush to the bathroom to vomit; staring back at me from the mirror as I splash water on my face. I saw it on Father's face, too.

Dirty copper.

Is Dominic Bell dirty too? I want to know *what* he's done. *Why* he did it.

I don't want to have to hurt him.

*

Cabs are plentiful in this part of town. The cabbie driving mine is far too chatty, and I'm really not in the mood. Still, that he showed up as Dominic Bell was leaving was lucky, as was his reaction to my instruction to follow the cab in front – a raised eyebrow and no questions. We've been driving fifteen minutes, heading south.

Every now and then the cabbie glances in the mirror at me. He's doing it now. I look down at the floor, avoiding eye contact.

He clears his throat. 'Off on a night out then?'

I pretend I haven't heard. Stare harder at the grainy rubberized floor.

'Meeting friends?' His voice is louder this time, and I realise he's not going to stop trying until he's got a reaction.

I avoid the mirror, looking directly at him instead, at the distressed collar of his leather jacket and the back of his shaved head. The close crop doesn't quite disguise his bald patch. 'Something like that.'

He nods, and for a moment I think he's done. Then he gestures outside. 'Bad weather, isn't it? Worst November for rainfall in ten years, they're saying. Not a problem for me, mind. Makes for good business. People don't want to be walking in this.'

'I guess not.'

'I've done this job six years and it's the worst I've seen.'

I stare past him, through the rain-splattered windscreen, watching Dominic Bell's cab turn right down a side street. Oncoming traffic stops us following. The cab is getting away. Its rear lights disappear from view behind the buildings. I grip the plastic seat, digging my nails in tight. We can't lose him now. I can't lose him. 'Can you—'

The cabbie spots a gap and lurches us across the road. He floors the accelerator. The doors rattle as we bump over a hole in the tarmac, and I feel a twist of tension in my stomach. I ignore it. Clutch the seat harder as we swing round a bend.

'That's them. Parked up on the left there.' The cabbie sounds triumphant.

He's right. Twenty metres ahead, Dominic Bell is climbing out of the cab. 'Can you stop here? I don't want to get too close.'

He pulls over. Keeps the meter running.

I watch as Bell's cab pulls away. The detective glances left and right along the road, then strides across. It's a residential street, terraced houses on both sides. He stops in front of a purple door. Knocks.

The cabbie twists round to face me. 'You want me to move a bit—'

'Not yet.'

I move across the back seat for a better view. Peer through the window.

The door opens, a few inches at first, then wider. A skinny blonde stands in the doorway. She says something, then Dominic Bell goes inside and she shuts the door behind him.

I want to know who she is, and what she is to him. Adrenaline buzzes through me, making my legs feel twitchy. I can't bear to be contained inside the cab any longer. I need to move.

I look at the meter. 'I'll get out here, thanks. What do I owe you?'

The cabbie presses a button on the meter to show the price of my ride; fourteen pounds eighty. 'Boyfriend doing the dirty on you, love?'

I stay silent. Don't deny it.

'Looks a bit old for you if you, ask me, and if he's messing you about he's a fool. Kick him to the kerb.'

I take a twenty from my purse and hand it to him. 'Keep the change.'

'Thank you, very kind.' There's pity in his eyes. 'You take care.'

I yank the handle, push the door open and jump out into the darkness.

41
DOM

Therese looks surprised when she sees him on the doorstep. She looks slim, too slim, her baggy jogging bottoms and faded navy sweatshirt hang off her. Unlike yesterday, her hair is clean, but it's lank, all its usual shine is gone. Her skin is so pale it looks almost translucent. She's holding her right arm across her ribs as if trying to protect herself. Who from, Dom wonders?

'Surprise,' he says, but there's no fun in his tone. 'Can I come in?'

'I guess you'd better.' She steps back, making room for him to go inside.

He walks along the hallway to the kitchen. He glances back at Therese. 'Any of the others here?'

Therese house-shares with three nurses from the local hospital. He'd never met them, was only ever allowed round when all three were out, but he'd often joked with her about them. He doesn't today, though. He's not in the mood.

She shakes her head.

He pretends not to notice her wince from the movement. 'Work?'

'They're on lates,' Therese says.

Reaching the kitchen, he props himself against the breakfast bar and asks, 'So how are you doing?'

She shrugs. 'OK, I guess. It feels weird to be home, but so far, so good.' She picks up a couple of miniature cups. 'Coffee?'

'Yeah, sure.'

Therese makes the drinks. Her fancy coffee maker makes more noise than it does coffee. It's espresso, not really Dom's thing, but he's never told her that.

She hands him one of the tiny cups. 'So what have I done to deserve a house call?'

He puts the cup down. 'You've heard about Harris getting pulled in for another interview?'

'Lindsay said. I don't understand why Holsworth needs to prolong this further. Surely he's got enough information?'

'He thinks one of us helped Genk get out.'

Her eyes narrow. 'Do you?'

'Yeah. I think at least one of us did.'

'Shit.'

Dom stares at her. The skin on her neck has flushed pink. He wants to reach out and touch her, hold her, but he can't.

'Don't look at me like that, it wasn't me!' She shakes her head. 'And Harris is one of our own, a good guy – Lindsay too.'

'Are you sure about that?'

She steps closer to him. 'Dom, what is this, how can you suspect your own—'

'Have you remembered any more about what happened after I got taken out?'

Therese frowns. Looks hurt. 'Are you interrogating me?'

'You'd know if I was.'

She shakes her head. 'I know I was with Genk and some of his heavies when shots were fired. I think someone else entered the room before it kicked off, but I don't know who.'

'Have you and Lindsay been reminiscing about it?'

Her eyes flit towards the door. She takes a sip of coffee before answering. 'I've asked him a few questions. He's been helpful, a good mate.'

'I bet he bloody has.' Dom's tone is hard. He knows she won't like it.

She looks part angry, part confused. 'Meaning what, exactly?'

'He was hanging around your hospital room every day from what I hear, holding your hand, mopping your—'

'What are you implying?'

'I'm not *implying* anything, I'm asking you, what did you tell him about what happened inside our operation?'

'*Our* operation?' There's a vein pulsing in Therese's jaw. She looks furious. 'It was my operation. *Mine*, get it?'

232

'I get it, all right.' Dom steps closer. He can smell the herbal scent of her shampoo. 'So tell me what you told Lindsay.'

'I told him about my patchy memory, just the same as I told you, you dick.'

'Did you tell him what Genk said? How you'd tried to get him to take the bait a different—'

'No.' Something flashes across her face: confusion. Hurt. 'I've only talked to you about that.'

'Come on, Therese! Don't lie to me. You tell him stuff, I get that, you confide in him.'

Therese hugs her arm around her ribs. 'I said nothing, OK? I didn't tell Lindsay a damn thing about what happened inside the house even though he banged on and on about it, pushed me to say who I saw, what I saw. I still didn't say, couldn't say.'

Dom frowns. 'Why did he push you on it?'

Therese looks down. Exhales hard. 'He said he was following the chain of command, that there's someone who needed to know, a higher-up. Wanted to be sure nothing *bad* for them would come out in the IPCC investigation.' She looks up, meets his eye. 'Something's rotten somewhere up the chain. Someone's protecting Genk. But I don't bloody know who. You happy now?'

'Fuck.'

She puts her hand over his and strokes the back of his hand with her finger.

He's acutely aware of her touch. He wants to tell her to stop, but he doesn't. His head's buzzing. Lindsay wanted to know what had happened, but Therese didn't tell him. Neither of them had told him. But if the comms really had been down from the moment Dom was taken out, and Lindsay didn't hear the abort command, there's no way he could have heard what Genk said next about Therese going back to her whore business. But still he *knows*.

Someone is lying.

'I meant what I said, Dom. I really am sorry. I didn't realise you'd got so . . . invested. I thought we were having—'

'Everything all right in here?' Lindsay appears in the doorway. His shirt's half-unbuttoned. His hair looks wet from the shower. 'I heard raised voices.'

Dom's stomach lurches. He looks from Lindsay to Therese. 'What the fuck is this? You lied to me?'

'I'm sorry. I—'

'Another sorry, that's just great.' Dom can't keep the bitterness from his tone. He steps closer to Therese. Heart banging. Anger rising. 'So *he's* why we can't have a future? You're shagging him, too. You've been playing me like an idiot, while you behave like some cheap tart—'

The slap is harder, connects faster, than he'd anticipated. It knocks him off balance.

He steps back, rubbing his jaw. 'I'll take that as a yes, shall I?'

Therese looks like she might cry. 'You're a real cunt, you know that?'

Shaking his head, Dom says, 'I'm not the one who's a cunt.'

Slamming the coffee cup onto the worktop so hard it shatters, he pushes past Therese and Lindsay and charges out into the street without closing the door. As he marches along the pavement, he realises that whatever Therese and him had before, it's gone for good.

As his anger dissolves, all he feels is sadness.

42
CLEMENTINE

Ten minutes later he leaves the house. I let him get a head start before falling in step behind him. I pull up my hood and am careful not to get too close. At the end of the street he swings left onto the main road. I follow him past a Thai restaurant and a few shops. He takes a right across the road. I wonder what he's planning, where he's going and what happened inside the house with the skinny blonde woman.

I wonder why I care.

I tell myself it's because of what Wade said yesterday; that Death Stalker's main advantage is his police contact, and that it would be a good idea for me to have a police contact of my own. I tell myself that's why I'm following him.

But I know it's a lie. That's not why I'm drawn to him.

Dirty copper.

What has Dominic Bell done? It matters to me. It matters like a punch to the chest. I want him not to be guilty.

Minutes pass. Then the detective takes a sharp right and disappears. I speed up. As I hurry past a pub, I spot a gap in the wall. Slipping through, I follow a narrow path between two high wooden fences. I still can't see Dominic Bell. I break into a jog.

I round a bend and the path ends as abruptly as it began. Ahead is a one-storey building set back from a narrow street. It looks like an old library or hall, the once-grand stone frontage now shabby, weeds growing in the cracks around the paving. But it's not abandoned. A couple of large guys in suits are standing outside, either side of a strip of grubby red carpet. The makeshift sign propped beside the door says Crème.

Dominic Bell approaches the entrance. The bouncers must know him as they nod him through with a slap on the back. As he opens the door I hear the banging thump of dance music.

I know that getting into clubs is all about attitude, but I hate the way the bouncers are staring at me. My heart's thumping against my ribs as I approach the red carpet; fake confidence, I need to fake it. I set my face in a haughty expression and the bouncers wave me through. I hide my relief I as enter the club.

Inside it's dark and hot. There's a small bar at ground level, where a few kids are drinking shots, but the rest of the action must be happening in the basement. I shudder at the thought of going below ground. The memory of my aborted attempt at taking the tube is still fresh in my mind. But there's no choice here. If I want to find the detective I need to go down.

I take the stairs. The rubberised treads are sticky beneath the soles of my boots. With each step the light gets gloomier, making it feel like the dead of night. The music gets louder. It vibrates through me.

The space is cramped and airless. A rotating strobe illuminates glimpses of the place: whitewash flaking from the exposed brickwork, low ceiling painted black, neon-lit DJ booth on the farthest side of the room, hundreds of bodies jammed against each other, dancing to the endless beat. Somewhere among them is Dominic Bell.

Fighting the desire to turn and run, I shove my way into the crowd. Sweaty bodies press against me, forcing me to move with them. I'm trapped, straitjacketed by the dancing horde, unable to escape.

I feel the tightness growing in my chest. Try to take shallower breaths to calm myself. I cannot give in to the panic. The fear brings its own sour taste, and I need a drink to chase it away and give me a little more courage. Ignoring the stares of the men around the bar, I order a gin and soda. Tell the barman to make it a double.

I down my drink in three gulps. I push away from the bar and move back into the crowd, letting them swallow me into their mass. I don't fight them this time; instead I flow with them, dance alongside them, all the time searching for Dominic Bell.

*

He's near the DJ booth, dancing with a beer in his hand, and it looks like it's not his first. There are a couple of fake-tanned blondes in short glittery dresses dancing near to him. They're clutching bottles of WKD, although they look like they've had more than enough already. One of them is obviously trying to catch his eye, but he seems oblivious, eyes closed, lost in the music.

I dance closer. The crowd around me whoop and laugh. The atmosphere is stoked with the forced euphoria of drink and drugs. I wonder if Dominic Bell's only vice is alcohol; or whether he's taken something extra. He's unaware of any woman who gets close to him. Ignoring the girls writhing against each other and making 'fuck me' eyes at any half-decent-looking guy.

The blonde with the shortest dress and the best legs taps him on the shoulder. He looks confused as she whispers something in his ear, then kisses him hard. Her lipstick leaves a candy-pink smear over his mouth. She necks her drink, then takes his hand and leads him out of the crush.

I squeeze through the crowd, trying not to lose sight of them. Watch as the blonde pulls him towards the ladies'. See him halt, shaking his head, and point upwards, towards the exit. They change course, head up the stairs.

I wait twenty seconds before I follow.

43

DOM

He was a bloody idiot to come here. To think that dancing in this club would be a substitute for working his frustrations out at the gym. To hope the music would help him forget.

He's shocked. This woman, little more than a girl, kissed him. He hadn't wanted that, isn't looking for company, just wanted to lose himself in the music for a couple of hours to stop himself thinking about Therese, about Operation Atlantis and about the case.

This girl has put a stop to all that. Now he feels responsible.

As they exit the club, the blonde trips. Giggling, she loses her balance and falls sideways. Dom reaches for her arm, helps her straighten up. Her dark eyeliner is smudged. Grinning, she shuffles closer.

He holds her at a distance. Doesn't want her getting the wrong idea. 'How old are you?'

The girl reaches out for him. 'Old enough.'

But she isn't, she's young, too young. Just like Chrissie had been when all those bastards took advantage of her. 'No, you're not. You shouldn't be here.'

'I'm fine,' she slurs, taking a step closer to him. 'Legal.'

Maybe just, but it still isn't right. She should be at home. Safe.

He backs away. Feels the rough brick of the building against his jacket. The music pulses through the wall into his body. As the beats vibrate through him, the things he's been trying to forget start flashing on a loop in his mind's eye. In the first beat he sees Kate Adams lying perfectly straight in the centre of the double bed; in the next he sees Therese standing in front of Genk. Then he sees Chrissie, arms around Darren Harris; her young son, Robbie, laughing as he plays with his toy truck.

The girl giggles again. Wobbles on her high heels.

I didn't think this through. Couldn't leave her inside, though. Not in this state.

Dom tries to hold her steady, but he's been drinking himself and the alcohol is playing silly buggers with his head. He sees Therese again in his mind's eye, standing beside Genk. He hears Lindsay prattling in his ear, then the gunshot. Sees the blood. Watches Therese falling. The image changes, morphs into Lindsay in Therese's bed, screwing her. Laughing.

Bastard.

The girl cries out, wrenching her arm from his grasp. Rubs it where he's been holding her. Dom hasn't realised he's been gripping her so tight.

He blinks. Forces away the images. Concentrates on the drunk girl in front of him. Her pupils are fully dilated, her eyelids heavy, half-closed. She looks like she's barely a clue where she is, what she's doing.

Just like Chrissie used to look.

'What's your name?' he asks.

She giggles. Turning, she tries to press her bum against him. 'Sophia.'

He puts his hands on her shoulders. Manoeuvres her back to face him. She's shivering. Her eyes are unfocused. She's totally out of it. He can't let her go back inside the club. She could end up sleeping with some man she won't even remember, or worse. He hates that he feels responsible for her. That he always feels responsible.

The music's still banging.

In his mind he sees Kate Adams. Her eyes open, gazing back at him. Dead.

With the next beat he sees Zara Bretton.

In the next, her face changes to Jenna Malik's.

Eyes open. Dead eyes. Their faces flash across his mind like a strobe.

He puts his jacket around the girl and leads her towards the taxi rank. 'You should go home.'

44

CLEMENTINE

The blonde is angry. I'm standing, shielded by the other smokers, watching the detective struggling to persuade the girl to get into a cab. Even I can see that he needs to back off.

I take a drag of my cigarette and wince as she slaps him hard across the face.

'Get away from me, you loser,' she yells. 'I've just had a few drinks, what's your problem?'

He's holding his hands up, trying to reason with her. 'Look, Sophie, I—'

'Sophia, you prick.' The blonde's tone is venomous and loud.

He's pointing to the taxi. 'Sophia, take the cab, get home safe and—'

'Don't fucking bother.' She turns and stomps back towards the club.

He watches the girl go. When she disappears inside, he leans through the taxi's window, saying something to the driver. He hands him a tenner.

The taxi drives off and Dominic Bell heads towards the smoking area I'm standing in. That haunted expression is on his face again. He looks beaten, broken. I take a step towards him before I realise what I'm doing.

It's too late. He's seen me.

He's staring right at me. Turning away, I crush my cigarette out against the top of the metal bin. Then take another from the pack and light up with trembling fingers.

'You got a spare?'

I know it's him before I turn to look. There's something about his energy that gives me a weird feeling; like a silent alarm tingling down my spine. I hold out the cigarettes. Remind myself to smile. 'Sure.'

'Cheers.' He takes one and leans forward for me to light it. Inhales long and deep. Exhales slowly.

I raise an eyebrow. 'Rough night?'

'I guess so.' He touches his cheek where the blonde slapped him, and winces. For the first time since I've been watching him, a smile twitches at the corners of his lips. 'I was only trying to help.'

I take a drag on my cigarette. Smile back. 'I guess some people don't want to be rescued.'

He takes another drag. Shrugs as he exhales. 'Yeah.'

'If you're thinking of making a habit out of doing the hero thing, you might want to think about getting a cape.'

This time his smile is broader. It makes him look younger, less hassled. 'I'll consider that, thanks.'

I laugh, but I'm confused; it comes easy, talking to him. 'You're welcome.'

'So, has your night been better than mine?'

'It's been all right.'

'That good?'

'Almost that good.'

He stubs his cigarette out on the bin. 'Look, do you fancy a drink or something?'

Yes, I do. But I don't say that. If I go back inside with him, if I drink more and let my guard down, bad things could happen. I don't want to show him who I really am. I don't want to hurt him. 'Thanks, but I've had enough of it in there for one night.'

He frowns, and the haunted look starts to take him over again. 'Somewhere quieter, then?'

I hold his gaze as I battle with my choices. No. Yes. Maybe. I'm thinking that he's broken, too, like me. But I'm a wolf in women's clothing and he is just a man. I think about Wade saying it wouldn't hurt to have a police contact of my own; right now I have an opportunity to make Dominic Bell that contact.

'A pub?' he asks. 'My place?'

The choices circle in my mind: yes, no, maybe. Yes. No. Maybe.

Yes. I decide yes.

We drink. Him fast. Me slower. At first it felt awkward sitting on the black leather sofa here in his pristine flat with its laminate floor and magnolia walls. But as the first drink gave way to the second, and he put on some music – old stuff, Radiohead and the like, we've both relaxed. It's bearable, no, more than bearable; it's almost fun.

The more he drinks, the more he talks. I let him. Listen to him. Think how trusting he is to tell me these things, and how much I like that he's telling me. Know it must be the alcohol that's loosened his tongue.

'It's not that I don't want to do it, you know? It's just . . .' He takes another gulp of whisky. 'I wish I could bloody well sleep.'

'Why can't you?'

He doesn't answer. His gaze is fixed on the telly in the corner. There's an Xbox with one controller sitting on the laminate underneath.

I stay silent, giving him time. That's what the books on inter-personal skills say to do – ask a question and allow the person the space to think about the answer. Keep your focus on them, even if they look away. Wait.

It doesn't take long. He looks back at me. 'All the stuff from work, it's there when I close my eyes. I try to make sense of it, solve it, but . . . it'll last as long as the job takes, I know. It always does. But this time, this job . . .' He shakes his head. 'I don't know. It feels harder. I feel responsible, for everyone.'

He hasn't told me what he does for a living and I've not asked. 'So what's different about this job?'

His eyes narrow at the question. He's wary, suspicious. 'I can't tell you the details.'

I shrug. Look unbothered, even though I really do want to know what's going on with him. He's an interesting puzzle; an incongruent mix of controlled, strong detective and doubting, troubled man. Isolated like I am, perhaps. 'OK.'

'It's just . . .'

I reach for the bottle of Glenfiddich and pour another measure into his glass. 'You don't have to tell me. I know what it's like, that's all. I've had insomnia since I was a teenager.'

'How'd you manage?'

'Sometimes well, other times not so much. There's stuff you can try, CBT, meditation, white noise apps. Some people find it helps.'

'And you?'

'Sorry. Nothing consistent. The bad stuff always finds a way of breaking through.'

He looks concerned. 'What bad stuff?'

Heat flushes across my cheeks. I don't answer right away. I'm not sure I want to answer at all.

There's a ticking sound against the laminate. I look in the direction of the noise and see a small black cat standing in the doorway. It's staring at me, unblinking.

'You don't mind cats, do you?'

They make me uneasy. It's like they can see my true nature. 'No, it's fine.'

As if on cue the cat stalks towards me. I keep very still. Try to act relaxed.

Dom scoops up the creature and plonks it onto his lap. 'Sit here, BC.'

I raise an eyebrow. 'BC?'

'Short for Black Cat.' He grins. 'Not very imaginative, I know.'

I smile. 'Indeed.'

The cat purrs as he strokes it. It's still staring at me, eyes half-closed. Dom's looking at me too. 'So what was the bad stuff?'

I down some of my whisky. 'I was in an accident when I was young. It messed up my memories. Stopped me sleeping.'

He leans closer. 'And you blame yourself for what happened?'

I flinch. Shift back on the sofa, widening the distance between us. The leather squeaks beneath my bare legs. Questions fire rapidly into my mind. How could he know? Why is he asking me? Why have I told him anything? I've never told anyone this stuff.

'Sorry. Look, I didn't mean to pry. It's just the not being able to sleep thing got worse for me after a . . . friend was hurt in an accident. It was my fault she got hurt. I should have protected her better.'

It's OK, this isn't about me, it's about him. Somehow knowing that makes me want to tell him at least some of the truth. I exhale. 'There was a fire.'

Dom nods and waits for me to keep talking.

I surprise myself when I do. 'My father died.'

He puts his hand on mine. 'I'm sorry.'

'It was a long time ago,' I say, moving my hand and picking up the bottle of Glenfiddich so I don't have to look at him as I speak, so he can't see the darkness of unspoken truths lurking behind my eyes. I top up my glass. When I go to fill his he shakes his head. 'What about you?' I ask. 'Why do you think you should have protected your friend?'

'Because that was my job. I was meant to be her back-up.'

Dirty copper. The words echo around my mind. I push them away. 'So why didn't you back her up?'

The haunted look is back in his eyes. 'I got taken out first. Didn't have my head in the game.'

Because you're on the take?

I feel the adrenaline start to pulse through my veins. Try to control it. Grip my glass tighter to disguise the tremor in my fingers. 'Why?'

Dom's eyes dart from side to side as if he's struggling to put what he's thinking into words. The cat gets up and moves to the armrest beside him, its front paws needling their claws into the leather. Dom doesn't seem to notice.

He exhales hard. 'I'd been jerked around. I was pissed off.'

'With her?'

'Yeah, too right with her.' He runs his hand through his hair, leaving a tuft at the back sticking up at a weird angle. 'We'd argued the night before. Not about work. We had a thing, outside of work. Turns out she didn't think it was as big a deal as I did.'

'So you—'

'I was thinking about what she'd said, and what I'd said the night before. Not concentrating enough on the situation we were walking into. That's why they got the jump on me. How it got messed up. I keep trying to figure out how it went to shit so fast. There's all this stuff that doesn't fit together. They're trying to blame me, but I think someone on the team was in on it . . . it's making me crazy.'

He's not dirty. Someone is, though. I lean closer. 'Who?'

'I don't know for sure.'

My heart's hammering. My true nature is straining to be unleashed; wants to rip and tear and destroy whoever it is. I fight the urge. Stay outwardly calm. 'But you've got an idea?'

'I've got two, and neither are good. One's meant to be a good mate. The other's family.'

'Shit.'

'Yeah. It's fucked up.'

'Yep, that sounds like family.'

'Yours are difficult then?'

I wait a long moment before I answer. 'It's complicated.'

'Complicated how?'

I shake my head. I'm not going there. Not telling him those things.

'Advice, then?'

I force a laugh. 'Believe me, I'm the last person you'd want that from.'

'You're the only one here to ask.'

I make a show of looking round the empty room. 'I guess I am. Well, for what it's worth, I think you need to tell someone about your suspicions. You need to know the truth. I doubt you'll be able to sleep well until you find out what really happened. Tell your boss; let them handle it.'

He rubs his forehead. 'Yeah. I probably should tell someone.'

I finish my whisky. I'm thinking it should be my last. Any more, and bad things could happen. I smile at him. 'You can always talk to me.'

He holds my eye contact until his phone buzzes and breaks the moment. Dom picks it up and, as he does, I read the message on the screen.

245

Watched the Black Rose dvd. Can't see any connection. Parekh.

Dom curses under his breath.

I check my watch; it's gone midnight. 'Look, I should get going. Any chance of a tea first?'

He gets up. Weaves unsteadily out to the kitchen. Moments later I hear him switch on the kettle.

Reaching across the sofa, I pick up his phone and press the unlock button. The message has disappeared from the screen. The screen won't unlock; it needs a passcode. I'm still trying to guess it when Dom returns with the tea.

THURSDAY

45

CLEMENTINE

He didn't see me with his phone. We drank our tea but before I'd finished mine, Dom fell asleep. Now he's slumped sideways on the couch, his head resting on my thigh. He looks relaxed, his usual frown lines gone. With most people, all people, I'm forcing the interaction with them – every gesture, every word is a chore. Tonight, with him, it's been different.

I *feel* different.

It's like the sensation you get when you've had a dead leg and the feeling starts to return, except this is throughout my whole body, across my skin and into my bones. I like him, I assume that's what this ache breaking through the numbness means. I feel the beginning of something; a connection, perhaps.

I touch his face. Stroke the flecks of grey hair at his temple. He sighs in his sleep. His eyelids flicker, but he doesn't wake.

'You asked about my family, why it's complicated. One of the reasons is money. When my father died he left me everything – his London flat, the Oxfordshire cottage, or what was left of it, the money in his accounts. When Mother discovered he'd cut her from his will she contested it.' I look down at Dom, checking that he's still asleep. His breathing is steady, regular. He hasn't stirred. 'Father's legal team fought back. Mother didn't see a penny. From the day she stormed out of that courtroom she's never spoken to me.'

I trace my fingers across Dom's forehead, over the faint imprints of the frown lines he wears so often while awake. I wish I could stay here, in this moment with him, but I know that I cannot.

Trust. It makes you vulnerable, weak.

There's a pressure building in my chest; a surge of emotion threatening to overwhelm me and tip my carefully constructed world off its axis. I feel it coming and it terrifies me. What if I let go and he sees me for what I really am?

Crazy.

Evil.

Murderer.

However much I want to stay, I must not. I cannot allow myself to get close.

I remove my hand. Ease myself out from beneath him and stand up. The tingling feeling begins to subside. The numbness is returning. I tell myself that it's better this way. If I'm to help True Crime London be the first amateurs to beat the police at solving a serial killer case, I need to use this situation to gain an advantage.

I scan the room for anything related to the case. There's nothing obvious, and there are few places to look; the furniture is minimal – couch, television, Xbox, and a bookshelf against one wall stacked with fantasy novels – Tolkien, George R.R. Martin, Philip Pullman. There's nothing soft about this room, no cushions or rug, no artwork. Nothing sentimental.

I glance towards the couch, checking Dom is still asleep. He is, but the cat has woken up and is watching me. From its disdainful expression I can tell it doesn't approve.

'Don't judge me,' I whisper, and step out to the hallway.

There's nothing here either, nor in the kitchen. The whole place seems unnaturally tidy, too sterile and lacking in the debris of everyday life.

Dom is the only thing here connected to the Lover case. My jacket is hanging in the hall. I remove my phone and head back into the lounge to take a photo of him.

When I unlock the screen the notifications appear.

Crime Queen, Witness_Zero and two others posted in Case Files: The Lover.
Death Stalker sent you a private message.

I press the alert for Death Stalker's message.

Death Stalker to @TheWatcher I need your help.
Death Stalker to @TheWatcher It's URGENT. Reply asap.
PLEASE.

I check the timestamps. One message was sent hours ago; the last one four minutes ago.

The Watcher to @DeathStalker What's up?
Death Stalker to @TheWatcher She's dead. I left it too late.
Couldn't stop him.
The Watcher to @DeathStalker You found the killer? Where
are you?
Death Stalker to @TheWatcher I got more information on the
brush. Went to dental surgery. I saw him there. Recognised
him. I followed him. Watched him break in. I left it too long to
go in there. She's dead. DEAD!!!!!!

She, whoever *she* is, is dead. I try not to think about that, about
what was done to her, because right now I need to know what
Death Stalker discovered about the Lover.

The Watcher to @DeathStalker Where's the killer?
Death Stalker to @TheWatcher I think he saw me.
The Watcher to @DeathStalker Who is he?

Three dots appear. He's typing.
Come on. Hurry up. We could catch the Lover.

Death Stalker to @TheWatcher I ran.
The Watcher to @DeathStalker You wanted to catch him before
the police. This is your chance.

No answer.
'Come on, come on,' I mutter. 'Don't bail on me now, not
when we're so close.'

Death Stalker to @TheWatcher She was still warm when I touched her. He'd just killed her. I was banging on the door, trying to get into her flat. He was in there. She was warm.

He's losing it. Able enough to talk the talk, but crapping out when he has to step up.

The Watcher to @DeathStalker Who is he?
Death Stalker to @TheWatcher Not saying online, beware hackers. A window was open on to the balcony. He got away down the fire escape.
The Watcher to @DeathStalker Did you call the police?
Death Stalker to @TheWatcher No, we need to find him. Help me?

I exhale hard. Finally he's thinking about finding the killer again.

The Watcher to @DeathStalker Yes
Death Stalker to @TheWatcher Meet me at my place. Basement flat. 248c.

A geotag pops up next to his message. Tapping the link, I open the maps app and find his location – it's in east London, but only just, pretty close to Liverpool Street station. It won't take long.

I grab my coat and boots. Ignore the nagging thought that this could be a set-up, that Death Stalker might not have told me the Lover's name because he's the killer and I might be walking into a trap. Glancing back at Dom, still sleeping on the couch, I wonder if I should leave a note. I decide against it. If Death Stalker is being honest, and we're going to beat the police, I need to keep this from Dom.

The Watcher to @DeathStalker On my way. ETA = thirty minutes.

46

He is gasping. Running. Hiding.

She is ruined. All his planning wasted.

Frustration. Desire. Rejection.

The aching burns through his bones, more intense with every step. Heat scorches across his skin. His breath rises like clouds of ash into the frigid night.

How did they find us?

How did they know?

He has been so careful, disguised himself completely and hidden all his tracks, yet they found him out. He's cleverer than that. Better than that. Should have been better than that.

He punches the wall. Bites back the pain but howls inside. Waits deep in the shadows beneath the fire escape. Hidden.

The source of his fury runs along the path on the other side of the street. They're walking fast, glancing round every few paces; tense and scared and on the alert.

Revenge. Avenge. Destroy.

He yanks his hood down further over his face. Pulls his jacket tight around himself and clenches the handles of his bag harder, as if they're a chicken's neck to be snapped. They're twenty yards ahead now, but they won't get away.

He will put this right, and he will make sure no one else can find him.

Then he will have her again.

47
CLEMENTINE

I know Death Stalker could be bluffing. If he's the killer, Death Stalker could have faked his distress to lure me to his home.

Wade told me to be careful. I am not being careful. I'm on Death Stalker's street a few minutes from the Queen of Hoxton pub, standing outside a tattoo parlour. The next building is 248.

I go down the stone steps to the basement flat, halting when I see the door is ajar. I look around, but see no one. Listen hard, but hear nothing. The stone here is swept clean, in stark contrast with the leaf-strewn pavement at ground level. A grey blind is drawn across the window; there's no way to see inside.

I wonder if Death Stalker was right; if the Lover did see him. I wonder if the killer followed him home or if this is the killer's home.

A frisson of apprehension ripples through me. Either way the killer could be here. I feel an overwhelming urge to turn and run, but I don't. I have to check Death Stalker's OK. I have to know what he discovered.

I nudge the door open with my toe and step over the threshold. I don't call out. Instead I pad along the pockmarked laminate towards a door at the end of the hallway. I catch a glimpse of myself reflected in the glass of the black and white photos collaged along one wall, and flinch. Look away. Focus on the door.

As I get closer I hear music playing in the next room; a dance tune with a thumping beat. My own pulse pounds at my temples. With every step the anxiety builds inside me. I keep my breathing steady. Ignore the scratchiness at the base of my throat. Keep moving forward.

Reaching the door, I wait two beats before peering inside.

I see the knife first.

It's lying on the white kitchen worktop, a pool of crimson beneath the blade. The metal is smeared with blood. Its contrast with the whiteness of the room is jarring – the white units and worktop of the kitchen, the white carpet in the living space beyond, the white couch that lines the opposite wall.

The tune changes to one I remember from the club. This isn't fun. It's dangerous.

I take a deep breath. Know that something very bad has happened here.

I can't leave, though, not yet.

Five paces into the room, I spot him. He's slumped on the floor beside the island unit: Death Stalker, or what's left of him. I stare down at him. See the cuts zigzagging across his body, his throat and his arms. The white top he's wearing is drenched in blood. The splatter has flicked across his jeans, drying reddish-brown.

I check the time on my phone. It's three-quarters of an hour since he last messaged me. If the blood is already drying, the killer must have attacked him soon after. What if the killer is still here?

My legs feel weak, trembling, but I have to be sure. My breathing is rapid, shallow, as I force myself across the room to the bedroom, then the bathroom. I check that they're empty. Use the end of my sleeve wrapped around my hand to open cupboard doors, checking every space.

There's no one else here.

I go back to Death Stalker. Stand over him, careful to avoid the blood splatter on the floor, and check for signs of life. There are none. Given his wounds, he must have bled out in minutes. I stare at the macabre criss-cross of cuts. Unlike the victims in the photos Ghost Avenger posted online, Death Stalker does not look peaceful. His eyes are wide, his face contorted in agony. His release is not one I envy.

My stomach lurches and I feel a bitter tang in my mouth. The metallic smell of blood fills my senses, and I cannot stop myself from staring at it; the scarlet against the white purity of the floor tiles, the crimson against Death Stalker's skin.

I think of Father. *Crimson flames. Burnt skin turned black.*

Fury ignites inside me and I lash out, kicking Death Stalker – a hard kick to the side of his thigh. He's more solid than I'd anticipated. He hurts my toe, so I kick him again. 'How could you do this? You've ruined everything.'

The track on the radio changes, the dance tune mixing into something slower. I gasp and it morphs into another sound – a sob. I feel a strange quivering sensation in my chest and recognise an unfamiliar feeling – sadness. I drop to my knees. Touch Death Stalker's arm and realise that he's already turning cold. My eyes start to water.

The pressure in my chest releases. The fury has gone. That's when my brain kicks back in. When the police come they cannot connect Death Stalker to the True Crime London investigation. If they discover us they will shut us down. I need to remove every trace and leave. Fast.

Crouching down, I search his pockets for his phone and take it. I check the room for anything that could link us. Find his laptop by the sofa and snatch it. In the bedroom, I find a tatty paperback called *Black Rose Chronicles*. Given the text on Dom's phone was about a *Black Rose* film, I assume the book is linked to the case. I take it too, stuffing it into the laptop bag I spot wedged between the desk and the wall.

I don't look at Death Stalker as I hurry back through the kitchen. Now he's just another victim, another inanimate piece of evidence. If True Crime London is to have any chance at solving this, we need the information that led Death Stalker to the Lover's latest victim and caused the Lover to find and kill him.

I shiver, think about the increasing danger, and for a moment I consider the notion of walking away and disappearing. But I don't. How can I, when that would mean Death Stalker bled out for nothing, died for nothing, and that our investigation comes to nothing?

No. I won't let that happen. I'm in too deep to stop when we're so close.

Hoisting the strap of the laptop bag onto my shoulder, I stalk out into the night.

48

DOM

There's another noise. His mobile's vibrating against the laminate floor. Reaching down, he grabs the phone and answers.

'This is Bell,' he says, rubbing his neck where it's sore from sleeping with his head cramped against the armrest of the couch. He notices there are two glasses on the floor. Remembers the woman from the club; how they'd talked, he'd talked. Glancing around, he wonders if she's still here. He can't believe he fell asleep.

'Guv, it's Parekh.' She sounds breathless, excited. 'I thought I'd get in early and keep looking for reported thefts of controlled drugs.'

Dom glances at his watch; it's almost 5.30 in the morning. 'It's very bloody early. What've you got?'

'Nothing useful on the drugs yet, but uniform have just called. There's been another attack, over near Farringdon. From the description of the scene and the victim it could be our guy.'

Fully alert now, Dom says, 'Why aren't they sure?'

'This one, it's not like the others.'

Parekh was right. As it is now, this crime scene isn't the same as the others, but give it a couple more hours and it would have been.

What made him stop?

The apartment is in one of those merchant banker dormitory-type buildings – the traditional Victorian facade hiding an interior of uber-modern loft-style living spaces. Emily and Abbott have cleared the room where the victim was left. Dom stands on the threshold, ready to go inside. It's a narrow area, little more than two yards wide; a walk-in dressing room, with rails of clothes lining the walls. On the shelves at the far end, clear plastic boxes filled with shoes are neatly stacked; there's a photo of each pair taped onto the corresponding box.

She's sitting at the dressing table. Abbott's already got a preliminary ID: Melissa Chamberlain, twenty-five years old, working as a trainee solicitor for a well-known legal firm.

Dead.

Melissa's head is slumped forward, her body held in place by the cable ties binding her wrists, ankles and throat to the high-backed chair. She's wearing underwear, white cotton briefs and a pink lace bra. There's a birthmark the size of a postage stamp above her left hip. A layer of concealer has been smeared over it. The shade is a few tones darker than her skin.

Dom takes three paces into the space. Now they're alone, Melissa and him.

He tries not to overthink things. Keeps his mind clear and lets his brain freewheel, taking in the room. The dressing table is clear and spotlessly clean. A large flowery make-up bag is sitting on the carpet beside it. The overhead light and the spotlights around the mirror are blazing.

It's him, isn't it?

This feels different to the previous crime scenes, and not only due to the over-bright lighting. The whole energy of the place is strange, out of kilter.

Dom moves closer to Melissa. Her brunette hair is held back from her face by an Alice band and shines with the gloss of recent colour. It's the same shade and length Jenna, Kate and Zara's was altered to.

There's a tightening in his chest. His hands start to tingle and he clenches his fists until he can feel his nails cutting into his palms.

Breathe deep. Get this done.

Dom kneels beside Melissa, twisting between her and the dressing table so he can look at her face. Her eyes are closed and only one has been made up. He peers closer, notices the eyeliner looks shakier and the eye shadow is smudged. Her mascara has run, leaving a tidemark of black dye across her cheek. There are black marks, he counts three, where it looks as though mascara tears have dripped from her jaw onto her chest. There's a fourth on the lace trim of her bra.

Why leave her like this?

He hears the rustle of bootie-clad feet padding across the floor behind him. Ignoring whoever's approaching, he stands, still looking at Melissa. The cable tie noose around her neck is new, different. Dom wonders why. The plastic has bitten into her flesh, blood is crusted around the wound. She must have fought back hard.

'Different, isn't it?' Emily's voice comes from behind him.

They never give me long enough.

Dom tries to hide the irritation in his voice, but fails. 'Looks like she tried to fight off her attacker. Can you make sure her nails are checked for scrapings?'

'I always do.' The doc is standing a couple of feet away, gloved hands on her hips. 'Something must have made him stop. I don't think our vic's struggling would have done it. He'd already got her into the chair. That would've been the hardest part.'

'Maybe he was disturbed,' Abbott says, stepping into the dressing room behind Emily.

'Yeah, but something spooked him. You said the door was open when the first responders arrived?'

Abbott nods. 'Wide open, they said.'

'Did you see this?' Emily steps closer to Melissa, and points to a needle-stick mark on the inside of her forearm. 'He didn't hide it this time, just shoved it straight into the easiest vein.'

The guilt punches Dom in the gut so hard he almost doubles over. He could have prevented this; should have got this killer already. He stares at Melissa, at her slumped shoulders, her bound wrists, the bloodied noose around her throat.

Who did this?

Why?

I'm sorry. I'm so sorry.

He swallows hard. Looks back at Emily and Abbott. 'He knew he wasn't going to finish his routine, but he killed her anyway.'

'She'd have seen his face, wouldn't she?' Abbott says.

Dom doesn't respond.

Abbott clears his throat. 'So far we've got no eye witnesses and no next of kin. I'll get the uniforms started on door-to-doors as soon as it's light.'

Dom looks at his sergeant. 'Who called this in?'

'One of the neighbours,' Abbott says. 'They heard some banging, and a man shouting. Thought it was a domestic.'

49

DOM

On the murder board, a picture of Melissa Chamberlain has joined those of Jenna Malik, Zara Bretton and Kate Adams. The photo is from her graduation. It shows a smiling young woman with naturally blonde, straight hair, wearing minimal make-up. Her eyes are bright, and filled with hope. They're staring right at him. He wants to look away, but won't let himself. Her gaze delivers the sucker punch of failure.

Abbott clears his throat.

Dom looks away from the board. The team come back into focus. Abbott's biting his bottom lip. Biggs hasn't shaved; his stubble is patchy and unkempt-looking. Dom knows they were called in early, but it still irritates him. He makes an effort to keep his tone calm as he says, 'Yes, Sergeant?'

'Shall I kick off, guv?' Abbott's got his pad open, ready.

'Go ahead.'

'So we've got a fourth victim. Melissa Chamberlain. She was twenty-five, single and worked as a trainee solicitor. Her dad's a single parent, lives in Surrey. The local police have made contact and he's on his way here to make the formal identification.'

'Do we know when he's likely to arrive?' Dom asks.

'Close to seven-thirty, I'm told. The post-mortem's scheduled for eight o'clock. Dr Renton's shifted her schedule to get it done early.'

'Thanks for bringing us up to speed.' Dom looks around the team: they might be knackered, but they're looking attentive, apart from Biggs. 'As you know, this scene was different. Melissa was part way through the transformation, her hair was dyed but her make-up only half-complete. The door was open, the window onto the Juliet balcony, too, so it's likely he left in a hurry, either out the front or down the fire escape. We need to know why.

Parekh raises her hand.

'Go on,' Dom says.

'The call came from the neighbour in the adjoining apartment, Lacey Beck, at 2.19 this morning. She heard shouting and thought it was a domestic. She's given a statement. She also told me the camera on the entry system isn't working – it was reported to the building manager a few days ago. I had it checked and she's right, so there's no video of the killer. But I've asked for the CCTV around the building and neighbouring streets to be pulled. I should have it in the next few hours.'

Abbott's phone starts ringing. He moves to the back of the room, turning away from the team as he answers.

Dom continues, 'Biggs, can you get over to the crime scene and work with the uniforms on the door-to-doors? Make sure they're asking about more than just last night – we need to know how Melissa lived, what her routine was.'

Biggs rolls his eyes. 'I know how door-to-doors work.'

'I don't expect any mistakes, then.' Dom looks back to Parekh. 'Did anyone pick up anything useful from the *Black Rose* film or the book?'

Parekh shakes her head. 'I read the book cover to cover and didn't notice anything that connects with the case. The make-up is wrong for the period, the setting is different and none of the women's descriptions fits our victims. I watched about half an hour of the film and saw nothing there.'

'So we're saying it's a dead end?'

'I think so.'

'All right. Park it for now then. Concentrate on Melissa Chamberlain, and on Patrick Bartlett's alibis – find out if he knew Melissa.' He looks at Biggs. 'When you're done with the door-to-doors go over to Masters and Rubenstein and find out what you can about Melissa from them – colleagues, friends, her habits and work assignments.'

'Right.' Biggs is typing on his phone. From this angle it looks like the name at the top of the screen is Lindsay.

Do they know each other? Is Biggs passing Lindsay information? Is one of them feeding the details to the press? Is Biggs the sieve? Dom can't think about that right now, but knows he'll have to tackle Biggs about it later. Shit. 'Look for anything that could connect her with the other victims.'

Biggs looks up. 'Understood.'

'We've got something, guv,' Abbott says, rejoining the group. 'That was the crime scene manager. They've found a latent print on Melissa's dressing table. It isn't hers.'

'How long until we know?'

'They're expediting it – an hour, maybe two.'

Dom looks at Parekh. 'Can you chase them in an hour?'

'Will do. I'll put in a request for Melissa Chamberlain's phone and financial records, too.'

'Good.' Dom looks at Abbott. 'We'll need to get over to the identification and the PM, you OK with that?'

Abbott nods. 'Of course.'

'Right, let's get to it. Our killer's claimed another victim, but didn't finish his ritual. He's likely to be frustrated and angry. He's going to kill again, and it's going to be soon. We have to catch him. Failure can't be an option.'

An effort has been made to make the public entrance to the mortuary look more welcoming than the business end, but it doesn't really pull it off. Like a party dress on a pig, the grey carpet and orange curtains can't disguise the building's true identity. The double-width parking spaces outside with plaques saying *Ambulance* and *Funeral Directors* are not at all subtle.

Mr Chamberlain has to walk past them to get inside. Not that they will distract him from what he's come here to do. How could it? His daughter is dead.

Dom spots him as he comes through the door. Walking beside him is a uniform; a short bloke with glasses. He removes his hat as he enters the building.

Dom hates this bit. There's nothing he can say to make the situation any better; never knows if a handshake is a good thing or not. It doesn't get easier with time. No one should ever have to outlive their own child.

The uniform recognises him. 'Detective Bell? I'm PC Drayton.'

He nods at Drayton, and with his eyes on Mr Chamberlain says, 'I'm Detective Inspector Bell and this is my colleague Detective Sergeant Abbott. Thank you for coming.'

The words feel too sparse, inadequate, but they do the job.

Mr Chamberlain asks, 'Where is she?'

He wants to get it over with. Dom understands that. Until he sees her, and confirms it's his daughter, he's in limbo, waiting to know whether it's really true.

'This way, please.' Dom leads him out of reception and along the corridor. There's no carpet here, instead vinyl tiles squeak beneath Mr Chamberlain's shoes. The noise seems comic, inappropriate for the situation. No one speaks.

Dom stops when they reach the fourth door on the right. He looks at Mr Chamberlain. 'Are you ready to do this?'

'Yes.' Mr Chamberlain's voice sounds tight, like it's a struggle to force out the word.

Dom opens the door and leads him inside.

The room is painted lavender. It's small with three chairs along the far wall and a purple curtain drawn across what looks like a window. They halt next to the curtain.

Dom explains the process. He asks Melissa's father if he understands, and he nods.

Abbott pulls the cord and the curtain opens. On the other side of the glass the young woman lies on a metal gurney, a white sheet covers her from toes to shoulders. She looks different to the last time Dom saw her: the mortuary technician has taken samples of the make-up used by the killer and cleaned it from her face.

Mr Chamberlain puts his hand out, touching the window. 'It can't be. It can't be my Melissa.' He starts to shake as recognition turns into shock. He claws at the glass as if he's trying to reach through and touch her, to check that she's real. 'Not my Melissa.'

Dom waits.

Mr Chamberlain turns to him. Sobs between the words. 'That's my little girl.'

Dom doesn't want to intrude. He steps back, giving him a moment. The ticking of the clock on the wall above the chairs seems to grow louder.

Mr Chamberlain looks at him. 'Can I go in with her?'

'I'm sorry, no, not at this point.' Dom doesn't want to go into the details of why. 'You'll be able to once the doctors have seen her.'

'Thank you.'

Don't thank me, Dom wants to say; if I'd found the killer, your daughter would still be alive. Instead he says, 'When you feel ready, it would be helpful if we could ask you a few questions, to learn more about your daughter, anything that—'

'Will it help you catch who did this?' Mr Chamberlain's voice is shaky but there's no missing the anger.

'It could.'

'I'll do it now, then.'

At first Mr Chamberlain is too shell-shocked to say much. They're in the family liaison room, another bland space dressed with peach curtains and a painting – reds and greens splatted onto a huge canvas – that Dom finds rather disturbing. Mr Chamberlain clutches a cup of lukewarm coffee fetched for them by the uniform. He hasn't taken a sip.

Dom keeps his tone soft. 'Can you tell me about her?'

Mr Chamberlain rakes his hands through his grey hair and hangs his head. 'She was a good girl. Dedicated. She made me so proud. But she was always working. She really cared. Wanted to make a difference. And now . . . I can't believe someone would do this. I . . . I only spoke to her a couple of days ago . . .'

'How did she sound when you spoke? Did she mention anything bothering her, anyone?'

Mr Chamberlain shakes his head. 'No, not at all. She sounded happy. She'd had a couple of days off after having her teeth done. Said she was feeling great. I thought the rest had done her good.

She'd been working herself too hard. I was pleased she'd had a break . . .'

Abbott's written *Dentist?* on his notes. Dom looks back at Mr Chamberlain. 'Do you remember the name of her dental surgery?'

'Why does that matter?' Mr Chamberlain's voice is getting louder. 'Shouldn't you be out finding the person who did this?'

'I want to do that, sir, I—'

'You need to find who killed my little girl . . .'

'I'm trying to—'

Mr Chamberlain stands. Comes towards Dom. He's shouting now. 'The other guy said you think it's connected to the other murders. The Lover killer? Why haven't you caught him yet? Why?'

Dom stands. Puts his hands out, palms up. 'Please, Mr Chamberlain, we're doing all we—'

'Well it's not good enough, is it? How many people has this man killed? Three, four?' Mr Chamberlain's face is turning red. His shoulders start to shake. 'Who would do it, who? I just don't understand . . .'

'That's what we're here to find out, sir,' Dom says, 'and to do that we need as much information about Melissa as we can. Who were her friends? Did she have a boyfriend, or a girlfriend? Was there anyone who'd been bothering her?'

'She was single, but she'd loads of friends.' Mr Chamberlain frowns. 'I'm not sure how often she saw them. She worked so hard, didn't seem to have much time for fun.'

'Can you give me their names?' Abbott asks. 'We'll need to contact them, see if they can help us build up a picture of what happened.'

Mr Chamberlain lists his daughter's friends to Abbott.

Dom feels his mobile vibrating in his pocket. Ignores it.

Mr Chamberlain scowls at him. 'Aren't you going to answer that?'

Dom pulls his phone from his pocket. Chrissie's name is flashing on the screen. He rejects the call.

Before he's pushed it back into his pocket, the mobile starts vibrating again. Mr Chamberlain swears, muttering under his breath about incompetence and complaints.

Dom's about to reject the call again, but he stops. This time the caller ID is different: Parekh.

'I'm sorry,' he says to Mr Chamberlain. 'I need to take this.'

Dom gets up and paces to the other side of the room. Answering the call, he keeps his voice low. 'This is Bell. I'm with Melissa Chamberlain's father, so—'

'It's urgent, guv.' He can hear the excitement in Parekh's voice. 'We've got a match on the print.'

50

DOM

Dom's stomach flips. It's the first time he's been in this kind of situation since Operation Atlantis. His palms are clammy. The stab vest under his jacket feels stiff and uncomfortable. He's not relishing the adrenaline kick the way he always has in the past.

The fingerprint match has led them here – Glen Eastman's flat. Dom motions Abbott to follow his lead. Biggs has gone round the back, taking a couple of uniforms with him.

Dom needs to make this happen, but there's a niggling doubt fogging his focus. Why has the killer been so careless this time? He had time to gather his make-up and erase his prints from everywhere else in Melissa's apartment – why leave a single print? It doesn't make sense.

Abbott glances at him. He's doing the rabbit thing with his lip.

Dom gestures at Abbott to follow him, and descends down six stone steps to a green wooden door.

On each side of the doorstep stands a small bay tree, leaves clipped into a perfect sphere. The rectangle of paving between the wall and the steps is swept clean. It's neat, just like the kill sites have been. Dom's not convinced, though. There's a gnawing sensation in the bottom of his belly. Something doesn't feel right.

He knocks on the door. It swings open. The hallway light is on.

Dom catches Abbott's eye. This isn't what they'd expected. He pushes the door open wider and shouts, 'Police. We're coming in.'

Silence.

Dom's heart is pounding. The stab vest feels tighter, constricting his ribs, stifling him. He wishes he hadn't worn the bloody thing. Trying to ignore it, he gestures for Abbott to follow and steps over the threshold.

They advance along the narrow hallway. The walls are covered with black and white photos in grey frames, all different sizes, fitted together like a jigsaw. Dom focuses on the closed door ahead of him. He hears the faint sound of music playing.

When he's half a metre from the door he shouts again, 'This is the police, Mr Eastman. We need you to show yourself.'

No response.

He grabs the door handle and eases it down. 'Mr Eastman? Please respond.'

Dom pushes the door wide. The music gets louder; some pop song. 'Mr Eastman?'

The room is a combined kitchen and living space with white, quartz-topped units and leather couch at the far end. Dom moves further in, between the range cooker and the island unit that divides the kitchen from the rest of the room. As he steps through the gap, he sees a splash of crimson, bold against the stark white of the counter. Turns. The guy with the pudding-basin haircut is lying spreadeagled on the laminate.

He's a real mess: throat slashed, torso carved up with long, deep gashes. What's left of his white tee is stained dark ruby. The wounds are crusted brown.

Poor bastard. He'd recognised the name Glen Eastman when Parekh told him it over the phone, but hadn't connected it to the freelancer until she'd texted him the old mugshot held in the system. He was younger in the picture. It'd been taken eight years previously, along with his fingerprints, when he'd been arrested and charged for being drunk and disorderly – stealing a road sign, disturbing the peace. He'd been a student then, a first-year at uni. There was no record of him having been in trouble since.

Dom looks over his shoulder at Abbott. Abbott's staring at Eastman's body. He looks shocked.

'Abbott, call the doc, tell her we need her.'

He doesn't respond for a moment, then looks at Dom and says, 'Yes, guv.' His voice sounds strained, nervous.

Dom turns back to Eastman and crouches beside him. The bright ceiling lights illuminate the body from all angles. His eyes are open, his lips curled back in a grimace.

Dom shakes his head. 'What did you poke your nose into this time?'

Thirty minutes later the place is heaving with people. One of the techs brings Dom a paper babygro. He thanks her and puts it on, secretly thinking he's most likely contaminated the scene already. As he zips up, he watches Emily examine Eastman.

She turns and beckons him over. 'Killed sometime in the past twelve hours I'd say.'

'Rough time of death?'

Emily shakes her head. 'You know it's too early, Dom. I'll tell you more once I've got him back to my place.'

'Cause of death?'

'Again, I can't confirm until I've got him back, but if I was a betting girl I'd say a number of his wounds could have been fatal. I'll give you a conclusive answer later. I'll bump him up the schedule, do him after the woman.' She gives him a faint smile. 'Two murders in one day, Dom. You're keeping me busy.'

Dom watches a male CSI packing the murder weapon into an evidence bag. 'It looks like the poor bastard was stabbed with his own knife; it's the same make and style as the others hanging from the magnetic strip by the hob.'

'Nice knife too,' Emily says. 'Designer, engineered steel for perfect balance.'

Dom looks at Eastman's bloodied body. 'Didn't help him.'

'Not today,' Emily says.

'That fingerprint we found at the Melissa Chamberlain crime scene; it's his. So there's a connection between the two kill sites.'

'Do you think it's the same killer?' Abbott asks, looking at Emily.

'Impossible to say.' She gestures to Eastman's torso. 'Look at the state of him. This is totally different from the other crime scenes. Could be the Lover has an accomplice.'

'Maybe.' The fingerprint places Eastman at the scene of Melissa's murder, thinks Dom. Then hours, maybe minutes, later Eastman himself is killed.

Abbott coughs nervously. He's got that wired look about him. 'What is it?' Dom says.

'I don't get how Eastman fits.'

Dom looks at Emily. 'This was a frenzied attack, right?'

'Absolutely. Look at the high arcs of blood splatter across the cabinets. There was force and speed behind each of these incisions.'

'Like they were done in anger?'

Emily gives a small smile. 'You're leading the witness, Dom, but I see where you're going. It's possible, but all conjecture. What we do have, though, is skin beneath his fingernails and defensive lacerations on his forearms. That tells us he tried to fight back.'

Dom's thinking; piecing the pattern together. 'It could be he's involved with the killer, or perhaps he discovers him, maybe interrupts him, but isn't in time to stop him killing Melissa. The killer escapes, Eastman realises she's dead and legs it.'

'Or the killer chases him off,' Abbott says.

'Yeah.'

Abbott frowns. 'But if he gets chased off from Melissa's, how does he end up like this?'

Dom glances down at Eastman's bloodied body. 'I'm guessing the killer was angry about not finishing his ritual. Maybe Eastman saw his face. Either way, he tracks him here and gets revenge.'

'So his usual restraint is gone,' Abbott says.

'Exactly,' Dom says. 'He hacks at Eastman until he's dead, then flees.'

Emily looks at Eastman's body and back to Dom. 'It's a good theory.'

'Sounds plausible, doesn't it? We just need some evidence to tell us if it's close.' Dom looks at Abbott. 'Get the door-to-doors started. We need witnesses, descriptions of anyone who visited Eastman recently, and we need to find out what Eastman was writing about, get hold of his research, and his contacts.'

The photographer's done his stuff, and the CSIs are bagging up anything potentially relevant. Dom feels like a spare part. Across the room, Abbott is keeping an eye on the search. Dom looks over to him. 'What have we got?'

'Nothing. Any tech he had has gone.' Abbott points to a power cord plugged into a mains socket. 'My best guess is the killer took Eastman's laptop.'

'Well, get his phone and any other devices pushed through to computer forensics fast. I need the results today.'

'We've not found any,' Abbott says, stepping aside to let a male CSI with ginger stubble and ironic black-framed glasses unplug the power cord and bag it up.

Dom stays rooted where he is. 'What?'

'He didn't have a mobile on him, and we've not found one here.'

Dom swears under his breath. 'I saw him using a phone at the press briefing, and he shoved a voice recorder in my face yesterday, so where the hell are they?'

'Not here.'

'Well, we need to find them. If Eastman was on to the killer we need to know how.' Dom shakes his head. 'Call Parekh at the office, will you. Get her to chivvy up this guy's phone records. Financials, too. Any damn thing that'll get us more information.'

'Yes, guv,' Abbott says, ever the diplomat. He moves over to the CSIs and starts briefing the team leader in hushed tones.

Emily looks like she's finished her preliminary examination. She's standing back, hands on her hips, letting the meat wagon guys remove Eastman's body. Her gaze is fixed on the side of the island unit, at the blood splatter pattern flicked across the otherwise pristine surface.

He moves across to her. 'What?'

Emily gestures to the arc of continuous spray. 'There are no voids, so it's unlikely the killer stood between the unit and his victim.'

'So?'

'Look around you. Other than the pool of blood, which would have formed as he bled out, there's much less blood splatter across the walls and the rest of the floor.'

She's right; the majority of the spray is concentrated on the island unit. 'Meaning the killer must have shielded them from it?'

'Precisely. For that he'd have been closer to the victim than would've been necessary just to stick the knife in. I'm talking about them being inches apart – it would have been more awkward to stab him at that range.'

Dom thinks about it; a frenzied attack, made from close range, looking into the face of his victim. 'He wanted Eastman to know who he was, to look into his eyes as he died?'

Emily nods. 'I think so.'

'So the blood would have covered him.'

'There'll be an evidence trail, certainly. The blood spray would have soaked into whatever he was wearing – he couldn't have avoided it. If you can find those clothes, you'll have your evidence.'

'*If* we can find them.'

'Let's hope that you do.'

'Boss?'

Dom turns and sees Biggs standing a few feet behind him. The portly detective is slightly out of breath.

'Yeah?' Dom says. 'What is it?'

'We've got a witness.'

51

CLEMENTINE

Finally, I crack his password. It's taken almost two hours, but as I scan through the files, I can see it's been worth the time. There are a lot of cases here. Missing persons, aggravated assault, other murders as well as the Lover; many investigations he'd been spending time on.

That's not the only thing he'd been doing, either. Death Stalker – real name Glen Eastman – had a job as a freelance journalist, but he didn't restrict himself to two personas. On the laptop, alongside the folders labelled with the names of each newspaper he wrote copy for and one named *TCL Death Stalker*, is a folder entitled *News Byte*.

There are hundreds of files inside. Opening the *News Byte* website, I scroll through the posts, checking them against the files. They all tally, each upload corresponds to the last time each of the files was accessed. Death Stalker was Glen Eastman, and Eastman was responsible for the best crime news in London.

News Byte is an impressive site; it gets hold of stories early and investigates them deeply. Death Stalker, Eastman, must have had sources feeding him information on more than just the Lover case. Perhaps something from one of them led him to the killer tonight.

I scroll back to the last uploaded article and scan the text. In it, the writer implies Dominic Bell isn't fit to lead the Lover case. There's mention of an undercover operation – Atlantis – of a female officer getting shot, and hints that Dom could be found negligent by the investigation recently taken over by the IPCC. A strong suggestion he was on the take.

Dirty copper.

I reread the article. Someone's dirty, but I don't believe it's Dom. I believed him when he said he was taken out of action and that he suspects someone else of foul play.

The memory of Dom telling me about his friend getting hurt at work replays in my mind. Was that the woman who got shot? Was she the skinny blonde woman he visited last night? I want to know what their relationship is now.

I feel my pulse quicken. Realise that I'm obsessing. Force myself to stop.

I have to stay focused. This is about finding the Lover, beating the police. Nothing else can matter. I read Death Stalker's last messages. He said the brush was key, that the dentist link was important. I scan through the files looking for something that relates to brushes or dentists.

I find nothing.

What now?

There has to be something on here. The most likely source of information would be the lab contact Death Stalker mentioned. I open his email, tap my index finger against the trackpad as I wait for the mails to load.

One thousand, two hundred and seventy-three emails, 63 unread. I scroll through to the last ones read, work my way through those received between our meet in the café and his messages this morning. I find no mention of dentists or brushes.

I search against keywords – dentist, brush. Still nothing. The lab sent Death Stalker the chemical formula for the powder found on the bristles, yet there's no trace of it. I grab Death Stalker's mobile from the desk and check his messages, his contacts, his FaceTime. There's no reference to a laboratory. No lead I can follow.

I put the phone down and stare at the laptop. Think. What else? What next? There has to be something here. Has to be.

My mind circles back to the undercover operation. Switching windows, I return to the *News Byte* folder and search the files. Towards the bottom I find what I'm looking for – a document with Atlantis in the filename.

Opening the document, I see it's a cut and paste of an email trail – an exchange between Eastman and an officer in DI Bell's team. I bite my lip as I recognise the name – Detective Sergeant Abbott.

I read the mails. The first is timestamped the morning of Kate Adams's death. In it, Glen Eastman is making contact with DS Abbott – he's asking Abbott to tell him what's taken the DI away from the crime scene early.

I read through the exchange – DS Abbott saying there are rumours about Bell's role in the failure of the Atlantis operation, promising he'll try to find out more. Eastman urging him to hurry; DS Abbott using some salty language to tell him to back off, Eastman reminding him of their arrangement – the money he's paying. What money, I wonder, and how does a freelance hack get the money to bribe a murder squad detective?

The final email from the sergeant says virtually the same as the *News Byte* article, with one exception. Abbott makes references to a crime scene photo he'd sent that morning, and asks Eastman to confirm it's been received. Eastman messaged back a single word: *Yes*.

What photo? I scroll through the files but don't find anything else mentioning Atlantis. I toggle back to his emails. Reordering them into date received, I search for the image from Abbott.

Nothing.

I slam my fist hard onto the trackpad. There's a crunch, and a split appears, fracturing the casing across the side of the laptop. The pointer flickers and disappears off-screen.

Damn. My hand's throbbing. I rub it, massaging out the pain. Maybe Abbott didn't email the picture. Grabbing Death Stalker's phone, I open the text messages and swipe down to the day Kate Adams was killed.

There it is. An image with four words: *How we found her*.

The picture is Kate Adams. Not the pretty blonde shown in the newspaper articles. No, this is Kate Adams the corpse – lying naked on a bed, surrounded by rose petals and burning candles. Her hair is dyed the same mid-brown as in the mortuary photos. Her pubic hair is, too. But the biggest difference in this image is her make-up. In all the pictures used by the media she looked close to natural – a smudge of eyeliner, a touch of mascara. This photo is a complete contrast; heavy black eyeliner, peacock-blue eye shadow and thick black mascara. Her lips are stained a pinky-purple.

I feel a quivering sensation in my chest. I cannot take my eyes off the picture of Kate Adams, but what I'm experiencing now isn't the envy I felt from the mortuary photos. I'm feeling horror, disgust, a sickness in my stomach that's making me heave. I can't restrain the anger for the loss of this woman, this victim. I feel it fizzing in every pore as the sadness and fury take hold. I don't understand why it's happening, but I do know what it means.

I have to find the Lover.

I have to kill him.

52

DOM

The witness lives in the first floor apartment. She's an older lady, hard to age due to her botoxed face and shoulder-length chestnut hair, but from the creping around her neck he guesses she's nearer seventy than sixty.

She flirts with him. Chattering away as she makes him coffee, after having insisted on giving him a drink.

Just tell me what you saw.

But she doesn't. She's drawing it out – having a murder squad detective in her home is exciting. Her eyes are bright. She keeps touching her chest and her face as she speaks. He's trying not to hate her. There's nothing exciting about a corpse, three corpses, five corpses and counting. There's loss, and pain, and anger, but never excitement. Never.

Finally, the coffee is made and she leads him to a dainty wooden table. She waves a hand towards one of the spindly chairs. 'Sit, please, Detective Inspector.'

He does as he's told, figures it's the best way to keep her on side. The quicker he finds out what she knows, the sooner he can leave. 'So, Mrs Edgecombe, DS Biggs tells me you witnessed someone entering Mr Eastman's apartment earlier this morning?'

'Yes, I saw her. Pretty young thing, she was.'

Dom tries to mask his surprise. 'Her? You're sure it was a woman?'

'I'm not completely senile, you know.' She winks. 'It surprised me, too – I always thought he preferred men.'

Dom doesn't comment. He takes a sip of his coffee. It's too bitter. He puts it back on the coaster. 'Lovely coffee,' he says. 'Could tell me what you saw, from the beginning?'

277

She touches her fingers to her chest, playing with the lace of her collar. 'Of course, Detective, it would be my pleasure.'

He nods encouragingly.

'I don't sleep so well these days. I woke up, let me see, must have been around one o'clock, no, later, about two-thirty.'

'And that was when you saw her?'

'Indeed. I'd gone to get a glass of water and realised I'd not pulled the curtains at the front.' She gestures to the long gold curtains dressing the front window. 'So I go to do it, and that's when I see her.'

'Go on.'

'She's trotting down the steps to Mr Eastman's.'

'And?'

'That's all. I pulled the curtains and went back to bed.'

'So you didn't see her leave?'

'No, as I told you, I went straight back to bed.'

'Did you hear anything from downstairs?'

She laughs. 'No, but I hardly would, now would I? There's another apartment between me and Mr Eastman. Even when he was having one of his parties it never bothered me.'

'Parties?'

She gives a wave of her hand. 'You know how young people are, always gadding about. He had all sorts over, you know, but never the same ones, always different.'

Dom nods. 'Can you describe the woman you saw?'

'Oh yes, I got a good look at her. She was about my height, I'd say. Slim, although not as slim as me.' She gives a little laugh. 'And she had dark hair.'

'What was she wearing, can you remember?'

She pats him playfully on the arm. 'Of course, Detective Inspector, I'm not *that* old. She wore a great big coat with a fur trim around the hood. I don't know what colour.'

Mrs Edgecombe's hand is still resting on his arm. He doesn't mind; she's been helpful, more so than he'd anticipated. 'That's great, thank you. You've been a star.'

'Well, I do like to be useful.' She flutters her eyelashes. 'Now, can you tell me about the murder? What did they do to Mr Eastman, how did they kill him?'

'I'm sorry, I'm not allowed to divulge that information.' Dom moves his arm, causing her to remove her hand. Her excitement at her neighbour's death sickens him. 'It would be very helpful if you could give the description of the woman to one of our trained eFit officers, and work with them to get a good likeness. It would really increase our chances of finding her.'

Mrs Edgecombe beams. 'Of course, Detective Inspector, whatever I can do to help. Now would I need to come to the station with you to do that?'

He's back at the office by 10.30. The open plan is busy, every team member chasing down leads, conferring over their notes, looking for new angles. Dom isn't feeling the buzz, though; he feels knackered. The lack of sleep is messing with his head.

Parekh accosts him on the way to his workstation and shoves a couple of forms in his face to sign. As he hands them back he says, 'Team huddle in five. I need anything we've got that's viable for the press conference.'

'Yes, guv.' She tucks the forms into her file and hurries away.

Dom reaches his desk. That's when he sees it.

Propped against a stapler in the middle of the desk is a white envelope. His name, rank and address are printed dead centre. *Private & Confidential* has been stamped in the right-hand corner. *Urgent* is stamped on the left. He can take a good guess at what's inside.

He snatches up the envelope and tears open the top. Pulling out the pages inside, he scans them. He was right. It's the transcript of his interview with Holsworth; the seeds of doubt he'd sown about Darren Harris laid out neatly in Times New Roman with double spacing.

'Guv?' Abbott says.

Dom doesn't acknowledge him. He speed-reads the letter paper-clipped to the front of the transcript. It tells him to sign the document to say it's an accurate reflection of the interview, and bring it to a follow-up interview that afternoon at 4.30. The

IPCC are looking to make a decision on their recommendations from the investigation by the end of the week. Dom wonders if Therese, Lindsay and Harris have received similar envelopes. He wonders what their letters say.

'Hey, you OK?' Abbott says, louder.

'Yeah. Fine.' Dom shoves the pages back into the envelope, folds it and tucks it into the inside pocket of his jacket. It feels as heavy as a brick. When he looks at Abbott he notices his eyes are focused on the spot where he put the envelope.

'More IPCC crap,' he says, then jerks his head towards the other end of the office. 'Incident room. Pre-press briefing.'

There's not much time. They stay standing, grouped around the murder board. There's a new photo on it: Eastman. Dom picks up a black marker pen. 'OK, what've we got?'

Parekh raises her hand.

He points the marker in her direction. 'Yep, go ahead.'

'The make-up, Glam Max, is in very limited supply. If our killer is solely using Glam Max, they could have got hold of some old products from an ex or family member who's been to South Africa, or they've ordered it and had it shipped. I'm trying to get a customer list from the only place selling the product online, but it looks like I'm going to need a warrant.'

'OK, keep on it. Anything else?'

She nods. 'As far as I can tell Eastman wasn't connected to Melissa Chamberlain romantically. I've spoken with her best friend. She confirmed Melissa did have a love interest, and that it was recent and got serious fast, but she's adamant Melissa told her he was blond.' She flips back through her notes. 'Enzo Metiz alibis out, Patrick Bartlett too; for all of the murders.'

'So they're off the suspect list?' Dom says. 'Shit.'

He puts a black cross through Enzo Metiz's photo and Patrick Bartlett's name. 'Can you recheck the dentist link? Melissa's dad mentioned she'd recently had dental surgery. I know we discounted it before as the victims had all visited different surgeries, but it's come up again. It's too much of a coincidence.'

Parekh makes a note. 'I'll do that. I'll also go through Kate's phone records, and back through Zara Bretton's and Jenna Malik's, to check for patterns. I've got Melissa's and Eastman's phone and financials on urgent request, so that's my evening sorted.'

'All right, good.' Dom looks at Abbott. 'Any luck with the eFit?'

'They're still working, it'll be ready soon.'

Dom glances at the clock. It's twenty to eleven. 'Look, I need it now. We'll have to work with whatever they've got so far. Can you nip down to the interview room and fetch it, and get enough copies to give to the media?'

'Guv.' Abbott gets up and hurries from the room.

Dom turns to Biggs. 'Anything else from the door-to-doors?'

Biggs looks unusually solemn. 'Nothing yet.'

'OK,' Dom says. 'Anything else to add?'

'I'm visiting the vic's work in a bit. Got an appointment with her manager at three-thirty, so I'll find out anything there that's relevant.'

Dom nods. 'Thanks, guys. Keep going, yeah. We've got to be getting closer to this bastard. Keep on doing what you're doing. We'll—'

The door opens. Jackson's assistant pokes her head round the door. 'He's wondering if you're ready, DI Bell?'

'I'm coming.' Dom looks back at the team. 'We'll regroup later. If you get anything meaningful in the meantime, call me, all right?'

He's in the corridor outside the press briefing room when his mobile starts vibrating. He pulls it out. Its buzzing sounds angrier than usual. Chrissie.

Dom rejects the call and switches the handset off. As he's tucking it back into his pocket, his fingers brush the folded envelope. How can he talk to Chrissie when he's about to sign a witness statement for the IPCC that says Darren Harris knew Genk, that he was inside the building when he should have been outside; that he most likely was the inside man for Genk? It'll wreck their lives. How can he do it to his own sister?

Through the open doorway he sees the journos seated on rows of chairs laid out theatre-style, facing the raised area where he'll sit beside Jackson. Every chair is full. The noise of chattering grows louder the closer they get.

Pushing away thoughts of Chrissie and Harris, Dom takes a deep breath and steps into the lion's den.

53

CLEMENTINE

Death Stalker's laptop is broken. I've reset his phone to factory
settings and destroyed the SIM card. I cannot risk the police
tracking it and finding me. They've found his body. I've seen
tweets about a murder near Liverpool Street station, and there's
been some speculation on True Crime London. It's not been
picked up by the Case Files group yet, but then, why would
it have been? The victim is male. That's not the Lover's MO,
not usually. There are rumours about another female victim,
though.

> **Ghost Avenger** posted in Case Files: The Lover
> Is there a fourth Lover victim? I just got to work so don't have
> full details yet, but there could be another Lover victim. From
> what the duty manager just said in handover the police want
> a rush job done on her. Vital stats seem to tally with the other
> victims. I'll find out more and report back.
> **Robert 'chainsaw' Jameson** Thanks GA. Not heard anything
> from @DeathStalker on this. He usually gives the heads-up.
> **Crime Queen** Not seen DS online today – anyone know where
> he's at?
> **Bloodhound** Please untag me if you post pictures of the victim
> on this thread @GhostAvenger.
> **Ghost Avenger** Will do @Bloodhound.
> **Ghost Avenger** Not spoken to DS today @CrimeQueen.

I don't respond to the thread. Instead I pick up the paperback I
took from Death Stalker's home – *Black Rose Chronicles*. It's seen
better days; the pages are yellowed and the corners dog-eared.
On the cover there's a picture of a mansion in ruins, standing

behind locked iron gates. Briars have grown over the ironwork, and among them are roses, withered and black.

Inside the book is a printed copy of an email sent by DS Abbott. It gives information held back from the media – how the killer uses anaesthetic on his victims, and how he applies superglue to their lips and eyelids.

The email refers to a retyped passage from the book – page 247. DS Abbott says the text was on a note found in Kate Adams's hand, and that a black rose was left on Zara Bretton's naked body. He says his boss believes the Lover is trying to recreate someone from his past. I think Dom's right.

I read the excerpt from the book. It's romantic, wistful – a lover yearning for their love – and I wonder if that's what the Lover believes himself to be.

I'm still thinking about it when a notification alert pings on my laptop:

Crime Queen posted in Case Files: The Lover
Crime Queen There's a press conference starting. The Lover is the topic. It's streaming live on www.capital-news-vlog.com

I click 'like' beneath the update and open the vlog in a new window. This press conference has been put together fast. I wonder if they've connected Death Stalker with the case; if they've found the woman he said he had found dead.

The press conference has already started. The video feed shows a long table with a bunch of serious-faced people in suits sitting behind it. One looks awkward, like he'd rather be somewhere else; it's Dom.

The older man sitting beside him looks more comfortable. He's talking about the case. Giving the names of two more victims – Melissa Chamberlain and Glen Eastman – found in different locations but believed to be connected. He appeals for witnesses to come forward.

I watch Dom. He's doing his best to sit still – elbows on the table, hands clasped together – but his leg is jigging beneath the table.

The camera moves away from the detective to focus on a man who can barely get his words out; his voice sounding increasingly strained as he talks about his daughter, Melissa. The effort of speaking about her looks like agony.

The man stops speaking and the camera pans back to Dom.

'. . . and so we're appealing for this person to come forward,' he says. 'We believe they may have critical information that can help our investigation of Glen Eastman and Melissa Chamberlain's murders.'

I lean forward. Is this witness the person Death Stalker got his new information from? Could this be the lead I've been searching for?

Dom is handed a sheet of paper. His expression changes from seriousness to shock. He blinks rapidly, fixes his expression back to serious and holds up an eFit picture. His voice sounds stilted as he says, 'And so, I repeat, if this is you, or if you know who this person is, please call us immediately on the number that's on your screen.'

I exhale hard. Slump back in my chair. A freephone number appears along the bottom of the video feed, but I don't register the sequence. I'm staring at the eFit.

It's a picture of me.

The notifications keep pinging on my laptop. I press mute. Need silence. I have to think through how I'm going to handle this.

I stare at the video feed from the press conference. The screen is paused and from the shock on his face, I can tell Dom knows the eFit is me. The thought makes me feel sick. What must he think? What does he believe me capable of?

He knows what you are. Murderer.

No. It wasn't me. Not this time. I want to stop more women getting killed.

I click on the notifications, and let them take me to the Case Files: The Lover page. Beneath Crime Queen's post about the press conference the replies are increasing.

Crime Queen @DeathStalker is dead. Eastman was him IRL. I just can't believe it. How did it happen?
Robert 'chainsaw' Jameson That eFit looks like @TheWatcher.

Seems weird. What would she have been doing at his home? I didn't think any of us knew where he lived.

Bloodhound What the hell's going on? Does this mean the Lover is on to us? Who spoke to DS last? What leads was he working on?

Justice League @DeathStalker's dead? I'm stunned. It's too horrible.

Robert 'chainsaw' Jameson Do you think, @GhostAvenger, that eFits are reliable? There have been instances when they point investigations towards the wrong person. How convinced should we be that @TheWatcher has some hand in this?

Ghost Avenger There's always room for human error, but it'd be quite a coincidence.

Witness_Zero: I guess it depends on what @TheWatcher was doing near @DeathStalker's place, doesn't it? Perhaps they have a thing? @TheWatcher – tell us what's going on.

Robert 'chainsaw' Jameson She seemed nice.

Bloodhound She did.

Crime Queen They're linking @DeathStalker's murder to the Lover killings. Do you think she's the Lover?

Justice League This is ridiculous!! How can you suspect @TheWatcher? She's one of us. It has to be a mistake.

Robert 'chainsaw' Jameson How could she be – the Lover sexually assaults his victims. At most, she'd be working with him.

Bloodhound Could it be a woman? Could the Lover use, erm, implements?

Robert 'chainsaw' Jameson IMPLEMENTS???? @Bloodhound?

Bloodhound Some kind of dildo?

Crime Queen I'm thinking about calling the hotline.

They're talking like I'm not here, watching. Maybe they find it easier to talk about me rather than confront me. I light a cigarette and take a long drag, holding it in until the smoke burns the back of my throat. I count to ten and exhale slowly, controlling the smoke's release. I have to respond.

> **The Watcher** It isn't what it looks like
> **Crime Queen** @TheWatcher EXPLAIN YOURSELF!

I stare at the shouty capitals and know I have to take charge of the situation. These people know what I look like and where I live. I cannot let them turn on me.

> **The Watcher** He asked me to come, but he was dead before I arrived. There was nothing I could do.
> **Crime Queen** So you left him there alone. YOU JUST LEFT HIM. YOU COULD HAVE STAYED. YOU COULD HAVE CALLED FOR HELP.

Even I can read the emotion in her reply. I wonder if Crime Queen and Death Stalker knew each other better, other than just from True Crime London. I click over to the private message screen and send her a DM.

> **The Watcher** to @CrimeQueen I am sorry, believe me. He must have died almost instantly. There was nothing I could do. If there had been, I would have done it.

No reply. I've lost her, and if she wants me out, I'll be cast from the group, maybe tipped off to the police. I need to get in front of this, address the situation so I can get on with finding the killer. I'm alone now, just as I always have been. It's probably better this way.

I toggle back to the Case Files: The Lover page and type a comment to the group.

> **The Watcher** I'm going to the police. There are things they need to know.

54

DOM

Dom legs it as soon as the cameras are switched off. The journalist's questions, and accusations, still echoing around in his mind: *Why haven't you made an arrest? Don't you think you should have identified more suspects? Why can't you match the DNA? Shouldn't someone better take over?* They jostle with questions of his own: *Who is she? Why was she at Eastman's flat? How does she fit with the case?*

His head's pounding. He rubs his forehead and tries to think about it logically, but it doesn't make sense. The woman in the eFit was at the club, too. It was a chance meeting; it couldn't have been planned, set up, could it? He took her to his home. Told her things. Liked her.

When did I become such a bad judge of character?

He's been compromised, that's the way the press will see it. Jackson, too. He's been in contact with a witness, or a suspect, in the hours before they were seen at a crime scene. Alone with them, getting drunk with them and, if the press gets a hold of it, they'll make out he was screwing her too. Jackson would have no choice but to take him off the case. He can't have that.

But if he fails to disclose and it gets out, he'll never survive it. Professional Standards will be all over him. Then the media coverage will become all about him, and he's the last person they should be concentrating on: it's about Jenna, Zara, Kate and Melissa. Eastman, too. It's about getting justice, but the journos won't give a shit. They're already hell-bent on making him the story, looking for a way to sensationalise it even more. If they discover his link to the eFit woman they'll succeed.

*

Behind him, the noise increases as people start to spill out from the briefing room into the corridor. He hears footsteps behind him.

'Bell?' Jackson's voice is raised above the chatter. Closer, too.

Dom turns. 'Sir?'

Jackson's expression is grim. He nods towards his office. 'In my office, now.'

Jackson plonks himself down onto his throne-like chair. On the desk, neatly lined up around his computer, smiling faces in silver-framed photographs look up at him like loyal subjects: his four daughters, his wife, his two Yorkshire terriers. But Jackson isn't smiling. When he speaks, his voice is calm with a core of steel. 'Is it my imagination or didn't we talk before about how I don't like being surprised?'

Dom's stomach flips. Has Jackson discovered he knows the woman in the eFit? Surely it's too soon. 'We did speak about it, yes.'

Jackson holds his gaze. 'You taking the piss, Bell?'

'No, I'm just being accurate.'

'You didn't think to tell me about the eFit?'

Relief floods through Dom, but he tries not to show it. 'It was being done right up to the last minute. Even I hadn't seen it before it went in the press packs. I made the call to include it. I thought that'd be what you wanted . . .'

'Yes, yes, it was a good decision – that's not the issue. I just wish I'd known about it first. I don't like to look a fool in front of the media.' He raises an eyebrow. 'None of us does, eh?'

Why haven't you made an arrest? Shouldn't someone better take over?

Dom looks down at his feet. 'No'

'So this woman, any idea who she is?'

Dom swallows hard. This is the moment to come clean. 'I didn't get a proper look at the eFit in the briefing.'

Jackson holds out one of the printed copies. 'What about now?'

He takes it, looks at the picture, at the woman's likeness. A memory of her handing him a tumbler of whisky pops into his mind. He hands the sheet back to Jackson. 'No.'

Jackson leans forward, putting his elbows onto the green blotter on the desk. 'Do you think she's got anything to do with the murder?'

'It's too early to say. We've been promised the forensics within twenty-four hours – we should know more then.'

Jackson nods. 'Hopefully we'll get something from the TV coverage, too.'

There's a ping from Jackson's computer. He looks at the screen. 'Message says the Crimestoppers number is flooded with calls, almost five hundred so far. Could be some good leads.'

'Yeah, hopefully,' Dom says. He doesn't hold out much hope, though. Although the public can and do help, often huge amounts of time are spent sifting through rubbish. He moves towards the door. 'If that's all, I'd best get back to it.'

'Holsworth's been in touch. Asked me to impress upon you the importance of turning up at four-thirty today.' Jackson fixes Dom with a hard stare. 'I told the jumped-up sod I would. So make sure you go. If it's any consolation he made it sound like it's the last time they'd need to speak to you.'

'I'll be there.'

'Good. We need an arrest, Bell.' Jackson gestures in the direction of the briefing room. 'That lot aren't going to keep snapping at your heels for long, you know. Pretty soon they're going to start leaping for your jugular.'

Dom thinks about the woman in the eFit and wonders how long it'll be possible to hide the fact they've met. 'Yeah. They are.'

As he heads back to the open plan, Dom feels the freeze-out even more acutely. The indexer from Ketterman's team has done a tea run, made everyone else a drink except him. Even Abbott seems to be avoiding him. He's about to ask Abbott what's eating him when his mobile buzzes. The number for the mortuary flashes on the screen. 'Doc? What have you got?'

'Not much.' Emily's voice echoes, like she's calling from a swimming pool. 'But it might help you narrow down your suspects.'

'All right, what can you tell me?'

Emily speaks, but the line's bad. Dom can't make out what she's saying. 'You're cutting out; say again?'

'I'll switch to the landline, this one's a—'

'No, don't.' He needs a break from the circus, from the people constantly surrounding him and judging him. 'I'll head over. I'm leaving now.'

He meets Emily in the morgue. The three most recent victims are laid on gurneys side by side – Kate, Melissa and Eastman. Emily is sitting over in the far corner, eating biscuits.

Dom raises his eyebrows and nods towards the biscuits. 'Those things will kill you, you know.'

'It's lunchtime, and at least I'll die happy.' Taking another from the pack, she dunks it into her coffee and takes a bite. She gestures to the other mug sitting on the stainless steel worktop. 'Made you a coffee. You know you look like crap, right?'

Ignoring her comment, he picks up the mug and takes a gulp of coffee.

'I saw the press thing on telly. They're bastards,' Emily says, offering him a biscuit from the half-eaten packet. 'You ever wonder if it's worth it?'

He waves the biscuits away. Glances across the steel and tile workspace at the three bodies laid out on the gurneys, their serene stillness disguising the brutality of their endings. He looks back at Emily. 'Yeah, and it is.'

She holds his gaze. 'You sure?'

He thinks of Melissa's dad, and his devastation as he glimpsed his daughter through the viewing window. 'Yeah.'

Emily munches her biscuit.

'So what have we got?'

Emily gets up and walks over to Eastman. 'Let's start with him.' She gestures to the wounds on Eastman's torso. 'From the angle and depth of these incisions, I've traced the trajectory the knife would have followed to the point of impact. From this, I'd say you're looking for a suspect of between six foot and six foot two in height.'

'Male?'

'Most likely, but the evidence doesn't conclusively indicate that.' She walks over to where Kate Adams and Melissa Chamberlain are laid out side by side. 'I noticed the other thing by accident.'

'What?'

'Come over to this side, so that you can view them together.'

Dom hasn't got a clue what Emily's going on about, but he goes with it and steps around the gurneys so he's beside her. 'What am I supposed to be looking at?'

'Always so impatient, Dom.' There's amusement in her voice. Her tone changes, becomes more serious, as she continues, 'Look at their left shoulders.'

Confused, Dom does as she says. He looks at Kate, then Melissa. All he sees are two young women who've been destroyed; lives cut short, families devastated.

Emily steps closer to the nearest gurney and points to Melissa's shoulder. 'Here, see these faint marks? They're bruises, finger-marks.' She walks to the second gurney, gestures to Kate's shoulder. 'We have the same pattern here, same angle.'

Now she's pointed them out he can see the yellowish marks on both women's shoulders. 'Meaning what?'

'From their characteristics and orientation I'm fairly sure the killer used his left hand to make them. He's been standing behind the victim, restraining them.'

'His left hand is his dominant hand?'

Emily nods. 'Precisely. Your killer's left-handed.'

'Anything similar on Eastman?'

'Unfortunately for us, no.'

55

DOM

Thirty minutes later he's back at the office. He pushes his way through the journalists gathered on the steps. Ignoring their questions and the taunts about lack of progress, he keeps his head down and hurries inside.

'Dom?'

Shit. It's Chrissie, in person this time. He shakes his head. 'Sorry, sis, I can't talk now, I'm—'

'Darren's had a letter.' She sounds flustered, manic almost. 'What's going on? Why are they doing this?'

Shit.

Dom takes hold of her hands. Feels her shaking beneath his grip. 'It's standard procedure. They're almost at the end of the investigation. I've had one too.'

'His meeting is five-thirty p.m.' Her words come out fast. 'He's been told to bring his rep.'

'So have I.'

She swears under her breath. Looks like she might cry. 'He's bricking it, Dom. You need to talk to him. Tell him it'll be—'

'I can't, sis. I've got the case.'

'Don't tell me that, not today, not now, it's not good enough.' Chrissie's voice is louder. 'Really not fucking good enough. He's family, he's—'

'Stop, please.' Over her shoulder, Dom notices the guy on reception watching them. 'I can't do this now.'

'I'm just asking you to—'

Dom lets go of her hands. Backs away, towards the door. 'I'm sorry, Chrissie, but no. I just can't.'

*

Upstairs, he tries calling Holsworth. He wants to warn him that he might have it wrong, that Darren Harris might not be mixed up with Genk, that it's possible DI Simon Lindsay sabotaged Operation Atlantis, or maybe even Therese. There's also what she told him Lindsay said about someone higher, one of the brass, being involved. He needs to tell Holsworth but he isn't answering, and Dom doesn't want to leave any details on a voicemail.

'Call me,' he says before hanging up. 'Call me urgently.'

Ten minutes later, at two o'clock, the team are gathered in the incident room. Dom takes a seat. He nods to Abbott. His DS points to a photograph pinned towards the bottom of the murder board. 'The lab's matched this shoeprint found on Melissa Chamberlain's door to the shoes Eastman was wearing when he died. That's a second connection to the scene, in addition to the fingerprint.'

'So are we considering him a suspect?' Parekh asks.

'No, we're fairly sure he's out of the frame for that,' Abbott says. 'I spoke to a writer friend of his, Freya Rowland, and he alibis out for the times Jenna, Zara and Kate were killed.'

'Not Melissa?' Parekh says.

Abbott shakes his head. 'No. He wasn't with Miss Rowland anyway, and given the evidence at that crime scene I think we can be fairly sure he was close to Melissa's flat around that time.'

Dom catches Abbott's eye.

'Yes, guv?'

'Emily, the doc, reckons the person who stabbed Eastman was between six foot and six-two. Probably male, although that's an assumption rather than confirmed.'

'That fits with the DNA results,' Abbott says as he writes the new intel onto the board. 'The DNA from the skin scrapings taken from behind Eastman's fingernails is a match for the DNA found at the crime scenes of Kate Adams, Zara Bretton and Jenna Malik. The DNA left on Melissa Chamberlain matches too. The woman didn't kill Eastman; the DNA is male.'

'Ruling her out as a suspect?' Biggs says.

Abbott nods. 'Possibly, although she could be his accomplice.'

Five victims. One killer.

'The doc also thinks the killer is left-handed, due to similar bruising patterns on Kate and Melissa's shoulders, but there's nothing to indicate whether Eastman's killer is left- or right-handed,' Dom says.

There's a knock on the door. One of the uniforms who has been helping them with the door-to-doors enters. 'DI Bell? I've got a message from downstairs. They're saying a woman's at the front desk asking for you. She'll only speak to you.'

'Did she say what about?'

'She says you're looking for her.' The uniform gestures towards the eFit pinned to the board. 'That's her.'

Interview room three is the biggest room in the interview suite, but today it feels claustrophobically tight. She's sitting opposite him. Clementine Starke, as he now knows her name to be; the woman from last night. She's seriously pretty; her long black hair accentuates the bright blue-green of her eyes. She's watching him, but he can't meet her gaze.

He looks down at his notepad, at the hastily scribbled questions he put together before coming in here. Grips his biro tighter. His mind's buzzing. Tension is making his jaw ache. He can't think how to start the interview; all he can think about is how he'd let her into his home, talked to her about his problems, and how he'd *liked* her.

Fuck. What kind of a game is she playing?

He can't let on that they've met before. Not now. If he was going to disclose that he should have done it after the press conference. He's left it too late. All he can do is treat her like any other suspect. If she's here to blackmail him, he's screwed.

He meets her gaze. 'So, Ms Starke, you—'

'Clementine, call me Clementine. Please.'

He nods. Keeps his tone businesslike. Tries not to let the tension show. 'All right, Clementine. Firstly, thank you for coming forward.'

She smiles. 'My picture is all over the news. I couldn't really not, could I?'

Dom glances down at the notepad. Uses the questions like a crutch, even though he's done interviews like this a thousand times. 'I need to run through some background stuff before we get started, is that OK?'

'Of course.'

Her smile doesn't waver, but he imagines he sees something in her eyes – confusion, doubt perhaps. 'You told the desk sergeant that this is your home address.' Dom takes a slip of paper out of the thin folder beside his notepad and slides it across to her. 'Is that correct?'

She glances at the location scribbled on it and nods. 'It is.'

He tucks the paper back into the file. 'And what's your occupation?'

'I'm a PhD student. Final year.'

Dom scribbles *student* on his notebook, and wonders how a PhD student can afford a place in such an expensive area of the city. What the hell is she mixed up in? 'What do you study?'

'People, and the psychology of how they interact online.'

He remembers what she'd said about her family being complicated and wonders if that's why she chose to study psychology. Last night, she'd been easy to talk to; it'd felt natural to share his fears about Operation Atlantis, and about what happened with Therese. Afterwards he'd slept for the first time in bloody ages.

Now she's a murder suspect.

He puts down his pen. 'As you know from the appeal, a witness placed you at the scene of a crime in the early hours of this morning.'

Clementine closes her eyes for a moment. 'Yes.'

'What were you doing there?'

She gives a little shrug. 'Just seeing a friend.'

But you were with me. Why did you leave without a word?

'At two-thirty in the morning?'

She meets his gaze and holds it. 'That's right.'

'Why?'

'He asked me to come over.'

Dom wonders if it was a booty call, if Clementine Starke and Glen Eastman were fuck buddies, or murder buddies. 'And was that usual in your relationship?'

'Sometimes.'

Dom glances towards the blacked-out viewing window, and wishes they were alone. Hates that Abbott is observing them through the glass. 'So you'd often meet him late at night?'

'No.' She looks away. 'But every now and then he'd message me and ask to meet up straight away.'

'And that's what happened last night, he messaged and you left where you were and went to him?' He lets the unspoken accusation hang between them: *you left me and went to him.*

'I'm parched, any chance of a drink?'

She's being evasive. What's she hiding, or is she just playing with him, delaying the moment when she talks about him?

'Answer the question, please.' Dom's tone is harder than he'd intended.

Clementine frowns. 'I thought I was here as a witness. Should I be calling a lawyer?'

He knows he should back off and try to recapture the connection they'd had last night. Get her to open up. That's what he *ought* to do. Instead, he leans forward and says, 'You tell me, should you?'

She slides her chair back, the legs grating against the floor like nails down a blackboard. When she speaks, her voice is whisper-quiet. 'I think someone else should interview me.'

She's going to say something.

Dom closes his notepad. Holds his hand up as if in surrender. 'Look, I'm sorry. Let me get you a coffee and we'll start over again.'

She stares at him for a long moment, then gives a curt nod. 'OK.'

56

CLEMENTINE

This isn't how I wanted things to go.

My heart's still pounding against my chest, as it has been ever since Dom closed the door behind him. I'm alone now, but I don't let my guard down. Can't. I know that I'm most likely being videoed by the camera wall-mounted high in the corner, and that there'll be people – other detectives, a psychologist, perhaps – watching me from behind the cover of the black-glass window. I hate them watching me, analysing me, judging me. I hate that Dom is, too.

Keeping my posture the same and my expression neutral, I look around the room. It's a poky box with no natural light. The vomit-green walls and lino floor give it a depressing, hopeless feel.

You belong here.

You deserve this.

I wonder what the psychologist is thinking about me. Do they think I had a hand in Death Stalker's murder? Do they realise that I'm capable of killing? Maybe they're telling Dom their initial impressions right now.

I fight the urge to retch, and focus instead on the fact that Dom didn't let on that he knew me. He acted like we'd never met. I wonder what that means. Is he trying to protect himself? Is he doing it to protect me?

You're not worth it.

I look down at the plastic wood-effect table. Run my hand through my hair, and twist a strand tight around my index finger. I wonder how much Dom knows about Death Stalker and what he was doing online; if he knows about *News Byte* and True Crime London. I wonder if he'll ask me about it when he returns with the coffee, and what I'll say in reply.

I've lied to the police before; when they came to interview me after Father died. I lied to save my own pelt.

I'm still in hospital, I don't know how much time has passed. Weeks, a month, it's impossible to say in the hot, muggy environment of the burns unit. I'm still on the painkillers, but they barely touch the pain. Under the bandages my arms feel like they're still burning.

They sit on either side of my bed, the police detectives; a woman and a man. The man is huge; tall and muscular. The softness of his voice when he speaks to me seems out of place with his size. The woman just watches, taking notes.

The male detective asks me to tell him about what happened before the fire started. Did you notice anything suspicious at your father's house? Was your father acting strangely? Did you see who started the fire?

As he asks the questions, the images from that day replay in my mind: finding the letter; discovering Father is a dirty copper; the shock of the cash, the drugs, the exploitation; Father's anger when he found me at the cottage. Starting the fire.

But I don't tell the detective those things. Instead, I keep my expression neutral, my voice flat, and I tell him I can't remember what happened before the fire started; that I saw nothing suspicious; that Father was just the same as normal; that I don't know who started the fire.

Lies. All lies. And yet they believe me.

Just like Dom will.

There's no proof for him to seize. I've destroyed the evidence – smashed the hard disc of Death Stalker's laptop, snapped the SIM in half and trodden the phone into pieces. I dropped them into various bins on the way, a one-and-a-half-hour detour from the straight route here, in places where the CCTV cameras are always vandalised.

But I want to tell him. I want to end the lies, the carefully constructed camouflage of my true nature, and come clean. I want to tell him the truth about last night, about the Case Files investigation. I want to tell him who I am, what I'm capable of.

The door opens and DI Dominic Bell enters carrying two mugs. He smiles as he sits down and pushes one of the mugs across the table to me.

Tell him now.

I put my hands on the table. The laminate's cold and sticky beneath my palms. I inhale, rehearse the words in my head: *You should arrest me. I've killed a man.*

57
DOM

Dom decides an apology is the best way to go. Clementine Starke looks serious, like she's revving up to have a go or say fuck knows what. He leans forward, keeps his voice low, speaking before she can. 'Look, I'm sorry if I came on a bit heavy . . . we, I, need your help on this.'

She bites her lip. Her eyes don't leave his as she leans forward and takes the coffee he's made her. Cradling the mug between both hands she says, 'OK.'

'Thanks. So, if we can pick up from where we left off, how would you describe your relationship with Glen Eastman? Was he a friend?'

Dom notices how the right corner of her mouth twitches at the mention of Eastman being her friend.

'I wouldn't call us friends. He was more of an acquaintance, I guess. He wrote for a news website. You might have heard of it, it's called *News Byte*.'

Dom clenches his jaw. *News Byte* – the website that's been churning out scandalised coverage of his investigation. 'I'm aware of it.'

'Well, I helped him out sometimes with his investigations, giving advice mainly, when something he was interested in crossed into my field of expertise.'

'And it wasn't unusual for him to ask to meet late at night?' Dom watches her closely, interested in how she answers, in the congruence, or lack of it, between her voice, her facial expressions and body language and the words.

'He'd get in touch at whatever time he needed help.'

'Did you ask him why he needed you to go to his apartment? What was so urgent it couldn't wait until morning?'

'It *was* morning, Detective, but I understand what you mean.' She glances away. The volume of her voice dropping as she says, 'No, I didn't ask.'

'Weren't you curious?'

'Naturally, but I thought I'd find out soon enough.'

Dom waits to see if she'll elaborate, but she doesn't. So far her responses have seemed genuine. He wants to trust her, he really does. 'It must have been a shock, finding him like that?'

'Yes.'

'I know this is difficult, but can you tell me how you found him?'

She puts the mug down on the table. 'The door was open and I remember thinking it was strange – he was a very private person, very security-conscious. He'd never leave the door unlocked.'

Dom nods encouragingly. 'Go on.'

'So I went along the hall and into the kitchen. At first I didn't see him, but I could hear the radio playing so I knew he must be around. I called out, but there was no answer, so I walked . . .' She flaps her hands as if to try and get rid of the memory. 'He was there, on the floor by my feet. I . . . I screamed. All that blood . . .'

Dom keeps his voice gentle, soothing. 'I know it's hard, but you're doing great.'

She closes her eyes a moment.

When she opens them, Dom asks, 'Did Mr Eastman have a laptop or a computer?'

'Of course, he was always writing.'

'We couldn't find it at his apartment. Do you know what happened to it?'

'I've got no idea.' Her eyelids flutter. 'I thought perhaps it had been taken.'

She's lying, definitely hiding something about the laptop. Dom holds her gaze. 'You saw it was missing?'

'Yes, I . . . I think so, I must have.' Her lower lip begins to tremble.

Despite her words and actions, in her eyes he sees nothing but calm. 'Why did you run, why not call 999?'

'I was afraid.' Her eyelids flutter again, and she looks away. 'I thought . . . maybe the killer was still there. I wasn't thinking, I just ran.'

Dom doesn't believe her. She's making the right moves, saying the right things, that a person reliving the horror of what they'd seen would do, but it's not genuine. The eyelid flutter indicates she's hiding something. He wants to know what it is and why she's not telling him. 'I'm sorry I have to ask you to go through it again, but it's important. I'll take down what you say, then ask you to read and sign it as your statement. Do you need a moment?'

'No, it's fine.' She smiles, and this time it reaches all the way to her eyes. 'It helps, you know, talking to you.'

It's one hell of a performance, but in that moment he sees a glimmer of truth. Her smile – the one she gave him as she said talking helped – that's the first genuine emotion he's seen from her since he started asking the questions. 'It's my job.'

'I know, but I feel I should help you out in return.' She leans across the table and whispers, 'Eastman had a lot of sources, people he paid to feed him sensitive information from live cases.'

Dom feels himself go cold. Shakes his head. 'You can't be accusing me of—'

'Not you,' Clementine Starke says. 'Never you. But you might want to take a closer look at that sergeant of yours.'

58

CLEMENTINE

Home.

I'm sitting at my desk, staring at the screen, but it's not the folder of Death Stalker's files that I downloaded onto my laptop I see, it's Dom's face – his disappointment that I was involved with Eastman. I *feel* it like a knife in my stomach, a dull ache leeching the energy from me.

The numbness is retreating, but I want it back. I try to banish his image, but I can't. He appears in my mind uninvited, and I find myself reliving the way he smiled as we smoked outside the club, the feel of his head against my thigh as he slept on the couch, the hard stare he gave me as I left the police building.

I run my hands through my hair, and clasp them over my head. Is this what addiction feels like? This craving sensation? This is pain.

A ping from my laptop alerts me to an incoming Skype call. It's Wade. I let it ring unanswered; two rings, three, four. The call aborts. Within a few seconds another call comes; it's Wade again. I know he'll persist until I answer. If I don't pick up on Skype he'll call my mobile, then the landline.

I press accept. Wade appears on-screen, looking unusually casual in a black t-shirt, greying stubble visible on his face. I've never known him not to shave. I don't give him the chance to speak. 'Look, Wade, I know what you're going to say, but it's all OK.'

He frowns. 'What happened?'

'It was a mistake.'

'So the eFit wasn't you?'

'It was.'

Wade curses under his breath. 'How? Tell me.'

'Death Stalker messaged me early this morning. He was panicking. Said he'd tracked the Lover and found his latest victim, but she was already dead. He was afraid the killer knew who he was. He asked me to meet him at his place.'

'And you didn't think to call the police?'

'We were so close. We could have found—'

'You could have been murdered too.'

I shrug. Pretend that wouldn't bother me.

He stares at me. 'You've invested heavily in this so-called investigation, but you need to end this now, Clementine. Before you get hurt.'

'Are you threatening me?'

'I'm serious, Clementine. You need to stop. If Death Stalker's gone, it's over. We can request to retract your thesis. You can rewrite your conclusion. It wouldn't take long – a month or two. You can resubmit, and no one will—'

I hold my hand up to stop him. 'That's not happening. Look, I've been to the police. I talked to Dom. It's sorted.'

'Dom? You're on first-name terms with that detective?'

'I've got everything under control.'

'No, Clementine, you haven't.'

'You were the one who told me to get my own police contact. I did what you said.'

'And how did you do it?'

I feel my cheeks colour and notice Wade's jaw clench as he sees. I don't answer his question. Stare straight into the webcam.

Wade shakes his head. 'You need to back off immediately. If he discovers what you've done – breaking into a crime scene, removing evidence – that's a prison sentence, Clementine.'

'He wouldn't arrest me.'

'Don't be a fool, and don't let this . . .' He waves his hand at me as if he's batting away an insect, '. . . this infatuation overrule your usual caution.'

Wade's furious; I can see it in his expression, I can hear it in the harshness of his tone. I've never known him this angry, but I ignore his jibe; refuse to rise to it. 'I said, it's under control.'

'You can't control people. Just because you've studied him, it doesn't mean you can manipulate him to do what you want.'

'I don't need to manipulate him or anyone else, I just need to be able to predict the killer's movements, and for that I have to work out what Death Stalker knew. If I go back through the information, follow each of the threads, I must be able to work out what happened, and then extrapolate that forward into what will happen.'

Wade's image pixelates before returning to sharp focus. 'With every new dynamic introduced, a new set of possibilities, actions and reactions become possible. You cannot control every variable, therefore you cannot predict all outcomes. Back off, Clementine. You are in danger here.'

Perhaps, but something Wade has said resonates: *every new dynamic*. The group has been changing, morphing from purely online to real world interaction. Each new dynamic has introduced new data, new perspectives. 'That's it.'

'That's what?'

'I have to go. I've got an idea. I think I can find him, Wade. I think I know how to reveal who he is.'

'No, Clementine, don't do this! You'll leave me no choice but to—'

I end the call, and Wade disappears from my screen. I know what I have to do.

I stare at the whiteboard. Everything I know about the murders – the evidence I've collected, all Death Stalker had on his laptop and phone, every bit of data the members of Case Files: The Lover contributed – is represented on the tangled mind-map of victims, suspects, places and evidence. I've tracked each piece of data back to its source. Along one side of the board I've written the name of each person in Case Files: The Lover. At the bottom I've written *LAB CONTACT?* – I've still found no details for him in Death Stalker's files.

I look for patterns. The victims are all female, all of a similar age, have all been made-up to look the same. All the places they've been killed are relatively central but, from what I can see, there's nothing that connects them. The killer's MO has remained the same: rose petals, candles and the changed appearance of the women. Killing Death Stalker was different, but then I'm assuming that was unplanned and opportunistic.

I know Death Stalker figured out the killer through the dentist link, but I can't work out how. There's something in the mind-map that I'm missing, not seeing, there has to be. Grabbing my phone, I take a picture of the whiteboard. I prefer to work alone, but time is against me and I need help. I open the CrimeStop app and upload the photo to Case Files: The Lover.

> **The Watcher** I've been to the police and answered their questions. I am not a suspect. I discovered that they don't know about us – they don't even know Glen Eastman was Death Stalker. Death Stalker shared some of the information he had with me. I've summarised everything into this diagram and added the data we'd already collected. If Death Stalker found the killer, there must be something here that tells us the Lover's identity. I can't see it. What do you see?

It's a selective version of what happened, but in essence what I've said is true. I hope they'll believe it, or at least believe it enough to work with me. Holding my breath, I press send.

I don't have to wait long for the comments.

> **Robert 'chainsaw' Jameson** That's an interesting perspective, but I see there are only two lines from my name to pieces of evidence. I can't believe that's correct. I'm one of this group's biggest contributors.
> **Witness Zero** We've got a lot of data, far more than I'd thought.
> **Ghost Avenger** I'm at work right now, but I'll have a proper look as soon as I'm on my break.
> **The Watcher** Apologies if I've missed anything, Bob. Let me know what and I'll add it.

Robert 'chainsaw' Jameson I'll DM you.

Justice League Glad things smoothed out with the police. I've printed the mind-map and will take a look now.

Bloodhound Well done for sorting things with the police. I'm assuming you didn't tell them anything about this group?

The Watcher You assume correctly @Bloodhound.

Crime Queen This is what you had planned all along! You wanted @DeathStalker gone so you could take over the group. EVIL TOXIC BITCH.

I stare at Crime Queen's comment. She could put what I'm trying to do in jeopardy by alienating the group from me. I need to get her onside, to persuade her I'm not her enemy. I've tried being practical; now I need another approach. Mirroring her might work; I decide to copy her shouty capitals style.

The Watcher I NEVER wanted this. I SAW WHAT THE KILLER DID TO HIM! I have to catch this bastard, FOR DEATH STALKER!

It's not the truth. I want to prove crowdsourced crime solving can triumph over the police, and make my thesis undeniably groundbreaking; I want to avenge these women, atone for my own wrongdoings and take down this killer who has violated them and changed them into something different from their real selves; I want to lead this team to victory and be accepted. I want Dominic Bell to respect me, like me, want me.

And, more than anything, the wolf inside me wants to taste blood again.

There's still no reply from Crime Queen. It's just gone half three, ten minutes since I replied. She's seen what I said, but she's choosing not to respond. I exhale hard and bang my fists down onto the desk. My coffee spills.

'Shit.'

There's a ping from my laptop.

Anonymous871 has sent you a direct message [click here to read]

I frown. Who is this? I don't recognise the name from True Crime London. Why are they messaging me? I click the link. The message is one word and a photo.

Anonymous871 to @TheWatcher BETRAYED

The picture is of Dom and me, taken last night when we were outside Crème in the smoking area. In it he's leaning close to me, whispering something in my ear. I'm smiling.

I reread the message. The avatar beside it gives me nothing to go on – it's a plain black circle, no photo, no graphic – but although the message is from someone calling themselves 'Anonymous', the accusation and capitalisation fits with Crime Queen. She hates that Death Stalker messaged me last night when he needed help. She thinks I betrayed him by not calling the police and staying with him until help arrived, even though it was too late. It stands to reason she'd think me talking to Dom would be a betrayal, too.

The Watcher to @Anonymous871 Crime Queen, is that you?

Three dots appear. Anonymous 871 is typing. I wait. The dots stop but no reply is posted. As I watch, Anonymous871's avatar disappears.

A standard notification appears beneath my message:

User **Anonymous871** does not exist. This account has been deleted.

59

DOM

Abbott frowns. 'So you think she was in on it?'

In truth, I don't bloody know.

They've been in the incident room debriefing on the interview with Clementine Starke for ages, but it's getting them nowhere. There's no evidence that she's involved, but something about her behaviour, the gulf between her emotion and her words, still grates on Dom. He's not shared that with Abbott, though. Could he really be the leak? 'She's hiding something.'

'Is it something relevant, though?' Abbott says. 'Could be she was shagging Eastman and is too embarrassed to 'fess up. There's nothing linking her to any of the female victims, and we know the killer is male.'

'True, but plenty of serial killers have hunted in pairs – Hindley and Brady, Fred and Rosemary West. She could be helping him find them, grooming them.' Even as he's saying it, Dom doesn't believe it's true. Doesn't want it to be true. 'And what about the missing laptop?'

The door opens and Parekh leans through the gap. 'Guv? Have you got a minute?'

Not really.

He nods. 'Sure.'

'We've been going through the phone records and financials. On the money side, there's a bit of credit card debt, but nothing dramatic. Their phone calls are all to known numbers. Melissa's check out as mainly work-related, Kate's are to friends and family.'

'I'm sensing a "but" . . .'

'I cross-referenced the spending of our four female victims, checking for patterns, and as you'd expect, dental work came up.'

'Yes, but not the same surgeries, we know that.'

Parekh nods. 'That's right, there's no connection on the face of it, but you said to dig more, so I've contacted each surgery and asked for the details of who treated each of our victims. I should have the data any minute now.'

'What about Eastman?' Dom says.

Parekh shakes her head. 'There's no debt on his financials. Nothing about dental work, either. I did find payments to a security company, though; he'd had cameras installed. I've asked for the footage from last night – they've promised it in the next couple of hours.'

'Good. How about his phone records?'

'All the calls and texts are to identifiable numbers, regular stuff – work, family and friends. He had a lot of internet usage, but we can't see what sites he visited.'

'Was Clementine Starke a friend he called regularly?'

'Not that we've found, but she told you he'd messaged her, didn't she? That could mean via an app – we wouldn't see that.'

'Good point. Look, keep on the dentist thing.'

'Will do,' Parekh says, ducking back through the door and closing it behind her.

Dom's phone vibrates in his pocket. Taking it out, he feels his heart rate accelerate when he sees it's from Chrissie:

Call me. Please. Darren needs you.

He knows he should call, but what the hell can he say? She wants him to talk to Darren and he can't do that, not right now. He needs to speak to Holsworth first; get his suspicions out in the open. Then he can repair the damage with Chrissie.

Dom checks his watch. It's nearly three; the interview is in an hour and a half. He can't be late, there's a lot to get through before Holsworth sees Darren at 5.30.

He looks over at Abbott, who's standing at the board, staring at the photos. 'I need to get off to the IPCC meeting. Can I borrow your car? I'll be a couple of hours. I'll call you if there's any news!'

Abbott hands Dom his car keys. 'No probs!'

Dom grabs his jacket and leaves the room. As he closes the door and heads for the stairs, his mobile goes again. He checks the screen, expecting the text to be from Chrissie. It isn't. Instead it's a withheld number.

The message says one word: BETRAYED

The photo attached shows two people: Clementine Starke and him, talking outside Crème. He's saying something in her ear; the pose looks intimate.

Betrayed – what does it mean? Is she working with the killer? Who sent this – and who else has seen it? Is she in danger? Is he?

He stares at the photo. Notices how she's smiling at him, and that he's smiling back. Remembers that in that moment he'd felt a spark of hope that he might be able to move on from what happened with Therese.

He needs to see Clementine. Needs to know what the message means and who sent it. He glances at his watch again; it's gone three. If he's going to detour via Clementine's flat before the IPCC meeting, he needs to leave now.

'Wait there, I'll come down.'

Dom stands two paces back from the doorstep, waiting. He knows this is risky; he doesn't have much time and he can't be late for Holsworth, there's too much at stake. But he has to know what the text means, and what the hell Clementine Starke thinks she's doing.

A minute passes. Then another. He wonders why it's taking her so long to come to the door, and why she didn't just buzz him inside and make him go up to her apartment.

He's debating whether to press the buzzer again when he hears the sound of the door being unlocked. She's wearing the same clothes as earlier, but her hair's twisted onto the top of her head in a messy bun. It makes her look younger. 'Hey.'

'I have a couple more questions.' Even he can hear the anger in his voice.

She frowns. 'Me first. Were you so very drunk last night that you didn't remember us meeting?'

'I remembered, I just couldn't say anything. When I first saw the eFit I thought it looked like you but I didn't see how it *could* be you. Then, when you showed up at the office, it was too late for me to admit we'd met before.'

'It was awkward.'

'Yeah, it was.' He keeps his expression serious, but he's feeling more hopeful; she isn't talking like she's out to blackmail him or betray him. If anything, she looks hurt he hadn't acknowledged they'd met. 'Look, can I come in?'

She shifts her weight from one foot to the other. 'I don't think so.'

'I got a text.' He holds his phone out to her.

Her eyes widen as she reads the message. 'Who's it from?'

'I don't know. I thought maybe you would.'

'Sorry, no.' She looks away.

'You sure about that?' Dom puts the phone back in his pocket. 'It says "betrayed", what do you think that means?'

She looks back at him. Holds his gaze a moment, then shakes her head. 'I really don't know.'

Although her words are calm there's worry in her expression. Dom thinks he's onto something. 'Did someone threaten you? Hurt you?'

She's shaking her head and moving back from the door. 'I think you should leave, Detective.'

He can't let her go yet. 'This text means something. Don't you want to work out what? We're both implicated.'

'I'm going inside now.'

'Don't.' Dom's phone starts buzzing. He ignores it. 'You know who murdered Eastman, don't you? You know more about the murders than you're telling me.'

For a moment she looks surprised. Then she shakes her head. 'No.'

Guilt. He sees it in her gesture. 'You sure?'

She recovers her composure fast. She looks at the pocket of his jacket where the phone's vibrating.

The call stops. There's a brief pause, then the phone starts again.

'Sounds like they *really* need to speak to you,' she says, stepping back and turning to shut the door.

With his free hand, Dom wrestles the phone from his pocket. The caller rings off. A moment later a text from Abbott appears on screen.

New suspect: Thomas Leopold. Answer your phone.

Dom looks back at Clementine. She's staring at his phone. Angling the screen away from her, he says, 'We're not done here.'

She gives him a sad smile. 'Yes we are, Detective.'

She shuts the door as he answers the phone.

'Guv?' There's a brief hesitation, then Abbott says, 'We've found the link between the dental work.'

'Tell me.'

'Thomas Leopold. He's a visiting specialist whose name came up on the consulting staff list at each of the surgeries. Parekh checked it out. He oversaw the work on each of the victims.'

Dom looks up at the top floor of the red-brick building. Wonders what Clementine Starke is doing now, before wondering why it bothers him so much. Shaking his head, he turns and hurries back to his car. 'And it's him?'

'The evidence points that way. He's six foot one, medium build, dark hair. The staff that worked with him described him as attractive, charming. A dental surgeon meeting patients, getting to know them on the side, that's how we think he did it. I mean, you'd trust a surgeon, right? They'd seem normal.'

'Yeah,' Dom says, opening the door and sliding into the driver's seat. 'You would.'

'We're en route now to pick him up.'

Dom taps the satnav screen on the car's central console. 'Give me the address, I'll head right—'

'Don't. Jackson told me you'd say that. He said I was to tell you to go to your meeting, that it's an order. We're pulling up outside now. I've got to go.'

Dom can hear Parekh's voice in the background, Biggs's too. They'll be hyped, adrenaline pumping and ready. He hates that he's not there with them. 'Do it then, Sergeant. Get the fucker and end this.'

314

'Yes, guv.'

Dom hangs up and drops the phone into the cup holder on the dash. He shoves the key into the ignition but doesn't turn it. Hesitates. Something doesn't feel right. He should feel relieved, excited, but he doesn't. He feels a void, like there's a gaping wound in his mind that won't stitch back neatly together. There's something more.

It has something to do with Clementine Starke.

Pain needle-pricks across the site of his old head injury. His eye flickers.

'Fuck,' he shouts, bashing his fists against the steering wheel. Gritting his teeth against the pain that vibrates through his body and into his skull, he fires up the car's engine and pulls out, accelerating hard.

A bloke in a suit is crossing the road twenty yards ahead. He jerks his head in Dom's direction, speeds up to get out of his way. Dom keeps his foot down. He knows he's driving like a twat, and doesn't care. It's almost four o'clock. He'll be lucky to make the meeting with Holsworth in time.

He hopes he hasn't left it too late.

60
CLEMENTINE

The buzzer goes again. Dom's persistent, I'll give him that. It is troubling we've both been sent the message *BETRAYED* and the photo, but unsurprising that we've each interpreted it differently. He doesn't trust me any more, he's probably right not to. I've lied to him, hidden the things I've done and refused to share information that could help him solve the case. He would be a fool to trust me.

I've already shared the suspect's name that flashed up on his phone – Thomas Leopold – with the Case Files group. We're closer – I'm closer – to finding the killer; I have to get to him before Dom.

And yet, even though I want to beat him, I'm happy Dom's come back. I want to answer the door. I want to see him. I take a step towards the intercom.

Wade's warning repeats in my mind: *'If he discovers what you've done – breaking into a crime scene, removing evidence – that's a prison sentence.'*

He's right. I can't risk letting Dom see what I'm doing. I close the lid of my laptop then snatch a cloth and rub it across the whiteboard, erasing the mind-map in large, sweeping arcs. When it's clean, I throw the cloth onto my desk, pick up the paperback of *Black Rose Chronicles* and shove it into a drawer.

The buzzer sounds again, longer this time. Hurrying to the intercom, I switch the speaker to two-way and say, 'Fine, Dom, if it's really that important, come up.'

I hit the button to release the main door. The speaker is still set on two-way, and I hear the bolt unlock four floors below, followed by the squeak of the front door as it's pushed open. Heavy footsteps. Then the door clicks shut. He's on his way up.

My heart's pounding. Excitement fizzes in my belly. The combination makes me feel both nauseous and elated. I tell myself I'm being ridiculous, that this is dangerous, stupid; I should not let Dom get this close. Still, I cannot resist this new feeling. I count to five, then draw back each of the bolts, undo the deadlock and unlatch the door. I don't open it, though. I can't appear too eager. I'll wait for him to knock.

He seems to be taking his time.

Going over to the window, I take hold of the curtains ready to pull them shut. That's when I see it. There's a gap between the vehicles parked lining the street; the gap is where Dom had parked his car.

I hear a creak on the landing.

Turning, I look at the door. The locks are unfastened. All my defences gone.

Why isn't Dom's car outside any more? Who have I let into the building?

What have I done?

Oh God, what have I done?

My heart hammers faster.

I hurry across the room. I have to bolt the door.

I manage three steps.

The knock on the other side of the door makes me jump. I'm too far away to reach the bolts. I'm trapped, a wolf in a snare. There is nowhere for me to run.

I watch the door handle slowly twist round. The door inches open.

It feels as if my heart might explode.

The man in the doorway has dark hair, but blue eyes rather than brown, a smile on his face instead of a perpetual frown.

Bloodhound smiles. 'Hey, Watcher.'

I'm confused. 'What are you doing here? How do you know this is my—'

'Loved your mind-map, very insightful. You might not see it yet, but you're closer than you think. The *Black Rose Chronicles*

317

connection and the dental brush, that's all you really needed. I was already on my way over when I saw you'd discovered my real name.'

'Your real name?' I frown. He's not making sense. I try to push the door shut. 'I don't think you should be here.'

He jams his foot against the frame. His blue eyes appraise me – scan from my face, down my body, to my feet and back again. 'You're wrong. I'm precisely where I need to be.'

I see the black holdall in his hand. The name badge hanging on a lanyard around his neck – Thomas Leopold. He lied. Bloodhound isn't called Colin Blunt; that's why there was so little information about him online, why I only knew the details about him that he shared with the group. Colin Blunt doesn't exist; Thomas Leopold is his real name.

'It's so easy to be anyone you want online,' he says, grinning. His teeth are white and too perfectly sized and straight to be natural. Lunging forward, he grabs me. His hand closes around my throat, and I realise my mistake too late; Bloodhound is a wolf in man's clothing. His threat level is off the scale.

He pins me against the wall. I punch at him with my fists but I'm too weak to do him damage. Ignoring the blows, he tightens his fingers around my throat, his eyes boring into mine; watching, waiting.

I open my mouth. Try to breathe.

Fail.

'Sweet how your detective friend rushed round here as soon as I messaged him that photo, isn't it?' Bloodhound winks. 'Could've been a keeper, that one.'

I can't escape. Black spots jig across my vision and the room blurs. My eyelids feel heavy, so heavy, and through the haze I see Bloodhound grin.

'Go to sleep,' he says.

I can't fight any more. Can't stay awake. I let the darkness take me.

61
DOM

He's over the river and almost at Holsworth's office when he gets the call. The phone vibrates in the cup holder, jumping about making one hell of a noise. Dom doesn't have hands-free; doesn't want to look a tosser with one of those earpieces. At this moment, though, he's regretting it.

Grabbing the phone, he presses answer and speakerphone and drops the handset onto his lap. 'This is Bell.'

'Guv?' It's Abbott.

'Yep.'

'Leopold's not here.'

Dom takes a left into the road the IPCC office is on. The traffic is stacked both ways. He brakes, taking his speed down to twenty. 'What?'

'He'd left the surgery by the time we arrived. We've got more evidence against him, though. The CCTV from Eastman's apartment came in while we were en route. We've got clear images of Leopold arriving and leaving. Parekh recognised him. He was in the Wetherspoons the night Kate and her friend were there – Parekh has an image of him from their CCTV.'

Dom grips the steering wheel tighter. Inches the car forward, closer to the bumper of the BMW in front with the *Princess On Board* sign in the rear window. 'So he's definitely our killer?'

'Yes, but we don't know where he is.'

'Fuck.'

'I've got an image, I'll send it to you.'

'Yeah. Do that.' Dom hears rustling at Abbott's end. 'So what's your next move?'

'We're driving to his home address now.'

Dom's phone beeps. He takes the handset from his lap and glances at the screen.

1 new message

'Hold on, mate,' he says to Abbott, as he opens the message. A photo fills the screen. Dom recognises him; the bloke crossing the road by Clementine's apartment as he'd gunned along the street. Dom only glimpsed him briefly so the memory is sketchy: dark hair, medium build, around six foot, carrying a bag. Dom shakes his head, can't recall what the bag looked like, but as he replays the scene over and over, something else does. The way the man moves – his gait, his posture – reminds him of the man on the CCTV footage outside Kate's flat.

'Guv? You still there?'

Dom's heart rate accelerates. He glances at the clock on the dash; it's 4.48. He's already late for the meeting with Holsworth.

He thinks about Clementine Stark. Thinks of how she looked as he asked her if she knew Eastman's killer; the shock she couldn't stifle fast enough. She knows more than she's letting on, Dom's damn sure of it, but what it is and what it means he doesn't know.

What if she knows what Eastman knew?

What if she saw the killer's face?

She could be next.

Checking his rear-view mirror, Dom yanks the wheel and does a U-turn. The noise of his heartbeat is thunder-loud in his ears. If he's right, if the man he saw is the killer, he's been at Clementine's place for over forty-five minutes already.

I can't let there be another one.

62
CLEMENTINE

The stench of petrol is acrid in my nostrils. I feel the one-two punch as I inhale the smoke and try to exhale. Breathless. Choking.

Father grabs for me, but we're too far apart and his fingers claw at the air. He's shouting, telling me to get out of the cottage. Telling me he's been set up. That he's not on the take. That he's doing his job; fighting against corruption at the very core of the police force. That he has to let them think he's been turned.

I'm crying. I don't know what to believe. But I'm afraid. The flames rise higher. The lights shut off as the electrics blow, cloaking us in murky shadows.

Father's gesturing, pointing above my head. The flames are licking along the timber beams, the embers glowing orange inside them like captive fireflies. He lunges for me, pushing me towards the door. The beam cracks and pops, buckling from the heat. There's a deep groan as it crashes down, hitting Father on the shoulder and showering us in sparks. Father loses his balance, stumbles onto his knees, his teeth bared in pain.

The burning timber divides us. The smoke thickens. Inferno hot. My eyes stream, my vision blurs. But I see movement, behind Father. A shadow dressed in black. It circles Father. I hear shouting, yelling, words too muffled by the hiss and roar of the flames for me to understand.

There's a strangled cry. Then no more voices.

I hurl myself across the burning timbers. Father's silent. His eyes are wide, bulging. He falls backwards onto the carpet of flames, his chest a mess of crimson and black.

Dropping to my knees, I press my hands against his chest. It's wet, sticky, hot. Smoke attacks my eyes. Blinking, I look down and see Father's blood dark against my own skin. I am crimson and black too.

I can't breathe. I gulp the air but there's no oxygen, only smoke and death. Through the gloom I see the dark shadow coming for me. Rough fingers force my hands open; press matches into my left, a knife into my right. I'm too weak to fight back.

Their footsteps fade and I hear the door opening. The flames leap and roar from the backdraught. I look down at the matches and the knife and I know they killed Father. I throw them into the flames. Hear the door slam. The key turns in the lock.

I'm blind from the smoke. My breath comes in strangled gasps. I smell my own flesh burning and I know that I will die here. I lie down beside Father and give in to the nothingness.

63
CLEMENTINE

It's as if a thousand volts have lit up every nerve ending in my body and brought me back to life. My skin tingles. My mind swirls with the memories of Father, of the fire, of the fresh memory that someone else was there. That dark shadow of a man killed my father and tried to frame me. I have to know why. For the last twelve years I've believed I am a murderer. Now I'm doubting that is true.

I hear footsteps behind me. That's when I remember what caused me to black out – Bloodhound.

Holding my breath, I listen. He's behind me. Muttering under his breath. I can't make out the words over the pounding in my head and the music playing; I can't even recognise the tune. I feel groggy, disorientated.

He moves closer and I hear snippets of his words. '. . . so messy . . . bad girl, Veronica . . .'

Panic builds like a rising pressure within my chest. I try to swallow the fear, but my mouth's dry and the sour taste of bile stings my tongue. That's when I remember Death Stalker's files – the police evidence said the Lover uses superglue to fix his victims' mouths shut and their eyes open.

I try to open my lips, but can't. I try to press them together and still I cannot move them. The pressure in my chest increases. I try to move my hand, to touch my mouth. My hand doesn't move. I'm powerless.

Behind me, Bloodhound is humming tunelessly to the music.

My breathing quickens. My heart rate accelerates as the flight response kicks in and adrenaline hits my blood. My vision is blurred. I try to blink but I can't. I try again, and feel my right eyelid flicker. I wait a moment before trying again. This time I'm more successful. Slowly, my vision clears.

I recognise where I am; my bedroom. In front of me is my dressing table. I'm sitting on my desk chair, and I'm naked, but my skin does not look like my own. The lighter patches on my forearms from the skin grafts used to cover the scarring from the burns now match the rest of my skin. My pubic hair is brown, not black.

My breath catches in my throat as I see the plastic ties binding my wrists to the chair arms. I feel the same tightness from ties around my ankles and throat. Slowly I raise my gaze.

The face that stares back at me, reflected in the mirror, isn't mine, but I recognise her from the picture on Death Stalker's phone – the mid-brown hair, the black eyeliner and blue eye shadow, the purple lipstick. It's the face the Lover's female victims have all shared. I am next.

Helpless, I watch Bloodhound in the mirror as he finishes lighting a line of candles along the top of my chest of drawers. He's draped a white sheet over my duvet. Rose petals are scattered across it.

This isn't how it's supposed to end.

He turns and sees that I'm watching. He steps towards me. 'Don't fight. There's no point – the drugs I've given you have seen to that.'

The pressure in my chest feels as if it will crack my ribcage in two. I open my eyes wide. Try to scream, but still my lips will not move. The sound is audible only inside my head.

I feel his touch against my cheek. His breath is warm against my skin, and when I inhale I catch the faint smell of mint.

He looks into the mirror and meets my gaze in the reflection. 'Do you remember how we first met?'

I can't speak. Can't move. All I can do is stare at him.

He laughs. 'Of course you do. It was a month before my twelfth birthday. I was on holiday in South Africa.'

He straightens up and moves behind me. Strokes my hair with his left hand. There's a wistful look in his eyes. 'About a mile outside the boundary of my uncle's farm was an old barn. My cousins and their friends met there every afternoon. They let me go too. We'd play games, daring each other to walk across the high beams, or trying to shoot rats with our pellet guns.' He glances in the mirror, meeting my eyes. There's an intensity to his gaze that wasn't there before. 'The afternoon we met there was a new game.'

I blink twice. It's the only way I can respond, to try and encourage him to talk. If I can keep him talking it'll give me more time to figure out how to get free.

'Because I was the youngest, I had to go last. I waited my turn, listening to the other boys with you, the grunts and the moans, the giggles and the whimpers. A single scream.' He frowns. 'You were quiet when it was my turn. I saw your flowered skirt and red t-shirt folded neatly beside your bag, a copy of *Black Rose Chronicles* peeking out from inside. You looked so still lying on the hay, the ropes tight against your pale skin, your eyes open but not seeing me . . . I shouted down to my cousins, told them something was wrong, but they called me names – coward, pussy, wuss – said they'd take the ladder away and leave me there if I failed, if I couldn't prove I was a man.' His cheeks flush red. 'I was just going to untie you at first, so you could rest more easily. I was young, I know, but all the films and books told me there should be romance – wine and flowers, soft light and music. Still, I told myself there would be other times for that. You were so beautiful, but you were so beautiful, and I really wanted to be a man.' He exhales, long and slow. Grins. 'You felt amazing.'

Bile rises in my throat and I gag. My mouth won't open, but I feel like I'm going to be sick. I try to move my head away from him, but can't. Try to move my hands, but they won't budge. After all these years of numbness, of believing I killed Father, I cannot let Bloodhound kill me, now that I've remembered the truth. I let out a muffled cry.

The grin disappears and his face contorts into anger. His fingers dig into my shoulders. Pain spikes through me. 'Why did you have to take Death Stalker's investigation so seriously? He wasn't a threat before you joined in. I had my eye on him, could misdirect if needed and keep the group in the dark.' He clutches my shoulder harder. 'But you went and broke into that crime scene. You had to get chummy with that detective. You ruined everything. I wanted you, but I promised myself I'd save you for last – a proper challenge – but then you met *him* at that club, and starting putting things together.' He's shouting now. 'You forced me.'

He was following me, not Crime Queen. He went after Melissa when Death Stalker was getting close, and that put him in his sights, too. I want to ask him how Death Stalker found him, but I can't. My jaw aches. Feels heavy as lead. I keep trying, fighting.

Bloodhound presses his finger against my lips. 'Hush, Veronica, don't cry. You're perfect now.'

I look into the mirror. Veronica's face stares back at me. She looks afraid.

Bloodhound rummages in his holdall and takes out a pair of scissors. They're large, like the kind that dressmakers use. As he steps towards me I start to tremble.

Bloodhound looks confused. 'I won't stab you. That's far too messy.'

Opening the scissors, he slips one of the blades between my left wrist and the cable tie that binds it to the chair. The metal is cold against my skin where the dull edge of the blade digs into my flesh. He cuts the plastic, and repeats the process with the tie around my other wrist, then those at my ankles. As he slides the blade between my neck and the plastic restraint, I hold my breath.

I'm released from my bonds and yet still I cannot move. I cannot cry out – even though inside my head I'm screaming for him to get away from me, no sound comes out.

He puts one arm around my back and slides the other under my thighs. Scooping me up, he lifts me from the chair and carries me to the bed. He lays me in the centre of the white sheet and, with a look of intense concentration on his face, pushes my legs apart. I have no choice but to let him.

I wait for the violation to come, but it doesn't. Instead, he turns away and lifts a small metal tin from his bag. Removing the lid, he takes out a syringe and a vial. His hands are steady as he inserts the hypodermic needle into the top of the vial. He draws the drug into the syringe and keeps going until the vial is empty, then he steps towards the bed.

No. It cannot end like this. I can't let it. I concentrate on my hands, my fingers. Will them to move.

Nothing.

I focus on my right hand. Feel my fingers twitch. Try harder.

His eyes are on mine as he leans over me and brushes his lips against my forehead. 'I'm sorry, Veronica. Now I'm going to have to hurt you.'

64

DOM

She's not responding. She's not fucking answering.

Dom stabs the buzzer with his finger again. Repeats the action, over and over.

Nothing.

He steps back from the doorstep, squinting up at the top-floor flat's windows. 'Clementine Starke,' he shouts. 'Clementine?'

Again, nothing.

He goes back to the entry system. Presses every button in turn. 'Come on, answer the bloody thing, someone answer, for—'

'Yes?' A woman's voice, not Clementine, answers. She sounds pissed off.

Dom talks into the speaker. 'This is Detective Inspector Dominic Bell. Please open the door, one of your neighbours is in danger.'

Silence. Then the intercom crackles. 'Show me some ID.'

He looks around. Can't see a camera. 'How?'

'The glass spyhole in the door, hold it ten inches away.'

Dom swears under his breath, but does as she says. He holds his warrant card up and shouts towards the intercom. 'There. See it? Let me in.'

The door unlocks. Dom shoves it open, not stopping to hear what the woman's saying through the intercom. His footsteps echo off the black and white tiled floor as he sprints along the hallway. Grabbing the banister, he hauls himself up the stairs, taking them in bounds, two at a time.

Clementine lives on the fourth floor, he knows that from the address she gave earlier. If that bloke crossing the road was the killer, if he came here and she let him in, then he could have been up there for almost an hour. An image of Kate's body laid out on her own bed pings into his mind.

Dom pushes himself faster. His lungs feel as if they're about to explode. He reaches the top floor. Sprints towards the only door: 48D. His breath is coming in gasps. He bangs on the door, shouting, 'Clementine Starke, this is the police.'

Silence.

He tries the handle. It's locked. Thumps the door with the heel of his fist, louder, harder. 'Open the door.'

Again nothing.

In his mind's eye he sees Melissa, dead but sitting upright, her head slumped forward, the noose around her throat holding her captive.

He steps back. Aims. Kicks hard, his heel connecting with the bottom of the lock mechanism and the wood surrounding it. The timber splinters on impact. Dom feels the aftershock vibrate through his leg, his hip. The lock's still holding, but the wood around it is not. He slams his shoulder against the door, once, twice. It gives way, swinging open, propelling him into the flat.

'Clementine?' he shouts, stumbling forward, just managing not to trip.

Still nothing.

Is she here? Am I wrong?

There's no sign of anyone. It's bizarre. There's music playing – some eighties crap, Simply Red, he thinks – but the volume's not that high. Whoever's here must have heard him kicking the door down, so where are they?

He spots a woman's bag half-open on the red sofa, its contents spilling out onto the turquoise throw. A phone lies on the floor; its screen is shattered and lifeless.

Is he here? Is she his prisoner?

There are two doors leading off the living space. One is the bathroom; he can see the tiled floor and the corner of the wash-basin from here. The other door is shut.

Four strides and he reaches it. Yanking the handle down, he shoves the door open. 'Clementine Starke, this is the . . .'

She's naked. The bed she's lying on is covered in a white sheet and strewn with petals. The man beside her has his back to the door. He's bending over her, obscuring the upper half of her body and her face from view. On the floor beside the bed is a black doctor's bag.

It's him.

Clementine isn't moving. Dom can't tell if she's dead or alive. He has to get to her. 'Stop. Police. You're under arrest.'

The man turns as if he's moving in slow motion. He twists at the waist but his feet don't follow. He drops to his knees.

He jerks his head to the right, and that's when Dom sees the syringe. It's sticking out of his left eye, the plunger depressed. Empty.

He looks at Dom with unfocused eyes. Tries to shuffle across the floor towards him. He's trying to say something, his mouth opening and closing like a landed fish. Dom can't make out the words.

He falls to the ground. Eyes open. Gone.

65

CLEMENTINE

'Clementine, can you hear me? It's over.' It's Dom's voice, close beside me.

I start to whimper. Don't open my eyes. Can't, not yet. The pain won't stop. It keeps building, the napalm in my blood sending a continuous ripple of explosions through me until it feels as though they will split me apart.

'Breathe, Clementine. You're in shock, but you're safe. Breathe in. Breathe.'

I exhale too fast. The breath grates across the back of my throat, choking me. The void it leaves in my chest is a vast ache of grief. Rolling onto my side, I curl into the foetal position. It feels as if I'm imploding.

I feel a hand on mine. Warm. Squeezing. I hear Dom's voice, closer now, saying, 'Clementine. For fuck's sake, breathe.'

Opening my eyes, I see Dom staring at me. I breathe in. The pain ebbs a fraction. 'Sorry,' I try to say, but through my closed lips the word is just a mumble.

Dom frowns, and for a moment it looks like he doesn't know what to do. He looks from me to Bloodhound's body lying on the floor at his feet, then back to me. There's a mixture of shock and relief on his face then, as he holds my gaze, his expression hardening into something else. Anger.

Murderer. He's seen what you are.

The voice inside my head was wrong about Father; it always has been. I know that now. So I cry. I really let go. Let the sobs burst from deep inside me, twelve years of stored-up loss and guilt and sadness. Tears that I've never felt the need for until now flow down my face, washing away the make-up. Erasing Veronica.

Dom grabs my robe from the back of the door and covers me. His scowl is gone. There's concern in his eyes. 'Clementine, are you hurt? Are you OK?'

Shivering, I pull the robe tighter around myself. I'm cold, and every nerve in my body is jangling, but I'm glad. I realise that it means I'm whole, real. Alive. I survived the fire and the dark shadow that killed my father, I survived Bloodhound trying to kill me and now I'm feeling something again – glorious and terrible, suffocating and overwhelming emotion. It's what I've yearned for all these years. I'm beginning to believe I can survive it too.

I look up at Dom and try to smile.

Everything happens so fast.

Dom's asking questions and I'm answering, trying to write down answers although the pen feels heavy, my movements unco-ordinated. More people arrive and they're talking, too. Dom is pushed further away from me. Then another detective, one I recognise from the press conference, says something to him and he frowns. He looks over at me, holds my gaze for a moment, then turns and follows his colleague out of my flat.

I remain, as do the people and their questions. As stern-faced people in white paper suits take things away in clear plastic evidence bags – the bed sheet, my laptop, my phone and Bloodhound's bag – questions and answers and more questions are fired at me. I nod, and I shake my head, and I try to tell them what I can, what I'm able to. I feel grateful, so very grateful, that I have survived, but I cannot rid myself of the nausea, the horror, the stifling fear I felt with Bloodhound and the knowledge that those other women, his previous victims, died with that feeling as their last.

I tell them what happened. They believe me, I think, but they keep on asking questions. Keep saying it shouldn't be possible for someone in my condition to have fought back. Say it's a miracle I'm not dead.

I nod. It's best if they put it down to a miracle so I don't tell them about the fury. How I gave in to it and let it take me over.

How I unleashed the wolf and let her fight to the death.

Murderer.

66

www.darkstreetsdarkcrimes.com

*Bringing you off-the-record crime news as it happens – pop back
soon for more . . .*

THE END OF THE LOVE AFFAIR [posted 17:43 by Crime Queen]
The rumours are true – THE LOVER is dead. Sources say it
happened this afternoon as he tried, but failed, to claim another
victim. She, according to my intel, is at Hammersmith Hospital
getting checked out.

UPDATE: THE LOOK OF LOVE
It's been revealed that the twenty-seven-year-old woman who
fought off THE LOVER was a friend of Glen Eastman, the freelance journalist who got too close and became the killer's fifth
(and first male) victim. Seems the amorous murderer spotted her
and decided he liked what he saw. Tried to make her number six.
More fool him!

UPDATE: ALL YOUR FEARS ABOUT DENTISTS CONFIRMED
Sources tell me becoming the object of THE LOVER's affections
wasn't down to chance. His first four female victims had dental
work done prior to their murder. THE LOVER selected his victims
from the women visiting him – a cosmetic dental surgeon – for a
consultation. Turns out we're RIGHT to be scared of going to the
dentist!

UPDATE: NO CHARGE – IT'S SELF-DEFENCE, DARLING
At last, the powers that be have decreed the twenty-seven-year-
old woman who wrestled THE LOVER's lethal injection from him
and stabbed him with it acted in SELF-DEFENCE. Hurrah for girl
power! I hope to be chatting with her soon.

NINETEEN DAYS LATER

DOM

'It's bollocks, that's what it is.'

Sitting behind his desk, Jackson frowns at the profanity but doesn't pull him up on it. 'It's the process, Dom.'

'Like I said, it's bollocks.'

'We've been over this already. The IPCC are within their rights to suspend Darren Harris. You didn't show at the meeting, so they made a decision in the absence of further information being forthcoming.'

Dom says nothing.

Jackson shakes his head. 'Look, with the next round of budget cuts coming we need to do anything that'll make the powers that be look at us with a bit of favour. You just need to sit tight. Do the interview with Holsworth on Monday, and get things straight. Things will work out.'

'Yeah.' Dom hopes his DCI is right. Once the stuff with the IPCC is done, he knows he'll need to tackle Abbott about the information he was allegedly leaking to the press. He hasn't forgotten what Clementine Starke told him, but he hasn't told Jackson about that yet. Wants to have evidence to hand when he does. He can only cope with one internal investigation at a time.

The only positive thing to come from his missing the IPCC interview is that they caught Thomas Leopold – the Lover. Or at least, Clementine Starke caught him. Dom shivers at the thought of her name. Of the lies she told him or, at least, the things she didn't tell him that she should have.

Jenna Malik. Zara Bretton. Kate Adams. Melissa Chamberlain. Glen Eastman. Leopold had picked his victims as they made arrangements for their cosmetic procedures, all except Eastman and Clementine. The DNA matched. They'd found a polaroid camera in the bag he took to Clementine Starke's flat, and at his home, hidden inside a battered old armchair, they'd discovered a stack of photos, hundreds of them, dating back to the eighties. All the women in them had been made up to look the same, although there were only five who'd been photographed dead; the last four and the first.

'Look, I know you had a few doubts about Clementine Starke, but she's been nothing but helpful. Her only crime was being a friend of Eastman.' Jackson says.

Dom purses his lips together. Doesn't speak. Jackson doesn't get why the truth about Clementine Starke – her involvement in True Crime London, and the research she's been doing online – bothers him so much, and he can't explain. She should have told them about True Crime London before, and she should have told them she knew Leopold as Bloodhound, even if she thought his name was Colin Blunt. And, even if she didn't feel she could tell him as a police officer, she could have told him off the record. She should have told him. He'd given her enough chances.

'She was in the wrong place at the wrong time, that's all – being on that online forum thing attracted the attention of our killer.' Jackson peers at Dom over the top of his glasses. A fatherly look that said *I know what I'm talking about.* 'You took her statement. Leopold was guilty, not Clementine Starke.'

He *had* taken her statements. She'd been subdued, in shock; speaking hesitantly and largely avoiding eye contact.

Dom rubs his forehead, trying to ease the pressure he can feel building. 'I still don't like it. I mean, self-defence, really?'

Jackson sighs, knowing they've been through this many times already, and knowing Dom's going to keep pushing. He sounds resigned to going over it yet again as he reels off the facts. 'You've seen the report. With the amount of drugs he'd pumped into her system it's a miracle the poor girl managed to move at all, but she did. When pushed to extremes, people can do remarkable things – it's the primal flight or fight response. Hers was very strong.'

The moment he'd held Clementine Starke in his arms replays in his mind. He remembers how blood oozed from where the plastic had scored into her flesh, staining his hands; how cold she'd felt; and the gut-wrenching sound of her sobbing. He tells himself he's being unfair. Letting his anger over her not telling him about True Crime London colour his judgement. 'Yeah, I know.'

'So let it go, Dom. It's over.'

'I guess.' But if it *was* over, if he'd got justice for Jenna, Zara, Kate and Melissa, why do they still haunt him? Why does he lie awake, unsleeping? Why does he punish himself in the gym for hours every night? Why does he see the dead girls' faces on every woman he speaks to? And why can't he stop thinking about Clementine Starke?

'Good. Don't forget, you owe me.' Jackson raises his eyebrows.

Dom gets the message. If the DCI hadn't stepped in to sweet-talk Holsworth things could have gone very wrong with the IPCC. He'd have been waist-deep in shit, even more than he is now.

Chrissie still won't talk to him. She'd left a message on his voicemail as soon as Harris told her he was suspended. Her voice was tight, her words stilted. Disappointment and anger were audible in every breath as she said it was his fault Harris had been suspended, and that there was talk of a criminal investigation. Told him if he'd bothered turning up to his own interview things would have been different, but that he never gave a crap about her, about family, and this bloody well proved it. From now on, as far as she was concerned, she had no brother. It wouldn't be much of a change.

It was the hurt, the fear talking, Dom knew that, but it didn't change the facts. He had not taken responsibility. She'd trusted him, depended on him to come through for her like he always had since their parents died, and he had let her down. He'd felt it, like a punch to the chest, as Chrissie's voice cracked when she said goodbye and he fought to stifle the sob welling up inside him as the voicemail ended. But still, he knew – Chrissie was right to get shot of him.

Out of habit he takes out his phone and checks to see if he's got any texts.

338

He feels a moment of hope, then he reads who it's from and adrenaline spikes his blood. Clementine Starke. Her words are brief and accompanied by a geotagged location.

I have to see you. Now. Please come.

ACKNOWLEDGEMENTS

Writing a book means sitting on your own at a keyboard for hour upon hour. It sounds like a lonely process, and it would be if it wasn't for the wonderful people I have around me, and who kindly forgive me for my reclusive ways when I'm absorbed in creating my story.

First thanks must go to Jock. *My Little Eye* started life as an idea that came out of one of our many conversations. I can't remember exactly what he said to spark the idea, but I know it was a long and lively debate about conspiracy, true-crime fans and social media. I was on the train home when I wrote the first scene with Clementine.

I also owe Laura Wilson a huge debt of thanks. Laura – without your expert mentoring and guidance this book would never have happened. Thank you so much.

Massive thanks to my subject experts – to Dave for teaching me about policing (and Cathy for keeping us piled up with food and wine); to Dr Chris for keeping me true on academic theory and research, and to Tors for her medical knowledge – these guys totally know their stuff, so any errors are absolutely mine.

I remain eternally grateful to Andy and Helen for reading sections of the story when I lost confidence, and for telling me it'd be OK – you guys are awesome, and your support means everything.

A thankful shout out to the City writers group – Rod, David, Laura, Rob, James and Seun – we started this journey together and I love that we're continuing it shoulder to shoulder. You guys rock!

As do my crime-writing sisters – Susi, Alexandra and Helen – who continue to keep me sane with a heady mix of laughs, hugs and wine. Your input is always spot on, and I love you muchly!

The crime-writing community is such a lovely place and crime writers are the most generous bunch of people. I've met amazing friends, laughed till I've cried and learnt a huge amount from you all. Thank you. Please keep the advice and the smut coming!

I'd also like to say a huge thank you to all the readers and bloggers who've been so supportive and cheered me on via social media and IRL – bookish people really are the nicest folk! A special mention goes to Liz Barnsley, who championed this book from an early stage, and continues to pimp it wherever she goes – Liz, you are legend.

Massive thanks to my brilliant agent Oli Munson and the team at A.M. Heath for having faith in me and helping me navigate a whole new world. And to the Trapeze team and my super-fabulous editor Sam Eades – for her tireless enthusiasm, pitch-perfect input and for helping me craft and polish this book into the story that it is today. I love every moment of working with you.

And last, but absolutely not least, to my family – to Mum and Richard, Dad and Donna, to Will, Rachael and Darcy – thank you for always being there and for supporting me no matter what. And to Pod, who showed me you can achieve anything as long as you apply enough determination (and gin!).

AUTHOR Q&A
WITH STEPHANIE MARLAND

Clementine Starke is a strong, complicated character. Did you have a clear idea of her from the outset, or did she develop as the story gained pace?

I had a clear sense of her voice and peculiarities from the beginning but it took me a number of drafts to get her side of the story to a place I was happy with. A lot of that was due to her unpredictability – as a character she's by nature inconsistent, yet I needed to have her actions consistent enough to be believable, while being inconsistent enough to be true to her nature. Another challenge was writing a character that's numb emotionally, and therefore has very little empathy or emotion towards others, but still making her someone the reader can get behind. Through the editing process, by tweaking her character and emotional journey a bit more each time, I was able to refine her into the character she is now.

Clementine joins an online 'true crime group' and becomes involved in the live pursuit of a serial killer. This is such an original idea - what inspired you?

The idea of Clementine came out of a conversation with a friend about conspiracy theories and true crime, and how through social media we have access to far more information, far faster, than ever before. The way true crime draws people into trying to solve crimes that have gone unsolved seems to have accelerated and there are an increasing number of television programmes and podcasts dedicated to true crime. Now there are numerous online groups of true crime fans that come together and try to solve cold cases. It got me to thinking about where the phenomenon might go in the future, and I wondered 'what if a true crime group decided they could beat the police at their own job?'. I wanted to explore the idea, the personalities attracted to doing something like that, and what lengths they might go to find out what really happened.

Another key figure is DI Dominic Bell, and the dynamic between him and Clementine is fascinating. As a writer, how do you get inside a relationship like this?

As Clementine is quirky and unconventional, and not used to allowing anyone to get close to her, any relationship she has is going to be rather unusual. Dom has his own baggage and is also, for much of the book, the rival of Clementine and the true crime fans. To get inside their relationship I found I had to write their joint scenes from first one of their perspectives (usually whoever was point-of-view character for the scene) and then switch into the other character's perspective and write their responses and reactions to the point-of-view character. This was how I wrote most of the book – by immersing myself in one character and writing all of their chapters in sequence, then swapping to the other character and writing their story from start to finish.

The London locations feel important to the telling of the story. Do you think the story could have worked so well in a different landscape?

For me it was always about London – there's something about the city that is both comfortably familiar and impersonally vast. It's a place where you can be completely surrounded by people and yet still feel entirely alone. I wanted to capture the contrasts within the city – the bright lights and the grimy underbelly – and used a variety of areas and locations I've spent time for inspiration when writing the key scenes.

The killer quickly becomes known as 'The Lover' as he leaves his victims carefully arranged and surrounded by petals. This was particularly chilling - where did the idea come from?

I've always found images more impactful if they're the opposite of what's expected. There's no blood and gore in The Lover's usual MO, but by taking what's usually a romantic gesture – candlelight, rose petals, wine, soft music – and subverting it, to me it seemed both more chilling image and a physical representation of the abuse of trust that each of the victim suffered. The Lover changes his victims' appearance to fit his own romantic ideals, robbing them of their own identity. The loss of identity is a continuing theme within the book – Clementine's struggling to face up to her true nature and finds it easier to interact using a fake online profile than her real life identity; DI Dominic Bell has become his work persona at the expense of his personal life – the serial killer's victims having their appearances altered mirrors this. It also highlights DI Dominic Bell's primary drive – that every victim deserves justice – he won't rest until he's caught the man who stole their lives and identities from them.

Did you always know how the story would end - or did that show itself to you during the writing process?

I had the climax scene with The Lover in mind from the very beginning and wrote towards it, eager to find out what led to that scene. I wasn't sure how things would play out in the aftermath though; that part showed itself to me during the writing of the first draft.

READING GROUP GUIDE

Topics for discussion

1. What is the effect of following the investigation from the true crime group and from the police perspectives? How do their detecting methods differ?

2. Clementine is a complex character, damaged by her past. Is she a hero or a villain? Do you like her?

3. Discuss the relationship between Clementine and DI Dominic Bell, and how it changes over the course of the story.

4. Did you suspect who was the killer was? What clues did the author leave?

5. Discuss the role of social media in the story.

6. How did the chapters from the victim and killer's points of view affect the story?

7. The ending is intentionally ambiguous: what does life hold for those characters? What will happen next?

8. Clementine and Dl Dominic Bell join forces to catch the killer. Share your favourite films/TV programmes/books about detective duos.

9. With the success of *Making of a Murderer* and *Serial*, true crime has never been more popular. Why are we so interested in real life mysteries?

10. What did you enjoy most or least about *My Little Eye*?